The Corescu Chronicles Book Two

ellen c. maze

DAMASCUS ROAD
The Corescu Chronicles Book Two
By Ellen C. Maze

ANNIVERSARY EDITION 2020
©2017, 2020 by Ellen C. Maze
All rights reserved.

ISBN-13: 978-1-7340474-2-4
V.2-9-2020
Little Roni Publishers
Byhalia, MS
www.littleronipublishers.com

The following is a work of fiction. Names, characters, places, and incidents are fictitious or used fictitiously. Any resemblance to real persons, living or dead, to factual events or to businesses is coincidental and unintentional.

www.ellencmaze.com

PUBLISHED IN THE UNITED STATES OF AMERICA

A MONSTER IN THE MAKING

Paul Black scratched at his blood-stained shirt. The grievous knife wound had healed and he was aflame with anticipation of what lay in store.

Yesterday, he'd been a servant; a willing slave to a magnanimous superman.

A scant half-hour ago, he'd almost died; bleeding to death on the forest floor with an impossibly evil blade thrust deep into his heart.

Yet, minutes ago, he'd been saved; transformed into the image of his master—immortal, invincible, a vampire.

Things were going to be different from now on.

The Corescu Chronicles Book Two

Damascus Road

ellen c. maze

PART ONE:
THE SERVANT

1

…Is it not from the mouth of the Most High that both
calamities and good things come?
Lamentations 3:37-38

THE WAITING WAS KILLER.

Paul forced his feet to remain in place. Fifteen yards away,
secluded in the shadows of the alley, his prey leaned with her back to
the slimy brick wall locked in a passionate embrace. Oblivious to her
upcoming demise, the woman moaned with delight while her furtive
fingers pawed her partner's pockets. Her happenstance paramour's
focus kept him enthralled as he worked to disrobe his companion.

Paul bit down on his bottom lip, using the discomfort to distract
his ballooning bloodlust. Two people at once, he really shouldn't; it
would make the headlines. One hooker, page six. But this drug-
addicted businessman *and* a lady of the evening, murdered together,
the same night? Even in his less-than-experienced mind, Paul figured
it best to avoid such print.

So, he waited.

Fingers twitching, stomach roiling, and his brain synapses literally
misfiring and causing intermittent shock-like jolts, Paul stood
immobile and worked to calm his nerves. It wasn't easy, he had no
formal training; the one who transformed him departed before
handing him the answers to such a life. Paul smirked; at least tonight
he was aware of his activities. Too many nights since he had become a
vampire, he would experience lost time, blacking out and awaking
hours later, usually with a nameless stiff in his clutches.

Just as he thought his heart might burst from its pounding, the
man in the shabby suit backed away from the woman, zipped his fly,
mumbled a few drunken pleasantries, and ambled out of the alley. He
shuffled past Paul hidden in the dark and disappeared around the
corner to the sidewalk.

Paul flew into action. He'd waited so long, his urge to play with his food had all but dissipated. Instead, he grabbed the woman from behind as she counted her bills, jerkily stepping out of the shadows to seek new customers. With only the most basic thought, Paul plunged fierce fangs into her throat, flicked his head violently to the right to open the access, and allowed the sweetest liqueur to slosh past his palate and head to his deepest parts. Lasting less than a minute, another woman he didn't know breathed her last in his embrace.

Was this what his master felt when he ripped the life from his victims? Paul dropped the corpse to the ground and backed away. He may never know what Mark thought when he judged them; Mark had abandoned him. Paul scowled and marched down the littered alley to the street. Tonight's meal satisfied, and with access to the full scope of Mark's wealth, he was living well. He'd be okay, and soon, he'd be reunited with his master.

It had been a good night, a clean kill, and unlike the last three occurrences, he remembered it all. Things were looking up.

2

…I will pour out My Spirit on all people.
Your sons and daughters will prophesy,
your old men will dream dreams,
your young men will see visions…
Joel 2:28

TONY SHOOK HIMSELF AWAKE AND ROLLED OUT OF
bed. Recurring nightmares had become commonplace since his stint
at the Corescu mansion. Jogging to the bathroom, he splashed cold
water onto his face and looked in the mirror. Repeatedly, the moment
Dr. Mark Corescu sank his fangs into his arm revisited Tony in his
sleep. It would be nice if God purged the image from his
subconscious, but so far, He hadn't.

Tony's eyes fell on the half-used note pad and capless Motel 6
pen at his side. This lodging wasn't as nice as the first one he had
rented, or even the second, but as his money ran thin, so did the
luxury. If he didn't find the guy soon, he'd have to abandon the
pursuit. Tony clicked off the lamp and lay back on the bed.

Paul Black, where are you?

Behind closed lids, Tony recalled details of the hunt so far.
Corescu fled the country the day after their altercation, but the
vampire's partner, Paul Black, was in the wind. Driven by a vague
prophecy delivered by a stranger and a compulsion from the Spirit of
God, Tony determined to locate him.

The vampire's estate had been put up for sale and the dozens of
rooms of furniture had been sent to a storage facility. Thus, Tony
found himself in a shabby motel in Atlanta, Georgia, two blocks from
the climate-controlled Store-All where Paul signed for his master's
belongings. Tony would get an address from the site manager
tomorrow. Not bad investigating for a drop-out seminary student.

Tony sighed. It wasn't late, but he needed to focus. He'd been seeking the most dangerous of fabled creatures, fully aware he was an army of one. Tomorrow, he would discover God's will. If the Store-All manager refused to give out Paul's address, Tony would be justified in going home. God opened doors and sometimes held others closed. It was conceivable that God might use someone else to help save Paul's soul.

That would be okay, too, Tony mused as he drowsed. *I've seen enough blood and horror to last me a lifetime.* He chuckled, feeling no joy in the act, and finished his thought. *Even though I do have plenty of experience with vampires.*

A metallic bell woke Tony with a start. He bolted upright and clicked on the lamp before he realized what caused the sound. Grabbing the receiver, he noted the time on the hotel radio/clock: 7:07 p.m.

"Preacher-man, did I wake you?"

The familiar voice sent chills down his spine.

"I've been thinking about you," the voice continued in an amiable tone.

Tony groped the bedside table for his glasses and fumbled them onto his face. Paul had been looking for him? Did he seek to finish him off? Tony cleared his throat.

"What a coincidence," he managed, smiling at his smooth response. "I've been thinking about you, too."

"I know," Paul replied, this time in a guttural whisper.

Tony rubbed the goose pimples that rippled his arms at the sound. The guy was as mischievous as he remembered. Tony hardened his voice. "Where are you?"

"Not too far away." Paul had resumed his normal tone. "I'm staying at Broadmoor Apartments on Union Street, number six. I'll leave a light on for you."

Tony didn't respond. Why would Paul invite him over?

Come to think of it, what did I intend to do when I found him? Take him fishing?

Even as the thoughts flashed across his mind, his eye fell upon his much-loved Bible. God would lead him as He always did.

"I'll meet you somewhere public," Tony said, tucking his dress shirt into his trousers. "I saw a mall nearby."

"No, it has to be here," Paul interjected. "If you want to see me, you'll have to come here."

Tony paused, hands on his hips, the phone pressed between his shoulder and ear. Inside, he sought a nudge from God.

"Look, I don't want to hurt you," Paul said, his tone sincere enough. "I was out of my mind last time you saw me. I'm much better now, honest."

God still hadn't spoken, but Tony decided to concede. "I believe you," he said with an audible sigh. "I'll come."

"Excellent, number six, see you soon."

Tony agreed with a grunt and shoved his wallet into his pocket.

"And Tony," Paul said, his voice soft again.

"What?"

"I've missed you," Paul whispered and was gone with a click.

Tony stared at the receiver in his hand. God would protect him, lead him, and tell him what to do when the time came. He had to trust. Tony grabbed his car keys.

I must be crazy.

Kneeling beside the bed, Tony bowed into his hands.

"Father," he mumbled, "You are the God who enables. Help me help Paul find you. You are my shield and my shelter. Amen."

Hoping that was enough, Tony grabbed his Bible off the dresser and walked to the door. Pray and proceed; it was all he could do. He allowed the door to lock behind him as he headed to his truck. Apparently, the nightmare was not quite over.

♦ ♦ ♦

Detective Jonah Miller rubbed his tired eyes and mumbled to his partner. The Whitford City Police Department buzzed quietly on all sides, but all Jonah could think was how nice it would be if the end of his shift would roll around. Then he would grab a bite to eat with his partner, and they would head home, each to their respective abodes. Jonah murmured his complaint again and his partner shot a rubber-band at his head.

"We speak-uh da English here, buddy. Say again?"

"I said we got nothing here, Speltz. Nothing." Jonah peeked over his palms, but most of his face remained obscured.

Jennifer Speltz, his partner for the better part of five years, leaned back in her chair across from him, her desk butting up to his, their corporate junk mixing on both sides. She was forty-seven, sturdily built, and sexy. Jonah had never told her so, but he went to bed many nights with her on his mind. He continued to stare at her over his hands as she righted herself and began to flip through a file folder on her desk.

"Stop whining, soldier. We have quite a few good prints, a hastily-chosen weapon of opportunity, a body, *and* an ID on said corpse. How can you say we got nothin'?"

She had a point. The corpse found behind the abandoned BP Station was six-months old at least, but the medical examiner sent them a remarkably detailed write-up.

"Okay, miss perky." Jonah rubbed his face once more and then sat up to rifle through the coroner's report. "This guy lived a good three minutes before he expired. I think we can assume he fought his attacker. Any corroborative evidence on your end?"

"Well, we're half a year after the fact, so there was no tissue evidence found on the vic, under the fingernails, in or around the wound site. Six months of rain, wind and frost didn't do us any favors. No footprints or blood evidence…" Jennifer scanned the report in her hand. "The vic's rental turned up at the bottom of the pond back in February, but since we're just now finding the body, that link in the chain of evidence isn't helping us. Wait," she said, and scratched her chin. "There's phys-ev on the oak at the scene. Low, at ground-level, as if someone sat down and leaned against the trunk bleeding. The tree bark definitely had traces of blood underneath it. Could be the perp just as well as the vic."

"Underneath it? Fortuitous, eh?" Jonah asked, using a big word he knew would elicit a remark from his partner.

"Yes, pard'ner," she replied, slurring her Maine accent into an exaggerated southern drawl. "We gots mighty lucky ta find dat blood under dat tree bark!"

Jonah chuckled and shook his head. "Very nice, Bubba. Do we have the report back on that yet from the lab?" Jonah dropped the file on the messy desktop and took a swig of his decaf.

"Not yet," Jennifer replied in her normal voice just as a uniform rushed by to drop a clear vinyl folder on her desk before disappearing around the next corner partition. "Wait, I think this is it."

"Perfect timing. What's it say?" Jonah stood, his back creaking.

"Making old-man noises now, Jonah?" Jennifer raised her eyebrows as he approached. "Is this what I have to look forward to when I get to be your age?"

"Hah, hah," Jonah laughed. "In three years? Yeah, better get to the gym before it's too late." He looked over her shoulder as she pulled open the lab report.

"I'm way ahead of ya, grandpa. I bought a Stairmaster last week. Haven't missed a day on it. Twenty minutes a day, three times a week for rock-hard abs. Or some other hogwash. Okay. Let's see," Jennifer traced the page with her finger. "Oh, good. The blood on the tree bark definitely wasn't the vic's."

"We got a blood type then? Too early for DNA?" Jonah tried to read ahead of her, but even after adjusting his glasses, the letters remained out of focus.

"Well," she began, her finger trailing down the page. "That's weird."

"What?" Jonah squinted and still couldn't make his eyes focus properly—it was time for a new prescription. Jennifer recommended contact lenses frequently enough, but he never could get the hang of putting his finger on his eyeball.

"The lab has nada on this point. They don't have a blood type or a DNA note here. I wonder if there's a screw up?" Jennifer flipped the report to page two and it ended with a few lines of procedure, but no additional information. "Have you ever gotten a summary from the lab that was incomplete?"

Jonah reached for the folder and brought it closer to his face. The unchecked square that normally revealed the blood type of the donor came into focus; the portion devoted to column after column of DNA information had been left blank.

"This is ridiculous," Jonah sighed. Whitford City was a small city, to be sure, but he'd always considered the police department to be first class. Jonah handed the folder back and returned to his chair to grab his jacket. "Get down to the lab and find out what the holdup is. This guy has a six-month lead on us and they send down shoddy police work? I can't believe it."

"Don't get your man-panties in a wad. I know these guys. I'll go get whatever they have. You can go to that rental place and see if the rep remembers our vic. They're open 'til nine. Maybe you'll get lucky." Jennifer stood and a tiny pop emitted from her own knees. Jonah smiled her way. "Don't say a word. That's the sound of knees getting stronger from riding my new toy. Not a word."

Jonah laughed and shrugged on his brown suit coat. "I wasn't going to say anything. Do unto others, my child."

"Hah, hah, rabbi," Jennifer joked. She shoved items into her briefcase and shrugged on her windbreaker. "I'll check back with you at nine. Meet ya at Twirlies?"

"'Kay," Jonah returned, ignoring the rabbi jibe. When she had disappeared around the corner, he turned for the men's room. Jenn sometimes called him rabbi because once she caught him carrying a Hebrew Bible to his car. He studied the Scriptures in his spare time and kept the book in his locker. And he wasn't full-Jewish. His great, great grandfather, Isaac Cohen, had been Hasidic, but he'd converted to Christianity and later married a goy, who's children married goyim, etc., etc., leaving Jonah's Hebrew lineage not worth measuring.

Jonah made it to the men's room and stopped to wash his face. He regarded his reflection, staring into his deep brown eyes through wire-rimmed eyeglasses. He looked enough like his Cohen ancestor to honor the name. He'd seen a silvery photograph of the barber from Milwaukee, and like him, Jonah had almost no gray hair at fifty years old. He wore his brown locks a little long so everyone would see that he not only had a terrific head of hair, but also enviable curls.

Jonah wrung his hands under the tap, his thoughts returning to the case. The captain had given them this hopeless case because he believed in them. (Or so he said.) Jonah had an inkling that Erkleson dumped it on them because the rest of the detectives were busy catching real killers. He and Jennifer had been on cold-case duty for over a year and it didn't look like they were going to be reassigned anytime soon. Any case that the chief thought may never be solved, he handed to Miller and Speltz. As a duo, they worked with quiet efficiency, requiring few departmental resources. If they were successful in solving an impossible case, they did it with professionalism and grace, and without media attention. Miller and Speltz served as the unit's unofficial cleanup crew, no recognition, no promotions, just work the case as far as you can, stamp it closed (or unsolved), and move on to the next.

Jonah shook his head at his reflection and headed for the door. Retirement was looking better and better. Maybe he could convince Jenn to come with him. It was a possibility. He was single, she was single, and they got along.

It could happen, Jonah thought as he crossed the parking lot to his battered Cutlass. *Nothing's impossible...*

◆ ◆ ◆

Paul rushed about the apartment turning on lights for his soon-to-be guest. He'd taken to living in the dark, relishing his newly-acquired night vision. From the moment his master transformed him, he explored his supernatural abilities. He sensed other powers within that could only be developed with a tutor's help. Until he could be reunited with his other half, he would push himself to the limit to see what he was capable of. He'd already discovered he had strength beyond his wildest imagination, as well as exceptional hearing, eyesight, and sense of smell. His extra-sensory abilities grew every day with telepathy bringing up the rear.

It was telepathy he most hoped to develop. Three weeks after the incident at Mark's, he attempted to contact his master with this invisible phoneline. Although Mark was thousands of miles away on another continent, their mental link was stronger than ever. Mark's replies so far had been minimal, but Paul gleaned plenty of information sideways. He learned that his master had hunkered down in a heavily-wooded European wilderness and rarely ventured out, surviving, but barely. Paul wasn't happy about it, but he didn't question Mark's motives. His master was sorting through emotional and spiritual trauma Paul didn't comprehend. Plus, Mark missed Agricola's friend, Hope Brannen, terribly. After consoling his old master long distance, Paul searched Mark's consciousness for the whereabouts of the preacher. As luck would have it, he knew every move Agricola made. This evening, when Paul contacted Mark telepathically, he was tickled to learn the preacher's exact location.

Quite a while had passed since their night together and Paul no longer desired to kill Tony Agricola. Over the last few months his hate for the godly mortal had dissipated and he toyed with the idea of making the man his servant. After all, it was Tony's fault Paul was alone in the first place. Paul stood quietly, but not patiently, and waited for his prey to arrive.

◆◆◆

A hundred miles away in Whitford City, Georgia, Hope walked in thoughtful circles in the moonlit pasture searching for signs of life. She caught a glimpse of a shimmering coat obscured by the pasture's scrubby brush. Hope moved toward the slip of white fluttering between the branches, but it wouldn't be her horse, Lucas. She'd sold her jumper weeks ago.

I must be dreaming…

With this new awareness, Hope picked up her pace to reach the tree-line, a dozen feet from the horse-shaped mystery. Whatever it was lay prostrate beside a small tree appearing a silvery-white apparition, slow and deliberate breaths puffing from its velvety nose.

"What are you doing there?" she asked the dream horse, close enough to see it looked nothing like her familiar mount. Lucas, an Appendix Thoroughbred, had been white, but slender and long-legged. The facsimile before her appeared an albino Clydesdale, with wide, bulging withers and thickly muscled hindquarters. It had bunched itself on its side in the dewy grass, its graceful neck endowed by a mountain of mane arched, its muzzle resting nose-down to the earth. It did not acknowledge her presence, even as she stepped close. The creature's coat glowed as if lit from within. Hope was compelled to touch it and she knelt to stroke fur as soft as down.

"There, there," she whispered. It did not respond to the contact, but continued its rhythmic breaths. "Let's get up now; it's not good to lie down too long." Hope prodded its shoulder with her fingers, encouraging it to rise. "Why do you lie so still? Can't you get up?"

The creature moaned and lifted its huge head, pivoting her direction, its movements languid and serene. Then, it resumed the previous position and fell into the same slow, cadenced breathing. Hope frowned, a memory of her childhood show pony that had died of colic, and she poked the beast with more fervor.

"Get up!" she barked and opened her palms to shove against the animal's wide middle. "You're dying! Get up!"

But it did nothing, as if accepting its fate. It would die and there was nothing she could do about it.

To hell with that! Hope crawled to the thing's enormous head. Grasping its jowls, she maneuvered it inches forcing it to meet her eye. *"I said GET UP!"* she shouted, her dream voice cracking with anger and frustration.

This time, the creature responded. Its brown eyes aflame, it gathered its energy, coiled its neck, and struck, taking hold of the dreamer's shoulder with the teeth of a lion—

Hope snapped awake, her breath ragged.

Oh, God! Oh, God! Her hand flew to her shoulder. It ached, the nightmare more real than ever. It took several moments to regain her composure, and when her heart stopped racing, she could only think of one name: *Mark Corescu.*

"Mark? Are you there?" Hope addressed the air as she'd been doing off and on since the vampire deserted her that crazy night at his home. She didn't fear him, and now more than ever, she wished he would call for her. She'd go in a heartbeat because together, they could make everything right again.

"The dream horse is you," she whispered.

Unsure if her own sadness built the odd night terror or his subconscious sent it, she couldn't bear the thought of him allowing death to overcome him, alone and thousands of miles away.

"Mark, don't disappear. I can help you. I love you. Won't you just call me?" Begging an invisible lover to contact her had become second nature and she brushed her fingers to wet cheeks. "I need you. Doesn't that count for anything?"

No answer. But so far, he never did.

Still… he might, he only needs time.

Hope fell asleep creating in her mind a *good* dream, one where they danced arm in arm in their own house overlooking a beautiful European landscape. This one could happen, too…

From his reclining position, the elderly gentleman grasped his head with both hands and moaned. Did he just have a vision of the woman? Was she calling him, her voice distant and detached? Was she dreaming of him? Maybe. Maybe not. She might not have been there at all. *I never should have left her. If only she'd come here, to Germany…*

"No!" The old man squeezed his eyes tight with a snarl. He would never wish that upon her. She must never see him as he truly was: a monster with nothing to offer an innocent. *No, I must never see her again.*

Mark cleared his mind with effort. Recumbent on his impromptu table-bed, he stared at the crumbling ceiling tiles illuminated by the light filtering through broken windowpanes. He had no need of electricity and an old-fashioned well out back provided what little water he sought. He needed nothing. He had lived his life, maybe wasted it; he hadn't yet decided which. But the revelation the woman and the preacher brought last Fall would not be forgotten: Mark was *unclean,* a vampire, a mythical monster doomed to an eternity of dozing and dreaming and wishing he had never been born.

I was a god once.

Yes, but he'd relinquished his presumed deity to save his soul. Gave up his kingdom and his sovereignty in an attempt to appease the one true God, the Almighty Creator who he *knew* existed. Since he *knew* Him, he had to *obey* Him. That obedience was what led him to his current living death.

For how can I feed when my food is forbidden?

The hollowed-out soul of a man sighed. The woods surrounding the dilapidated mansion held blood. A clan of Gypsies sang, worked, played, and fought not two miles from his broken home. Skillful hunters, they traipsed through the protected forest, poaching various prey. Aside from the human residents, various animals roamed the property, carrying the crimson fluid that would nourish the vampire if he were to arise and seek it.

But don't only devils drink blood?

So he lay, surrounded by food and unable to bring it to his lips.

Yet not every hour is interminable...

No, with effort, he had learned to depend on God for his daily bread. When he became intoxicated by the recollection of the great power he enjoyed in his former life, he would be reminded to whom he belonged, hearing in his black heart how much God loved him.

Is that enough?

So far, no. Even though several months had passed since that night at his house in Georgia, deep in his spirit, he often vacillated between trusting God and playing with the devil. Mark's mind turned to Paul and the peace he enjoyed with the young man by his side. As if on cue, his longtime servant arrived in his mind.

"Mark, master, show me the preacher."

Mark smiled. Paul didn't call him master for most of their century together. Only when The Other arrived in force did their existence begin to morph into something else, something new, something that in the end turned his favorite man into a bloodthirsty monster.

"I want to find him. Please. Where is he?"

Mark closed his eyes to the sound of Paul's voice. His son, his creation, three thousand miles away, still called to him, seeking wisdom, encouragement, and love.

Love? Mark didn't have it in him. All he could offer was pity.

"Yes, go ahead, yes..." Mark sent and allowed the man to use his mind as he saw fit, holding sacrosanct only the dark secrets that made Mark Corescu such a powerful vampire. His face broke into a crooked smile. Paul didn't need anything to increase his evil nature; he was

wicked enough with what was thrust upon him at his second birth. Sighing, he bid Paul farewell and pushed him away.

◆ ◆ ◆

Paul checked his watch imagining the preacher would be half-way there by now. *Why is it taking so long?* Paul crossed to the front window and peeked through the slatted blinds.

The Whitford City police never caught up with him. As far as he knew, they hadn't even investigated the loose ends he and Mark left behind. In those last days, Paul killed two people with his bare hands. One an immortal like himself named Reuben, but the other man, a busybody reporter, had been ended behind an abandoned gas station. Both were killed for the master's sake; both had been trying to ruin and expose Mark. So far as Paul could ascertain, the police hadn't yet discovered either corpse.

Paul fidgeted with his thumbs wondering what would happen when the preacher arrived. Would Tony be safe in his presence? Paul couldn't say for sure; his behavior had become erratic since his transformation.

When first changed into his master's likeness, Paul endured an intimate and terrifying presence inside his head referred to as *The Other*. Mark confessed later this entity had once been his master in the flesh, the original vampire that four hundred years ago changed Mark from priest to supernatural being. Mark's recollection of the old master's spirit enabled it to speak to all who carried Mark's blood— this meant his servants, Paul and Reuben. And The Other had much to do with Paul's current condition. When Mark left the country and Paul hunkered down to hide, the disturbing voice faded and ceased its telepathic communication. But he wasn't gone; Paul sensed it within, as if this alien creature had melded with his subconscious, and he never felt released of its despicable possession.

And how long will I have those blackouts?

Paul sometimes awakened in a strange place after a kill, wondering what happened and where he was. Should he worry about the lost time? Was it normal for vampires? He had no teacher. Mark had not been forthcoming with the secrets of the trade and Paul found it difficult adjusting to life without a master.

As for eluding the police, Paul moved to an apartment in the city under an assumed name. The only time he used his real name was when dealing with Mark's estate. As the doctor's executor, he carried the burden of making sure his master's material wealth remained secure and hidden. If the authorities found Nixon's or Reuben's body, even then, they wouldn't have reason to search for Paul Black. He and Mark destroyed everything the reporter had collected on the doctor from Whitford City.

So where is Tony? Come on!

Paul narrowed his eyes and focused on the entrance to the apartment complex. The preacher would make life interesting. Tony Agricola had an insane obsession with sharing his God with everyone he met, even vampires. His bravery had been impressive and his conviction compelling. Shivering with anticipation, Paul forced a deep exhale; very soon, the evening would begin and Paul would make certain he showed his guest a good time.

3

For we are God's workmanship,
Created in Christ Jesus to do good works,
Which God prepared in advance for us to do.
Ephesians 2:10

TONY STOOD AT NUMBER SIX AND TOOK A DEEP BREATH,
the red leather-covered Bible flexing in and out of a tube in his sweaty
hands. *I'm here to help Paul find God...* Tony huffed at the realization.
Because of a restrictive budget, he had no formal ecclesiastical
education; his vocation had been church administration. But he loved
the Lord, studied His word, and followed Him blindly.

This is how he found himself here, knocking on an *honest-to-god*
vampire's door. He would *again* face the devil that smiled through
Paul's little-boy face. Tony lifted his fist to knock, but before his
knuckles made contact, Paul swung the door in wide.

"There you are!" Paul exclaimed, grinning and running a furtive
gaze across Tony's face. "Aren't you a sight for sore eyes?"

Tony stepped back and corralled his courage. "You look
different," he managed and remained on the mat. Before his
transformation, Paul had been a normal-looking guy with shaggy
blond hair and a surfer's tan. Something compelled him since their last
meeting to die his hair and eyebrows black, giving him a fake,
Halloweeny appearance. Still, he looked barely eighteen, which Tony
learned was the age at which Dr. Corescu found him, turning him into
a sort of immortal manservant a century ago.

What's wrong with his eyes? They had always been bright blue, but
today? An icy gaze laced with malice held Tony's eye. *It's the vampire
spirit doing that,* Tony assured himself as Paul smiled under the scrutiny.

"Tell me how handsome I am," the vampire said and stepped

back, gesturing for Tony to enter. Tony remained in place.

"You look like you're in disguise," he told him, inside ramping up the courage to enter the house. *Once I cross the threshold…*

"I was," Paul said and motioned again, sweeping his hand across his body. "It'll wear off and in a month, I'll be the adorable blond boy you love and remember so fondly."

"You're not in hiding anymore? Did the police give up?" Tony asked delaying.

"Give up? Turns out they aren't looking for us. Never have." Paul lowered his chin, holding a friendly grin. When Tony still did not move forward, he backed three steps, holding the door by its edge, creating a wide berth. "Please, Mr. Agricola. Welcome to my home."

With a tight grin, Tony stepped through the door and tucked his Bible under his arm to put out his hand to shake. Paul rolled in his lower lip looking at Tony's offered fingers.

"Like a man, eh?" he said teasing and grasped the hand to shake.

Two firm pumps and Tony yanked free, still in the open doorway, and looked around the space. From where he stood, the apartment was of good size, the foyer leading to a living room walled with empty built-in shelving.

Paul reached for Tony's sleeve and gave a little tug. "All the way in, preacher-man," he said and Tony walked past him. Paul closed the door and when Tony turned to face him, Paul smiled anew exuding childish excitement. "This is great. Just great. So, how have you been? How's that miserable woman-friend of yours?"

Tony kept out of his reach not encouraged by the vampire's demeanor. From the moment he met the duo of Mark and Paul, he considered them both unbalanced and dangerous. With his heart in his throat, Tony remembered God. He ignored the jab about Hope and tried a new opener. "Can I have a glass of water?"

Paul's eyes widened and he nodded. "Sure!" He stepped around Tony toward the kitchen and stopped before entering. He swiveled and covered his mouth. "I don't have cups. Sorry, man." He giggled into his hand. "What use have I of cups?"

"It doesn't matter," Tony said, swallowing hard. Paul's intention had been to remind his guest he was a vampire; Tony did not need any help recalling that tidbit. He considered Paul's boxed belongings and lack of décor and changed the subject. "It looks like you're moving."

"I am. I was waiting for you." Paul tipped his chin to the side tossing Tony a wink. "You're coming with me."

"Oh?" Tony held his face static but his mind raced, wondering at his meaning and the implications. *I'm not staying here. I'm not moving in with this guy. Father, are You seeing this?*

Paul dropped his hands into his jeans pockets and waited for Tony's eye. "You praying? Like right now?" Tony narrowed his eyes and Paul shrugged. "It makes light. My eyes are amazing now. I can see the craziest stuff I could never see before."

"Paul, look, I know why I accepted your invitation to come here, but why did you want me to come? What makes you think I'd go away with you?" Tony only held Paul's gaze in flashes, spending every other second to look aside.

"You look like you've been losing sleep," Paul offered, ignoring Tony's question. He softened his gaze and smiled. "Were you worrying about me? About how you caused my master to abandon me and turn me out into the world with a brand new life and no one to spend it with? Was that keeping you awake at night?"

Tony held his breath, gauging Paul's emotional state. Was he growing angry or only teasing to get a reaction?

Paul continued with sarcasm, "Because if that's what's been keeping you away these past six months, good. Because it's been hard. I've decided all of this is your fault and you're going to put it right."

Tony shook his head with a woeful eye. "No, this isn't my fault. Mark wanted me at his house. Your master wanted me to remind him about God. Mark wanted this—not me. I am here to help you the same way. God wants me to tell you that He loves you—"

"Hah!" Paul laughed and stepped into Tony's space. He put his hands to Tony's shoulders and held him firm. "You didn't help him. You *killed* him. He has holed up in Germany, lying on a broken table in a disgusting abandoned mansion. Flies and worms and rats run his estate now, Tony. *You* did that. *You.* And I want to hear you admit it."

Paul's contact had not grown uncomfortable, but the immoveable strength reminded Tony of that night in Corescu's mansion, when the vampire and Paul returned bloody and full of evil intent. At the memory of the doctor sinking sharp fangs into his inner elbow, Tony's free arm curled to his chest, the Bible in his other hand.

"I read you like a book, Tony," Paul said his voice low now, raspy, and his eyes danced about Tony's face. "I couldn't see you up here..." Paul touched his temple. "...until we met eyes, but I read you now. No more secrets, my friend." Paul sent him a victorious smile.

"You're thinking about that night in the garage."

An easy guess. Tony monitored his tone. "Please let me go."

"Not until you say it. Say, *I'm sorry I ruined your life, Paul. I will do anything to make it up to you.*" Paul's brow raised but Tony did not look into his eyes. "Say it."

"I am sorry you're unhappy, but I didn't ruin your life." Inside, Tony asked questions of God, mostly of, *what now? What now? What now?* "Please step back so we can talk," Tony said low looking aside unable to converse with the vampire mere inches away.

"No, I don't want to talk. You won't say it so I'm not letting you go." Paul slid one hand to the side of Tony's throat and cupped his neck, still holding Tony in place. "If you don't say it, I think I might get a little closer."

The hand on Tony's shoulder lifted and he moved to Tony's cheek. When his fingers made contact with Tony's short beard, he flinched backward. Paul positioned the hand at his throat to brace his forefinger to the base of Tony's skull, discouraging future resistance.

"Say the words or take your medicine," Paul said his whisper guttural. His hand returned to Tony's beard and he ran the fingers through the coarse hair. "I could never grow a beard," he said at the same volume. "Neither could Mark…"

Tony closed his eyes, still looping his mantra to God.

"See, I had just turned eighteen," Paul continued, his whisper turning wistful. "I hadn't started shaving. This tan…" He moved his free hand to his collar to flip the material. "…I got this tan shoeing horses in the sun in 1910. It's exactly the same. The length of my hair, it never gets longer. I weighed a hundred and thirty-one pounds then and I weigh precisely the same now…"

"Paul," Tony whispered, still averting his gaze in the close proximity, "I'm sorry your life's been turned upside down, but I can help you…"

"Same for my master. Mark's always been cleanshaven, the same weight, the same beauty, his amazing power that thrilled me to the core. *Every. Single. Day,* that marvelous man turned his eyes on me and loved me."

"I only wanted to teach him about God," Tony whispered. *He's not going to leave me alive. This is bad…*

"What about me? Do you want to tell me about your God?" Paul asked now leaning in to speak in Tony's ear.

The movement put them cheek to cheek, with Paul a few inches taller. Tony's blood curdled with the vampire so close. There would be no stopping him if he decided to attack. Tony said very small, "Yes, He sent me here to help you. I know it…"

Paul allowed his lips to brush the outer lobe of Tony's ear as he whispered, "Will you say it?"

"I don't want to have to hurt you…"

Tony thought about the second phrase. It hadn't been in his ear, but in his mind. *Can he speak to me telepathically?* He could think of no scripture backing that up. More than anything, Tony needed Paul to move away so he gave in.

"I'm sorry I ruined your life and caused Dr. Corescu to abandon you…" Tony said in his softest voice.

Paul's fingers massaged the back of his neck. "And?" he breathed, still against Tony's ear.

Tony swallowed. "And I promise to make it up to you."

"Whatever it takes," Paul whispered.

"Yes," Tony said and closed his eyes.

"Okay…" Paul backed away in increments, the contact with Tony's throat and cheek dropping just as slowly. "Good. We have that straight…" He backed one step remaining within reach, and crossed his arms. "This is what we'll do. You will be my partner, move with me to Montgomery where I bought a bookstore. You're going to run the store for me and we'll use it to be our legitimate income."

Tony's face flushed, his entire future flashing before his eyes. As always, his heart tossed dozens of complaints to the Lord. *"I'm supposed to be a preacher, remember? I was going to seminary, honor my dad and preach in his church? Remember all that, Abba? You didn't get me to thirty-three years old to play businessman with this monster! Why aren't you doing something? Hello?!"*

Paul released a chuckle that built into a hearty laugh before Tony looked up from his inner monologue.

"I don't hear words, but I see pulses…" The vampire flicked both hands like staccato stoplights. "It must be Morse Code for angels," he said with a final laugh. "At any rate, if you and the heavens are finished, this is what we'll do. Would you like to hear my threats?" he asked, his expression as sweet as a child asking for candy.

"No," Tony said and turned for the door. He hadn't instructed his body to flee, but he was heading out. *You want me to live with a vampire? Do You think I'm that brave?* He didn't reach the door before Paul zoomed past too fast to track. The vampire leaned his back to the door, facing Tony, his expression calm.

"If you leave, I'll go to your house and kill everyone you care about. Your family, your pets…" Paul raised his brow. "Do you have a dog? I'll kill it, too."

"Just stop!" Tony replied and thought over his options. His father had passed already, but he had a mom. One look in Paul's eyes told him the vampire meant what he said. Add to that, he'd enjoy it. "Okay, I'll stay. We'll do it. I'll set up house with you. For a little while. Just until you feel better about what's happened."

Hearing it aloud, Tony nodded. Yes, that made sense. The guy had endured a horrible loss and had no one to help him figure out his new life. *Why not me? Only I can help him. I'm the only preacher in his life…*

"Fantastic," Paul said and took a dramatic inhale. "So this next part…"

The vampire grasped Tony's nearest arm and although he jerked away, as before, the grip was like iron. Tony shuffled backward and Paul followed, until Tony's rump met the low counter of the nearest built-in shelving.

"Wait, wait, wait," he hissed the claustrophobia returning. "What are you doing? What do you mean?"

Paul held his wrist and leaned one palm against the bookcase, looking upon him with psychotic affection. "You look scared."

"I said I'll stay. You're too close." Tony set his Bible down on the surface behind him and put both palms to Paul's chest. "Please…" Paul held his eye with ferocity and Tony could not look away. This was Mark Corescu's trick and Tony had become the hare in a trap.

"You mesmerize me. Why is that?" Paul asked, his pause indicating he sought an answer. Tony didn't have one. "I never wanted to touch anyone more than I want to touch you. Why do you think that is?"

Suffocated by the proximity, Tony withdrew the final inch, rapping his head against the wall. "Because it makes me so upset," he whispered, speaking what he believed to be true. Paul's face dawn with revelation.

"Hey, I think you're right!" He leaned in and lowered his free hand to Tony's face, again in his short beard. "Your heart is really hammering. I hear it like a drum."

Tony offered a rapid nod. *Be cool. Be cool. Be cool. Don't let him scare you. You got this.* Tony looped new mantras inside and Paul came in close enough to touch his lips to the skin under Tony's eye. Tony had shut his eyes and the vampire's eyelashes flutter the hair at his forehead.

"Huh, not bothering you, eh?" he teased still in place. "Let's see what this does…" Paul released Tony's wrist and used that hand to stabilize his neck as before. The hand on his face ran into Tony's hair and shoved his chin aside.

I'm cool. I'm cool. I'm cool. Don't let him scare you. I got this, Tony said inside, his eyes closed. The sound of Paul's lips smacked and the vampire opened his mouth against Tony's throat, then his tongue, flat and at rest. He wanted Tony to be afraid, but inside he chanted, *This is nothing. I'm fine. I'm fine. I'm fine..*

Paul closed his mouth and leaned out to look into Tony's face. Running his hands against his scalp until the fingers of both hands were entwined in Tony's longish hair, Paul said, "Look at me."

Tony opened his eyes. His host looked insane, his blue eyes now steel-gray and rimmed red.

"I want you to pray," he commanded in a raspy whisper. "Like you did when I grabbed you at Mark's."

"I'm not afraid of you," Tony lied and Paul gave him a sugary grin and moved his hands to Tony's inner shoulders.

"Yes, you are." Paul leaned in like before to Tony's ear. "I think I'll make you immortal. Think how many souls you can save in a thousand years."

He wants to make me a vampire!

Tony snapped into action, pushing with all his might into Paul's chest. "You're crazy!" Tony said with urgency. "Wait! Back up!" His panic growing, Tony squirmed and twisted, but against the vampire, still weak as a baby.

"Pray," Paul whispered again in Tony's right ear, his fingers fleshy daggers at his inner shoulders.

Tony's righteous mission dissolved and he lost all sense of reason. He filled his lungs to shout for help and one of the vampire's palms covered his mouth. He did not call out to God, and as he prepared to be attacked, no one came to his aid.

4

"I will set My face against any
Israelite or any foreigner residing
among them who eats blood."
Leviticus 17:10

THE LUST THAT FILLED PAUL'S SOUL OVERWHELMED HIM
as he held the preacher close, his aching fangs inches from his pulsing
carotid. Tony had asked repeatedly to be released, but...

How can I? I can't.

But he needed the man to pray. He needed that light—if he
could take Tony's blood when under that light, the nirvana would be
complete. He whispered again for the man to pray and he uncovered
his mouth to press his lips tight to Tony's. It wasn't sexual, but a way
to breathe in the man's abject terror. Until the preacher's will broke
and forced him to reach to the heavens, Paul would wait.

At least he would try.

The bloodlust had turned his vision pink and if the man didn't
utter something to his God very soon, Paul would waste him. Rip out
his throat and lap up the blood.

Oh, what an unfixable wound I would make!

"Please! Jesus! Help me!" the preacher barked after yanking free
of Paul's fierce suction. The kiss worked; the man fell into the same
supplications he spouted at Mark's. Oh, those hateful words Paul's
master adored, the words that caused Mark to abandon the one in the
world that loved him most of all.

Paul's incisors elongated into fangs and he plunged them into
Tony's throat, deftly hitting his mark. The man's prayers fell to a
whisper, but the ambrosia had been released, his lifeblood packed
with adrenaline and despair, and Paul drank it all. Then Tony relaxed
in his grip, prayers still dribbling upward, and an incredible joy filled
Paul's heart. The liquid coursed faster and faster, with more volume
than he normally drew from his victims. Somewhere in the back of his

22

mind, he heard the man moan.

I need to stop…

Tony's heartbeat skipped. Once, twice, and returned to its rhythm. Paul drank on. The prayers ceased and Tony lost consciousness.

I have to stop. This is my preacher-man. I want him alive. I have to stop…

But he couldn't. And Tony's blood scratched his itch more than any in the past. Whatever happened in the minutes to come, this moment Paul would treasure forever.

♦

Tony's eyes rolled back and his knees buckled, a hundred miles away from the sensation of Paul's attack. The fire that raged where the monster's lips touched his skin subsided and Tony drifted into nothingness.

But ahead…

Tony focused on the sliver of light evident beneath his partly-opened lids. Wind rushed by with palpable sound; could it be God?

Father, is that You?

Tony wanted to call out with his voice, but had no mouth. He was afloat on the wind, without a body, without anything.

Is this what happens when you die?

Tony allowed the mighty wind to carry him along, the only sound the comforting rush of air. A white light enveloped him on all sides. In his mind, he was smiling, arms outstretched, enjoying the flight. But then, he began to decelerate, the wind lessened, and the clean white-brightness of his surroundings dimmed. Tony was returning.

No! No! I can't go back! No! Please!

Returning to the pain, the humiliation, the disgrace... Below him, his body's outline filtered into his awareness. Tony recognized his pale complexion, his nerdy accountant's face, his unfortunate physique. His body lay on a bed, its eyes closed with the form of a man bent over him.

Why can't I stay with You, Father? Haven't I done enough?

"Just think how many souls you can save in a thousand years?"

With the sudden recollection of that phrase, Tony fell into his physical body. Had he been rejected by the Light?

"No, not rejected. Go and make disciples of men," he heard in his spirit as sensation returned to his arms and legs with a syrupy feel. He

hadn't been rejected; he was reborn. And he'd do the Lord's work with more zeal and boldness than ever.

Not rejected, means accepted. What else could he ask for?

◆

Paul sat on the edge of the bed watching the preacher's face. He'd been surprised when the man's heart stopped, but as had happened in recent past, he blacked out. He moved Tony to his bedroom and looked at his pale face, no heart-sounds; his pet was dying.

"Oh, no you don't!" Paul shouted and scooted to sit upon one leg next to Tony's quiet form. With barely a notion that it would work, he bit down hard on the heel of his hand, and since his fangs had not been aroused, he gnawed and dragged the flesh with his cuspids until it split. He slapped Tony's face with his other hand and shoved his leaking wound to the preacher's mouth.

"SWALLOW! Swallow, dammit!" he barked, squeezing his fist over Tony's half-open mouth. The oxygenated blood fill the orifice and overflowed, trickling into his beard, down his neck, and onto the mattress. Paul's hand healed in another fifteen seconds and he used that hand to slap Tony again. "WAKE UP!"

Tony sputtered, red mist floating from his mouth and then he snorted, his upper body convulsing. Paul raised up and watched, waited, and when Tony fell quiet, he checked his pulse at his wrist.

His heartbeat had returned, strong, steady, and even.

"YES!" he shouted and got to his feet. "Yes," he said softer, his own respirations returning to normal. The man remained pale, but he was breathing. He hadn't opened his eyes, but his lids fluttered with REM sleep. Paul used the sheet to daub at the blood drying fast on Tony's face. This was how Mark first shared his immortality with Paul, a century ago, when he offered Paul his blood in a glass of wine. Tony would not have the amazing power that Paul enjoyed, but he would not age or die. Tony would be his servant.

...And an ever present blood slave.

Paul shivered with pleasure, his plan coming together. For once, his lost time resulted in an enormous prize. He would get the two of them settled in Montgomery, and when enough time had passed, Tony would help him bring Mark home.

Yes, by the end of this year, we will put Mark's house back in order...

And Tony would help, he'd have no choice.

After fifteen minutes, Paul stretched out alongside Tony snoring on his back in the narrow bed. When Paul clicked off the bedside lamp, reducing the room to shadows, he rolled onto his side to watch Tony's profile. It was done, Tony survived, everything would be fine. Paul dozed off, more content than he'd been in a long time.

♦♦♦

From another continent, Doctor Mark Corescu telepathically spied on his protégé. He watched with morbid humor as Paul harassed the man of God. Although the old vampire had chosen to sleep away his life, he enjoyed eavesdropping on his offspring, and Paul's bloody misadventures never ceased to amaze him. Paul's lust for death and chaos left Mark heavyhearted; all the while he was sending souls to heaven in his former life, he pointed his most precious one toward hell.

Those days are gone...

God didn't need a repentant monster. The Most High may have had a use for him before he allowed the devil to swap blood with him in that Hungarian cave, but now? What good was a four hundred-year-old vampire to a perfect and Holy God?

None at all.

Mark put all thoughts of poor Tony Agricola and his lost son out of his mind. Paul was in over his head; God held Tony close and would keep him safe. Like all men, Tony could expect trials and tribulations, but only when his Creator was ready, would he die.

Mark sighed at Paul's antics.

"Paulie, Paulie, I warned you not to seek trouble…"

Mark didn't mind if the sentiment he pondered trickled to his former servant, but he did not send it as a communication.

"You're pitting yourself against God by attacking his man. You never have understood your place in this world. It's not about you. It was never about you…"

Soon, Mark dozed off, and thankfully, did not dream.

5

"Because of the oppression of the weak and the groaning of the needy, I will now arise," says the LORD. "I will protect them from those who malign them."
Psalm 12:5

"RIGHT ON TIME, DETECTIVE SPELTZ," JONAH SAID AS Jennifer dropped into the seat across. From the beginning of their partnership, he had avoided using her first name. Previous experience with female coworkers taught him to keep things professional. So no matter how casual Jennifer behaved, he would always address her as a detective and not a woman. This didn't come easy; he liked her a little more than he should and hoped she never discovered that weakness.

"You first. Any luck at the Hertz place?" she asked once settled

He shook his head. "The clerk on duty wasn't hired until last month. Seems the turnover is pretty high. I'll start interviewing Nixon's next of kin in the morning. Your turn," Jonah said and swigged his coffee.

"Okay, but you're not going to like it." Jennifer retrieved a notepad from the pocket of her Levi's and flipped it open. "The alleles for the sample under the bark are contaminated. Instead of being obviously human or obviously animal, it's neither, and the lab guys said we should consider the sample too degraded to read. They put it away. They're not working on it anymore."

"You're kidding." Jonah searched his partner's eyes; she was as frustrated as he was. "The alleles are contaminated'? That's scientific mumbo jumbo. Why can't they say that they just don't know?"

Jennifer shrugged and set her memo pad on the table. "That new firebrand they got—Billy Austin—he said there were a few more tests they could run, but his supervisor nixed the idea, told him to move to a live case." Jennifer's eyes flashed in his as she must have read Jonah's determination. "I know that look. What do you want to do?"

"Talk to Billy tomorrow. Get him down to the precinct away

from his geek buddies. You speak his language—talk some science with him and dig into those other tests he wanted to run." Jonah flagged the waitress and she took Jennifer's drink order. When she had sauntered away, a question fell from his lips that he had intended to keep in his head a little longer. "Be honest, do you ever think about leaving this game?"

"Retiring?" she asked, her voice soft and humorless. When Jonah nodded, she shook her head. "I can't retire. I have to put in my twenty. I am a late bloomer." She shook her head again with more fervor. "No way. I've only been on the force twelve years, buddy. I'm not old like you."

"Jenn, I'm serious." When her name slipped, her eyes flickered. Jonah's gut knotted; she knew about his quiet infatuation. Jonah feigned innocence. "*If*, Speltz, *just if* you retired early, what would you do next? I'm just making conversation…" Jonah gave her a moment to think of a reply and then filled in his answer. "I'll tell you what I'd do. I'd move out to my land and raise organic mushrooms."

"Mushrooms?"

"Yep. I have seventy-two acres in north Georgia, it's very fertile for farming. There's a nice flat spot in one corner for a house, another flat spot for my button-mushroom greenhouse. I might even have shitake logs. The market is a niche, but it's lucrative. I've done my research," Jonah said with a serious nod. "And there's plenty of land left for cattle."

"For compost, I guess," Jennifer said with a straight face. "You're a complicated individual under that tough-cop exterior, Detective Miller. Know that?"

Jonah shrugged. "Just planning ahead. My brother Jacob raises organic spinach and cauliflower. He has rabbits, too. He sells those in the raw-food pet food market."

"You lost me."

Jonah grinned, happy to be at least for a tiny moment discussing something other than murder and alleles. "People who like their cat to eat raw food. They buy rabbits. Whole frozen rabbits, preserved organs." Jonah chuckled at the discuss in her face. "No, I'll do cows. But Jacob showed me around his farm last Easter. The numbers are good."

"Well, good for you," Jenn replied, her expression neutral.

"I'm serious." Jonah wanted to brave another direct query and he did. "Jenn, do you think you would go with me when I leave this place? I've been thinking about it a lot lately. You could be my partner in the mushroom business as well as policework." Jonah watched her rub her eyes with both hands.

"Jonah, gee-whiz, *God*," she lamented exasperated. "We're in the middle of a murder investigation. One thing at a time. Let's find the guy who knocked off this reporter and *then* talk about the mushroom farm. Deal?"

Not ready to give up, Jonah had to know if she'd even consider it, to give his heart a chance to accept her flat rejection of the idea. "Will you think about it?"

She groaned with drama and covered her face.

Jonah smiled at her histrionics and said in a serious tone, "This is my last case. When we put this one to bed, I'm puttin' away my saddle." Jonah couldn't tell her that he was in love with her, because that wasn't true, but he didn't want to cut her out of his daily life. "Just say you'll consider it."

Jennifer met his eye and tapped her spoon. "Dammit, Jonah, you're a good friend and the best partner any cop could want, but you're really ticking me off—"

A server drew near, refilled Jonah's coffee and walked away before Jennifer continued.

"If I agree to think it over, will you promise not to mention it again until we're done with this case? Do we have a deal?"

Jonah let her off the hook, leaning back and grabbing a breadstick. "Sure, partner. Sure. Deal." He poked the bread into his coffee bringing a grimace to her face and he laughed. She hadn't said no and that was all he needed to put the issue to bed.

"I'll take care of Billy Austin. Who does Nixon have available to interview?"

"I found his mom in Kentucky, his father in Missouri, a cousin in Alabama, and another cousin here, in Georgia. They've all been notified of the man's demise, but not interviewed. I'll knock all four out by noon. How's that sound?"

"Sounds like we're back in business." Jenn tested her sweet tea and then in a sudden movement, reached across the table to touch his hand. "And Jonah," she said lowering her voice to an almost intimate timbre, "I appreciate what you were saying, you know, about how you feel. And I think about you, too, when we're not at work. Maybe there's something there, maybe not. But it's important that you know you're not alone."

She had leaned in and her green eyes danced at her words. He'd seen those eyes when they solved a case, the joy this woman experienced would always shine in her eyes. Jonah didn't let her smile distract him, but he heard in his heart she was the most beautiful woman in the world.

"Yeah, that's right, but listen old man—if you're gonna fantasize about me, put in the bad stuff, too. I'm not fun when it rains, I'm crabby before I've had my coffee, I'm a terrible cook, and I don't keep kosher." She squeezed his fingers until he smiled back. "Okay. Now, we focus on poor old Craig O'Neal Nixon, victim, deceased."

"Good deal." Jonah pulled his hand off the table and rested it on his leg. He didn't need to tell her that her touch made him feel alive.

Mark concentrated on a tingling sensation in his leg, working to divine its cause without rising. After a full minute, he lifted his head. A sizeable rat gnawed on the cuff of his pants, it's ears on a swivel. Mark huffed with muted humor. Did it matter? Maybe he should let the rodents devour him. Would he die? If they ate his flesh, would they become as he was? In a spasm of revulsion, Mark jerked his leg sending the rodent flying across the room with a disgusted scream.

I need a box to sleep in. A coffin. Bram Stoker had quite a good idea there, to put the vampires in a coffin. *Why didn't I think of that?*

Mark took some time to rally his strength and swung his legs over the edge of the table. He sat up with a groan and took a ragged breath. Weak and emaciated, he hadn't eaten in more than four months. His first little while in Europe, he had attempted to sustain life by living off the blood of forest animals. The distasteful practice wore thin within days and he afterward ceased feeding altogether. If he couldn't have his ambrosia, human blood, he would have nothing at all.

Mark lifted one palm, rotating it in view, studying the skin that draped over his phalanges like leathery cloth. He didn't need a mirror to assure that his face would be similarly affected. How could he purchase a coffin in his current state? *I should have thought this out…*

Outside his curtain-less windows, the sun had set. Mark sat in silence, his weight balanced on his palms, and he pictured Paul in his mind. Paul Black had been a loyal servant for almost a century. Their days had been filled with contentment. Mark smiled as he recalled sweet moments when Paul tended his needs with unimaginable devotion. But now, Paul had become an infant monster, stranded in a land of bloodlust and desperation. Guilt plagued his soul when he followed Paul's antics; Mark could hear, see, smell, and taste everything Paul experienced. And the new vampire had tasted much his first few months. Learning the efficient kill took practice, and now Paul had a pet. Mark shook his head.

Poor Tony. Now you have real trouble. Because the nature of the transfer, Tony Agricola was tainted not only by Paul's blood, but Mark's also. *But is this so different from the way I received my baptism into this unholy life? I had also been a man of God, forced into this existence. How can God hold me accountable?*

Mark withdrew his mental probe and considered the dark room in which he slumbered. The house was crumbling and drafty, but he didn't care. He sought death, but it wouldn't find him. He would have to be decapitated to die; even then, would he regenerate through demonic intervention? How could he know? His master was murdered by men from Mark's parish, burned to ash in a fire. Yet, he lived on and may even still be in Paul's mind giving him the worst kind of advice.

A part of Mark wish the preacher was with him. Tony Agricola reintroduced Mark to his Maker. Tony helped an old vampire open his eyes to what he had been doing to mankind all of those years. As a result of his awakening, Mark chose to avoid drinking blood. One task remained; lie down and wait. Wait for death, which never comes. Wait for Salvation, which was uncertain at best.

I should have bought a coffin and been buried. I'll call Tony to this task. Paul would never go for it. But the preacher? He'll do it. He understands better than anyone...

Mark peeked into Tony's psyche to plant the required seeds. It would take time for the idea to grow and bring fruit, for the man was now a new supernatural creature himself. But he would remember the old vampire he laid waste through the Spirit of God. He would come and do the decent thing and put Mark in the ground. With a determined sigh, he reclined once more on the table and closed his eyes. Maybe Tony would hurry.

◆ ◆ ◆

Happy the barn was deserted, Hope sauntered down the main aisle, past clean-smelling stalls, soft blowing noses, and the whitewashed bathing rack. Vestiges of her old life. Only a scant five months earlier she had rid herself of the whole scene to focus her energy on reuniting with Mark Corescu. Yet, he never sent for her; he never called. To make things worse, she could not reach her friend Anthony who had been with her throughout the ordeal.

It's just not fair!

She had sold her horses, dumped her cat onto a neighbor, and put her house on the market. All to wait for her vampire boyfriend to call for her. Had she lost her mind?

Glorie did…

Hope sniffled and stopped at Lucas' stall. The gelding ignored her, as if she hadn't trained and ridden him for three years.

Glorie hated my horses.

Hope swallowed, her twin sister's horrible crimes and unexpected demise flowing back. If her twin sister had gone crazy, was Hope destined to do the same?

Lucas snorted, startling her out of her thoughts. The horse she had trained from a yearling and recently sold wore a new Rambo stable sheet and munched the best alfalfa hay. Amber Gwyn was spoiling him rotten. Hope frowned.

If Mark were here, Hope thought, *I could be happy, too.*

She pictured him in her mind, the night they walked together in the moonlight, Mark's strong arms around her when they embraced. Hope fists clenched. If he was so great, where was he now? Hope loved him, he said he loved her. How could he dump her as he did?

Even a vampire could have manners…

Hope headed back to her car and fell into the driver's seat. Maybe she should ask God. Mark believed in God enough to give up everything he knew. Hope concentrated and tried to think of something to say. No words came.

God? Have you disappeared, too?

Despite herself, Hope's eyes welled with tears. Why would God listen to her? She only spoke to Him when she needed something.

Hope reversed out of the parking space and turned toward the road. Maybe God was waiting for her to *do* something. Anthony had taught her that God gave believers chores. What was Hope's chore? After only seconds, she nodded. She'd find Anthony. She'd find her friend and he'd help her find Mark. Hope wiped her cheeks and smiled. God might help her, but even if He didn't, Hope would not stop until she accomplished her task. It was time to get her life back.

ƀ

When you pass through the waters, I will be with you;
And when you pass through the rivers, they will not sweep over you.
When you walk through the fire, you will not be burned;
The flames will not set you ablaze.
Isaiah 43:2

BIG JOHN JENKINS SHOOK HANDS WITH THE PASTOR AND his wife and strode onto the stage. Opal had drawn nursery duty and would miss his message, but she could depend on him for the highlights on the ride home from church. John preached once a month and was pleased at tonight's turnout.

Smiling and waving to the gray-hairs on the first row, John gathered his thoughts for the night's sermon. He gave their pastor Reverend Elijah Prince the thumbs up and the older man grinned with an enthusiastic nod.

"Brethren," Big John Jenkins began, the chocolate brown skin of his forehead glistening with sweat. He surveyed the crowd before continuing in a deep, rolling voice. "Is it just me, or is this room slam full of the Holy Ghost?"

The crowd broke out in approving applause and John waited for quiet before continuing with a broad grin.

"Reach your hands to the sky and *give Him praise!*"

As the congregation cheered and high-fived their neighbors, Big John came off the stage and engulfed many of the elderly with his huge arms and kissed their cheeks. At six-foot-six he towered over everyone he met, but they all knew him to be a gentle giant. Reverend Prince clapped his stand-in on the back and sent him back to the pulpit.

Once in place, John's attention swiveled to the worship leader who sat at the piano behind the podium. A musical genius, Franklin Short played like an angelic Mozart. He was the only white man on the praise team, but at DBC, there were no racial lines to be drawn.

Big John watched Franklin a moment longer and stepped close to the piano. The young man appeared stoned out of his gourd.

"Brother Franklin?" Brother John said and he shook the boy's shoulder. "Brother Franklin? What do you see?" After a moment, the youngster's eyes closed and he turned his face to the ceiling.

"I see the Lord...."

Brother Franklin's voice poured like fine wine past his lips and into the air as chill bumps arose on Big John's arms.

"And His train, it fills the temple...."

Big John Jenkins went down on one knee next to the piano.

"Angels cry...Holy, Holy, Holy, is the Lord..."

John had no idea why he was suddenly on the floor, but his one-knee stance soon converted to both, and before long, he lay flat-out on the stage floor. All around him, the church sang to the Lord, while he remained prostrate, unable to move or join in. John looked up and visually searched the north end of the stage.

"I see the Lord...and His train it fills the temple...."

John was at peace in his heart as he watched the north end of the stage run with blood. At first, the thick liquid ran from the drywall in a thin line, but as the congregation's voices swelled in one accord, the torrent poured forth fast and thick as a crimson waterfall.

What does it mean, Lord? Is this just for me?

Slowly and with effort, he wrenched his head around to survey the crowd. No one showed interest in the macabre flooded stage.

Okay, so this is for me. What does it mean? You have to be real plain with me, Lord. I'm not the brightest crayon in the box...

Then, with a dramatic movement, Franklin turned his attention from the piano keys to the prone man at his feet, and sang the next verse to John.

"The Lord asks... 'Whom shall I send?'"

John met Franklin's gaze, who sang the last line looking *through* John, instead of *to* him.

"And I said...Here am I. I ...will go... for You."

John was released then from the force that held him to the ground and he scrambled to a standing position. The song finished and the blood no longer washed the north end of the stage. With a violent head shake, John walked to the podium, his mind running like a wild deer.

Yes, I will go for you, Lord. But where? Where are we going?

When the house was seated, John flipped through his notes,

allowing the silence to rule the room for almost a minute. From his seat, Reverend Prince sent him a knowing wink. Had he seen the blood? John stared at his notes, wondering what to say while his mind whirled around the vision.

What do you want me to do? Why all the blood?

John launched into his prepared message, tying it to the vision and Jesus' shed blood on the Cross. In his heart, he knew the vision meant something else entirely, although at present, he had no idea what it could be. As he spoke to the congregation, he asked the Lord burning questions that squeezed his heart.

What do I look for? How will I know when it is time to act? What am I called to do for You, Lord? Then, *...I hope You know what You're doing.*

Smiling, John focused on his sermon. Of course, God knew what He was doing. He was God after all.

Tony opened his eyes, he was not in his room.

Not rejected...

Like film developing in a tray, the vision returned to his consciousness, the details sharpening every new moment.

"What the devil intended for harm, I have turned for the good."

Tony cocked his head to the side. That voice... pondered the spontaneous bit of Scripture before he turned his attention to his body. Rolling his head to the right, he regarded Paul's sleeping form beside him.

That's not right....

Tony sat up and swung his legs to the floor, taking a deep breath. He felt amazing, as if he had slept a century and awoke a new man. Paul stirred and Tony jumped to his feet.

Wait a minute...

Tony searched his memory and recalled Paul's mouth on his throat. Now the same monster lay sound asleep three feet away. The entire attack came back in a painful instant and Tony gasped.

That was real? It can't be! There's no way! No way!

Dizzy, Tony backed from the bed, stepping into the hallway, never taking his eyes off the sleeping vampire. He drew his hand to his throat and found he had no wound, no raw laceration, nothing.

But if last night was real... Tony's throat would be shredded. But it wasn't. Could he have dreamed the attack?

Tony grit his teeth and tip-toed into the hall, finding a bathroom halfway down. Without making a sound, he slipped inside and closed the door before flipping on the light. Tony gaped at his reflection. Dried blood ran from his lips into his beard. Clucking his tongue, a stale and coppery taste assaulted his senses. Tony leaned on the counter peering into his face. He felt great; he looked a mess. What was going on?

"I have your glasses. Don't you need them?" Paul said through the door. Tony froze, glancing toward the sound.

What do I do, Lord? He looked back to his reflection and asked himself the same question.

"Do you still need them? Maybe my blood fixed your eyesight." Paul's knuckle rapped the wood. "What'cha doing in there?"

"Leave me alone," Tony said through clenched teeth still staring at his reflection.

"Maybe I can help you," Paul said, his voice plaintive.

Tony opened the door. "Haven't you done enough?"

"I don't know. How do you feel?" Paul asked, standing in the hall holding Tony's wire-framed glasses at chest level.

Tony snatched his eyewear from Paul's hand and placed them on his face. His vision sharpened.

"So you still need them. *Hmph.*"

Tony didn't respond. Instead, he paused to take better stock of his body. Besides the blood crusted shirt, he looked normal.

"How do you feel?" Paul asked moving to stand behind Tony over his left shoulder and they both looked in the mirror.

Tony mustered a growl. "I feel fine, no thanks to you."

"Oh? I beg to differ. It's all due to me, and you're welcome." Reaching around, Paul pushed Tony's chin to one side. "Let's have a look."

Tony did not resist, but watched the two reflections with interest. "What are you looking for?"

"Your wound healed," Paul marveled, using a tentative prod to examine the skin under Tony's ear. "I did it, you're immortal."

"Don't be stupid," Tony replied and swatted Paul's fingers away. Shouldn't he have a wound? *If* the attack occurred and his wound had healed… "Don't be ridiculous," he mumbled with less gusto.

Paul rested his hands on Tony's shoulders again and met his eye in the mirror. "You sure are stubborn."

"I gotta go," Tony said quietly, planning his ride home. He

wanted to get away from Paul. Would the vampire let him leave? Would God? Since he survived last night, would he be allowed to go back to his life? His job at the church? Had he made a promise to stay? His memories before the attack were still filtering into place, but it seemed in his terror, he may have vowed to move away with Paul.

Tony's eyes flit to the vampire's reflection in the mirror. Paul was watching him, hi grin to the side, with both hands on Tony's shoulders.

"Where are you going?" Paul asked humor in his tone.

"I can't stay with you. You know that, right?" Tony said in his eye. "I'll help you from my own house. You get that, right?"

Paul only tilted his head the other way and continued with the eerie smile.

"I did it. You're immortal..."

Paul's words replayed in Tony's head and he returned to gazing into his own eyes. That was ridiculous. Yes, he attacked me. Yes, I can't find the wound. But why would that make me immortal? Corescu bit me in his garage and nothing happened.

Me, immortal? That's just plain silly.

♦

"That'll do, preacher-man," Paul said, irritated at being dismissed. He wrapped his left arm around Tony's chest and held him tight. "Watch and learn."

"Dammit, Paul!" Tony hissed and struggled in his grip, but Paul held him in place with no effort.

Finding Tony's eye in their reflections, he pressed his thumbnail into the man's healed throat. Tony gasped and then gagged at the pressure. To Paul's amusement, his guest's expression was *surprise*. Tony was *annoyed,* not afraid. Paul smirked and trained his eyes to the four-inch gash he'd opened in Tony's skin.

"Watch," he whispered and with a comical eye strain to see the site, Tony complied. The preacher grew still, his eyes glued to the awesome and immediate healing of the wound. When it had closed, Paul swiped the blood that had escaped and sucked his finger with flourish.

Tony jerked his shoulders free as Paul released him. "That can't be!" he barked and leaned close to the mirror. He pressed the skin where the laceration had disappeared. "That's impossible!"

"Aw, now, don't say that," Paul teased and resumed the same

hold to his body, his right arm snugging Tony to his own chest and the left hand headed this time to Tony's cheek. With the same thumbnail and pressure, Paul opened a smaller tear in the skin above Tony's beard. Tony squirmed free with surprising strength. He again leaned in to the mirror and touched his face.

"I can't feel it! Why can't I feel it?" Tony yanked a washcloth off the rack and shoved it under the tap. Before he could squeeze out the excess water, the gash in his face had closed as well. "This can't be happening!"

Paul grabbed him again, prepared for another demonstration. This time, Tony caught his hand before it reached his flesh and pushed it away.

"Stop it! I get the point!" Tony wriggled free and stomped from the bathroom. "Back off, dammit! Let me think!"

With a tight grin, Paul trailed him into the living room and watched as Tony located his discarded Bible and lifted it off the shelf. With his back to Paul, he opened the book, flipped a few pages, and grew quiet. Paul walked up behind him and looked over his shoulder.

"What does it say about immortality?" he said with false sincerity.

"It says no one is immortal, but God," Tony answered without hesitation.

"Well, then it's wrong," Paul said in a chuckle and turned away. Tony remained in place another minute and Paul dropped onto the couch eying him with curiosity. He was going to be fun to watch.

♦

Tony wasn't angry, he wasn't afraid. He was... what? Disappointed? Frustrated? His emotions jumbled and he stared at the pages without reading. Had God set this up for His purposes? Tony considered the holy Book and closed his eyes.

So, what does this mean? Paul served the Doctor as his partner for almost a hundred years. Paul wasn't a vampire until the end. If my body heals instantly and stops aging, I can still do God's work, right? And what about God? Does He blame me? Didn't I come here yesterday to do His will?

"Come here," Paul said and Tony did not look over. "Sit down," he said and pat the couch beside his leg. With a twitch in his left eye, Tony got his feet moving, eyes still on the pages, and his mind pondering the next move. He settled on the opposite end of the two-seater sofa and took a lung-filling breath. Once he exhaled he turned his face to Paul.

"Okay, what's different. Why did my skin heal up. That didn't happen after Corescu attacked me in the garage."

Paul leveled his gaze and sucked his teeth in slow motion. "How'd that blood get on your beard? I know you tasted it in your mouth." Tony's fingers went to his chin and he narrowed his eyes. Paul nodded. "You ingested my blood while you were unconscious. I did some magic on you!" The vampire flashed his eyes with humor and Tony snorted.

"No, I did not." His weak retort only made Paul giggle. The guy was right; Tony had tasted blood, but had hoped maybe he'd bitten his tongue in his struggle.

Beside him, Paul reached over to clap his back once before stretching out long and propping his head in upraised arms. "You're a new man. My little man-pet."

"No, I'm not," Tony said and drew his palm down his face. Then he whispered his next question. "So, I'm not a vampire?"

Paul laughed. "Do you want to be?"

Tony sent him a glare but softened soon after at his internal reminder: *God has this. This is about Him, not me.* Nodding his entire body in thought, Tony asked, "Okay, so what's different? Besides being a quick healer?"

Paul wiggled his eyebrows. "For starters, you won't age. That Tony Agricola you got there is the one you'll have forever. And you're so cute!" Paul teased and swatted his back again.

Ignoring the last job, Tony studied his hands. There had to be more, he felt amazing, marvelous. In fact, he was all but bursting with positivity. He looked to Paul. "What are you leaving out?" Paul shrugged. "Why do I feel so… so weird?"

"Oh," Paul said and grinned, "the high. That'll wear off. My magical blood did that. Same thing happened to me with Mark."

This is real. We're doing this. After a brief moment to close his eyes and set his spirit forward, Tony put away the final vestige of the denial flooding his psyche. Time to face facts and move ahead.

"Okay, start over. What do we do now?" he asked Paul, looking at him on his right.

Paul remained leaning back and looked to the ceiling. "Today, we go get your stuff and in a few days, we drive to Montgomery. I have some properties lined up, we choose a house, move in. We check out the bookstore, get that going. I suck your neck when I'm hungry, and as soon as it's right, we'll contact Mark and see how he's doing."

Tony regarded the vampire's reply. It sounded like the truth, the whole plan laid out at once, and he didn't take the bait on the threat. Paul hadn't mentioned one thing. He lifted the Bible, the cover toward the vampire.

"I have one condition and I guess you know what that is," Tony said and Paul rolled his eyes. "Every day, you will submit to hearing five minutes about God."

"No problem," Paul said low, eyes closed, his face upward.

"And part of that is letting me pray for you like this," Tony added and put his palm open on Paul's leg.

"Pervert," Paul whispered with a grin and remained still.

"God, we're ready. Please have your way with us today. Amen."

"Amen," Paul said by reflex and peeked at Tony's hand as he moved it away. "You can touch me any time, preacher-man. I like it."

Tony held his eye and shared the first line in the Bible. *Introducing a monster to God,* he thought. *May as well start at the beginning.*

♦

"In the beginning, God created the heavens and the earth," Tony said, reading directly from the book in his lap. Paul listened with a grin. Why not? If this was all it took to keep the guy happy, he'd invest five minutes. At least for now. Somewhere along the line he'd get the preacher in line, subjugate him properly, but for now? Paul would play nice.

"…And God said, 'Let there be light,' and there was light…"

Paul peeked at Tony and then re-closed his eyes, setting an internal timer. Religion made him angry, reminding him that he lost his former life because of his master's infatuation with God.

When Tony paused to take a breath, the time had elapsed and Paul sighed with drama. "That book, those words, that religion, it's just a silly obsession."

"I hear you," Tony said, surprising Paul with his neutral tone. Mark never allowed Paul to speak against God, and he never would; causing Mark distress was something he avoided with fervor. And then that Hope woman came along. Paul's jaw clenched at the memory of her. His master still wanted her, that was obvious, for each time Mark allowed Paul access to his mind, he'd see her there. Tony touched his knee, maybe thinking Paul's sudden frown came from the lesson.

"You don't have to work at it. You only have to hear the words.

They're supernatural." Tony withdrew his fingers and got to his feet. "The Lord's will is stronger than your stubbornness. You might be surprised to know that even now, right this second, God knows what will become of you. He has it all planned out. You're being controlled whether you know it or not."

Paul scoffed. "It seems like I would know if someone was controlling me," Paul said meeting Tony's somber gaze. "I made you like this. I did it, all by myself."

Tony shook his head. "On the contrary. I'm a child of God. I'm here because God put me here. Not you, or Doctor Corescu, or Hope, but God. If God didn't want this to happen, it wouldn't happen. He's in control."

Paul snickered, but Tony wasn't done.

"And one day, God will put me back the way I was. This is some kind of curse, that's all. I'll carry it as long as God needs me to, but it's not mine. It's yours."

Paul stifled another laugh. The man was still utterly convinced of his powerful delusion. It was downright entertaining to see him so serious. Paul also got to his feet and cupped Tony's near shoulder. "I say you've been neutered. Neutered by God." Paul pulled himself to his feet and stretched. "I'm going to enjoy having you around."

"I'm sure you will," Tony replied.

"You need a shower," Paul deadpanned covering his nose. "There's soap and towels in there." Paul reached the bedroom and closed himself in, listening for Tony's movements. Would the guy try to leave? *Nah, I don't see that happening.* No matter how much he trusted his book and the words in it, the guy had seen bad things happen to people he liked, and Paul would carry out his threat. If Tony abandoned him, everyone he knew would die. The shower went on in the hall and Paul smiled.

Big John nodded at passersby, awaiting his wife. They'd stopped by Walmart and enduring her third trimester, she needed the facilities every hour. He pondered his recent vision and what it might mean for his family.

Why now, with the baby coming so soon? I've been a servant of Jesus since I was twelve years old. Why would You wait until now?

It was the timing that bothered John the most. He studied the

Scriptures but dropping his day-job to become a preacher had never been possible. Was God urging him to go full-time? John huffed. He should be able to keep a day job, making real money, and still do the will of God. Didn't he talk about Jesus to Scully and the guys at work? And when he was bouncing clubs, didn't he pray for the drunks and tell as many of them as he could about the Lord?

John frowned. Had he made the right choices by God? Did he marry the woman God picked out? Definitely. And wasn't it God who placed him at the helm of his father-in-law's moving business? What did God expect? He was no Apostle Paul.

Big John sighed and redirected his thoughts. A rotund and rosy woman drew near toting an equally round baby. She offered a tight smile at the eye-meet and looked John up and down. He was huge, he knew it, and since he hit puberty, he collected *the looks*. John gave her a grin and a "good evenin'," and she scooted to the exit.

If I was supposed to go into full-time ministry, I would've known about it. I'm sure of it. So why that dramatic vision?

The ladies' room door opened and John joined Opal at the water fountain. As she sipped, he held her waist-length, reddish-gold hair aside. *God, I love her so much…*

She finished and turned to give him a kiss, funny now because when he bent to her level, she poked out her rump to make way for the baby. She was perfection. Her pink skin flawless and before and after the pregnancy, her shape drove him wild. How did he ever score such a beauty queen?

Father in Heaven, he prayed, *just hold off, okay? Don't let anything dangerous happen right now. Just hold off. I'll serve You when the baby gets old enough to defend himself. Please…*

By the time he had Opal tucked into his rusty Cadillac, he decided he had misinterpreted the vision. God wouldn't spring a deadly trial upon him with a baby on the way. It didn't make sense. When he pointed the car to the interstate, his wife began to sing, her voice causing his love to swell anew. Yes, God would wait. He *had to.*

"Are not two sparrows sold for a penny?
Yet not one of them will fall to the ground
Apart from the will of your Father."
Matthew 10:29

EXITING THE SHOWER IN HIS RELATIVELY UNSTAINED slacks from the night before, Tony found the bedroom empty. He padded to the front of the apartment in his socks looking for Paul. Then he reached the front door and pulled it open.

"Hey!" Paul said with an open grin, pushing indoors to pass Tony for the kitchen. "Nice of you to get the door."

Tony followed and Paul set his sack on the marble countertop. "I was only in the shower ten minutes. What's that?" He peeked into the bag as Paul unloaded eggs, cheddar cheese, milk, butter, cream, and a box of plastic cutlery.

"I'm really, really fast. Plus, you'll be hungry. You had a big night." Paul removed a miniature frying pan from the bag and placed it on the stovetop.

Tony touched his middle. He wasn't hungry. Maybe he'd lose some weight. He pushed his tummy, measuring too many donuts consumed late night at the church.

Paul caught his movement and waited for Tony to look up. "Let me feel it," he said joking and when Tony only leveled his gaze, Paul added, "remember what I said. You'll stay just like this from now on. You can eat all you want and never gain a pound. I really deserve some thanks, Mr. Pudge."

Tony dropped his hand. He wasn't *that* out of shape... Anyway, he wasn't hungry. He sat on a bar stool and watched Paul's movements. With expert care, the vampire cracked the eggs into the pan, stirred, added cream and butter, stirred, and plopped cheese on as it hardened.

"I'm not hungry," he said and Paul shot him a glare.

"Yes, you are. And you'll eat this." He adjusted the heat as the eggs finished. "I was quite the cook back in my day. Of course, I only cooked for myself." He send Tony a grin, bringing the memory of Corescu around for them both.

Tony made no reaction, unwilling to be drawn into a discussion about Paul's perfect existence under the thumb of the vampire doctor. Tony stood to reach for a plastic fork near Paul's position and the vampire popped his hand. "I got this, preacher-man. Go sit down."

"Whatever," he said and settled on his stool and watched Paul sprinkle copious amounts of cheese over the sizzling eggs. Why not? If calories no longer counted, Tony might start eating cheese with every meal. Paul removed the pan from the heat and spun with drama. Tony gave him a thank you when he placed the frying pan where Tony sat getting a glimpse of what daily life alongside the megalomaniac vampire was going to resemble.

"Gobble, gobble, turkey," Paul said, and ran his eyes to Tony's middle and back again. "I think you look great." Tony had no reply. He looked at the eggs and Paul handed him a fork. "Anyway, what do you care? I'm not dating you. Do you have a girlfriend?" Paul tilted his head awaiting an answer. Tony didn't reply and after a few seconds, Paul huffed. "I don't think you'll need a girlfriend anymore."

"I guess not," Tony agreed, setting his fork to the eggs. He couldn't have a romantic relationship with a homicidal vampire on his heels. Maybe this was the reason, that at thirty-three, he remained the oldest bachelor in his congregation.

The omelet was good and after two bites, he was glad Paul had insisted he eat. As his stomach reacted to the sudden nourishment, Tony looked at Paul leaning on the counter.

"Can you eat this?" he asked, pretty sure the answer would be no. Paul grinned and shook his head. "Then what have you been eating?" The man was a vampire and it had been many months since he was transformed. Tony would need to find a way to keep him from killing people during their tenure together. Paul didn't answer and Tony allowed it to finish off his meal. Then he took a deep breath and cleared his throat. He met Paul's eye. "Well?"

Paul offered a tiny smile. "Are you sure you want to know? Might make you throw-up. You were sort of squeamish at Mark's."

"I'm not squeamish," Tony replied, indignant.

Paul shook his head. "You faint at the sight of blood. I remember holding you off the ground when Mark made a tiny hole in your arm."

Tony wiped his chin with his forearm and frowned. "I fainted from blood loss, not the sight of blood."

Paul smirked and crossed his arms at his narrow chest. "If you say so."

Tony reworded his question. "Have you been killing people since that night at Dr. Corescu's?"

"Yep," Paul said and leveled his gaze, daring a confrontation. Tony steeled his nerve. He had to know what he was dealing with.

"You'll have to stop. We can't leave a trail of bodies everywhere we go." Paul didn't reply and Tony turned his chair to face him, now wondering how long it would take God to deliver the guy. How long was his new sentence?

"Your pulse is up." Paul hopped onto the counter and dangled his legs below. "I can hear your heart? Pretty cool, huh?"

"Amazing," Tony dead-panned. "Who have you killed?"

Paul studied his fingernails. "A few derelicts, and a hooker."

Tony broke out in gooseflesh, worry over the vampire's victims piercing his heart. He peeked back to Paul's face. "Were you merciful?" The vampire gave a single nod. "That's hard to believe." Tony had said the words aloud, but meant them inside. Paul replied with an edge.

"I only torture *you*, preacher-man. Them? I was gentle."

"Praise God for that," Tony whispered, and gave Paul a slow shake of the head. "Look, no more killing. *Period.*" Tony ignored Paul's growing irritation. "How long can you go without blood?"

"Four days. Five—if I can stay distracted," Paul replied. "But it's moot. Why should I go without? No, that's not an option."

"What about animal blood?" Tony asked and Paul's grimace answered the question. "Dr. Corescu never drank animal blood?"

"Why would he? He had a new victim every night for four hundred years." Paul's eyes flashed. "And he had me…"

Tony got to his feet. "Calm down, Dracula. I'm not going to be donating any more blood. *Period.*" Tony shivered at the memory, life draining out like water from a sieve.

"I'm not going to be donating any more blood," Paul said, mimicking Tony's voice with an uncanny accuracy. He looked at Tony with a playful wink. "No more killing, *period*. No more sucking my blood, *period*," Paul laughed into his hand. "You can't stop me."

Tony watched Paul's impish expression.

God, that's not what You're thinking, is it?

Tony's heart pictured it, the vampire latching onto him night after night after night. And each time, another innocent is saved. He exhaled with drama and looked to the ceiling. *Father! I can't do that!*

But he could.

And he would.

He grumbled aloud and met Paul's eye. "Maybe so, but I'm not going to be your servant."

"We'll see about that." Paul sent his threatening reply telepathically and Tony frowned.

"Let's get moving." He turned for the other room and Paul followed. When they reached the driveway, Paul pointed to the Tahoe.

"I'll drive." He opened Tony's door on the passenger side and then climbed in the driver's seat. "Hah, did you see that?" he remarked aloud. Tony didn't answer so he continued as he switched on the truck. "I just fell back into servant mode there."

Tony *humphed* and stared out the windshield. Whatever was going through the vampire's mind was nothing he would be able to comprehend.

"You are *my* servant, Tony. I'm not yours." Paul's voice hardened. "And if you want me to stop biting strangers, you're gonna have to pony up your own blood every week, maybe twice a week."

Tony's throat constricted, but he nodded without looking over.

"Good," Paul said with finality and pulled away from the curb. He patted Tony's shoulder.

Tony rolled in his lips and counted his blessings.

Jennifer Speltz sat across from the newest CSU Lab Tech tapping her pencil against her temple. Jonah was fifteen minutes late and she didn't know how much longer the kid would wait. He had dodged his boss to come by in the first place, but what could she do? She'd already called her partner's apartment as well as his cell with no luck. Jennifer put the pencil behind her ear and opened the lab report.

"Okay, Billy, I know you've gone out of your way, so maybe you could just begin and I'll fill my partner in later. Tell me what you think of the sample we sent down yesterday."

"Off the record?" Billy asked as he combed his goatee in quick jerks. When she nodded, he snaked the comb into his back pocket and leaned his elbows on Jonah's side of the messy desk pair. "I was excited after those first results. I mean, the blood is human, no doubt about that, but it had a few misplaced markers and it *might* have had a mutated DNA indicator."

"That happen a lot?" Jenn pressed. Billy laughed.

"I wish. Everybody has an allele from their mom and one from their dad. *One.*" He held up his pointer finger. "I detected several weird things about this blood sample, and one was multiple alleles."

"Like it's contaminated with several blood donors?"

Billy shook his head. "No, but that's what my boss said to close the issue. I saw the initial results, Detective. Those multiple markers are in one person. Whoever spilled that blood had mutated DNA. Mutated in a way we've never seen before."

"And that didn't make those other guys excited?" Jennifer kept her voice low, aware of Billy's conspiratorial nature.

"Brown-nosers," he scoffed. "We run the same old tests every day, always the same old thing, same old thing…" Billy rolled his eyes at his repetition. "And then we get this novel blood sample and I think, 'Hey! Something new! Let's see what it is!' But my supervisor nixed the investigation after that."

"Is that standard procedure down there? Find something odd and tuck it away instead of investigate it properly?"

"No. I mean, we never saw anything this weird before, but in the past, if a sample was degraded or peculiar, we'd send it to Atlanta and use their resources to get answers. I think that if they gave me that sample from your case, I could have some answers for you in a few days. It would only take a little manpower. I wouldn't even need any outside equipment." Billy shrugged and leaned back in Jonah's desk chair. "But they won't give it to me. They got me on another case altogether. In fact, I better get to the lab before they start wondering where I've been."

Jennifer stood as Billy rose to his feet. "If I get permission for you to work on it again, will you?"

"Sure. But I won't hold my breath."

"Just keep your options open. I think I can get Erkleson to put a few more hours in on this one. Give me 'til the end of the day, okay?"

"Sure. Tell Detective Miller I said hi and bye." Billy shook Jennifer's hand and turned to leave.

Jennifer settled back into her seat and dialed Jonah's phone number. It rang four times and went to voicemail.

"Jonah, you missed Billy Austin's report. Call me or get your hiney into the office."

Jennifer had been working alongside Detective Miller for four years and eight months, and it wasn't uncommon for him to not be sitting at his desk by nine. He often ran down leads before work and showed up when he was done. It wasn't because he liked working alone, but because he didn't have anything better to do from 6 a.m. when he awoke, to 9 a.m., when he was due at work. He had no hobbies that she knew of other than studying his Bible, he didn't have a relationship with his ex-wife, and his only daughter was married and living across the country in L.A. He had his work and it filled his time. That was why Jennifer was surprised to hear him talking about retirement. She thought of Jonah Miller as a career man, the kind of guy who would stay with the department until he could no longer wield a gun. So why the sudden interest in giving it all up?

Jennifer picked up the phone, preparing to try his house again. As she dialed, she was reminded of his invitation. What made him think she would want to leave a lucrative career with the police department to raise fungus on a farm? For twelve years, she'd been serving the public, first as a patrol cop and the last eight years as detective. She assumed she'd stay at least twenty years and then consider her options, maybe ride a desk and make some real money. But leave now to move into a farmhouse with Jonah Miller?

Jennifer shook her head, but she was smiling. Jonah was a keeper. Handsome and mature, and probably a lot tougher out than he was in. Jennifer imagined he would be a particularly attentive lover. Spending every day with him the last few years *had* been fun... Jennifer shook her head. She would focus on the case and not on her partner's preposterous invitation. At least for now.

Rising from her desk, she headed for the captain's office. If he'd give her Billy for one day, they might get the break they needed to solve the case of the dead reporter from Kentucky.

And then onto mushroom farming.

One thing at a time, Jennifer told herself as she pushed open Erkleson's door.

8

I have commanded My sanctified ones;
I have also called My mighty ones for My anger—
Those who rejoice in My exaltation."
Isaiah 13:2,3

JONAH AND JENNIFER SAT ACROSS FROM ONE ANOTHER
in a rear booth at Twirlies, their favorite last stop for chow before
heading to their respective homes. It had been a good week, with a
couple of decent breakthroughs, but they were far from finished.
Jonah took a bite of his spaghetti and flipped the pages of his pad.

"Nixon was a bonified jerk. Nobody liked him, 'cept his mother
and she seemed pretty senile. I spoke to a cousin in Columbus named
Opal Jenkins. A red-head knock-out," Jonah said and caught Jenn's
reaction. His partner shot him a look and he snickered. "She said that
they didn't get along, but he had contacted her via email during the
period just before his death."

"That's interesting. What did he want?"

"Maybe not that interesting. He sent her a j-peg of a carved knife
and asked her to determine its value. I don't see that the knife she
described has any bearing on our case. The one she described was at
least eighteen inches long with a serrated edge."

"A hunter's knife," Jenn offered and Jonah nodded.

"Nixon was killed with a pocketknife. Looks like a coincidence."

"What else you got?" Jennifer asked, munching her bread.

"I was unable to reach his cousin in Alabama, a man named
Snack Peters. All the phone numbers I found for him were dead
ends."

"Snack Peters? Funny name…"

"Huh, yeah. I thought so, too. But there's a light at the end of the
tunnel. I spoke to Nixon's editor, a pleasant enough fellow named
Grouper. He said that Nixon was a scumbag who blackmailed him to

get published each week. He also indicated that Nixon was dirty and had a lot of enemies. I had him fax me copies of his stories for the past year. Maybe we'll get lucky…"

Jennifer swallowed her ravioli. "Yeah, I'll go through as many of those stories as I can tonight. I want to draw up a list of suspects. Despite its mutated nature, Billy determined that the donor of the sample from the tree bark was human and male. He'll match it to a perp if we find the right guy." Jennifer's eyes flashed, her smile tight. "This case is not sleeping anymore, Jonah. We got a real investigation going and the captain has taken notice. He came to my desk today to get an update."

"Erkleson asked about our case?" Jonah couldn't believe his ears.

"Sure did." Jennifer took another bite with a triumphant smile. She glanced at her watch and wiped her mouth. "You know what? I'm going to go ahead home and start with those files. Hand 'em over."

"It's only ten o'clock. Let's work them together until midnight. I'm just as anxious as you are to get this thing closed." Jonah took the last swig from his coffee and set the cup down. "We'll work at your pad so you won't have to be driving home late. Deal?"

Jennifer shrugged. They had poured over evidence at her house before and had even solved a case or two over a pot of her lavender tea. "Fine with me. But I want to get them all read before midnight. Can we do it?"

Jonah stood and dropped a five on the table for the server. "Let's quit jabbering and find out," he said and followed her out the door.

◆ ◆ ◆

Tony rubbed his eyes and sat up in the dark. The clock read midnight. Thank God, he was alone, having convinced Paul to stay on the couch. It was the only way Tony would get any rest by having a locked door between himself and the vampire who kept him.

Not that a stupid push-in lock would stop him.

Tony frowned. But… he *had* survived six impossible days so far. Thursday night, Paul had not returned home until well after two in the morning and Tony was too horrified to ask him if he had been out hunting. As much as Tony wanted to prevent the innocent from dying, he delayed the vampire latching on to him again.

Apologizing to God and asking for courage, Tony rose and padded to the front of the house to grab a sip of cold water from the fridge. The plan was to return to his room unmolested and he tiptoed past the living room entrance. At the refrigerator, an uneasy sensation washed over him. He spun a circle in the dark kitchen nook, peering into the corners illuminated by the icebox light. He saw nothing, but his instincts told him otherwise.

"Paul?" he whispered. No reply. Was the guy planning a stealth attack? It seemed like something he would do. Tony left the nook without getting a drink and shuffled back to his room at speed. Tucked into bed once more, the eerie presence lingered and a cold chill filled Tony's bones. The bedroom door remained closed and Tony pulled the sheet over his head like a child.

"Tony, relax before you hurt yourself…"

Tony squeezed his eyes small. The telepathic voice was not Paul's, but his master's; the creature in the semblance of a man whose infatuation with Hope Brannen set the dominoes of their lives tumbling down.

"That's harsh, don't you think? I am your brother…" The voice paused and Tony detected a chuckle. *"Now in more ways than one…"*

"What do you want?" Tony hissed. He had no inkling that the vampire would be able to, or even desire to, contact him after all of this time. Why now and did he have to listen?

"Come to me, Tony. I need you. Put me in the ground. Hurry."

Then, in a wisp of nausea, the presence was gone. Tony sat up in the dark. "Dr. Corescu?" he whispered to the empty room. Just as he gave up, his bedroom door opened with a pop and creak as if it had not been locked.

"You locked the door?" a voice from his now open doorway questioned. Paul chuckled, wiggling the broken doorknob, when Tony met his eye in the dim light.

"Like it did any good," Tony mumbled, pondering his ethereal conversation with a vampire that was supposedly on the other side of the globe.

Paul leaned against the doorframe. "Who are you talking to? Did you say Corescu?"

"No, it's no one, it's nothing." Tony stumbled over his reply. "Bad dreams. Go away. Good night."

Paul sneered. "I can hear a pin drop across the apartment, so you know I hear every noise you make clomping around the place." Paul stayed put, enjoying his partial invisibility. "What does Mark want with you?"

"I don't know. He hung up." Tony rolled over, away from Paul and shut his eyes.

"You all packed to leave?" Paul lowered his voice so that Tony was forced to poke his head out of the covers to hear him.

"What? Yes. Of course." Tony re-covered his head. "Now, please let me sleep."

"You should be excited. We're going to buy a big, beautiful house in the next few days, and you can get whatever you want. The sky's the limit. I'd think you'd be a little more appreciative."

"Thank you, Paul," Tony said, then added, "It'll be great."

Tomorrow, he and Paul were driving to Montgomery, Alabama. A Realtor had been contacted and houses in their price range lined up to visit. It might be a nightmare living with a vampire, but so far, Tony was thankful that things were fairly comfortable.

"You never told me how it went with your people back home," Paul said, his voice almost too low to hear. Tony heard enough to answer.

"I took care of everything," he replied, just as quietly. "Now, please, for God's sake, let me get back to sleep."

"You know, if I wanted to, I could yank you right out of that bed."

Muffled, beneath the heavy comforter, Tony mustered a sarcastic reply. "I know. You're very powerful. I'm very frightened. Now good night."

He waited as silent moments passed. Did Paul care if Corescu contacted him? Would he make good on his threat and attack? When nothing happened, Tony fell asleep; only one thought rolling around his head: *Put me in the ground. Hurry.*

◆◆◆

Hope taped the last box and sighed. She didn't have a buyer, but packing helped to remind her of her determination. She toted the heavy box to her dinette table and the phone on the wall filled the kitchen with bells. The last person she knew with an actual landline, Hope yanked the cordless phone off the charger.

"Hope?" a male voice said and she sank into a chair. It was Jimmy Hershey, her dead sister's husband.

"Hey, Jimmy. How're the kids?" Hope asked. He'd lost his wife and been saddled with three boys, all children of other men. How was he taking it? Hope was ashamed that she hadn't spoken to him since the funeral. Glorie died in a car wreck the same night Hope discovered her twin's dirty little secret, that Glorie had murdered her previous husbands and been poisoning her living children with household ammonia. But Jimmy was nice, and right now, awful quiet.

"Jimmy, you still there?"

"Sure. Sure, Hope. Look, remember at the funeral you offered to come up and stay with the kids?"

"Uh-huh…" Of course she had offered; everyone had.

"Well, does that offer stand? I have a situation here."

Hope listened patiently as Glorie's husband detailed his needs. She was to go to their house and keep the children a few weeks so he could go out of the country on business. He offered to buy her a plane ticket, but she refused, preferring a long, meditative road trip.

"Tell them that Aunt Hoppy is coming and I'm going to give them all horsy back rides when I get there."

"I will," he replied. "And Hope…"

"Yeah?" She knew what he was going to say. She could feel it.

"Thank you. You're the best sister-in-law a guy could ever have."

"Yeah, yeah. I know. I'll see you soon. Love ya…"

Hope allowed him to hang up before she clicked the phone back into its holder. Then she slumped onto the floor and considered her boxed treasures.

Uprooting my life for a man. Unbelievable, she mused now staring at the dark shadows in the living room. She imagined Mark there, tall, handsome, so sexy.

Hah, don't forget immortal, inhuman, uncaring, and selfish.

Unbidden, her heart swelled with the memory of his arms around her at the Block's party last fall. Hope closed her eyes and meditated on his face. Just this once, she'd allow herself to go as far as she could, to slip away from her little house and fall completely into thinking of her lost love. The recollections rolled past like images on a movie reel, and she smiled. Hope's pulse quickened as she remembered their more intimate moments. Those had been the best and she was not ready to let them go.

Mark, she said in her mind, focusing on his eyes, *I'm not giving up. We're going to be together if it kills me. I'm going to find you and you'll be so happy to see me that you'll never let me go.*

"Hope."

Hope's hand flew to her throat. Had she just heard her name or was it her imagination? She became as still as possible and waited for more. Inside, an unexplainable sense that Mark had heard her tickled her consciousness. Could he be listening? Was he waiting to see what she'd say next? Mark wasn't a mortal man. He was supernatural with abilities she didn't understand. Maybe he *could* hear her lamentations.

Maybe was good enough.

Taking the same posture, Hope formulated a more exacting transmission. *"If you're listening, Mark, I love you. You need me. I'm going to find you and we'll straighten this out. Mark? Mark?"*

There was no reply, but Hope could not shake the feeling that she had been heard. For the first time in months, Hope sighed with relief. Maybe she could survive a month with Glorie's kids, away from home, away from her friends, if she thought Mark was listening. And she'd call him often until he replied.

9

"Call to me and I will answer you
And show you great and mighty things
Which you do not know."
Jeremiah 33:3

THE HOUSE ON HIBISCUS LANE WAS PERFECT. PAUL crawled out of the Realtor's dazzling white Lexus and stared at the simple beauty of it. The two-story executive home was very much like the one he had left in Georgia, and Tony would notice the similarity. Painted a soft eggshell, it had green shutters on the front-facing windows, and elaborate beds on both sides, immaculately planted with assorted flowering plants. A closet horticulturalist, Paul pointed them out to Tony whose gaze was trained to the far left behind the house to a professional tennis courts. Paul punched his arm. "You play?"

"Sure," Tony replied without meeting his eye.

The guy was sullen, but he'd perk up. Paul eyed the back of the Realtor's head as she chattered on the phone. "Remember to call me Saul, and you're my big brother." Tony nodded and Paul put his hand to his chest, palm down and then to Tony's forehead as if measuring their height differences. "I'll bet you've never been the 'big' anything." Paul laughed at his insult, but Tony said nothing.

The Realtor finished her call in the front seat and was gathering her paperwork. Paul smoothed his hair and sent Tony a friendly wink. The guy had softened over the past few days, which was nice. Maybe Tony was just a serious guy. Today's cover story was simple: Tony and Saul, step-brothers and co-inheritors of a huge family fortune. They opted to continue using the name *Saul White*; it had worked well keeping the law off their case and Paul enjoyed the game, playing someone else.

"Gentlemen, this is the Cherry Tree Estate." Stepping from her car and tucking away her phone, the Realtor, chirped in interrupting Paul's thoughts. "It is so-named because of the cherry tree grove on the back of the property. She sports a Wimbledon-worthy tennis court, twelve fenced acres, and a barn-slash-workshop behind the house. And there's a one-acre pond stocked with bream and sunfish."

The agent did her dance, pointing and gesturing with every word. Sold from the moment he laid eyes on the place, Paul ignored her. Tony, though, was paying close attention, which was fine. Only one of them needed to be boring.

♦

Convinced of the pending sale, Real Estate agent Veronica Law sashayed up the front steps and turned to the buyers. The setting sun reminded her not to work too late; her boyfriend had planned an elaborate birthday party for her after work. But she needed this sale and the commission would more than make up for her tardiness. Veronica maintained her pleasant demeanor and kept her mind on the dollar signs. At first sight, she would have taken these two as renters. They didn't dress G.Q. and they drove a hunky SUV, like good ol' boy rednecks. But her boss confirmed their bankroll; they were filthy rich. Veronica thanked her lucky stars her name had come up for the sale. To the men, she smiled and spoke up in her sing-song voice.

"Would you like to see inside?" She jingled the keys and watched the taller man's eyes. Sold on the place already, his smile gave him away. Veronica pushed open the door with flair and Mr. White wandered in like a child in a candy store.

The serious-looking Agricola walked in after him, scrutinizing every detail. Veronica couldn't decide if the man was unfriendly or simply being prudent. He carried a well-worn Bible in his hand that had Veronica thinking. If he was a preacher, he may be unable to relax. In her fundamentalist Baptist past, she had never met a laid-back pastor. They just weren't wired for repose or recreation. Thankfully the guy was polite, because he did all of the talking. Veronica jogged ahead to walk beside his more expressive brother.

"Mr. White, this house has a 20' x 18' master bedroom, four full-size guest bedrooms, and seven toilets—three on each floor and one in the basement. Two multipurpose rooms could be used as bedrooms as well, here on the main floor. There's a beautiful skylight in the solarium and recessed lighting throughout most of the house. The basement is semi-finished and we can discuss carpeting or flooring if that is your pleasure. This is a fabulous modern home with top-of-the-line security built right in to the wiring."

"How about a garage? My brother and I enjoy a really big garage," Mr. White asked and sent a strange wink to his brother. Veronica cleared her throat; in her experience weird and wealthy went hand in hand.

"Of course!" she exclaimed, keeping the air alive with her energy. "The garage is around back, access from the mud-room off the kitchen, and it will hold up to six average-sized vehicles."

Mr. White nodded and smiled with her every point. Despite looking a little haggard, he was a cute kid. The fading dye-job on his hair and eyebrows had been distracting at first, but now she hardly noticed. His compelling gaze threw her off and she made an effort to look away. Her distraction rolled into a minute and when she looked around, Mr. Agricola had wandered off.

"So, shall we see the upstairs?" her young client asked and Veronica startled. Blushing and confused by her sudden alert status, she offered the youth a wide grin.

"Yes! And please, Mr. White, call me Ronnie." Veronica headed up the staircase and her client followed two steps behind. As she reached the landing, the hairs at the nape of her neck stood on end.

What is going on? she admonished inside, matching stride with the client. *Don't freak out. This sale will set you up for a long time! Straighten up!*

Feeling better after her internal pep talk, Veronica pasted on her best smile.

♦

Paul strode past the agent and poked his head in the first room on the right. She described the designer wall-covering and he spun with drama to catch her gaze.

"Ronnie," he said with a secretive rasp, "did you lose my brother?" Paul looked past the woman as if trying to see down the hall. The afternoon was winding down and shadows reached the corners.

"Your brother?" Veronica repeated with a nervous titter. "I suppose he went to look at the barn before it got too dark."

Paul entered the room and walked the depth of it, forcing the Realtor to follow suit. Her respirations had hyped and Paul smiled. "Tell me more about the basement." He attempted to catch her eye, but the woman expertly avoided his gaze.

"With pleasure. The basement is partly finished with oak paneling, but the floors are bare cement. It wouldn't take much to carpet. Do you think we should have it carpeted for you?"

"Hmm…" Paul murmured, still waiting for her to meet his gaze. She was uncomfortable, but compelled to secure the sale. Paul shook his head at her question. "No, I have no need for carpet. I rather like the cold hard floor beneath my feet."

The woman looked up to nod and he grabbed her eye. The color drained from her face and she cleared her throat. Paul released her to look out the window. She was his type, but weren't they all?

"Let's see if my brother went to the barn." Paul leaned on the sill to look into the yard below. The four-stall barn sat within view, tucked against the fence line. The sun had set and he pretended to have difficulty finding Tony in the gloom.

"I think I see him down there." Paul pointed without looking at the woman. "Come here… is that him?" He moved over to make room for the agent to squeeze in next to him. The Realtor stood her ground.

"I have some flashlights in my car. I wish he would have waited," the woman said.

Paul listened without turning, sensing her inner struggle. She wanted the sale and didn't want to offend. He turned the screws.

"Come over here, Ronnie. Something wrong?" He didn't look at her and she stiffly joined him at the window. Paul gestured outside. "You were right. He's checking out the barn."

She leaned back and exhaled as if she'd been holding her breath. "Well, let's go downstairs and meet him."

Paul stopped her with a question. "First, tell me about the barn."

Veronica remained at his side to describe the stables. Paul ignored her well-rehearsed script and studied her profile. She was in her forties, trim, and well put-together. She wore her make-up tastefully and her perfume was delicate and floral. Paul inhaled and Veronica's voice hitched as she continued her practiced monologue. His scrutiny made her nervous, which egged him all the more. As he studied the way her jaw blended into her neck, he became aware of his growing hunger. It had been more than four days since he had fed and going without hadn't been part of the deal.

Paul leaned in and took in her aroma again, this time with purpose. All the more aroused, he sensed her flight response. Veronica spoke faster as Paul's agitation increased. At one point, he touched her arm with his fingertips and she spun on her Prada pumps for the door. Paul stayed put as she scooted out of his grasp. *So close.* If she hadn't peeled off when she did, he would have attacked her. Instead, he softened his voice to disguise the edge of his hunger.

"Ronnie, will you send my brother up here? This is the one, I know it."

The woman released a decidedly audible sigh. "Oh, Mr. White, you'll be very happy here!" She almost came back into the room to shake his hand, but caught his eye and stopped herself.

"Huge commission or not, I can't use the money if I'm dead."

Paul overheard her thought and it made him laugh aloud. The agent pursed her lips, wrung her hands, and stood in the doorway wondering which way to go. Paul waved her away. "Sorry, I'm just so happy we finally found the right place."

"Good! I'll ask Mr. Agricola to meet you up here right away! Ya'll take your time. I'll wait in the car."

The agent left the room and took the stairs down two at a time. *Smart woman,* he thought. The preacher would be better food anyway.

♦

Tony reached the grand staircase as the agent marched down at speed. She was spooked and he kicked himself for leaving her alone with his unruly partner.

"Is everything okay? Where's my brother?"

The Realtor stopped in front of Tony panting, and pointed upstairs, her smile more a grimace. "You brother wants to buy the house," she said and took a couple of breaths. "He asked me to send you up to see him."

"Great, thanks," Tony replied, then lowered his chin. "Everything okay?"

"Of course," the woman huffed and grinned wider. "I'll wait in the car. Take your time. I have some calls to make. Mr. White is in the last room on the left."

That said, Veronica Law bolted out the front door. Tony watched her leave, slamming the door behind her.

"Oh, Saul?" Tony called, climbing the glossy waxed steps. "Saul?" he said again, certain Paul was ignoring him. If Paul's hunger had returned, what were the chances of Tony being able to calm him? Tony reached the top of the stairs and headed down the dark hallway, flipping on the hall light. "What did you say to that sweet lady? She's scared out of her mind." Tony stopped in the doorway of the last room and peeked inside. Paul leaned against the windowsill, facing the doorway. He was smiling, but no emotion touched his eyes. Tony swallowed and remained by the door.

"You'll be happy to know that the barn looks good," Tony began. "I don't see why we can't put a couple of cows or horses or even pigs in there for you to get blood from when you need it." Tony held his breath and waited. When there was no reply for several seconds, he shifted his feet and waved his hands in the air. "Paul, did you hear me?"

"Cows and horses and pigs, oh, my!" Paul snickered and stepped off the sill. "Preacher-man, always putting my needs ahead of your own." He approached with an enigmatic smile opening his arms wide. Tony backed out of reach.

"No way." Tony raised his hands.

"You waited too long," Paul said in a low voice, putting a hand to his own middle. "But think of it as a learning experience." In a flash, Paul stepped forward and grabbed Tony's forearm. The worn Bible slipped from his hand and Tony grunted with surprise.

"Wait. Hang on. Just a little longer. I didn't realize how much time had passed, really," Tony reasoned, straining against the vampire's grip. Paul reeled him in, a devilish glint in his blue eyes.

"Don't fight, Tony. It's you or that woman downstairs. I can get her to come back up here," Paul teased, now toe-to-toe. "You know I can. She's desperate to sell this house and somebody is going to feed me *right now.*"

Tony groaned; it was useless. The hunger in Paul's eyes was undeniable. Carefully nudging his Bible with his toe so that the pages closed, he prepared for Paul's attack. After unbuttoning his long-sleeve dress shirt, he presented his arm.

"Stay away from my neck," Tony said and hunched his shoulders to his ears.

"Don't you look silly," Paul said, not asking a question. He hooked his fingers into the collar of Tony's shirt. "Behave, preacher-man. I'm not biting your stupid arm." He tugged at him with one hand and waited for Tony to lower his shoulders. Tony opened his eyes and thrust his arm forward again.

"Paul! I'm serious. Take it from my arm. Here!" Pleading, Tony was losing the battle of wills. "Dr. Corescu took it from my arm, remember?" Tony shrank against the wall, searching Paul's eyes for any bending. When Paul remained absolute, Tony looked to the ceiling and said aloud, "Why do You let him abuse me like this?"

Paul seized the opportunity and pulled Tony violently to his chest, his face forcefully nuzzled under Tony's jaw. After the initial pressure and then stab from the vampire's sharp incisors, Tony clenched his teeth. This time, he had no pain, but the straw in the cola bottle sensation was as horrible as he remembered. Tony brought his knee up into his partner's groin. No response.

"Paul!" Tony gasped into his ear, his mind going numb. "Just take what you need, for godssakes! We both have to walk out of here and ride home with that nice lady!"

Paul made an indeterminate noise and held on. When he finally released Tony, he pushed himself away. Tony slid down the wall and sat on the floor, his fingers pressed to his quickly-healing wound.

"I miss the praying," Paul mumbled, squatting beside Tony. He wiped his mouth with the back of his hand and popped Tony on the head. "Hey, I'm talking to you. How come you didn't pray? Next time I want to hear that prayer. You know the one I mean."

Tony monitored his expression and gained his feet, using the wall as support. "I don't pray for your amusement," Tony said. "And there's not going to be a next time. If you do that again with people around, I'm leaving. It's too risky. I'm dead serious."

"Don't be mad," Paul cooed and waited for Tony to make for the stairs. "I was good. I was *really* good. For four whole days."

Tony inhaled and released the breath, counting to five, the feeling of violation hard to overcome. Still, his sacrifice saved Veronica Law's life; that had to be worth something.

"Come on," Tony said and took the first steps down the hall toward the staircase.

"Cut me some slack," Paul interjected, not willing to let the subject lie. "I didn't hurt that lady," he said and smacked his lips, "but she really had it coming."

"No, she didn't." Tony turned to catch his eye. "None of them do." Tony gestured for the front of the house. "They shouldn't have to worry about vampires." Tony took a deep breath and nodded to himself. "I don't know how long I can stand this, but if you hold out as long as you can, we might make it longer. Understand where I'm coming from?" Paul shrugged, neither yes or no. "At least wipe your chin." That said Tony tromped down the steps and out the front door.

10

It is the glory of God to conceal a matter;
to search out a matter is the glory of kings.
Proverbs 24:2

JONAH PUT THE CAR IN PARK, BUT LEFT THE ENGINE
running for the A/C. Jennifer was on her cell speaking to someone at
the office, so he waited, his fingers tapping the wheel to the beat of
the '80s pop music on the radio. When she lowered her phone and
turned to him, her eyes were bright and hopeful.

"Okay, I have good news and bad news. What's it gonna be?"

"Good news. I haven't had my coffee," Jonah replied half-joking.

"Okay, we collected eleven suspects from our efforts last night,
right? Well, the lab has on-file fingerprints for all eleven. They're all
politicians, so they've been printed. That saves us a lot of footwork,
eh?"

"Then what's the bad news?"

"The lab ran their prints and we don't have a match. We're
looking for someone else." Jennifer shrugged and popped a bubble
with her gum. "Of course, he was working on a story the week he was
killed…"

"That's right. His editor sent him to Atlanta to investigate a slew
of cold cases. I think that is where we'll go next. What'cha think?"
Jonah wasn't opposed to trekking over to Atlanta for a few days of
real detective work. He preferred the small-town crime they had in
Whitford City, but it was not uncommon for an Atlanta case to mix
now and then with one of their own.

"I was thinking the same thing. I've already contacted the APD
and they hooked me up with a lady who knows Nixon pretty well."

"I thought he was from Kentucky?"

"Apparently, he gets around. She told me he got an address for a kid named Reuben Stuckey. Let's roll to Stuckey's pad and start with him." Jennifer buckled her seatbelt and Jonah did the same. "Do you have any other CDs in here? I'm not too keen on that pop stuff."

Jonah groaned and opened the glove box. "Have a look, kid."

"Thanks, Pops. Forty-five minutes of *Kiss on My List* and I might start shooting people." Jennifer plucked through the five or six CDs her partner carried for such an occasion. She settled on *The Best of Marty Robbins* and popped it into the player. As Marty crooned to them about the hazards of living, loving, and dying in the Old West, Jonah steered the car toward the interstate.

An hour later, they found Stuckey's address. The guy lived in an upscale neighborhood where the average rent must have been three grand a month. Jonah rapped on the door before peering into the beveled glass insert. Jennifer stepped off the small porch landing and headed for the picture window gracing the front wall.

"Nobody home, partner," she said.

Jonah scanned the yard. "The grass is mowed and the flowers are wet. This house is serviced regularly. Maybe they can tell us when Stuckey was last here."

"There's a lady by the pool next door," Jennifer replied and stepped toward the path. "Tell me you heard that decidedly southern drawl as I did when we got out of the car."

Jonah looked at the neighbor's house. He hadn't heard anything. "Okay, let's go ask her if she's seen him."

Once they were close enough, Jonah caught glimpses of the woman through the gaps in the privacy fence. She lay by a pool wearing a small pink swimsuit. Jonah followed Jennifer through the monkey grass that separated the two yards. Jen gave the gate an authoritative rap.

"Police, ma'am," she said in her cop voice and Jonah smiled. "Can we speak with you a moment?"

"Coming!" the woman called in a lilting accent. "My lawd! The police, no less." The wooden gate swung open and a woman in her fifties wrapped a towel around her waist as her eyes settled on her visitors. "You'll have to excuse my attire, officers, but I was busy gettin' my sun." The woman stepped aside, inviting them to enter, then latched the gate behind them as they passed. "I have a little doggie, but he doesn't bite."

"Ma'am, I'm Detective Miller and this is Detective Speltz. What can you tell us about your neighbor, Reuben Stuckey?" Jonah asked, but the woman was busy scrutinizing his badge.

"Whitford City?" she asked, eyebrows raised. Jonah nodded and repeated his original question. The woman looked him up and down and smiled. "Mm-mm, I likey."

Jonah maintained his expression and Jenn piped in from behind. "Ma'am, do you know your neighbor, Reuben Stuckey?"

"Huh," the woman laughed, her eyelashes fluttering for Jonah. She answered without meeting Jenn's eye. "Mistuh Stuckey has never been so populuh, I'll give ya that much, offissuh."

"What do you mean?" Jenn asked, her tone belying her irritation.

"Name's Pearline Bonner, Detective Miller." The woman reached out her hand to Jonah who shook it and backed up Jennifer's question.

"Has someone else been by looking for Stuckey?"

"*Lawd*, it's been like…maybe last fall? There was a fella from the city looking for him. You know what? To tell ya the truth, I ain't seen Reuben since. We all lease from the same cooperative, you know, so they keep his house up. But, I ain't seen him in a *long* time."

"What about your husband? Is he home?" Jennifer prodded to ask the same question of him.

"Larry!" The previously demure Southern Belle shouted at the top of her lungs toward the house and a balding older man came to the screen door.

"What, Pearline?" he barked through the screen door.

"When did ya last see that Stuckey kid?"

"Dang-it, Pearline, you interrupted me for that? I ain't seen that kid in forever. Now leave me alone."

Jonah watched the man disappear into the house and slam the door. He turned back to the woman who regarded him with a hungry gaze. "Mrs. Bonner, can you tell me more about this man from the city asking about Mr. Stuckey?"

"Well, he was some kind of reporter from Tennessee or Kentucky or someplace like that. Told me that Mistuh Stuckey won an award for writing or somethin'. Heck, Reuben wasn't home that day either. I told him to go look for him where he worked. At the Corescu place. Are you familiar with Doctor Mark Corescu? He runs the Hematology Department at Whitford City Memorial."

"Doctor Corescu. Got it. What does he do for the doctor?" Jonah asked, eyes on his pad.

"Well, he's his *driver,* of course. The doctor's the type who likes a nice lookin' black man to chauffeur him around town on the weekends. We should all be so lucky to have such a person workin' for us." Mrs. Bonner shrugged and then gestured toward the house. "My husband won't even let me hire a *pool* man much less a driver, the tight wad."

Jennifer reached into her pocket for Nixon's driver's license photograph and thrust it in Mrs. Bonner's direction. "Is this the man who questioned you about Mr. Stuckey last fall?"

The woman recognized him right away. "Oh, yes, that's him. Nice-lookin' fella, even though he's not from the South. He came off like a Yank, you know? Talkin' fast and not meaning anything he said. Yanks are like that, you know."

Jonah nodded and didn't look at Jennifer. She transplanted from Maine in her thirties. If she'd been allowed to talk a little more, the Bonner woman would have no doubt recognized her Yankee remnants. Jonah had been born and raised in Georgia, and fit right in.

"So, you goin' to go see the doctor now? I don't really keep up with everyone's business, but I think he lives in your neck of the woods, Whitford City." Mrs. Bonner peeked at Jonah's notepad as he scribbled his notes. He asked her for her contact information and folded it closed.

"Thank you, Mrs. Bonner. You've been a real help." Jonah gestured to Jennifer who began to trek back. "Can we call you again if we have additional questions?"

"Of course, *dah-ling.* You come see me anytime."

Jonah smiled and disappeared around the house to join Jennifer at the gate. She pulled out her cell and followed him to the car.

"I'll get the number for the hospital and call ahead," Jenn said, opening her door. "If this Corescu's at work, we'll ask *him* about Reuben Stuckey."

"I'll call Atlanta PD and see if anyone's reported this Stuckey guy missing. Something weird's going on for sure," Jonah mumbled as he piled into the car.

"What'cha thinking?" Jennifer asked before looking up the number.

"Nixon came to Atlanta to investigate some cold cases, particularly some unsolved murders. According to the copies of the files he took from the APD information services gal, most of those murders from the '70s had missing person's attached to them."

"Yeah? And?" Jennifer set down the phone to hear her partner out. "What're you thinking?"

"We have us a murder and perhaps a missing person. What if Nixon stumbled upon a serial killer that had never been apprehended? What if the killer didn't like being sought after all these years and did away with the nosy reporter?" Jonah didn't like where his rhetorical supposition was leading and he clammed up. Jennifer picked up where he left off.

"That would mean that Miller and Speltz are on a very important trail. We might just have us a killer, Jonah. A *serial* killer. That's gonna look good on our records. This could be our ticket out of the Twilight Zone."

Jonah's mouth went to the side. Serial killers were handled by the FBI. On top of his thoughts, his partner continued in a rush.

"Worry wart. Just let it unfold; isn't that what you always tell me?" she asked, and Jonah nodded. "Okay, how about you call the hospital and I'll call the captain. He'll decide when to call in the Feds."

Jonah liked the idea of handing off the case if it exploded into serial murder. He had worked homicide for ten years and had seen enough of the hard stuff. He pushed redial and got the APD dispatcher who put him through to the hospital switchboard. He asked the volunteer who answered to get him the hospital administrator and after a few moments, a male voice piped into his ear and introduced himself.

"This is Stan Watkins, the Hospital Administrator. What can I do for Atlanta's finest?"

"Thank you, Mr. Watkins, Detective Miller with Whitford City. I need to find a doctor named Mark Corescu. Is he in today?"

"Corescu? No, I'm afraid he doesn't work here anymore. He left about, hmmm, let's see…"

Jonah waited a few quiet seconds as the man looked up the information. Right off, he noted that Watkins was familiar enough with Corescu to know in an instant that he was gone. That could mean several things, so Jonah tucked the information away. Finally the man cleared his throat.

"Detective Miller, he's been gone since September last year."

Jonah noted a tweak in the man's intonation and he pried for more. "Why did he leave, sir?"

"Hmmm… I don't have that information. I'll tell you what, his supervisor may have more. Shall I connect you to his office?"

"Hang on. You seem to know the doctor. What was he like? If you don't mind."

"I don't mind, Detective. Dr. Corescu is a competent physician with an immaculate resume. Anything else?"

"Did you *like* him, Mr. Watkins?"

The man paused, cleared his throat, and then resumed his politically correct banter. "Of course. Shall I get his supervisor?"

"Yes, thank you. Only, get him on the line right now. Don't put me on hold and run off, or put me in the hands of some volunteer. Can you handle that?" Jonah kept his tone civil, but he meant his words.

"Of course. You will be speaking to Dr. McCary. Nice talking to you, Detective."

Jonah mumbled the same and waited a few seconds before another male voice picked up the other end. This one decidedly older and less jovial.

"Yes? What is it, Detective? I'm in a meeting."

"Just a quick question. Dr. McCary. Why did Mark Corescu leave your employ last September? Mr. Watkins didn't have that information so he sent me to you."

"Of course, he did. I can't depend on him to handle my surgeons. Let's see... Corescu took a leave of absence and hasn't returned. Looks like he took a week off after handing over his patients to one of his partners. As far as I am concerned, he's still employed. Payroll will send his check to him for up to a year even if he never comes to work. That's his contract. Nothing to do about that. In August of this year, he'll be up for renewal and that's when I'll get involved. Anything else?"

"Yeah, I'll need to know where his paycheck is going and a list of his associates."

"That's fine, Detective. Come on down and see my receptionist. I'll have her get everything you need. Anything else?"

"Dr. McCary, what sort of man is he? Do you like him?" Jonah asked expecting a similar response.

"What? Dammit, yes, of course. He's very competent. Anything else? Please," the man stammered losing his patience.

"I guess that does it. Thank you. I'll be over within the hour." Jonah let the man offer a quick goodbye and he hung up. When he put the car into gear, Jenn set her phone down, and she was glowing.

"Well, I filled the captain in and he's very encouraged. He put

Stansfield on standby to do legwork in Whitford City. What do you have?"

"I thought Stansfield was working the 7-Eleven robbery homicide with Baker."

Jennifer shrugged. "Not anymore. So what do you have, big boy?"

"Dr. Mark Corescu has disappeared. We'll go to the hospital and ask around. I've already ordered a list of associates and payroll information."

"Sweet. Let's roll," Jennifer pounded the dash and punched the on button on the CD player. Randy Travis began to tell the stories of love lost and love gained and Jennifer sang along. Jonah pretended it was Billy Joel and piped in during the chorus.

11

Stop trusting in man, who has but a breath in his nostrils.
Of what account is he?
Isaiah 2:22

BIG JOHN JENKINS WINCED AT THE SQUEAL OF THE AIR
brakes and received a playful jab from his Scully.

"You got a lot of skills, John, but mechanic ain't one of 'em," his
coworker joked as they rolled to a stop.

John smirked; since taking over from his father-in-law, he made
every part of the company his business. Lately, that meant doing oil
changes, replacing belts, and fixing brakes. By the screech emanating
from under the moving truck, he hadn't done such a bang-up job.

"Look at that fool," Scully was saying on his right. "Don't he
know we gotta get around 'im?"

John didn't reply. The homeowner had reached the house first,
driving a white Tahoe and had blocked the driveway. John was
patient. With a calculated maneuver, he circumvented the vehicle and
pulled through to the front door of the enormous estate. He had
accepted the run at the last minute, hoping to finish the job before
seven and get back home to Columbus. He hadn't thought much
about his vision from the Lord; as the days and weeks passed, it sank
into his subconscious. Sighing at the sudden memory of the blood-
filled stage, John climbed down from the truck. Peace of mind was
what he needed more than anything, especially with their baby coming
any day. John kicked himself for the millionth time for not having a
savings account. It hurt being strapped when Opal needed more and
more baby stuff every day.

A loud rumble rocked the circle drive as Scully unlocked and
opened the side bay doors. John tracked around the truck to speak to
the homeowner. The smallish, studious-looking fellow walked up to

meet him, a worn Bible in his hand.

"Mr. Agricola?" John asked, putting out his hand. The other man supplied him with a firm shake.

"Just Tony, please. And you're Big John Jenkins?" he asked, sounding unsure. John nodded and gave him a grin.

"That's right, just John is good," John smiled and gestured to Scully already unloading the first boxes. "That's Scully. We intend to be finished by seven and we'll break at noon."

The homeowner nodded. "Perfect. Can I bring you some lunch?"

John shook his head. "No, thanks. We brought our own. So we'll get started." John turned for the driver's side and Agricola headed for the house.

Once he'd grabbed his cell, John rounded the truck and noticed a second man—a boy, really—asleep in the white truck. On impulse, he knocked on the glass, only to see the kid awaken and look at him with amazing sky-blue eyes. John nodded hello and turned to continue about his business. Two steps away a strange light-headed sensation washed over him. *Whoa. That was weird,* John thought, a peculiar tightening in his gut. He stole another glance at the youngster and managed a smile. When he turned away, he sensed the guy was still watching him. Folks often stared at John because of his size, and after another minute, he put it out of his mind and got to work.

♦

Tony sat on the porch steps, out of the way, flipping through Ephesians. Engrossed as he was, he didn't hear Paul leave the truck and take a seat behind him. The vampire tapped his shoulder and Tony jumped.

"Geesh, Paul! Don't sneak up on me like that!"

"Did you get a look at that giant?"

"He's just a man. Now, please, don't sneak up on me," Tony hissed, embarrassed by his reaction. Paul scooted down one more step so they were side-by-side.

"I just sat down, nothing supernatural about that. If you want to see sneaking," Paul said lowering his voice, "I can show you some sneaking." When Tony didn't smile, Paul leaned in. "And you called me Paul. You're having real trouble with my new name, aren't you, big brother?"

"You surprised me, *Saul,*" Tony emphasized. He closed the Bible and wedged it between them on the step. "Also, keep your voice down. He'll hear you."

As Tony spoke, the big man stepped into view and removed his light jacket. Tony and Paul watched in stunned silence as his huge arms came into view, his entire frame rippling with muscle.

"Did you see his eyes?" Paul asked, his voice full of wonder. "They're gray—that's rare for a black man, right?"

"Stop staring. That man could squash you like a bug," Tony remarked, hoping he would leave the guy alone.

"I'm not afraid of giants. Are you?" Paul asked, his voice teasing. "Aren't there giants in that book? Giants brought down by a little rock?" Paul snickered and made as if to stand. Tony put a hand to his forearm.

"Correction, brainiac. The Philistine giants were killed because of the power of the Most High God working inside a man with a rock." Tony put his hand to his heart. "A man like me."

Paul laughed and yanked his arm free. "Whooo, I am really scared!" he said and slapped a hand to his cheek. "I'm about to faint from terror!"

Tony steeled his jaw and got to his feet. Paul started toward Big John in the foyer.

"Take a chill pill," he said in a low voice, his earlier grin dissolving. "I'm serious. Look at that guy. I want to feel his arm."

"Stop," Tony hiss-whispered. "Don't make trouble. Let them get this stuff unloaded and be on their way."

"Oh, they'll get unloaded, don't worry," Paul mumbled and took another step toward the mover. "You think he can take me?" he scoffed. "I'd like to see him try. It'd be fun…"

Paul crossed to within a few feet of John and Scully putting a china cabinet against an interior wall. Tony caught up with him and took a hold of his shoulder.

"Leave them alone," Tony said through clenched teeth. His efforts failed as Paul made it to John's side and put both hands across the span of the big man's bicep.

"Look at that! Do you see the size of this man's arm?" Paul said incredulous and motioned for Tony to join him in measuring the man's muscles. "Is your name really Big John?"

John pointed Scully off into another room and smiled down at Paul with humor in his eyes. "That's my name, little fella."

When the big man locked eyes with the vampire, Tony noticed

0

John's unease. Still, he held Paul's gaze and even smiled when Paul remained close. The silence grew and Tony grabbed Paul's arm.

"Leave him alone, these guys are working," Tony said, but Paul yanked away.

"Big John, how did you get so big?" Paul asked, pressing his hand now into John's pectoral muscle through his blue work shirt. Tony increased his objections.

"Sorry about my brother, John. Everything's a game to him these days." Tony again pulled Paul's arm and again Paul jerked out of Tony's grip. He faced Big John, his stance a challenge.

Raising his brow, Big John put his hands on his hips and nodded to Paul now removing his jacket.

"Let's see it, little fella. Show me your muscle."

"Hold this, big brother," Paul said as he tossed the garment to Tony. Making a fist to flex, Paul bared his bicep for the mover. "Take a gander at this, big man. Arrgghh!"

Mortified and wondering what Paul was up to, Tony looked at John. The moving man's reaction was to laugh two short bursts and then clap Paul on the shoulder with an enormous paw.

"Keep working on it, son. I was as tiny as you once when I was about six years old." John's tone was jovial. "Just keep workin' it." With that, John turned away, still chuckling, and headed out to unload the trailer.

Paul ran after him and Tony threw up his hands. The vampire was incorrigible and Tony prayed the friendly giant came to no harm.

◆

"Big John, I challenge you to a round of arm wrestling."

John forced a laugh and looked to see if anyone else heard the man's claim. Granted, the kid was probably six feet, but he was slender as a bean and his game had become a nuisance. The image of the kid's little hand clasped in his for a battle of strength made him shake his head. When Paul didn't back down, John dropped his grin.

"I'm sorry, kid, but I'm afraid you'd get hurt." He patted the guy's shoulder. John just wanted to unload and head home before dark. Opal was waiting; she'd warm up his dinner and then massage his shoulders. She deserved so much better than he could provide, but before he could begin wishing he could buy her diamonds, the strange blue-eyed boy's gaze intensified.

"Okay, here it is," he said, holding John with his eyes as sure as with steel bonds. "If you finish unloading by seven," he said, lowering his voice, "we'll set up the card table and see who's stronger." Paul rose to his tip-toes and spoke into John's right ear the last of his directive. "And I'll pay you five hundred dollars just for humoring me."

John leaned down. "Five hundred dollars? For arm wrestling? That's kind of strange, Mr. White," John replied, confused. He had taken the kid for a jokester, not a lunatic.

"Not strange—*eccentric*. Aren't rich folks supposed to be eccentric? Humor me. We'll have to do it in private, though. No audience."

John huffed. That part he understood. If their positions were reversed, he wouldn't want anyone to know he had challenged Goliath and lost.

"Let's see if I hear ya," John reiterated. "If we finish unloading by seven, you and I will wrestle in private, and win or lose, you'll pay me five hundred dollars?" John watched the kid's eyes, and then his widening grin. What did he have to lose? It would be the easiest money he would ever make. As sure as he was going to get, John shook Paul's hand and marveled at the shine in the kid's eyes. Paul then backed out of John's way and clapped his hands.

"Chop-chop, Big John. You only have six hours to go!"

John shook his head and got to work. The wealthy could be dumb as a stick but their money did spend.

◆ ◆ ◆

Hope sat at her dead twin sister's kitchen table and stared at nothing. Jimmy Hershey departed for the airport an hour ago and for the moment, all three of Glorie's boys were engrossed in a loud and sassy cartoon in the other room.

Now I'm the mom for a while, she mused, her thoughts darkened by depression. *What have I gotten myself in to?*

A yelp sounded in the other room, and Hope stepped to the living room entryway and checked. It must have been the puppet on-screen. All three stair-stepped, blond-haired, blue-eyed cherubs were lying on the carpet. Six little knees bent, six little arms tucked behind three little heads. Their tummies were full of Honey Combs and everything was right in their world. Did they miss their mom? Had she loved them at all? Hope didn't know, and the more she pondered, the worse it made her feel to think she had overlooked her sister's psychosis.

Ugh! Stop it, Hope! It's over! Glorie brought this on herself! Hope rubbed her face and returned to her chair. *So what do I do when Jimmy comes back? Am I really going to go find Anthony? And if I do, will he lead me to Mark?*

Tears threatened and Hope squeezed them back.

"Mark! I know you hear me!" Speaking in a hiss, Hope turned her face to the ceiling. "You can't ignore me forever. I will find you. I will." She paused and then pointed at the ceiling. "Mark Corescu, answer me!"

Tears overpowered her will and before she knew it, Hope was sobbing away at the dinette table. All of the months of fantasizing and scheming, every evening she dreamt of him, every corner she turned and thought she'd see him. All of her disappointment channeled through her tear ducts. Thankfully, the children were too self-involved to notice and they left her alone. Hope cried a long time, wiping her nose on the sleeve of her thick terry robe. Only when she couldn't breathe for the hitch in her chest did she wipe her face and make an effort to sit up. With a ragged inhale through her clogged nose, she stood and rested her hands on the table surface. Then the hair stood straight up on the back of her neck.

"Mark?" she whispered.

Nothing.

But I feel him here. I know it!

"Mark?" Louder this time, she waited, holding her breath. Twenty seconds passed. All she heard was the cackling of the kid's television.

Forty seconds. Nothing.

"*Please, say something…*" Hope pleaded in a whisper.

"*I know a man that once held the world in his hands…*"

It was Mark, speaking to her finally. Hope held her breath and closed her eyes.

"*…and he gave it all up for love.*"

Hope dared not speak for fear of losing their tenuous connection. She took a shallow breath and concentrated on quieting her mind.

"*That same man then held love in his hands…*"

Silence.

Hope waited, the perspiration of frustration appearing on her brow. Just when she thought he would not continue, she heard him once more.

"...*but he gave her up for death, which is infinitely sweeter. Hope, do you love me?*"

"Yes! Yes, I do!" Hope answered emphatically, no longer concerned about distracting the children.

"*I'm dying, Hope. If you will love a dead man, then come. Come.*"

"Mark!"

He was gone.

Hope looked desperately around the room as if he might materialize before her. But he was gone. His eerie presence had dissipated and Hope wondered if she had imagined the entire ethereal conversation.

I could have manufactured the whole thing. I might be as crazy as Glorie. What am I going to do?

But if she wasn't crazy, Mark was telling her to come. *Inviting* her to find him. Asking her to join him. Maybe to save him? Hope wrung her hands. How would she find him? How would she get through her current baby-sitting job with this new invitation on her mind?

"Aunt Hoppy, can I have some juice?"

It was Brown, adorable in his Spiderman pajamas. Hope poured him a sippy cup and sent him into the other room.

As soon as Jim gets back, I'll find him. The kids first.

With a heart alive with promise, Hope took off for her room to dress. There was a lot to do. *I'll get my passport in order...* She began her mental list and smiled.

◆ ◆ ◆

Mark wavered between waking and sleeping; had he actually contacted Hope. Lately he was not certain of anything. It seemed he had dreamed of Hope crying over him again and his heart broke at the sight. Did he really make contact and ask her to join him? Though it was the last thing he wanted, he was afraid that maybe he had.

What does it matter if she comes? I can't move. She wouldn't recognize me if she did somehow make it to this room to gaze upon this shrunken pile of bones. I need to sleep. Please, God...let me die.

Mark worked to quiet his mind, but it buzzed with images and sounds from thousands of miles away. Helpless to hinder the visions, he caught glimpses of Hope going through the motions of dressing for the day, and then just as easily, he would grab a vision of Paul and Tony in their new house. Mark's body had wasted away to a papery shell, but his mind grew sharper in equal measure. He had discovered a living hell and he would not see true death any time soon.

I am reaping what I have sown. I deserve this…

Despair wracked his soul and Mark sighed a shallow breath.

"Dr. Corescu's paychecks are going to a sleeping bank account in Atlanta, Georgia," Jonah reported, reading off his notepad. "No one's made any withdrawals in over a year. The money's piling up, too, over seven figures and counting, apparently forgotten. Must be nice."

Jonah handed Jennifer the notes he'd taken when interviewing Corescu's partners, and she handed over her notes that she'd taken from his subordinates. They were back at their own desks in Whitford City mentally readying themselves for another day of chasing down leads in Atlanta. Jonah skimmed the top page and pointed to the first name on the list.

"Fran Booker? She was the man's receptionist?" Jonah waited for the absent nod as Jennifer examined the papers in her own hands. He continued to read her scribbled notes to get a firmer picture of the man they sought. Every doctor he questioned who had ever worked with Corescu said the same thing: He was competent and efficient, but equally reclusive and misanthropic. Reading Jennifer's notes concerning the receptionist gave him more reason to be optimistic. Finally, he had an acquaintance of the good doctor that wasn't afraid to speak her mind. Jonah read a few of the comments under his breath and Jennifer looked up.

"'Creeped me out,' 'Reading my mind,' 'Scary dude.' I think Mrs. Booker might be the only one giving us the truth, you think?"

Jennifer shook Jonah's notes. "Yep. These doctors sound like robots, but Booker didn't hold back. She said he paid well, but was very weird. And get this; right before he disappeared he had a couple of women visiting him in his office. A *social* visit."

"Oh? Girlfriend?"

"Uh-huh. Mrs. Booker said that her friend… let's see." Jennifer pulled the papers from Jonah's hands and looked over her notes. "Her friend, Hope Brannen, of 321 Ellen Lane, was dating him. Pretty hot and heavy too, by her description. She thinks they were getting ready to elope right before he disappeared. And get this. There were *two* women visiting him the day before he left the office for good; Ms. Brannen and her twin sister, Glorie Hershey. Hershey had come to visit from Cumberland, Maryland. And you'll never guess where she is right now…"

"I'm afraid to ask…"

"In the ground. She was killed in a car accident. Fran Booker was also involved. DUI."

"Did you speak to APD about that accident?"

"Yep. Single vehicle. The driver was Hershey, DOA, and Booker had a concussion and fractured a couple of ribs. I also saw on the wire that there was an APB for Hershey the day of her accident. She was under suspicion of poisoning her three children. Can all this possibly tie together? Is this sick, or what?"

Jonah huffed. "This case keeps getting more and more twisted as we go along. We have a dead reporter from Kentucky who was looking for a now-missing man named Reuben Stuckey, who worked for and was supported financially by a now-missing doctor from Whitford City Memorial, who just so happened to be speaking to a now-dead possible murderess in his office the day before *he* disappeared. Does that about cover it so far?"

"That's the way I see it. Pretty cool, eh? It's like we're real detectives or something," Jenn said with a smile.

"I'm glad you're enjoying yourself. Let's try to find this Hope Brannen. Maybe *she's* not missing."

"That would be a pleasant change." Jennifer shuffled through her pages a few more seconds. "I have a phone number for Ms. Brannen. I'll try it and see what happens."

"Go for it." Jonah leaned back in his chair and stretched his arms as Jenn made her call. The Detective Den was quiet as the other men were out following their own leads. Stansfield was the only one in the room, and he was playing solitaire on his PC awaiting orders.

"No answer at her number. Think we can get a warrant for her financial and phone records? Maybe she left town. In the least we might get a break and see where she last spent some money on her credit card and when she last called any of our other suspects." Jennifer dropped the handset into the cradle and lobbed a pen at Stansfield.

"Yeah?" the young detective asked.

"Go get warrants on Hope Brannen of 312 Ellen Lane." Jenn

watched with approval as he spun away with purpose and headed out of the office. "That ought to give us a few moments to grab a bite to eat. Twirlies?"

"Where else?" Jonah grabbed his coat and prepared his gut for another round with the café's famous spaghetti.

The two laborers locked the doors of the moving truck at six-forty-five. The one called Scully climbed into the driver's seat and started playing with his phone, apparently aware that Big John had something going on inside. Paul led the burly foreman to an upstairs bedroom and had him sit down. Paul sat opposite and Big John returned his smile. The giant put his elbow on the table, hand open, ready to begin. Paul leaned back in his folding chair and crossed his arms at his chest.

"First, Big John, what's your real name?"

John sat up. "John Mallory Jenkins the Third. I've been big since third grade so my friends called me Big John. It stuck."

"It suits you beautifully," Paul agreed. "I want you to call me Paul. Saul isn't my real name." Paul noted a question on the big man's lips and he offered a more detailed explanation. "I use that name for business. But you and I are going to be friends." Paul paused and his guest made no reply or response. He clasped his hands together on the table top and grinned. "Big John, you have a family. A pregnant wife?"

John's eyes widened then returned to normal. "As a matter of fact, yes."

"And money is tight with a new baby coming, am I right?"

"We do okay." John bristled and offered a forced smile. "What does this have to do with our wrestling match?"

"Don't let your feathers get ruffled, Big John." Paul reached across the table and put his hand on John's forearm. "I'm in a position to help you. I have a job for you."

John looked at the hand on his arm and then back to Paul. After a moment of silence, Paul took back his hand and put his elbow on the table, ready for battle.

"John, true strength has very little to do with muscle," Paul said and John grasped his hand, allowing their fingers to intertwine.

"You're talking about mind over matter? You really think you can beat me?" John asked, incredulous. *I might even let him win. Might be fun.*

Paul's lips made a tight smile. He heard the big man's internal monologue more clearly than Tony's. The evening was going to be a success; he had no doubt.

◆

"You won't have to let me win, John," the rich kid said, his gaze boring into John's.

"What makes you say that?" John asked, spooked. Had the man just answered his thoughts?

"Are you ready?" Paul asked and John nodded.

For the first few seconds, the kid did nothing but match his effort. At the half-minute mark, John applied real pressure, and Paul effortlessly held his ground, giving back the same. John leaned more into the battle, his arm ten times the size of the slight character across from him. Sweat broke out on John's forehead, but the odd youngster's expression never wavered. Forty-five seconds later, the tiny *S.O.S.* hammering a warning deep in his spirit grew louder. As Paul Black matched his incredible strength tit for tat, John began to give out. Before another minute passed, Paul shoved John's hand down with enough force to buckle the flimsy table.

John exhaled and stared at his arm pressed against the card table like so much sausage. While water dripped from the tip of his nose and landed with a splat on the surface, the kid across from him had not even changed expression. His face was still plastered with the same bemused and haughty look it had when the battle began.

This isn't normal. This isn't right. This man isn't normal.

"You're quite right, John," the kid said without releasing John's collapsed fist. With his free hand, he dug into his pocket and retrieved the money. "You wanna go again? Two out of three?"

John shook his head and looked back to his losing hand. Not only did the strange man before him prove to be of superior might, he seemed to also be reading his thoughts.

But that's crazy. I must be more tired than I thought…

"You're not crazy, John. Just lucky," Paul said and closed his other hand around John's. "I have a job for you. It's unorthodox. Even more unorthodox than me arm-wrestling a giant."

John didn't react.

"It pays twice as much and you would be needed only four times a month. What do you say?"

John's head shook of its own accord.

"Four thousand dollars a month. Cash," Paul continued, his fingers caressing John's on the table.

John desired greatly to withdraw his hand, but remained still.

"Do you think your wife can find a use for that kind of tax-free money?" Paul waited for an answer, then sat up and took his hands to himself. "Are you afraid, Big John?" he asked, obviously using John's moniker against him. "You can leave any time you want."

"You got that right," John said; an automatic response, yet he had no confidence that he could do any such thing. Being bigger and stronger for most of his thirty-six years did not prepare him for what haunted him now.

"John, I'm not going to hurt you." Paul lifted his folding chair with his fingers and flipped it around to be seated beside the foreman instead of across. "I think you'll find this is the sweetest deal you'll ever get. Hear me out. Four thousand dollars a month, paid out with services rendered, in cash, for as long as you want it. No contracts, nothing further to buy." Paul chuckled at the end.

John didn't laugh with him, his mind racing. What did the guy have in mind? Could it have to do with drugs? Or worse, did he take one look at Big John and consider him a hitman? John cleared his throat and hoped he did not look as terrified as he felt. "Are these rendered services legal?"

"Legal schmegal, Big John. Let me explain it like this."

Paul placed his hand on John's shoulder as he talked. John didn't move away, but he wanted to.

"Do you donate blood to the Red Cross?"

John swallowed. Did he say blood? In his mind, the stage at Damascus Bible Center began to flood with a sea of the stuff, coating, covering, devouring everything in its path.

What does blood have to do with this man? John glanced at the hand on his shoulder. *And what does God have to do with this man?*

Recovering his concentration, John stumbled over his reply. "Sometimes, when they have a shortage."

"Well, I need you to donate blood to me," Paul said, kneading the muscle through John's thin shirt. "How about it? You'd come by here once a week, give blood, and then take your cash and buy your baby some new clothes. Heck, buy your baby a pony."

"Whom shall I send?"

79

Recalling the words Franklin sang to him during his vision, John's mind grew fuzz. The kid continued to talk, but his voice garbled as it reached John's ears.

"Here am I. I will go for You."

Franklin's song again. Was the Lord speaking to him? Should he agree or run away?

"John!" Paul said and popped the table with his palm.

"Wait a minute," John said, his voice a near whisper. "All I have to do is donate blood?"

"That's all. But there's one condition."

"What's that?" John asked, *"Whom shall I send,"* rolling around in his mind over and over.

"You can't tell anyone about the blood. Make up whatever story you like regarding our arrangement, but never mention the blood."

The baby was coming soon, maybe this week. Their cottage was too small for a family and he didn't have the equity to trade up. Opal didn't have a car and she'd need one by the time the baby had his first outing. A cover story cooked in his brain, and his right hand snaked forward to shake hands with Paul.

"Fantastic!" the kid exclaimed and leapt up from the table. "I want you to start on Wednesday. Can you come?"

"This Wednesday?" John's mind reeled. He rose to his feet and wiped his face with both hands. "Wait. What do you need the blood for? Are you qualified to draw blood?"

"We'll go over all of that on Wednesday. Go join your friend." Paul slipped ahead of John and opened the bedroom door. "Remember," he said placing his palm on Big John's forearm when he was close. "This is our little secret. Wednesday night, anytime between 5 p.m. and midnight, one grand, cash money."

"Okay, okay." John started away suppressing the instinct to run down the hall. He would come, how could he not? Four thousand dollars, even for one month, would buy peace of mind.

"See you Wednesday," Paul called and John trotted to the ground floor without looking back.

12

For I have been crucified with Christ.
It is no longer I that live, but Christ lives in me.
Galatians 2:20

"THIS IS IT?" TONY LOOKED AROUND THE DUSTY STORE. Paul's idea of a mortal cover required a lot of work. It wasn't that Tony thought it was a bad idea, he just couldn't see Paul working in a retail setting.

"I think it's cool." Paul shut the front door behind him and shook the dust off his hands. "They closed six months ago and left most of the inventory. I think the former owner died in a fire." He lifted a hardcover book from the closest shelf.

"It's great, but are you serious about working here? You?" Tony asked, running a finger across a dusty counter top. Paul laughed aloud.

"No, dummy. My days of labor and servitude are over."

Tony smirked and turned back to survey the room. "So you'll hire a manager?"

"You're the manager, Tony. I'm the owner. You hire folks, whatever. Just call me boss."

Tony headed for a short staircase that led to a landing at a door marked *Office*. He started up the steps with Paul right behind.

"So, I expect you'll either hate the idea or love it," Paul said keeping up with him as he ascended.

"It's a good idea," Tony replied. "I'll do it, if—and I emphasize *if*—you keep out of it. I don't even want you in the store. If this is going to be my responsibility, I don't want to have to think about you popping in and hurting anyone."

Paul snickered. "I'll stay out of the way, but I'll be around."

"Way out of the way, then," Tony replied and surveyed the small upstairs room. Inside, sat one old desk and two chairs, with two bracket shelves on the wall. He imagined setting up shop in there, and relished the idea of spending the majority of every day far away from Paul Black.

"What? You getting sick of me?" Paul asked. Tony turned and squeezed past him to the narrow stairs.

"Stop trying to hear what I'm thinking," he mumbled and reached the ground floor again. No matter how idiotic the vampire behaved, Tony had to admit that his plans were panning out. His bookstore idea looked fun, the giant moving man had agreed to come and donate blood, and maybe Tony wouldn't have to feed the vampire as often himself. That last thought gave him the most peace.

Tony crossed the tiled floor and reached the information island. He thought again of Big John Jenkins. Tony hadn't pried and Paul hadn't given any details, but what would make a sane man donate his blood like that? Was God about to move the burden on to this other guy? Instantly, Tony was ashamed of trying to shirk his duty. From behind, Paul slapped his back and laughed.

"Can you keep all that whining down to a minimum? I'm not *reading* your mind—it floats over. It works like that." Paul came around him and caught his eye. "So please, will you just shut up?"

Tony bit his tongue and turned his back. The cash register tray was empty and he wondered where they kept the inserts. Overtly, he made small calculations regarding how much money they would spend getting the place ready to open. In a separate compartment, he pondered how to keep his thoughts to himself.

Maybe I can think up a way to block him, he thought, jotting down figures on a loose slip of paper.

Behind him, Paul sighed. *"Yeah, that'll be the day."*

Tony turned; Paul was much too close. "You're in my space again. Five feet away, please," Tony said, sensing the return of Paul's impish behavior. His partner had entered the three-sided counter area where the employees would work when the store opened. He blocked the exit with his body.

"So, you know what day it is?"

Tony held Paul's gaze and shook his head. It was Tuesday, but his demented partner was leading up to something else.

"It's Paul-And-Tony-Buy-a-Store-Together Day! Let's celebrate." Paul stepped closer, still blocking the opening. "Isn't this exciting?"

"Paul, come off it. What're you talking about? What kind of celebration?" Tony remained where he was, but perspiration beaded on his forehead as it did every time Paul came too close.

"Let's have a drink," Paul said. He covered the distance between the two of them too fast for Tony to follow. In a heartbeat, he was in Paul's grasp and Tony trained his eyes to the front door.

"Someone will see you! Don't you have any sense?" Speaking in a low whisper, Tony's voice cracked. As in times before, why couldn't he be brave?

Paul snickered and knelt down, pulling Tony with him. "Why would anyone see us? It's getting dark. The lights are off in here…"

Tony came to rest on his knees, still held firmly by the upper arms. "Paul!" he hissed.

The vampire shook his head. "The door is locked, we're behind the counter. Now, how about that drink?"

"Please, how can you be hungry so soon?" Tony strained and attempted to stand. Without changing expression, his partner's cruel grip tightened and Tony slumped back to the floor. "Tomorrow you'll have that moving man…" Tony looked up to the white ceiling. "I can't keep doing this!" he said to the air.

Paul laughed and pulled Tony close. "Oh, come now, big brother, why are you being such a baby? Aren't you just practicing what you preach? Aren't you sacrificing your blood to protect the innocent?"

Tony put his hands to his throat, covering the exposed skin, and again tried to stand. It was futile, but maybe, just maybe, if he delayed the attack, God might send help. *It could happen.*

But it didn't.

"I don't want you to fight," Paul said and increased the pressure in his grip. Tony whimpered as his wrist bones creaked and began to fracture.

"My wrist, Paul, my wrist…"

"It'll heal." Paul forced Tony's hand out of the way and buried his face in his neck. As he opened his mouth wide and sank his fangs into Tony's throat, he said telepathically, *"You agreed to this. Be still and take your medicine."*

Tony did fall still, but he grumbled inside. His broken wrist bones had healed, but they throbbed with an alien sensation he'd never felt in his old life. His heart ached, too, as he realized that, once again, God had not come to his rescue.

Is this what I'm reduced to? he thought, dismay clouding his purpose. *To serve as food for demons?*

When Paul released and began to tease him for praying, Tony

tuned him out and got to his feet.

"That's okay, Paul," Tony said aloud, only to finish the thought silently for the vampire to overhear. *"You will get yours. God is watching. My God will break the teeth of the wicked."*

Paul snickered and goofily bared his teeth. Tony looked away, leaning on the counter for support. When Paul stepped aside, he headed for the exit. His wrist was fully restored and the wound in his throat had closed. It was Tony's turn to smirk, and he did so inwardly.

I guess it isn't so bad. It's almost like it never happened.

"Yeah—you're just a big, whiny baby," Paul said and shoved Tony ahead of him toward the front door. "Of course, I feel pretty good..." Paul rubbed his belly for emphasis. "...for something you pretend never happened."

"Aww, I'm so happy for you," Tony replied, not hiding his sarcasm. Paul reached the exit and draped an arm across Tony's shoulders to pull him in tight.

"You make me laugh, preacher-man. Let's go home and see what's on TV." Paul held him to his side until they reached the truck.

Tony said nothing, happy when Paul released him to climb into the driver's seat, *thinking, this can't go on forever.*

But he wasn't really sure.

◆ ◆ ◆

It took three days to track down Hope Brannen. Jonah led the way through the airport foot traffic with Speltz in his wake, making way with an intimidating glare at the other travelers. He made an effort to hear Jenn over the crowds as she touched on various topics.

"I still can't believe the captain approved this trip to Maryland," Jenn shouted over the Hartsfield-Jackson throng. "Things are sure different around the station."

Jonah nodded, but did not reply. There would be plenty of time to chat on the flight, and screaming over the heads of a hundred strangers was not his way of expressing sensitive case related information.

Hope Brannen had left a paper trail a mile long, as if she had no fear of being tracked. At first, Jonah wondered if that was a sign of her innocence, but when he added all the coincidences, he and Jenn both decided that she had to be the key. She might be their octopus, as his partner put it; the center to all of the tentacles found so far.

"Jonah…" Jennifer yanked on Jonah's coat to get him to stop. "I need to step in here. Wait up."

Jonah sighed and leaned against the wall. What Jenn had said about the Whitford City Police Department's change over the last couple of weeks was accurate. Ever since they hit the break about Reuben Stuckey, they'd been getting more respect from the rest of the squad. There were only six detectives on the whole force, but lately, Jonah felt like the elite team. The captain was nicer, their fellow officers more helpful, as if the entire department shared in the glory. Although they'd made no official claims to the Feds, they all wanted to be part of catching a serial killer. Also, Stansfield wasn't the only junior detective at their disposal. Four uniforms had been added to their team, waiting by the phone to hop-to when Jonah had a need.

With all of the support they'd been receiving, Jonah had forgotten how rewarding police work could be. Maybe he had the answer to why Jennifer found her work so exciting and he had been growing bored. He'd become jaded, plain and simple. He was approaching twenty-two years' service to the city, and Jenn had barely cut her teeth.

Waiting for her to emerge from the brightly-lit ladies alcove, he was suddenly embarrassed that he had asked her to retire with him a couple of weeks ago. He cleared his mind so he wouldn't preoccupy himself with self-doubt. She would probably not bring it up unless he did, and as the days passed, he didn't think he would.

13

"I have come that you may have life,
And that you may have it more abundantly."
John 10:10

BIG JOHN JENKINS HAD NO TROUBLE CONVINCING HIS WIFE
Paul White's offer was a good one. He omitted the gruesome details
and she sent him off with a kiss. From the moment the deal was
struck, John anticipated the appointment with a mixture of curiosity
and foreboding. Now that he was in his battered Caddy, barreling
southwest toward the Alabama line, the fear he had experienced in the
man's presence crept into him anew.

But what have I to fear? John asked inside. *He's just another weird white
rich kid. It's not as if he's more than human...* But deep in his heart, John
wondered at the validity of that position.

He eased his foot off the gas. Full of nervous energy, he had been
traveling well over the speed limit. His insane mission made so much
sense from a practical viewpoint, that he hadn't the inclination to
think about it too hard. Was there any other way to earn such easy
cash? Opal had given him her blessing, knowing full-well how much
money went out and how little came in.

*What's the big deal? So, I donate a little blood at a guy's house instead of the
hospital?* So what if he had to drive ninety miles to earn it? Wasn't the
trip worth the wage? So what if he had to take off from work every
Wednesday afternoon to let blood for a freako? He never made a
thousand bucks a day in his regular job. The pros more than
outweighed the cons and he knew it.

Then why am I breaking out in a sweat the closer I get to his house?

John knew why; because of the blood on the stage. And because
maybe, the odd kid wasn't a man at all. John swallowed unexpected
bile and zoomed down the interstate, clearing his mind and preparing
his heart.

"Now remember, don't interfere," Paul said, shaking his finger in Tony's face. "If you booger-up my plan, I'll have to take it out on you."

"Unbelievable," Tony said, his tone serious. "Let me get this straight. That huge man agreed to let you drink his blood for money?"

"Yep."

"I don't believe you." Tony frowned, but Paul sneered and held out his hand.

"Don't worry about it. Did you go to the bank?"

After a huff, Tony placed a stack of hundreds into Paul's palm. Paul fanned out the bills, nodding his head.

"Excellent."

"Paul, look at me. This is important." Tony tugged Paul into the light and met his eye.

Paul concentrated on the man's thoughts, but none trickled forth. He opened his eyes wide to exaggerate that he was paying attention.

"I'm serious," Tony said and waited for Paul to drop the face. "How did you know where to find me?"

Paul read his master's name in Tony's head at that moment; the guy wanted to know if he'd been talking to Mark. Paul didn't think it was his business. He sent Tony a coy smile.

"Would you believe that I'm just really, really, really smart?" Paul put his hands on Tony's shoulders, holding his gaze. As usual, Tony became agitated when he couldn't break free.

"No, I think you're somehow stealing information from the doctor."

Deflated, Paul released Tony and plopped down on the sofa where they had been standing. "He lets me in. Stop nosing in on my business. You don't know him. *You* are the enemy; you practically killed him with all that God-talk. I am his friend."

"He lets you in?" Tony repeated. "I doubt that. From what you've told me, he's practically a vegetable. You're squeezing information out of him against his will. That's cold. Even for you."

"Mind your own business," Paul warned. "Mark is living through me now. And I know he has spoken to you. I know he asked you to bury him. I say we go, now, right away."

Tony frowned and Paul waited to see what he would say. Finally, the preacher sighed and looked to the ground.

"Soon. The timing has to be right. I'll know when it's time."

Paul smirked; Tony was talking about *feeling* God, or some other nonsense. Standing, he straightened his clothes and headed for the door.

"My dinner's here."

Tony followed and seemed about to comment, but Paul shooed him with a hand behind his back.

"I got this, Tony. I don't need any help."

"Be careful," Tony warned. "Remember your promise—no dead bodies, *period*."

"There you go with your periods again," Paul chuckled.

"I'll be in my study," Tony said and then raised his voice. "Paul, I'm not helping to hide any corpses, do you hear?"

Paul laughed louder and reached the front door to meet John. Tony was a funny little guy and there was no way his sour attitude could dampen Paul's excitement. Paul giggled again and stepped onto the porch.

◆ ◆ ◆

Hope led the two detectives into the living room and offered them something to drink. The female detective had a friendly smile and a pretty face, but she looked hard, as if she'd looked down one too many gun barrels to be totally feminine. The man was hefty and tall with thick bushy hair and a sweaty brow. Both detectives politely declined her offer and the three of them sat in her sister Glorie's living room.

Hope was terrified. The detectives had phoned her an hour earlier and foretold their arrival. Hope had nowhere to run and she couldn't leave if she wanted to. She was in charge of Glorie's three boys. Where could she go with them in tow? She had put on a fresh outfit and waited for the police to arrive. If they began to ask her about Mark, she would do everything within her power to leave him out of it. Unfortunately, she'd never been a very convincing liar.

Hope pasted on a smile and waited to see what kind of mess she would get them all into.

◆

"Ms. Brannen, thank you for seeing us. We only have a few questions and we'll be on our way." Jonah flipped his note pad to a clean sheet as he spoke.

The Brannen woman was nervous, fidgety, as well as unusually attractive for someone not in show business. Seeing her in person gave him an inkling of how the men in her life may have operated.

"Okay," she said, crossing her ankles, "but I don't know what I can tell you. I'm here taking care of my sister's kids. She died in a car accident a little while ago. Or did you already know that?"

The woman was fishing for information and stalling at the same time. Jonah sucked his teeth and leveled his gaze so she would quiet down. She did and clasped her hands in her lap.

"Just a few questions," Jonah reiterated and took a deep breath. "Ms. Brannen, what can you tell us about a Kentucky newspaperman by the name of Connie Nixon?" Jonah gestured for Jenn to show her the photo. The woman looked at it and both detectives gauged her reaction.

"Connie Nixon? That's his name? Oh," she mumbled and held the photograph in her hand. "Did something happen to him? Is he in trouble?"

"Please just tell us what you know about him," Jenn piped in, her voice gentle. Her handling of the frightened beauty was working and Jonah allowed Jenn to take the lead.

"You recognize him, you know him," Jenn said, her tone soft but firm, like an elementary school teacher. "Tell us how you met, how long you've known him. Stuff like that."

Blondie scratched at nothing on her sleeve. "Well, I-I didn't know his name, but I've seen him before." She looked to both of the detectives in turn before continuing, her voice shaky. "I don't see what the big deal is about this guy."

"We do the police work, ma'am," Jonah offered, matching his partner's manner. "How do you know him?"

Ms. Brannen paled and stiffened her back. "I don't know him, but I met him once. Last fall, I was with a friend of mine, and this Nixon guy walked up to our car and started asking questions about this other guy I knew…"

Jonah held his tongue and glanced at his partner. Jenn's eyes said what he felt: the Brannen woman was up to her eyeballs in trouble and was trying her best to cover her steps on the fly.

"Ma'am, we're going to need you to fill in those blanks. Names and places and times. This is a murder investigation and you should take it seriously." Jonah lowered his head and looked at the woman over his glasses.

"Murder? I don't know anything about a murder…"

Jonah caught Jenn's eye; Ms. Brannen had inadvertently told them more than they had hoped to discover. She actually knew quite a bit about at least one murder, her guilt evident in every word uttered in her own defense.

"Just tell us that story again, but insert the names and places. You're doing fine," Jenn coached. "You're not a suspect, but we need to know as much about this man as possible. So please, Ms. Brannen, then we'll be on our way."

"Oh, God, I'm confused," she gushed and rubbed her face. When she looked up, there were tears on her cheeks. "Look, I met that guy in the photo one time. That's all. He asked me and my friend Anthony—that's Anthony Agricola—about this guy named Reuben Stuckey. He told us that Reuben had won a writing award and he wanted to do a story on him. I knew the guy was lying, so I shined him on to get him off Reuben's trail. Does that help?"

"When was this?" Jonah stepped in. "Can you give a precise date?"

"Uh, mid-September—I think it was a Monday. I just don't remember the exact date. I'm sorry."

"How did you know Reuben Stuckey?" Jonah asked, his tone cordial.

"Reuben? Uh…" Ms. Brannen stammered, and rolled her eyes. Jonah resisted the urge to shake his head. "He used to work for another friend of mine…" She trailed off, looking to both detectives for empathy. Jonah sighed, fed up.

"Look, Ms. Brannen, it's really hard to come up with lies on the fly, isn't it? Let me help you a little. We've already spoken to Fran Booker who told us everything she knows about you and Dr. Corescu. So please, come clean and let's get this over with. I don't think you're in any trouble, but if you withhold information right now, I could charge you with obstruction."

"You talked to Fran?" The woman uncrossed her ankles and gripped her own forearms. Jonah drove it home.

"Yes, and so far, we have one dead body, and at least two missing persons. If you don't start helping us soon, I'm going to have to extradite you back home, and who would watch your sister's kids then?"

Ms. Brannen began to openly sob. "I'm so confused! I don't know who you're talking about. Is Reuben dead? Or that Nixon guy? Or someone else?"

"Ms. Brannen, please, start over, from the beginning," Jenn urged and handed her a Kleenex from a nearby box. "The truth this time, please."

She was silent and sniffling several long moment before the woman hid her face in her hands and began to talk. Jonah readied his pencil and jotted notes when appropriate. She told them that she had met Dr. Mark Corescu last fall at Mrs. Booker's office and the two had hit it off. She related how she met his household staff, Reuben Stuckey, and a man named Paul Black. Then she told them that one day she ended up in Corescu's driveway where the Nixon fellow questioned her about Reuben Stuckey.

"Now, that wasn't so hard, was it?" Jennifer asked and tried to lighten the mood with a laugh. It didn't work. Hope Brannen was still in tears.

"Who died? Did Reuben kill that Nixon guy?"

"What makes you think Stuckey would kill Nixon?"

"Well," Ms. Brannen sniffled, "Reuben seemed kind of… you know… mean. Maybe he didn't like the Nixon guy. Maybe the Nixon guy was following him for some reason and Reuben didn't like that."

"Interesting theory," Jonah offered. "It's Nixon who's dead. Stuckey's missing. No one has seen him since last fall. In fact, no one has seen Mark Corescu since then either. How about you? Can you tell us where he is? We're very anxious to speak to him."

"You think Reuben killed the Nixon guy and then disappeared?"

"Please answer the question. Where is Dr. Mark Corescu?"

"Mark? Why do you need to see him? What does he have to do with any of this?" The woman sounded panicked and Jenn jumped in with the next question.

"We need to ask him about Stuckey and Nixon, of course."

"Well, I certainly can't tell you where he is. He left the country. He dumped me. Did I mention that? I haven't seen him since that same day. The day I met the Nixon guy was the last day I ever saw Mark." She looked to both detectives. "That's the truth."

Jonah believed her. "Where did he go?"

"He took a plane to Europe, I think. He said he was going home. I don't know where. He just left."

"And Paul Black? Did he go with him?" Jonah asked, checking off names.

Ms. Brannen was quiet and then shrugged her shoulders. "I don't know. I don't think so. They had a fight that night, that last night we were together, and Paul left alone."

"What did they fight about?"

"I don't know. Maybe they were fighting over me…"

Jonah didn't buy it. "You have no idea where Paul Black is?"

"No, honest," she said and Jonah continued to the next question.

"Can you give us a description of this guy, Black?"

"Uh, he's about as tall as you and he was really, really skinny. And he had blond hair, kind of wavy, and blue eyes. And a suntan. He looked like a surfer. Like from California."

Jonah nodded as he jotted notes. "And how old would you say he is?"

Ms. Brannen paused long enough for Jonah to look up. Her gaze flickered and her fear response arced. What was going on? Finally she squeezed her arms and shook her head. "I don't know his exact age, but he looks like he's about nineteen. Maybe twenty."

"Okay," Jonah said, making a mental note that the age of the Black character made their host very nervous. He began to add appropriate information to his pad and fell quiet, thinking. He had photographs of Stuckey and Corescu already from their driver's licenses. Maybe they could get Paul Black's next. He'd set the guys back at the office on it as soon as he was done with Blondie.

"Okay. Got it. So how about Anthony Agricola? Where is he?" Jonah put a check mark next to his name as he spoke. "When did you last see him?"

"I haven't been able to reach him since last Fall."

Jonah must have sighed too forcefully, because the woman offered more information in a rush.

"Anthony worked at his dad's church in Whitford City, Green Oaks Presby. You might get some idea from them where he went."

"Thank you, we'll look into it," Jonah said and closed his notebook with a finality that gave the Brannen woman hope. "Is there anything else you can tell us that might help us?"

"That's about all I can think of," Ms. Brannen said, her grip loosening on her arms.

"Thank you, Ms. Brannen." Jennifer stood and shook the woman's hand. "Can we contact you with any additional questions?"

The woman nodded. "And call me on my cell. I'll be here for a little while. I'd like to know if you find Anthony. I've been looking for him for months."

"But not Corescu or Stuckey?" Jonah tried one last tactic, but the woman did not flinch.

"No. I didn't know Reuben that well. And Mark? He dumped me. Why would I go looking for him?"

Jonah nodded; she was almost convincing. "Good point," he agreed and followed his partner to the door. They made a hasty exit and piled into the rental car.

On the road, Jenn went over the facts of the case aloud, making guesses and posing theories. Jonah didn't feel any closer to solving the puzzle than before they questioned the Brannen woman. Still, they knew who to look for next. The newest name to the list: Paul Black.

"You know," Jonah said as he pondered Jenn's theories. "Corescu and Black lived in the same house with Stuckey for years. Let's send teams down to dust for fingerprints. The new owners will just have to put up with us for a day."

"Great idea. Even if we don't know which prints go to which man, at least if we get a hit on the prints from our murder weapon, we can narrow our field of suspects down to those three. This is big. I'll call Stansfield. He's the best man for the print job."

"And tell him to set the uniforms on getting me driver's licenses for Agricola and Black. Also, current stats."

Jennifer nodded and began making calls. Jonah's pulse quickened. *Finally a break.* He hoped they'd find a match by the time they got back to Georgia.

◆◆◆

Big John spotted Paul Black's silhouette in the front door as he pulled up. It would be fine; John gave blood three times a year at the church Red Cross drive. No need to panic. Once out of the car, Paul watched him approach, his gaze much too severe for a casual male/male meeting. John glanced down at his attire: a snug tank top and loose-fitting workout pants. He told Opal that he would be the man's physical trainer. Now that he was at the front steps and Paul seemed so anxious for his arrival, John wondered anew at the mysterious deal he'd struck.

"Big John! You made it. Come in," Paul said putting out his hand and John forced a smile. Paul pulled him by the arm and into the house. "We're all set in the room upstairs. You know—the wrestling room." Paul laughed and turned to lead the way to the stairwell.

John blanched and forced his feet to move. *Calm down, Big John! It's just your imagination!* Aloud, he said, "I hope you weren't waiting too long. You said any time after five…"

"Any time you get here suits me. Come on, let's get started." Paul was half-way up the stairs and motioned for John to hurry. With a quick prayer, John trotted after him and joined him at the door.

Paul flipped on the light and John's eye widened. The previously bare room was now filled with an elegant bedroom suite consisting of a four-poster bed and an elaborately carved dressing table set between the two floor-length windows. These pieces hadn't been on the moving truck. Had they been hastily purchased directly after Monday night's move-in? Paul allowed him to gawk only a second more before he stepped to a huge chair astride a polished oak dressing table.

"Come over here. I want you to sit in this chair." Paul turned the substantial chair to face the center of the room, and when John tested his weight in it, it did not creak in the slightest.

At the absence of medical equipment, John's internal alarms sounded. "Are you going to draw the blood yourself?"

"Yes." Paul came around to face him and pulled several bills from his back pocket. "One thousand dollars. I want you to hold it during the donation."

John's eyes lit up at the sight of the money and he was instantly ashamed. He clutched the cash as Paul cocked his head to the side, studying below John's chin. John looked down and Paul reached out to lift the flat-gold cross off John's wide chest.

"What's the story behind this?" Paul asked, his interest hard to read. "Are you a religious man or is this just fashion?"

In slow motion, John removed the cross from Paul's possession. "Both, I guess."

"I like that." Paul chortled. "Tony carries a Bible and you wear a cross. He's a preacher, did you know that?"

John *humphed,* but said nothing else.

"Are you a preacher, too?"

John swallowed and answered in what he hoped was a normal voice. "Now and then."

Paul scrutinized him a few uncomfortable moments, sighed, and walked out of view. John sensed him only inches away and before five seconds passed, Paul put his hands on John's shoulders from behind.

"The deal," Paul said behind him, his voice growing breathless, "is one thousand dollars for approximately one pint of your blood. Does it really matter how I draw it?"

John's spine stiffened at the insinuation. "You aren't using a phlebotomy kit?” The wad of money in his left hand gave him little comfort as his heart rate increased. He didn't start praying, but he wanted to. *Why am I so frightened?* John was a huge man, not given to hysterics. He waited to hear Paul's response.

"I'll take care of the details," Paul said. "It's best if you concentrate on being very, very still…" Paul's voice grew softer as he spoke, his palms quivering where they rested on John's shoulders. "Just hold on to that money and close your eyes."

John felt breath on his neck and knew Paul had leaned in. An image from the latest vampire movie came to mind, and he turned part-way to catch Paul's eye. He was sorry he did.

"You can still leave, John," Paul whispered.

John heard the words with his ears, but also somewhere deep in his mind.

"You won't get that money, but you can go. I release you."

"No, it's okay," John rasped. "Do what you gotta do." He steeled his nerves. The man was not about to bite him, that was ludicrous. He closed his eyes as his brain fuzzed around the edges. The sensation soothed him and he realized through a hazy fog that he really didn't care how the little guy drew his blood. He was holding ten Benjamins in his hand; did it really matter how the services were rendered?

It doesn't matter a hill of beans, really…

At that moment, the gentle touch became claws as Paul gripped John's shoulders and bit his back hard. John snapped awake as if he had been shocked. He stood, hardly noticing that Paul had not loosened his grip and hung onto his back like a demonic child. For a split second, John forgot where he was altogether. Then, just as quickly, it all came back. He looked at the cash in his hand and bent at the knee to allow Paul to regain his feet.

"Atta boy, Big John," Paul whispered, his breath hot and damp on John's back. "Be still, be brave. Shhhh…"

As he spoke, Paul's right hand slid down John's arm and grabbed his wrist. With his arm pinned hard and fast against his own back, John's knees buckled and he cried out. At that moment, John came to the conclusion that a thousand bucks wasn't enough.

"Are you gonna be still?" Paul whispered in his ear and his head, his spittle mixed with John's blood.

John didn't speak, but he relaxed in Paul's grip, calmed once more by the man's voice in his head. Paul resumed his feast from the rip he had made in John's flesh.

"Come on, Big John," Paul telepathically whispered into John's frayed mind. *"You're a Goliath. That's why I chose you. What're you afraid of? A little mosquito? That's all I am to you. Be still. It doesn't have to hurt. Shhh."*

Still on his knees, John squeezed his eyes against the pain of his wrenched arm. He no longer felt anything except the throbbing of his over-extended shoulder joint.

How can I be so helpless against this guy?

Then John recalled his earlier assessment that questioned that the man was a regular *guy* at all. Maybe he wasn't even human.

"Shhhhh."

Paul's telepathic voice further tranquilized and John's toes grew cold in his shoes. Dark spots dotted behind his closed lids and just before they overtook his inner vision, he mumbled to Paul very quietly, "Better stop. Better …stop."

Paul removed his mouth with a loud smack. From his kneeling position, John fell forward in slow motion and landed on the carpet, face down. The last thing John heard before he passed out was Paul telling him that he was a delicious fellow.

♦

"Paul, you didn't!" Tony sprinted to the big man on the floor and looked at Paul with real fear in his eyes. "He's not…?"

Paul laughed at Tony's histrionics. "Of course not, idiot. He's fine. He's *very* fine." Paul rolled John onto his back with one foot and pointed to his legs. "Let's put him on the bed."

"Praise God," Tony said and bent down to grab the huge shins. He grunted with the effort of lifting him the four feet to the bed, but Paul found it easy work, grinning at Tony's complaints.

"Wimp," Paul mumbled as he adjusted the pillows under the man's head. "He's as strong as a horse. You have to admit, this was a very clever plan and I concocted it all by myself."

"Yes, you're very clever," Tony deadpanned. "He's bleeding. You need to bandage him up." Tony removed his handkerchief from his pocket and slid it underneath to reach the raw wound.

Paul chortled. "Nuh-uh. You do it. That's what I have you for."

"Do you have a first-aid kit?" Tony asked and Paul gave him a blank look. "Go to the drug store and get what we need." Tony pointed Paul to where he held the cloth. "Hold this on there a moment. It'll probably clot soon enough. Thank God you missed his jugular vein."

Paul took over pressing the cloth to the man's wound. "I know what I'm doing. Why don't *you* go get whatever we need at Walgreens?" He turned back to look lovingly at the giant man on the guest bed. "He sure is a healthy specimen. I wonder if he'd like to live forever."

Tony stepped closer over Paul's shoulder. "Don't even say such a thing! If you ever…"

Paul cut him off before he could complete his threat. "Hush now, preacher-man. I gave you an errand. Shouldn't you be getting to it?"

Tony huffed, his face red.

"I know what's happening. Don't get jealous. You're the only one for me, Pudgy." Paul smiled and Tony growled his reply.

"God! You know what? Get your own supplies!" Tony turned away and stopped at the bedroom door. "I hope God gets through to you before I'm forced to give up!"

Paul watched Tony stomped from the room. It was pretty funny, seeing the preacher so upset. Paul had located Tony's buttons and would press them as often as possible. The wound no longer seeped and he dropped the cloth.

"John? Big John Jenkins? Wake up." Wiping his chin with the palm of his hand, he leaned against the bed and shook John's arm.

John stirred. "What happened?"

"You earned your money."

"Why am I lying down?" John squinted, focusing on his whereabouts.

"Give it a moment. It'll come back." Paul crossed his arms. He watched John's expression as he turned his head to survey the room. *What will he think when it hits him what has happened? Will he come back?*

John strained to sit up and Paul stood to give him room to swing his legs off the side of the bed. His eyes finally fell upon the overturned chair and they grew wide with understanding.

"The blood. You needed my blood. Why?"

No emotion in his voice, but Paul saw plenty in his eyes. The man battled for his sanity and Paul was ready with a rehearsed response.

"Does it matter? You have a thousand dollars in your hand and next Wednesday, you'll have a thousand more. What's the big deal?" Paul spread his hands apart in supplication and shrugged.

John looked into his hand and found that he still clutched the cash. "So you're some kind of …vampire?"

"Don't be silly. I'm a six-foot mosquito." Paul clapped John on the shoulder. "Lie down and rest. You can stay overnight. This is your room. I set it up just for you."

"No, I have to call Opal. She'll be worried," John said, still too shaky to stand. Paul shrugged.

"Suit yourself. The phone's over there." Paul turned away and headed for the door. "I'll be downstairs if you need anything."

With that, he left the man alone with his thoughts.

14

And pray in the Spirit on all occasions
With all kinds of prayers and requests.
Ephesians 6:18

BIG JOHN FOLLOWED THE AROMA OF TOASTED BREAD
to the kitchen. He hadn't seen his host or his brother since he'd
awoken to find himself tucked into bed. When he reached the
threshold to the sunny dinette, he paused. Tony Agricola sat, head
bowed, lips moving as if in prayer. When he mumbled amen and took
a bite of his toast, John cleared his throat.

"Oh!" Tony said, startled.

"Sorry about that. I was just leaving," John said. He caught a
glimpse of his reflection in the side-by-side refrigerator, and he
swiveled to see the left side of his back. As suspected, a 4" x 4" gauze
pad belied the bite he received the night before.

Tony stood and met him, gesturing to his reflection. "Let me
have a look."

John turned and presented his left shoulder where Tony peeled
up the tape to examine the wound.

"Good," he said and resealed the bandage. He patted John once
and returned to his seat. "That Paul sure can dress a wound."

John remained by the fridge, wondering what to say. He
remembered everything; how did this man fit into the picture?

After another moment, Tony looked at him and motioned a
chair. "Have a seat. Want some toast?"

Seeking answers as well as breakfast, John pulled out the offered
chair. He accepted the orange juice Tony poured and drank it in one
effort.

"So, Big John," Tony started, "are you okay?" John felt great and
he said so. Tony plucked grapes off a bunch on the table and popped
them in his mouth. "Good. Praise the Lord."

John swallowed the rest of his toast and pointed a knuckle Tony's way. "Are you ...a ...a ...are you like him? A *mosquito?*"

Tony stopped chewing and then after a pause, shook his head. "No, no way. Not hardly."

"Good," John exhaled relieved. "I'd hate to think of two of him buzzing around."

"Yeah, one's too many, if you ask me," Tony said, sipping his juice. "How did you sleep?"

"Fine, I guess. Don't remember waking up in the night."

Tony chuckled. "I'm not surprised. You took quite a hit." He met John's eye. "I'm glad you're okay. I was praying for you."

John said thanks and his head whooshed. Placing his palm against his eyes, he winced. "I guess I lost more blood than I realized. Your brother might have to pay me double if he's gonna do that each time."

Tony cleared his throat. "First off, he's not my brother. And secondly, you're coming back?"

It was John's turn to laugh, his head clearing. "I didn't think ya'll could be real brothers. But, yeah, I'll come back. I mean, I'm not hurt, and the money's good." John shrugged and left off there. He had never considered it to be a question of integrity, but Tony intimated that it was. He suddenly felt the need to defend himself. "I mean, does it really matter? No harm done, right?"

Tony swished the crumbs from his hands. "It's your body. I guess Paul had you pegged."

"What do you mean?"

"Paul picked you out the moment he saw you. He said you tapped on his window while he was sleeping. He opened his eyes, took one look at you, and concocted his ingenious plan right there."

"Is that right? I don't know what made me tap the car. I never would have thought he was... I mean, I thought he was kind of funny. Hah-hah funny, I mean. He was so puny and fierce. And his eyes, they capture you, you know?"

"I try not to look into his eyes," Tony quipped and wiped his mouth with a napkin.

Neither man said anything for several long moments and John didn't care for the silence. He gestured for Tony's Bible.

"Paul told me you were a preacher."

Tony inhaled, laying his hand over the gold embossed title of the Book. "I was in seminary before I met Paul." Tony hooked a thumb back the way John had entered.

John's skin crawled at the thought of running into the kid and he finished his impromptu breakfast and got to his feet.

"You leaving?" Tony asked without standing.

"I better. My wife will be looking for me."

"Are you a God-fearing man, John?" Tony asked, his eyes trained to the cross around John's neck.

John touched it with his fingers. "Are you asking me if God approves of this deal?"

Tony held his hands up in surrender, his expression grave. "I just wanted to know what side you were on, that's all."

"I'm on God's side, and I got bills. What about you? Do you think God approves of this—of this guy, Paul?"

Tony rose from the table. "Approves? No. Wants to save? Yes."

"You're trying to help him get saved?" John was amazed. Could this soft, nerdy-looking fellow turn the vampire from his evil ways, or was the young preacher deluding himself?

"God-willing, yeah," he answered.

"How did you get mixed up with him? Is he a… like a movie vampire? A real one?"

"He's a real vampire, not a movie one." Tony nodded, frowning.

"God help us," John exhaled. "And you met him, how?"

"God's will, John," Tony said and sighed. "It's a long story and you probably want to be gone before Paul comes in. He's probably the last person you want to see right now."

"You're right about that," John said and crossed to the doorway.

"I called your wife for you last night. Told her your appointment ran late and that you'd be home in the morning. I hope that's okay."

John was puzzled and Tony read his expression.

"I had to go through your wallet to get your number. Hope you don't mind."

John relaxed.

Tony—safe. Paul Black—stay the Hades away from my wife.

◆

"I was happy to help," Tony said, listening for Paul as he shook John's hand.

"I appreciate that a lot," John said. "She doesn't need to be worrying at a time like this. We're expecting a baby this week."

"Congratulations," Tony said with sincerity and turned to lead

John to the door. John held up a finger, paused, and turned for the hall restroom.

Tony continued to the front door and leaned against the wall and planned his day. The bookstore idea had grown into a renovation of sorts. After their initial visit, the floors needed to be replaced and Tony hired a pair of local college students to do a complete inventory. In a week or so, they might be ready to open their doors, Tony even more relishing the idea of spending his days away from Paul's lair. And Paul had been keeping his hands busy, too. This morning, the vampire headed out at first light, presumably to work in the barn. He liked to tinker, and Tony liked to see the vampire's imagination go beyond *who do I bite today*. The guy had to learn a new mindset now that he was his own boss.

"Yeah," Paul said in a sarcastic voice as he joined Tony in the foyer. "And who's fault is that?" Paul draped an arm across Tony's shoulders and offered a brief squeeze. Tony stiffened and waited for the embrace to end. "Where's my giant?"

The toilet flushed and Paul's question didn't require an answer. Tony shimmied free and stepped away. Paul again took Tony under his wing and dragged him toward the door.

"Leave him alone, okay?" Tony said as he wiggled free. "He's a good guy."

"He's *very* good." Paul licked his lips and leaned against the wall.

The sink water started up and Tony said low, "Just be cool. He's pretty shaken up."

"No, he's not. Not everyone's a wimp like you." Paul stood off the wall. "He's going to need a car. Did you get a look at that clunker? It's not going to last long traveling to and fro every week."

Tony's gut clinched as he realized who would have to pinch-hit for John if his car broke down. "Definitely," Tony agreed. "Get the man a new car."

On top of his thoughts, Paul shot him a glance and chuckled. "Don't worry, I won't neglect you, Pudgy."

Tony opened his mouth to retort, but John entered straightening his clothes and jingling his keys. Paul stepped up to him before he reached the foyer threshold and put both palms to his chest.

"It's a beautiful day to buy a new Caddy," he said, staring up into the big man's face. Tony read the moment of panic in John's eyes, and just as quickly, it faded, becoming accustomed to Paul's eccentricities.

"Say what?" John asked and turned his gaze to Tony's. "What

does he mean?"

"John, look at *me,*" Paul said under his nose. "I'm speaking plain English. That old rat-trap you drive won't get you there and back every week. I aim to buy you a new car. Right now."

John looked down at him and tried to smile, but it came out a grimace. Paul didn't release John from the close quarters.

Tony ruined his moment by opening the front door and pulling Paul outside by his T-shirt. "Let's get moving."

As soon as all three men were outside, Tony pulled the door closed and locked it. "How about it, Big John? That okay?"

"You want to give me a car?" John asked. "You mean like a company car?"

Tony held his hand up to shush Paul and he took John by the arm, drawing him aside. "No, a replacement. A gift." Tony waited for a flicker of understanding to appear in John's eyes, but he was still confused. Tony tried a more direct tact. "Look, you're coming next week, right? And every week as long as needed, right?" Tony waited for John to nod. "We don't want you to break down on the way here." Tony glanced at Paul who eavesdropped from a few feet away. *"I* don't want you to break down," Tony said after lowering his voice to a whisper. Paul would still hear him, but it made him feel better nonetheless. "If you don't make it one day, I'm the only other person here and I don't make a thousand bucks each time."

"Oh." John nodded with understanding. He shook Tony's hand and glanced at Paul, who was laughing to himself. "I accept."

"Great, let's go." Paul fished around in his pocket for his truck keys. "You drive my truck, Tony."

Tony rushed to the Cadillac and winked at John "No, we'll follow you. I'm going to ride with Big John." Tony fell into the passenger side of the rusty red Caddy and hoped Paul didn't fly over and yank him out. Surprisingly, he smirked and turned for the Tahoe.

"He's in a good mood," Tony said as John turned the ignition.

"That's a blessing, right?" John asked. The engine sputtered but then roared to life with a huge burst of black exhaust.

Tony grinned and tapped the dash. "He made a good call with this car." John chuckled and fell in behind Paul's white truck toward the security gate. Tony looked at John's profile and then out the windshield. "Paul is fixated on you and he doesn't want you and me getting too close."

John sighed and stole a look Tony's way. "Why does he have to be so weird about it? I've never known a real life monster, but I never would have thought a demon would be so… *huggy*."

Tony gave a sad laugh. "He does that because it makes you—it makes *us*—uncomfortable. He could inflict physical pain easily, but he's figured out that emotional and spiritual torture is much more effective. And fun."

"Watch it… it can get much worse."

Paul's voice rolled past Tony's mind, but he continued. "And he's been through a lot this past six months. If you stick around, you'll learn that he wasn't always a vampire. I get the impression that before I ever came into the picture, he was really pretty pleasant."

"That's better…" Paul sent telepathically.

Tony rubbed his eyes and sighed. "If I'm lucky, he won't drive me insane before I can help him. Be thankful you only have to deal with him once a week."

"Well," John started, his voice low, "he scares me to death. And I'm a big guy."

"Size is relative," Tony mused, watching the houses go by as they approached the bypass. He suddenly remembered what he wanted to say to John before Paul had interrupted him in the foyer. "By the way, you know that all of this is confidential, right? You can't tell anyone. Not your wife, family, or even your pastor."

"Yeah, I know. I won't tell anyone," John said under his breath, and then added, "No one would believe me anyway."

Tony agreed with a *humph* and had another thought. "Also, did you realize that Paul can hear some of your thoughts?" John gave a slow nod. A car-length ahead, Paul waved in his rear view mirror. "Distance has very little to do with his ability," Tony said gamely waving back. "But recently, I've had some success in blocking him."

"Really? I'd like to know about that."

Tony winced and touched his temple. Paul had pinged him hard. John caught his movement out of the corner of his eye and he looked concerned. Tony forced a smile. "You'll figure it out."

The big man sighed with a shake of his head. "I'm doing this for my family. I belong to God, and I trust Him to keep me safe. As far as I'm concerned, this little vampire thing you and Paul have going on here is a temporary stint. Just to help me get on my feet."

"Have you considered that maybe you're here to help me help him?" Tony wondered if he was simply applying his wishes to the situation, but John considered his words.

"Yeah," he said after a moment. "I think God sent me a vision about this a few weeks ago. I'll stay as long as God wants me to."

"I appreciate that. And John…" Tony lowered his voice again. "Paul hates God. None of this will be easy."

"Yeah, I got that."

"You're one cool customer, John Jenkins."

"Well, thanks, but I'm not as cool as I look." John gave a nervous titter that did not match his appearance. John laughed then and shook his head at something in his mind. Tony waited for an explanation and it came shortly. "I'm thinking about my pastor. He's a powerful Seer. I wonder if he'll see any of this stuff."

Tony shrugged. "From what I understand of prophecy, he'll only see what God wants him to see. We'll just have to count on that."

"I guess so."

"You believe in the power of the Holy Spirit?"

"Amen," John said with sincerity.

"John," Tony began, understanding dawning. "I know why Paul is attracted to you. Besides the novelty of your gigantic physique—" Tony gestured his way. "He can't resist the energy inside us. The *Spirit*. The Light attracts him. He's hijacking the Holy Spirit off us."

"Is he a demon?"

Tony shook his head. "He's just a man, but he turned his life over to demons by choice. They control him and he doesn't know it."

"If he has devils in him, they could be cast out," John said with hope in his voice.

"Exactly." Tony nodded.

"Good luck with that, preacher-man…"

Paul's retort sounded in Tony's head and he kept it to himself.

Within moments, they were parked and Paul jogged over to walk John into the sales office. Tony hung back and let the vampire do his thing. In the past, he had purchased dozens of vehicles for Mark Corescu; buying a Cadillac should be a cinch. While he waited, he wondered how to cast the devil out of a vampire and if John would help him do it.

15

The eyes of the LORD are on the righteous
And His ears are attentive to their cry.
Psalm 34:15

THE SANCTUARY OF EAST MONTGOMERY UNITED Methodist Church was packed and from his seat in the rear of the huge congregation, Paul watched Tony prepare the room for his opening prayer. Tony had been invited to preach Sunday evening's service and Paul came along for laughs. Plus, church was a good place to nap; he felt most at peace when dozing to one of Tony's monologues. He had no plans to cause trouble, even though Tony glared at him twice by the time he started speaking. After a long moment, Paul closed his eyes.

The bookstore could open any time they chose. Tony had arranged for new laminate flooring, fresh paint on the walls, and two boys he wouldn't let Paul meet came by and logged every book into the computer. Paul assumed he'd next hire cashiers and that would be fun; once the store was up and running, Paul intended to haunt Tony often. Put an innocent and Tony alone with Paul and he could make the preacher do whatever he asked. The man's drive to *protect* was hilarious. Paul smiled to himself and from the stage Tony spouted a new prayer to his God.

After a few minutes, a high-pitched whine came through the speakers. Paul opened his eyes to see if anyone else noticed but there was no sign that they did. Paul put a finger to his temple—the sound was for *him* and magnified by the second. At first, he pretended it wasn't there, but when he thought his head would explode from pain, Paul stood and covered the fifteen feet to the exit, both hands pressed against his head.

Once outside the sanctuary, the noise abated and Paul looked about, bleary-eyed. The lobby was empty save a woman pouring herself a cup of coffee. Paul walked in the opposite direction for the huge glass doors that opened to the parking lot. At his truck, reached for the door handle and heard a tiny shuffle directly behind. Turning, Paul forced a smile to the stranger.

"Excuse me. Can you help me with my car?"

Paul gave her a hard look, his mind seething, *do I look like Triple-A?* But Tony's be-polite lessons were working and he remembered he was a monster undercover. He managed a half-smile and said hello.

"I'm Pastor Sarah Tracey. Do you have any jumper cables?"

Paul shook his head. The woman was in her late thirties and nearly as tall as he was, with dark blonde hair cropped close and the errant wisps flipped in the evening breeze. She looked toward a dusty Volvo.

"Do you know anything about cars?"

"I'm afraid not," Paul said and returned his keys to his pocket. The parking lot was well-lighted by large sodium lights and he surveyed for witnesses. Maybe she would like a ride.

"What's your name?" she asked, stepping back giving Paul the sense that she was frightened of him. That made him smile for real and he leaned on his truck fender.

"Name's Saul White. Can I give you a lift?" Paul fantasized about taking her blood. The woman's breath-rate increased and she backed another step. *She knows...* This intrigued him very much and he widened his smile. "I'll take you home."

"No, thank you," she said, her keys in one fist. "I'll call my husband," she said, her voice wavering and her eyes wide.

"Well, if you're sure," Paul replied. The more fearful she became, the more he wanted to kill her. Then, the woman blinked twice, hardened her gaze, and seemed to grow two inches as she stood erect. Now it was Paul catching a whiff of danger. Something strange had occurred and he now wanted as far away from the woman as possible. He backed and watched her expression as the air between them crackled with electricity.

I have to get away from this crazy church!

The woman inhaled and held his gaze. "You can't get away from God, young man," she said, her voice shivering, but her words forceful. "The Lord wants you to know that He loves you and He's watching over you. He has always been looking after you, hedging you in and protecting you. He's not going to let you leave this world without knowing Him. You will travel to a distant land seeking one master, but you will find another. As you go, listen to your little shepherd and do as he says." That said, the woman made a quick turn and jogged toward the church entrance.

Paul stood, mouth ajar, processing what he'd just heard.

What in the world was that?

He was spooked and hated the sensation prickling up his spine.

Crazy woman!

Paul stumbled to his door and locked himself inside waiting for the hair to stand down on his arms. *This is Tony's fault!* The preacher constantly undermined Paul's authority, calling on his God every time he had a problem. Weak, pathetic, and disobedient. Why did he want the guy around? He had Big John; did he really need two preachers?

Paul rest his forehead against the steering wheel and closed his eyes. The Sarah woman's words tried to float back and he pushed them away. The woman was insane. *Religion makes people nuts!* Paul asserted. He thought of Tony, trying to rehabilitate him as he did Mark. *I won't let him. I'll get him to bow to me. He can respect me, or die. Big John worked out fine. Tony's not irreplaceable...*

Feeling better, Paul resolved to work Tony over when they got home; see if he could get the little man to see things his way. He formulated his attack sequence to pass the time.

16

Therefore confess your sins to each other and pray for each other
So that you may be healed.
The prayer of a righteous man is powerful and effective.
James 5:16

"BROTHER TONY, YOU DON'T LOOK SO GOOD."

Tony didn't meet the big man's eye as he took the initiative to sit across from him in the front room. Tony used the entire couch, head on one arm and feet propped on the other. His wounds may have closed, but he hadn't changed clothes nor showered since Paul's attack. He was too busy arguing with God to care much about hygiene. What John was seeing, he could only guess.

"You look like a man with a pest control problem," John said. Tony met his eye, but not getting his humor. John tried again. "You know—the mosquito man. Has he been bugging you?"

Tony forced a smile and sat up, but was in no mood for small talk. "It's nothing, I'll be fine."

"Where is he? He's usually waiting at the door tapping his foot."

Tony only shrugged.

The room had fallen into darkness and John switched on a table lamp without rising. Tony flinched at the extra light. He hadn't slept in thirty-six hours as Paul tortured him without mercy. As much as he wanted someone with which to commiserate, he did not think it prudent to reveal Paul's darkest side to his new accomplice.

"How's the bookstore going?" the big guy asked.

Tony mumbled it was fine. In reality, he hadn't been by since the renovation completed, mostly because of Paul's abuse. Tony had grown weary to the bone and spiritually, he had reached the lowest point in his memory. John fidgeted preparing a new question.

"Do you think he'll be back soon?" John asked in a soft voice.

Tony decided to hide what he could. He ran his hands through his hair and tucked in his shirt. "Yeah. He wouldn't miss your visit for the world." Tony watched the big man's face. He was petrified of Paul, that was evident, but he had a duty he believed in and needs Tony didn't comprehend. He might have appeared judgmental because John sat up and asked his own query in a humble tone.

"Am I prostituting my blood, Tony?"

Tony sighed. "John, you have to follow your heart. I can't tell you what to do."

"What are you reading in the Bible, there?" he asked, changing the subject.

"Lamentations," Tony answered. The sad utterings of the prophet Jeremiah gave him comfort as he babysat the monster God saddled him with.

"Yeah, well," John began, "I guess you know about suffering."

Tony smiled. "Yes, sir, I do."

John fidgeted in the chair. Paul was close; maybe he could sense it. They had been seeing each other a few weeks now and Tony didn't know how far Paul's power extended.

"Tony," John said, "tell me what's going on. Did Paul do this to you? You look awful."

Tony leaned over his lap. He was exhausted, his head screaming with pain. John was an oasis of sanity in the whole crazy business. He decided to share something, if only to increase their bond.

"I don't want to scare you," he said in John's intense gaze. "Or maybe you should be scared..."

"I *am* scared, but I have bills."

"I know. Just be careful. Consider everything your conscience tells you. Paul is dangerous and he could kill us, or worse, at any time. The only reason I stay is because I am *certain* God put me here. If He opened an exit for me, I'd be gone."

John leaned in. "This is your blood, then?"

"Yeah. Paul has been very angry. Something's bothering him and I don't know what it is. He, um..." Tony paused to choose his words. Finally he swallowed and continued. "He has attacked me every night this week, starting on Sunday night when we got home from the church where I was preaching."

"He attacked you?"

"Every night for three nights. Thank God you're here tonight, or he'd do it again." Tony read empathy in John's face. He lowered his eyes. "I fought him as well as I could, but it's like fighting a machine."

"A man of steel," John whispered.

Tony nodded without looking up. "I fell into praying and the louder I prayed, the angrier he became." Tony added in a sad whisper, *"And God didn't help me at all."*

"Jesus," John mumbled. "You gotta leave. He's gonna kill you."

"Leave?" Tony leveled his gaze. "You don't get it." John's face remained a question mark. "Do you think you and I are the same?" Tony watched his face and waited for something to dawn.

"Well, yeah. I mean, you're not like him, so I assumed…"

Tony gave his head two quick shakes. "Look at me. I was attacked, my throat literally torn out and my skin ripped apart. The next two nights, beaten to a bloody pulp. Look." Tony pulled down his collar and turned his head away to reveal his healed neck. Then he straightened out both arms to show that they were also wound free.

"What are you saying?" John stammered. "Are you saying that he… that you…?"

"I'm bound to Paul by his blood. I promised God I would keep him under control and try to keep him from killing innocent people."

"Wait. How did you become bound by blood? Am I going to catch this disease?"

Tony frowned. "No, it doesn't work that way. Paul fed me his blood when I was unconscious. When I awoke, I was like this. Immortal."

"Did you just say that you're *immortal?* You're losing me."

"If you drink a vampire's blood, then you become a regenerating slave. Except I'm already a slave to God and I'm not serving Paul. That's why he's so angry. His vampire master was very powerful and terrifying. And in comparison, Paul is impotent." Tony crossed his arms in front of his chest now indignant and the entire story. "And I can't be concerned with his complaints. I serve God. I've told him that from the beginning."

John cursed and rubbed his bald head. "How long have you been like this?"

"A few months."

"How did this happen? When are you going to tell me the whole story?"

Exhausted in mind and spirit, Tony leaned back and closed his eyes. "Ask Paul. He would enjoy telling you of his days of glory."

John didn't say anything else and let the room fill with silence as they waited for the night to begin.

♦ ♦ ♦

Sarah Tracey towel-dried her hair and combed it through before shutting off the bathroom light and heading to the living room. She had spent the day meditating on God's word. Ira had only interrupted her once and he only did so because he had no other choice.

Ira Tracey was a kindly Charismatic Evangelist that she married with the Lord's blessing two years previous. Ira had just celebrated his 68th birthday and his forty-fifth year in the ministry. She was half his age. Sarah snickered as she recalled the amazed admissions of her more outspoken friends and family when they heard of the Tracey's betrothal.

"He's old enough to be your father."

"What could you possibly have in common?"

And the one that they all thought, but only her cousin Sheryl was brazen enough to ask, *"Do you guys have sex?"*

Sarah shook her head. What they didn't know was that she was barren. Worse, the conformation of her uterus prevented comfortable intercourse. She and Ira never intended to consummate their relationship in the conventional manner. Thankfully, Ira had come to an age that his own sexual drive had decreased enough to ignore. To her doubting friends, she offered a quiet decree, "God has a plan, and He knows what He's doing!"

Sarah sat down on the couch to check the Weather Channel. Ira had gone out an hour ago to teach his Wednesday night Bible group and would be home soon. Since her encounter with the frightening young man in the Methodist parking lot almost a month ago, she had brooded in her prayer closet about the incident. The man oozed evil and she saw with her spiritual eyes that he wanted to kill her. Sarah shivered; God protected her then and He'd continue to do so.

What is that?

Sarah clicked off the television and sat upright. Her mind went over a mental check-list of general safety requirements; *the doors are locked, the alarm is set, the dog is loose in the back yard...*

She lifted her cell from the coffee table and held it to her chest. She hadn't heard a sound with her ears, but her spirit was alive with uncomfortable sensations. She stood and faced her front door. What she was sensing now was brand new. Under compulsion of her own mind or that of God, she crossed to the foyer and peeked out the oval inset. Instantly, the source of her dismay became evident; the monster from the church stood at the curb in front of her house.

Jesus! Send him away!

She backed from the window, praying under her breath that it had been a hallucination. Didn't she specifically ask God to keep them apart? Sarah was shamed by her cowardice and cleared her mind. Then floating on what had to be God's strength, she returned to the door, unlocked it, and called out to the silhouette in the streetlamp's glow.

"Come on in, Saul."

Without delay, the kid with the ancient eyes stepped toward the door. Sarah steadied her nerves by reminding herself that her house was robustly protected by angels. Any evil would be powerless within her walls. God wanted her to minister to the kid and she wouldn't say no. Even if it killed her. Mostly convinced, she watched the man approach only to stop ten feet away.

"Won't you come in?"

"Why don't you come out here?" he asked, jittery and unsure.

Did he fear her or God *inside* of her? Sarah firmed her tone. "You'll have to come in here to talk with me. House rules." Sarah stepped back to make room for the man to enter, but he hung back beyond the reach of her porch light.

"I'm fine right here," he said, his voice edgy. "What was that you were saying to me that night? Are you a witch?"

Sarah considered his question. How badly did God want him to come in? How much should she answer through the door? She decided finally to answer the one bit of truth he should go away with if he chose to run off.

"No, I'm not a witch. I'm a servant of the Living God. *Our God.* Your Creator. Do you know Him?"

"I should have known." Her visitor managed few steps forward. "Religious nuts, all of you."

Sarah prepared for his entrance, but as his foot touched the threshold, he winced and grabbed his head. With a burst of courage, she grabbed his shirt and pulled him inside as hard as she could. "There you go!" she barked. The man was knocked off balance and he tumbled into her foyer.

"My head!" he cried before opening his eyes to notice where he was. Lowering his hands, he turned a full circle, his eyes round with wonder. "Why did you do that? Aren't you afraid of me? A stranger, here with you…" He seemed to listen to the house before completing his thought. "With you all alone."

"I'm not alone and I'm not afraid. I pulled you in because you didn't seem to have the power to do it yourself." Sarah left the foyer and led Saul to her dinette.

"Oh," he replied and sat in the closest chair. "I feel numb. Is this place moving?" The kid swiveled his head to catch Sarah's eye. "Why did you say those things to me that night..." Her visitor was lethargic now, slurring as if intoxicated. He planted his palms to the table top and stared at her hard. "Why did you..."

The kid's voice undulated and Sarah assumed that the evil forces inside him were being forced into submission by the spiritual forces on her side.

"Saul, God is real and He's trying to touch you. I don't have all the answers and He only shows me tiny pieces of the puzzle. I can't put them together any more than you can disappear into thin air."

"I don't believe in God," the kid that wasn't a kid sputtered, "but my master did. And now he is dying a slow and painful death; a death that will never end."

Sarah's visitor covered his mouth then, eyes narrowing, as if he'd said too much. Perhaps God had loosened his tongue. At any rate, she prayed for words of wisdom and continued her impromptu ministry.

"I don't know you, but I want to help you find your way to God."

"What? I'm not going that way—you can forget it," the man stammered, his eyes wide.

"Look, God is speaking to me about you right now. You're not doing right and God will hold you accountable." Sarah had run out of words and she stood to send the young man out. "God is trying to communicate with you. My suggestion is that you let Him in."

Her visitor followed her to the door moving in jerks. He looked to have more to say, but spoke only when the door was opened and he stepped into the night. From the first step, he turned and met Sarah's eye, his face red with new anger.

"You *are* some kind of witch!" he hissed then held up his hands like claws. "If you were a normal woman, I would have squeezed the life out of you right here!"

Although startled by the threat, she was not afraid. Sarah offered him a sad smile and backed to close the door. "God bless you, Saul and do not come here again." With that, she shut the door in the man's face and shut off the porch light.

♦

Paul sputtered and cursed most of the drive home, wishing he'd never laid eyes on the church witch. A plan to hunt her down and kill her tickled his psyche as he turned onto his street. Once he'd coded the gate to open, he sent a mental greeting to Tony and found him drowsing indoors. The man had been sulking because of the rough treatment he had been dealt. But he had it coming. Eventually, he would come to realize who was in charge. In the front room, he caught snatches of a morose conversation between John and Tony; John feared Paul would attack him in a like manner. Paul snickered.

John opened the front door as Paul was climbing the last porch step. Paul lowered his chin and sent John a wink.

"Big John Jenkins, *you* waiting on *me*? How marvelous! Spent last week's money, did you?" Paul poked at the man's pride knowing it would hurt and that he would never strike back. Being superior had its merits. He glanced into the adjacent room and spied Tony on the couch. "Look at the baby sleeping in his cradle."

The big man cleared his throat and ignored Paul's insults. Unsatisfied with his reaction, Paul prodded again.

"John, I've discovered that Tony Agricola is hardly a man. He can't take near as much of my attention as you can. Such a disappointment."

John shook his head. "Come on, you know Tony's not—"

"Shut up," Paul snapped. "And don't go feeling sorry for him. He got what he deserved." Paul passed John and started up to the second floor. "You shouldn't take everything he says so seriously. He's so emotional and blows everything *way* out of proportion."

John remained in the foyer, watching Paul ascend the stairs. "Maybe you shouldn't be so hard on him. He only wants what's best for you."

"Hah!" Paul said and turned to look down at John on the first floor. "He has no idea what's best for me, and until you know the whole story, you won't either." Paul took a calming breath, but it didn't help. He leveled his pointer finger at the big man below. "You two zealots are out to convert the world when the world is perfectly happy the way it is. Now, get up here!"

John looked in the direction of the sleeping Tony and turned begrudgingly toward the stairs. Paul watched him climb, admiring the way his muscles moved beneath his skin. The man might be a giant, but Paul would have him in tears before long. When he reached the landing, Paul gestured for him to lead the way to the room. Once there, he pointed for the bed and John sat down with an *umph,* as if weary to the soul.

"Buck up, John. I'm the victim here. Worry about me for a change!" Paul crawled behind John and sat on his knees. Chunky scars from previous donations puckered in several places and he rubbed them as he vented his frustration. "My master was everything to me and that preacher down there destroyed him. Don't feel sorry for him, feel sorry for me!"

John grunted and Paul clenched his jaw. The man was as hard-headed as Tony, maybe worse. He grabbed the hem of John's tank and pulled it over his head with no resistance from his guest.

"I am a marvelous and rare being," Paul said, his hand already seeking the place he would attack. "I will not be controlled by an insignificant preacher man and his ancient voodoo rituals." John still hadn't spoken and Paul smirked. "You're going to be as bad as he is one day, aren't you? I don't want to have to hurt either of you, but I could. I could snap your thick neck like a twig."

Paul placed both hands around John's neck from behind, his fingers not even coming close to touching on the other side. The big man's heart rate was up so Paul's words were getting through. Why couldn't he get a response? Where did the man get his courage? Paul squeezed John's neck enough to cut off his breathing.

"I've killed many times and I could easily do it again."

"Huh," John managed, and Paul loosened his grip so the man could speak. As Paul watched, Big John closed his eyes, and began to pray. "Heavenly Father, Creator of Heaven and earth, this man You made is not a total loss, is he? There's always a chance that he can be saved. You have said that anything I ask for in prayer will be answered if I believe..."

Paul had frozen in place as the big man began his prayer, but then returned to choosing the best place to draw his blood. He listened to the words his second preacher man uttered and his mouth twisted into a wry smile. His supplications made a similar light as Tony's and Paul enjoyed seeing it seep out of the man's pores. As if he could hurt their God by having his way with His servants.

"Don't you dare stop praying, Big John. If you do, I'm going to kill you," Paul said in John's ear when he paused. John flinched and continued, this time, his voice wavering.

"…if I believe, and I do believe this, O Lord. Heal this man from his affliction. Scare that devil right out of him. Remove this terrible blood…" John grimaced as Paul ignored his back altogether and stabbed his nape with dagger-like teeth. When he realized he'd stopped praying he started up where he left off. "…remove this terrible bloodlust that has darkened his very soul. Protect me, Your son, from evil this night."

John grunted as Paul's fingers dug into his shoulders, holding with cruel claws although he did not resist.

"And Lord, if it is Your will that I return home after this, please get me home safely." John paused longer this time, his words slurring from blood loss. "There's a demon on my back and I sure would like You to pull him off…"

Paul abruptly snatched his lips away from John's skin and laughed, carelessly spitting on John's back and arms. Giggling like a child, Paul smeared the blood with his hands so that when he was done, the giant's chocolate flesh was coated with sticky crimson fluid.

"Amen, Big John! Amen," Paul sputtered. "Now, explain this mess to your sweet wife!"

He whipped out a handkerchief from his back pocket and pressed the folded cloth against Big John's wound. It was not a deep puncture, but a nasty laceration nonetheless. The fountain had flowed freely and although it would heal sufficiently, it was liable to sting worse than any he had received thus far. He prodded John's shoulder with his free hand.

"I wonder what you'll tell your little wifey back home. Here's one for you, how about this…" Paul lowered his voice to a comical warble to fall into a vocal impression of Big John. "Baby, remember how I told you I cut my back last week on a nail? Well, I ran right into that nail again last night and this time, it went right into my neck! Yes! Isn't that awful? I'm so clumsy and that guy's gym is full of dangerous pointy objects!'"

Paul laughed anew at his joke and climbed off the bed, still holding the hankie firmly in place. John had not looked up, humiliated and at a loss for words. Plus, he was close to passing out.

"Thou shall not lie, *Preacher John*. What a hypocrite!" Paul peeked under the cloth, satisfied that the blood had clotted well enough to begin healing. "There you go, my giant preacher man. Lie down and count your money." Paul reached into his other pocket and pulled out the familiar wad of hundreds. "For services rendered." He pressed it into John's lax hand and pushed his shoulder until he fell back.

John reached for the raw injury on the back of his throat and winced.

"Let this be a reminder to you. Respect me and I'll respect you, otherwise…" Paul paused and walked to the door. "Otherwise, you're no use to me." John lost consciousness without a retort, his fingers to his wound. Paul was pleased; it had been a marvelous time.

◆

Tony tip-toed in to check on John. The big man was fast asleep, one hand full of hundreds and the other arm draped over his face. Tony rolled him onto his side and tended his laceration. He had been standing outside the door for most of the attack and felt sorry for the guy. If he'd only known what he was getting into that first day.

He would have run from the house screaming and never returned, Tony sighed to himself. *That's what I wish I had done…*

He headed to his room and his cell phone rang, startling him with its sudden noise. The caller ID revealed that it was the assistant pastor at his home church, Green Oaks Presby.

"Harry? What's up? Everything okay?" Tony asked. Harry hadn't called him since he left, so he couldn't imagine what the man needed.

"Hey, Tony. Been lifting up the Lord there in Montgomery?"

"Sure have. How are you?" Tony asked, irritated by the small talk and then instantly sorry for his bad mood. No matter what his state, he was supposed to be a Light to the world.

"We're fine. Tony, the police called here for you yesterday. They wanted your phone number so I gave them your cell. They wouldn't tell me what it was about, but I thought I'd let you know."

"The police?" Tony's heart fell and he sat down on his bed. "The Whitford City Police?"

"Uh-huh, homicide detectives. They seemed pretty intent to question you about something. I thought you should know."

"Yeah, of course. Thanks, Harry. How weird." Tony's mind whirled with possibilities, but he was able to close his conversation with Harry and disconnect.

Homicide? Did they find Reuben's body? What can any of that have to do with me? How can they connect me to Mark and that bunch? Tony lay back on his bed, the overhead light stinging his eyes. *And why haven't they called me? What are they waiting for? They're not looking for me, are they? Can they find me? Who has my address? I haven't given my address out, have I?*

Tony concentrated on his internal questions, seeking answers. He'd been purposefully vague with all of his contacts since he'd hooked up with Paul, and now he was truly thankful. The solution was simple: don't answer the phone. Tony was making a conscious decision to be deceitful.

But I can't talk to the police. What could I say? he asked himself and God. *I can't help them if they found Reuben dead. They'd never believe what really happened.*

Tony's cell phone buzzed, startling him all over, and he fished it from his pocket. The ID said name unknown, but the area code was Whitford City. Tony tucked the phone back into his pocket and ignored it.

I'll think of something… he thought, his mind still racing. *I need to get my story straight. I'll work up something to tell them that won't lead to the topic of vampires.*

The phone rang again as if the caller tried back after hanging up. Tony checked the ID and then shut off the ringer all together.

Jonah hung up the phone and made a note of the hour and date. Jenn was gone for the night and he was tying up loose ends. Agricola's father was deceased, mother didn't answer and Jonah left his number, no brothers, or sisters. He had plenty of friends at his church and a pizza place he sometimes delivered for. All persons vouched for his character and painted him as the epitome of a godly man. He was a seminary student, currently on Sabbatical in Montgomery, Alabama, and had left no forwarding address.

Jonah sat back in his chair and tried to link him to the man found dead behind the BP off I-65. The connection was tenuous. Brannen said that Agricola was with her when she saw Nixon, but that didn't predicate that Agricola knew Nixon. Basically, Jonah was looking for the Doctor. Seeing as he was his employer, he was the man who would most likely know Stuckey's location. And how likely was it that Stuckey killed Nixon? Jonah scratched his head and glanced down at the first file he'd started. *Nixon APD files.*

It was Jenn's shorthand for the stuff the APD ISS gal gave her on the case files Nixon collected before his death. Nixon had asked for a list of every unsolved case headed up by a Detective John Q. Buckley. Jonah's precursory glance needed to be upgraded, so he pulled back the cover. Scanning the stack ate up forty-five minutes. As the clock chimed eleven, Jonah yawned and reached for a slip of notepaper.

Nixon had pulled precisely twenty-two Buckley cold cases from APD. Twenty of those cases had evidence of staged suicide. Four of the twenty-two had filed missing persons reports. Jonah nodded as he put it together. Someone killed twenty-two people, tried to make it look like suicide nearly every time, and sometimes, took one of the family members hostage. Did he kill them, too? Why hide one body and leave another for the police?

Jonah shook his head. The MO did not fit the profile of any serial killer cases he had ever studied. Serial killers were methodical and predictable once you discovered their pattern. The this guy's pattern-that-wasn't-a-pattern didn't fit.

Jonah flipped through the cases more quickly, making sure to notice the victims' ethnicity and social status. After going through the whole set twice, he could see no common denominator. Apparently, the victims were sought at random. And the crime scenes were all over the city map, in every neighborhood, high and low. Black, white, Asian, Hispanic, young, old, rich, poor, ugly, pretty, male, female—every type was covered in the twenty-two cases. Jonah coughed and flipped through again.

I must be missing something. They have to link up somehow.

Jonah found the ME report for the first case and read it over. A woman, forty-eight years of age, whose throat was slit. ME put cause of death as blood loss. Jonah looked at the next file. This one had a broken neck from a fall, but the throat was also slashed. ME report said cause of death—blood loss. Jonah blinked a few times and pulled open the next case. It was a man again, middle-aged, appeared to have strangled himself with a rope, but his throat was also cut. ME said—blood loss. Jonah sat up in his chair and flipped hurriedly through the rest of the cases. In every one, the ME had put blood loss as the primary cause of death.

This is nuts. Nobody caught this back then?

Another odd comment caught his eye as he flipped the cases again. He'd seen, "evidence of unexplained blood loss." Peeling the pages, one a time, he found the specific report. It was a woman, sixty years old, who had fallen to her death from a fifth-story window. The policeman on the scene made a note that if she had died of blood loss, as the ME reported, why was there no blood at the scene?

Good question, Jonah thought and skimmed the police reports an additional series. Only one other made that observation, so he began to scrutinize the crime scene photos. Not a single photograph showed the victim's blood pooling where they lay.

Where's the blood going?

Another thing grabbed his attention. The file on the bottom had been for a woman named Clara Stuckey.

Jonah slapped his head and dug it out. Clara Stuckey—Reuben Stuckey. Although he was alone, he found himself embarrassed to have missed such an obvious connection. Jonah adjusted his glasses and stared at the woman's second sheet. Her mother had reported a missing child—the victim's son, a five-year-old boy named Reuben.

Five years old in 1971? That's over 40 years ago. Reuben's driver's license says 1985. So the kid Nixon was hunting must have been the missing Stuckey's son? Jonah didn't like it. He pondered the facts from several angles, but no matter where the conclusion took him, he simply wasn't satisfied with the logic. Clara Stuckey was a known drug addict and prostitute. Cause of death—blood loss. And unlike the others, there was blood splatter at the scene.

Jonah was tired. Forcing his eyes open and his mind clicking, he worked the case a little longer before the sound of his watch beeping the midnight hour shook him out of his fugue.

"I'll think about it tomorrow," he said aloud as he stood, stretched, and shrugged on his coat. "Brand new day. Brand new brain." But he'd probably keep working on it all through the night; at least in his subconscious. And he'd keep trying to find out what the Atlanta police force in 1970 apparently didn't even try to discover.

What did Nixon know that got him killed?

And of course, where was all the blood?

12

They say "God has forsaken him; pursue him and seize him,
For no one will rescue him."
Be not far from me, O God; come quickly…to help me.
Psalm 71:11-12

THURSDAY MORNING IT WAS POURING RAIN WHEN BIG John awoke. He rolled out of bed with sleep in his eyes and headed to the bathroom. As before, his memory of the past evening's donation was vivid. It wasn't natural, it wasn't *wholesome,* and it bothered him that it was probably sinful. Still, it had become old hat, and by the time he washed up and had a bite to eat, he'd have nary a concern. As he washed his face in the sink, he purposefully avoided looking for his newest wound.

The money was going to good use on the Jenkins home front. The first two weeks saw some hefty payments on Opal's credit cards, but after that, John took a breather from paying bills and splurged. The third week, after the baby was home and doing fine, John bought his wife a proper wedding ring.

Five years ago when they married, he barely made ends meet as a bouncer for various clubs in downtown Atlanta. The beautiful and perfect woman who had chosen him as a husband didn't care about money or comfort. She was in *love,* and the old-fashioned sentiment was the only thing that sustained them the first year. Twelve months into their marriage, Opal's dad handed over the reins to his moving company. The pay was good, and before long, John was able to move Opal into a sweet little house in the suburbs of Columbus. He also moved the business base from Alpharetta to be closer to home.

Race had never been a problem between the two families, and they ignored the prejudiced society surrounding them. Opal assured him whenever anyone raised an eye at them in public, they were most likely curious or jealous and they ran into very little overt bigotry.

Opal's parents could not have been more open-minded when she brought the big man home. They were genuinely pleased with themselves more than anything; as if their daughter's marriage to a black man reflected on how progressive *they* were. And John's family was not surprised when he told them his bride was white. He had dated Caucasian women exclusively since his teens. The African American girls he knew growing up were intimidated by him none had ever considered him a good mate.

John checked his watch; he was losing time. If he could be out the door by nine, he could be home by ten-thirty, have lunch with Opal and John Junior, and be to work by one. Precisely calculated, it had worked so far. Ironically, the success was due in part to the car that Paul had purchased. There was little chance it would cause him to be late for anything ever again.

He dried his face and hands and headed toward the stairs. The odor of bacon and eggs told him that Paul was downstairs cooking. Since his second week, he found that he could count on the vampire to be making them breakfast when he arose. Strange as that sounded, it was always delicious. The guy could cook, and John had always been a big eater.

◆ ◆ ◆

Jennifer Speltz closed the captain's door without a slam, and Jonah sensed her restraint. The Nixon case had stalled and Erkleson had lost patience. But what could they do? Agricola proved difficult to locate despite the fact that they had a good phone number for him. He hadn't answered their calls nor returned their voicemail messages. The church in Whitford City paid his bill, so the police couldn't sit back and wait for him to contact the company when he needed to renew his contract. His social security number hadn't popped up in the fifty States, nor had he used any credit cards in his name. So how could they find him? Jonah was in touch with the Montgomery PD, and Agricola hadn't shown up on their radar, either.

Obviously as frustrated as her partner, Jenn plopped down across from him, grumbling.

"No good, eh?" Jonah asked, chewing his roast beef sandwich on one side of his mouth. Eating lunch at the office wasn't so bad when Twirlies delivered.

"No good. If we don't get something soon, Cap's gonna pull the plug. Damn! We were on a roll for a minute there. Why doesn't Agricola return our calls? He's *got* to be guilty. Some preacher he turned out to be…"

"Hold on there, missy. Maybe his phone's busted. Don't assume he's crooked until you *know* he's crooked. All his friends vouch for him and I'm convinced that they were being honest about that." Jonah took another bite and watched his partner's eyes.

"Hogwash. You're taking his side because he's a preacher. I know you."

"Yep." Jonah smiled, but Jenn did not smile back.

"I know you have a blind side when it comes to preachers, but you need to face facts. Agricola is hiding something. We've called him dozens of times and left messages with his people in Whitford City. If he was a stand-up guy, he would have returned our call."

"I'm just saying—" Jonah's phone rang at his left and he swallowed to answer it. "Detective Miller."

"Good afternoon, Detective. I understand you've been trying to reach me? This is Tony Agricola. My phone has been out of commission and I am just now getting your message. What can I do for you?"

Jonah sat up in his chair and gestured for Jennifer to pick up the extension. *It's him!* he mouthed, spitting pieces of bun, and cleared his throat for his caller.

"Yes, Mr. Agricola, thank you for returning my call. I need to ask you a few questions regarding a Kentucky reporter by the name Connie Nixon. Are you familiar with that name?"

"Connie Nixon? No, the name doesn't ring a bell. Should it?"

So far, the man sounded confident and forthcoming. Jonah gave him the benefit of the doubt despite Jennifer's suspicious glare.

"Apparently, one day last fall, you were out with a woman named Hope Brannen and Nixon came up to you and began asking questions about a Reuben Stuckey. Does that ring a bell?"

"Oh, that guy! Yeah. Hope and I were in my truck and sure enough, a reporter came up and asked us if we knew where to find Reuben Stuckey. I don't know Reuben, but Hope did. She thought the guy was hunting Reuben for some reason so she tried to send him on a wild goose chase. He said thank you, got in his car, and drove away."

"Yeah, that jibes with what Ms. Brannen remembers. You don't know Stuckey or Nixon?"

"No, I'm afraid not."

"Okay. What can you tell me about Dr. Mark Corescu?" The line was silent for a heartbeat and then the caller's voice returned strong and clear.

"Mark Corescu? Yeah, I know him. We were at his house that day, in his driveway actually, when we saw Nixon."

"Yes, Ms. Brannen said as much. Will you please give me your side of what transpired at the Corescu house? I'd like to compare it to what Ms. Brannen reported." Pencil ready, Jonah sent his partner a wink, her countenance brightening.

"Well, is it important? I mean, do I have to tell you? I don't understand why you are interested in Mark Corescu. Did something happen to him?"

Jonah sighed, but maintained his friendly tone. "We're investigating the murder of Connie Nixon and our investigation has led us to this point. It's imperative you tell us everything you know about Mark Corescu and that night at his house."

"But I don't know anything about this Nixon guy's murder…" Agricola began a plaintive reply, but Jonah cut him off.

"Mr. Agricola, *Tony,* I know you're a man of God. So am I. God is no doubt wondering why you're dodging my questions. Let's be honest with each other and honest with Him, because you know He's here with us right now." Jonah gave Jenn the thumbs up as she rolled her eyes. *That'll get him,* he mouthed as he waited for the man's reply.

"Detective Miller, I appreciate you acknowledging God like that, and I'll try my best to answer your questions. I wasn't trying to be dishonest or evasive. I'm trying to avoid betraying a confidence between the doctor and myself. See, I'm his pastor. I'm bound by my conscience to avoid discussing anything he and I may have shared during our session. Do you understand?"

Jonah's shoulders drooped and Jenn rolled her hand. "Okay, Tony. Just tell me as much as you can about that night without betraying Corescu."

"Fine. Let's see… Hope and I went to Mark's house about ten o'clock that evening because he was struggling with some theological issues. We prayed together for a couple of hours and around midnight, Hope and I left together by Uber. I never saw Dr. Corescu again after that night."

"Isn't that kind of odd?" Jonah asked because Jennifer was about to horn in and ask the same thing.

"Not this time because once we finished praying, he asked us to leave. He might have left the country. I left the room and called the Uber while Hope stayed behind to say goodbye. That's all I know. I haven't seen him since then."

"Have you talked to him on the phone since then?" Jonah stuck the question in quickly because in the past he had been able to trip the suspect up. But Agricola did not miss a beat.

"No, sir, I haven't spoken to him on the phone since that night."

"So you've spoken to him some other way?" It was the way he repeated *on the phone* that reminded Jonah of how he himself phrased questions when he was trying *not* to lie. Men of God are horrible liars.

The caller paused.

"Sir? Tony? When did you last speak with Dr. Corescu?"

"Not since that night, Detective. I told you."

Jonah and Jennifer's eyes met. *Liar,* she mouthed and Jonah looked back to his notepad.

"Okay, thank you, Tony. One more question. What did Paul Black do all this time?"

Another long pause. Jonah's pencil hovered over his paper as he waited. He let two seconds pass before he rephrased his question. "Hope Brannen told us that Black had a fight with Corescu that night. Can you tell me about that?"

Another pause, shorter this time and the man cleared his throat.

"Paul Black? Oh. Mark's assistant. I only met him that day. He lived in that house with him as far as I know. Paul Black…"

"Yes. He fought with Corescu?"

"I guess you could call it a fight. I mean, they quarreled, but I've seen worse. I was praying when he left, so I can't say exactly when or how. I had my eyes closed."

"Convenient," Jenn whispered to Jonah and he frowned.

"So when did you last see Paul Black?"

"I haven't seen him since that night either. Sorry, Detective, I wish I could be more help."

"One more thing, if I may. Hope Brannen said that Paul Black might be dangerous. Do you concur with that assessment?"

"I do. Can I speak off the record?"

"Yes. Off the record."

"I didn't trust Paul Black from the moment I met him. I think if you run into him in a dark alley, have your gun drawn and aim for the head."

Jenn narrowed her eyes at Jonah who nodded with her

expression. To Agricola, he said, "Okay, thank you, Tony. You've been a big help. If we have more questions, can we count on you to answer the phone?"

"Hah, yes, sir. I apologize again for my cell service being down. It's working fine now."

"Okay, bye, then." Jonah hung up and sat back. Jenn was not sure whether to be happy about their new interview or not. She opened her mouth to speak just as Stansfield stopped by her desk holding a file folder from the lab.

"It's from forensics. We have a match on the prints." Jenn grabbed the folder and flipped it open.

"Jonah! One of those three men killed Connie Nixon. Corescu, Stuckey, or Black. Three sets of prints from the house on an interior door that the new owner's claimed to not have used. We're back in business!"

Jonah took a bite of his sandwich and smiled back.

"That sure does smell good," Big John announced as he entered the kitchen. Paul didn't look up, but concentrated on the meat he pushed around in the skillet. The rain outside had produced a somber gloom to the usually bright room, and Paul hadn't slept. Being a vampire ruined his REM and he hoped he'd eventually grow used to it. For now, he'd gripe and complain and keep the two preachers on their toes.

Big John fell into his chair and Tony entered, looking at his cell but then met John's eye and clapped his arm.

"Big John! Sleeping-in these days?" He settled across with a smile. Paul glared at Tony and scooped scrambled eggs onto both men's plates.

"Thanks," John said and waited for Tony to finish grace before telling him good morning.

"Morning," Tony returned and gave Paul the side-eye as he turned to say something to John.

"How do you feel?" the vampire asked.

John held up his hand and bowed his head.

Paul prodded his arm. "Are you asking God how you feel?" Paul leaned on the table and John did not reply. "Both of you are pitiful. I am what I am, and there's no escaping one's nature," Paul said and returned to the stove. "I won't apologize to a made-up god for something that comes natural."

"God exists even if you don't like it. Tell him, Tony." John ate his eggs in huge mouthfuls.

Tony opened the novel in his hand and didn't look up. "You are not your own. You're a creation of the Almighty. You only think you're in control."

"Shove it," Paul replied, his back to both men.

"Paul, God uses you like a puppet to perform His will. People who choose to ignore God, ignore their Maker. Therefore, God places them on the board anywhere He wants. It's a cosmic chess game."

"He shoots, he scores! Bam!" Big John whooped at the table and drank down his juice.

Paul scowled remembering what the woman Sarah had told him when he last saw her. "That makes no sense. I can't believe millions of people are under the same delusion. My master fell prey to its insanity, and I'm never going to let it get me."

Paul turned the water off in the sink where he was working and left the room. If Mark hadn't been so infatuated with an ancient Savior, he'd still be around today, in glorious vigor, commanding mortals, directing the spin of the world. Now he was a mere shell of his old self, flesh withering, alive but locked in despair and loneliness. Waiting to die but not being able. Paul sat in the parlor and rested his head in his hands. Maybe it was the rain outside or the weeping in his heart, but Paul was more and more compelled to rescue Mark from his self-induced prison. If he didn't go to Europe soon, he may not be able to find him. The last few weeks, Mark's mental contact had been weaker and less frequent, as if finally comatose, his body shutting down. Yet he would still be in there; still alive.

Paul pounded his knee, ready to leave. Now. With or without the preacher, Paul was going to save Mark from his self-induced hell.

◆

At the kitchen table, Tony looked at John and shrugged. Tony put down his book and sipped his coffee.

"What's wrong with him? He's not usually so touchy."

"He only has one thing in the whole world to worry about so he worries about it constantly." Tony saw John was waiting for more and he continued. "His master. Did you ever ask him about that? About

Doctor Corescu?"

John shook his head. "I haven't had the inclination."

Tony gave him a sad smile. "That's understandable. Paul is grieving the loss of the vampire who changed him. This vampire refuses to drink blood and he's starving himself somewhere overseas."

"He won't drink blood? Then, you did it. I mean, you were able to at least help one of them. That's a miracle."

Tony shook his head. "I'm as surprised as you are. Paul and I are going to go find him soon. He has asked me to bury him."

John's eyes grew wide and he gasped. "You're going to bury him *alive*?"

"Well, yeah." Tony shrugged and finished his coffee. "He's wasting away. If we bury him, he'll be safe from animals and townsfolk who might find him and try to burn him at the stake. There's no telling what those rural people will think if they discover him." Tony nibbled his toast and continued as John listened. "In the ground, he can wait for the Lord. It's the only thing that makes sense."

John nodded. "There's no other way? Can't they drink the blood of animals?"

"The Bible says that God detests the drinking of blood, so Mark won't touch the stuff. Paul said that he even refuses volunteered blood. Like what you do for Paul."

"Like what *we* do for him. Aren't you still donating once a week?" John asked, surely not meaning to offend. Tony's cheeks reddened.

"I never *volunteer*." Tony put his hand to his neck and frowned. Tony's fists clenched and he knew Paul could hear him from the other room. To ensure that Paul knew that he was aware of his eavesdropping, Tony shouted in the direction of the parlor, "And it's going to STOP!"

John looked toward the door and shushed him. "Don't make him mad. Wait 'til I get out the door before you guys start fighting." John wiped his hands and took a deep breath.

"Well, the police are on to him, to us. I'm going to try to throw them off, but who knows? I don't have any idea why God would throw the police into this nightmare. I don't want anybody getting hurt." Tony removed his glasses to rub his eyes.

"I hope you'll tell me if I need to keep away. I don't want the cops to know I have anything to do with this. How do you explain something like this? They'd never believe it. They'd lock us up."

"Yep." Tony had no other response.

"Well, tell me about this master vampire and what he has to do with anything."

"Are you familiar with vampire movies?" Tony started with something easy.

"Well, sure," John answered.

"Good. Forget what you saw. These monsters aren't afraid of garlic or sunlight or crosses. They have incredible strength and a terrible lust for blood." Tony shook his head. "Paul's master is four hundred years old and killed a hundred thousand people before I met him."

"Oh, my God," John mumbled.

"That's right."

"Was he unstable, like Paul?" John whispered.

Tony chuckled. "No, Paul is half-crazy. It's sad, really."

"I know he's childish, but maybe we shouldn't beat him down so much. He's getting pretty sensitive to it." Tony caught the big man's eye; he knew Paul was listening. Tony sent him a woeful frown.

"No, it's the best medicine. He's more sensitive because he's starting to face reality. Mark is not coming back and Paul will have to learn to face this life without him. On his own. Paul will need a new god. I want him to choose *the God*."

"Yeah, me, too." John lowered his voice. "How did you lead this old vampire to Jesus but not his disciple?"

"Paul wasn't a vampire at the time. He was changed somewhere in the fracas. He served Mark Corescu for a hundred years. Devoted to the vampire's every whim."

"Sounds like Stockholm's syndrome," John remarked and Tony didn't disagree.

"Paul lost his identity in Corescu. But when Mark took up with my friend Hope, the Lord had His way with all of us."

"Hope? Where is she? I assume she's okay?"

"She's still around," Tony said, nodding, although he hadn't spoken to her in a long time. "She and I escaped with our lives, but when Paul took off alone, God compelled me to track him down. That's where we are now." Tony fidgeted with his fork, nervous that Paul had overheard their conversation. At least Big John finally had the story plotted in his mind.

John sipped his juice. "So, you're leaving soon? To find the master vampire?"

"Soon," Tony said, then gave a wry smile. "Have a passport? You're welcome to come along. I'm sure Paul will find a use for you."

John was not amused. "Uh, no thanks. Opal and Junior need me right now. I'll be happy to keep the home fires burning for you." John stood and tucked his tank into his pants.

"I know, sorry," Tony said, and reopened his book. John waved goodbye and left the kitchen. Tony prayed for God's will on them all so he wouldn't have to worry about a thing.

♦

John shuffled to the front door, and Paul beckoned before his hand touched the knob. His drastic mood swings left him feeling restless and unhappy. Maybe John would show him some empathy. Of the two men, Tony was more belligerent, and John's responses in the kitchen had been empathetic.

John entered the parlor. Paul sat on an ornate oak stool, stooped over with his elbows on his knees and John came up beside him, squatting.

"What's up?"

"How's that baby of yours?" Paul asked, increasingly interested in John's home life. "And Opal?"

"He's fine. Opal's fine," John replied, anxious to leave.

Paul huffed. "I want you to move here. I'll give you a raise; you can move the whole family. Money is no object."

"Paul—" John began, but Paul cut him off.

"I want to see you more than once a week," Paul said. His roller coaster emotions swung upward, and Paul found himself angry to be slave to them.

"You know I can't do that. I can't get my wife and son mixed up with a…a six-foot mosquito. That's *my* one condition—that you stay away from them," John said. "I can add another day, if that helps. I can come on Sunday nights. Would that help?"

Paul shrugged, it wasn't enough. Tony wasn't enough. "I like having you around. I feel more alive when you're here."

"Yeah," John said with sympathy in his gaze.

"Don't you think I am doing a pretty good job of handling my superiority here? A *vampire*, a supernatural being, behaving. Worrying over every little thing to keep his human companions happy. My master killed a different person every night for four hundred years.

Don't I deserve some credit?"

"Yeah. I for one am glad you haven't killed me yet," John said with forced levity.

Paul leveled his gaze at the big man kneeling before him. "I would never kill you. I just wish you lived here with Tony and me."

John shook his head. "I can't make that deal. Not for all the money in the world." He shifted his weight onto his heels.

After a few silent moments, Paul sat up straight and looked away. "You can go," Paul said and clenched his fists in his lap.

The big man left the house and Paul growled low in his throat. How could he be so impotent? He had strength, but couldn't use it. He had power, but couldn't wield it. When his master wanted something in the old days, he simply took it. Paul thought his life would be the same when he joined ranks with the mighty Dr. Corescu. But no. The master fled the scene and Paul's current companions regarded him as a joke. A target of their disdain. So what was the problem?

The preacher man. Tony had vowed to desert him if he didn't do as he commanded. *Why do I let him command me? He should be subject to me. Forever. Anthony Agricola is a naughty puppy that I allowed to mature into a bad old dog.* Would he really leave? Could he leave? Paul could never let him go. They shared too many secrets. Tony had the ability to bring higher authorities and law enforcement to Paul's front door. He could supply them with proof of everything. And someone would invariably believe him. Maybe even one of the cops who recently called Tony. Maybe the police had finally found the reporter's body. At least Tony didn't know anything about that.

Paul thought his recent attack-and-subdue methods would cow the man, but they did not. Instead, they made him more disgusted. Suffice it to say that if Tony considered Paul his cross to bear, Paul thought the same way about the preacher. He was more trouble than he was worth.

No, he's not. He just needs more time.

Paul listened out for Tony's whereabouts. After a moment or two, he heard the man turn a page of his book in the kitchen. Suddenly, thinking of Anthony nonchalantly reading some religious garbage in the kitchen while he sat alone in the parlor fuming angered him further. He ground his teeth and tried to calm down.

I don't want to be tamed. I want to be all that I can be. I can't let that preacher push me around. Paul stood and walked quietly to the kitchen entry. He watched Tony read, his lips moving as his eyes traveled the page. After a long minute, Paul sighed and Tony looked up, obviously startled.

"What? Why do you insist on sneaking up on me all the time?" Paul leveled his gaze following Tony's harsh tone. He focused his energy and replied to the man's rhetorical question in his mind only.

"Because I can do whatever I please. And you'd do well to remember that." Unnerved, Tony set down his book without responding. "What did the police want?" Paul asked, leaning against the doorframe.

"I covered for you," he said softer but with his usual disdain. "I'm sure you know everything I said."

"No matter. Get my papers in order. I'm flying to Germany." Tony lowered his gaze, a sign of respect that Paul hadn't realized he'd been craving. If only the guy would keep it up.

"I'm going with you," he said in a soft voice.

"Good," Paul snarked. "I'll need a snack."

Tony turned for the stairs to make the necessary arrangements and Paul watched him. He wouldn't have gone without Tony and the guy must have known that. Paul headed for the shower to start the day, hoping that within the week, he would embrace his master once again in the flesh.

◆ ◆ ◆

John Junior had not cried all day for which Opal was thankful. The baby had been so easy, certainly it was not normal. She walked into the nursery to make sure he was breathing. He was her first child and every little thing worried her sick. Is he too hot? Is he too cold? Did he get enough to eat? Is he growing right? The whole business was a never-ending guessing game between the new mother of thirty-two and a seven-pound, three-week-old bundle of gurgles and saliva.

Opal returned to the kitchen and checked the meatloaf. Big would be home any minute from his Alabama appointment and he'd be famished. The heavenly aroma of beef and spices brought a grin and she adjusted the temperature.

Come on, Big. Ten more minutes and you'll be late!

Opal peeked out the front window in case he had driven up while she checked on Junior. No such luck. Making sure that the table was set and ready, she collapsed on the couch and grabbed a magazine from the coffee table.

The Alabama appointments had been strange, yet the man who paid John had been true to his word. Every week, Big came home with a wad of hundreds, which went to good use. Still, there was something mysterious and unsettling about the whole business. Big packed his gym and described a job resembling fitness coach to an eccentric and reclusive millionaire. Whatever the details, Big John Jenkins was not easily manipulated and was good to the core. In addition, her husband would never lie to her, so no matter how uneasy she felt about the weekly jaunts, she leaned on that truth. Big would explain in his own time. Their bank account was in the black. What more could she ask?

The new Cadillac growled with power as Big pulled up to the house and she hopped up to open the door. She watched her husband climb out of the car, his bulk making the huge luxury automobile look small by comparison. He lumbered over and met her with a grin on his handsome face.

"Hey, Babe. Did you miss me?" Her husband took her into his arms and kissed her hair. "You smell delicious!" he said and playfully grabbed her behind as they entered the house.

"Keep it down!" she hushed through the giggles. "Junior's asleep!"

"Did you miss me?" John repeated his question in a whisper and tried to swipe her rear as she deftly moved out of range.

"Yes," she said. "Now, go wash up for lunch."

Opal disappeared into the kitchen and John followed.

"How was Junior today?"

"Perfect...just like his daddy." Opal turned in time to see her husband washing his hands in the kitchen sink. She stopped herself and approached his back. "Big, what is this on your neck?"

John's hand flew to the site. "Oh, that? It's nothing. Gee, this lunch smells terrific! What did you make?"

"John Jenkins," Opal said sterner than she meant. "There's something going on that you're not telling me. What are you and this guy up to over there in Montgomery?"

"Babe, I promise. It's nothing. It's just part of the job. It's perfectly safe and I am making a ton of dough. Let it drop." His gentle tone did not convince her and she narrowed her eyes.

"I don't like it. This looks nasty. Worse than before. This looks like a *bite.*" Opal tried to touch it, but her husband moved away and took his seat at the table. "Was it a rat?"

ellen c. maze

"A rat? What makes you think I was bitten by a rat? Drop it, Babe, or I could lose this job. Trust me. It's perfectly legit and sometimes I might come home with a little cut." Opal frowned, John disregarding her concern. But she had to trust him, and she would.

"Okay, but I have a bad feeling," Opal said and took her seat. She tried to let it go, but by the time they finished eating, she decided he needed to let her bandage it up. He acquiesced as he dressed for work. After applying Neosporin and a gauze pad, Opal released him for the afternoon. *He'll tell me eventually. I'm sure it's nothing.*

Still...

That looks like a bite!

◆ ◆ ◆

"Make mine roast beef." Jonah ordered his sandwich from the server and waited for Jenn. She looked tired and he was sure he did not look any better. But at least she wasn't grumpy.

"Same," Jennifer said to the waitress and handed over the menu. To Jonah she smiled and batted her eyelashes. "Did I tell you the lab came back with Agricola's prints? Yeah, just before we left. He was very helpful. He went to the Montgomery PD, was printed, and they faxed us his prints."

Jonah frowned at Jennifer's scornful tone and he glanced over his glasses. "And? He is not our killer? Imagine that."

"Right. No match. He wouldn't leave a good address and they had no PC to compel him. He gave them a hotel address on Union Street, but it was no good. Some preacher, eh?" Jennifer prodded, but Jonah only grunted. "We also ran the Brannen woman's prints the FBI had on file from her childhood. No match. Everywhere we turn, we're looking at Stuckey, Corescu, or Black for the murder. And we can't catch a break on any of them."

"I know. It stinks. Erkleson handed me a new case today. Did he tell you?" Jonah watched his partner's face curl into a scowl and he prepared for a rant.

"What?! What is he thinking? How did he ever get that job? He makes me sick!..." Jennifer ranted for a full minute, cursing now and then, before she ran out of breath and fell quiet.

Jonah lifted his hands in surrender. "I gave it back to him. I asked him as nicely as I could to give us one more week."

"And?"

"We have five days. Then we have to tuck it away."

Jonah sipped his decaf as Jenn went into another noisy tirade against their boss. What could he do? She was mostly right. He ignored the offended looks of the nearby patrons. Fortunately, Jennifer had removed her coat to sit and her badge and gun were readily visible. Perhaps they'd cut her some slack.

18

Have no fear of sudden disaster
or of the ruin that overtakes the wicked,
For the Lord will be your confidence
and He will keep your foot from being snared.
Proverbs 3:25-26

"WE NEED TO PUT A TAIL ON AGRICOLA," JONAH SAID, sitting with Jennifer in the Cutlass at quitting time, deciding the next move. Four days remained before their deadline and they weren't ready to admit defeat. "I want to like the guy, but he was holding something back in the interview. He might not have stabbed Nixon, but he knows something. I think we should put a tail on him."

"I agree. Maybe if you contact your buddy in Montgomery, he'll plaster his photo on the wire and try to get him spotted. If he's driving the S10 on file, they can watch for his tags, too." Jennifer looked out the window as she spoke and watched the rainwater collect in the gutter. In a faraway voice, she added another suggestion. "Should probably watch the Brannen woman. She lied to us, too. She might be getting ready to make a run for it."

"Yeah. You could be right. A woman who looks like that can really mess a man up. She might have been playing all these guys at the same time." Jonah raised his eyebrows when Jennifer shot him a look. "I mean it. She was with *Agricola* on the way to see *Corescu,* which just so happens to be where she might find Paul Black and Reuben Stuckey. Who knows? Maybe she seduced Nixon and he was killed in a jealous rage by the others."

"You've been watching too many TV shows, Detective Miller. Take it from my woman's intuition: Brannen's in love with Corescu and is hiding something that she thinks might implicate him. Agricola knows something about Corescu *and* Paul Black and he's not talking; maybe he is protecting them, too. Pastor/Penitent Confidentiality, my ass. If we could catch these guys doing something… I don't know. If they'd just slip up…"

"Keep dreaming, partner." Jonah switched on the car, but didn't put it in gear. "Anything on the bookstore Black purchased?"

"No, it's not open. I think we should watch that location, too. Could be bodies hidden in there."

"Now who's been watching too much TV?" Jonah laughed and then exhaled. "We'll get the MPD to locate Agricola for a casual tail. If he tries to run, we'll follow him."

"And maybe he'll lead us to Black, Stuckey, or Corescu. Get their photos up in the airports, car rental places, and bus stations, too." Jennifer rolled down her window and spit out her gum. She turned in her seat to better see her partner. "Did you come to a dead end on the Clara Stuckey file?"

"I guess. Whoever killed Clara Stuckey slashed her throat, took most of her blood with them, and might have abducted a five-year-old boy. But there's no sign of him. It looks like Nixon saw Reuben Stuckey's name in the phone book and went to his house to speak to him. I think Nixon thought that our missing Stuckey was maybe the offspring to the missing kid."

"This would mean that the kid wasn't missing. The police screwed up." Jennifer frowned.

"Uh-huh. Our twenty-year-old Reuben Stuckey could not be the same little boy from the 1970's crime scene. It's a dead end. I don't think we're looking at a serial killer."

"Are you so sure?" Jennifer asked and Jonah nodded. "Because the MO is different on our murder."

"That's right. Nixon was poked in the neck and left to die. No unexplained blood loss—the ME stands by his findings that the corpse had exactly the right amount of blood in him for a wound like that. No staged suicide, no missing person. No match. Nixon's killer is a different guy."

"You mentioned unexplained blood loss twice. Is that significant?"

"Could be. Every single Buckley case stated exsanguination as the cause of death, but most of them had little or no blood at the scene. Maybe it was a cult, but the blood was missing. Pints of it. Weird."

"And Nixon's blood was all there?"

"That's right." Jonah couldn't hide his disappointment and his partner shared his sentiment.

"Well, that explains Erkleson's change of heart. He's not so interested in catching a guy who kills one petty newspaper reporter from out of state."

"Exactly. So, in the morning, where to?" Jonah put the car in reverse and headed out of the police parking lot.

"Heck. Let's go to Montgomery."

"Montgomery?" Jonah checked her expression. "What do we tell Erkleson?"

"Nothing. We'll just go there in person and speak to our contact. It's less than two hours from here. What have we got to lose?"

Jonah nodded and headed for the interstate. He wasn't afraid to face the captain's wrath upon their return, but he was surprised that Jenn was taking such a risk. She had always been fairly political in the way she handled the department's higher-ups. Jonah decided he liked the new, bolder Jennifer and he told her as much. She smiled and reached over to pat his shoulder.

"I guess you're finally rubbing off on me."

"Uh-oh," Jonah laughed.

"Plus, we have that mushroom farm if this detective gig doesn't work out."

Jonah glanced her way. Jenn was looking out the windshield, a half-smile on her face.

◆ ◆ ◆

Paul sat in his truck just out of the reach of the parking lot's bright lights. He had been thinking about the Bible witch who spoke to him so boldly. Where did she get her courage? As far as she knew, Paul could have been a murderer of the worst kind. Why was she not afraid? He couldn't wrap his mind around it. He had successfully contacted Mark for a short moment earlier in the evening and almost gotten a response. He had pleaded with him to share the answer, but his master only laughed.

"It's God, my son. God. He gives these mortals bravery. Seek God and you will find your answers…"

Mark's reply infuriated Paul more than ever. He trained his eye to the rear doors of the Sears mall entrance. Sarah Tracey had entered that door an hour ago and Paul maintained his stake-out. Tonight, he would show her the vampire. As he again pondered the woman's crazy words against him, she exited the building alone, walking with purpose across the wide lot. Paul stepped from his truck without a sound and waited as she reached her driver-side door. As soon as she put her fingers to the handle, Paul closed the distance to her side.

"Got any jumper cables?" Paul asked, imitating her voice. She clutched her purse to her chest scanning the lot for help. Paul grabbed her forearm. "I have a few questions for you." He tugged with extra force enjoying her shocked expression. But within two abrupt yanks, her hand came out of her purse and she dispensed mace at his face. His inhuman reflexes enabled Paul to dodge the spray and then he grabbed the vial, depressing the trigger at the woman's head.

"You like this? You like this?" he snarled in fury as she shrank back. But the product would not dispense. Paul pressed the trigger twice more and gave up, tossing the vial aside.

Determined, Paul resumed pulling her toward his truck, cursing her in a hiss. Instead of fighting, the woman prayed, silly words in a foreign language Paul did not recognize. He maintained his smile but inwardly, his rage grew—why wasn't she terrified? He'd had enough. In a blur, he whirled to square off and he shoved her to the ground. She landed hard, her head slapping the asphalt, yet she made no sound except her continued soft prayers. Hidden from the mall behind the Tahoe, Paul dropped into a straddle over her cringing form. She had drawn her arms across her chest and squeezed her eyes closed tight. Her lips quivered and spoke and she still would not scream. Paul's face heated.

"Beg me for mercy!" he hiss-whispered. "Don't you know that I hold your life in my hands?" The woman's next words left him speechless with rage.

"You control *nothing!* Every bit of power you have comes from my Father in heaven and He's not going to allow you to hurt me this night!"

On her back, and in obvious pain, Sarah Tracey's words were clear. Paul slapped her face with all of his might, her body recoiling beneath him and the air huffed from her lungs.

I'll kill her! Her religion can't save her!

Paul dove down, her shoulders in his claw-like grip and opened his mouth, elongated fangs heading for her throat. He never reached his target. A fierce blow crashed against his head only to travel across his cheek and knock his nose out of joint. Paul yelped, enraged and confused by the vicious strike. *A brick!* Despite the fact he'd seen no such item when she went down, the woman still held it in the offending hand. Through vision tinged red, Paul pinned her arms, blood from his nose discoloring her cheeks and teeth and she began a new set of prayers.

That's my blood… She spilled my blood?

"I'll kill you for that!" he growled, but was unable to threaten her further as an unseen force lifted him up and sent him sprawling twenty feet from his victim.

What was that?! This is impossible!

Even as he connected to the blacktop, landing on his back and forcing the air from his lungs, he wondered at the invisible power. Then Mark's words filtered in as he found his feet, backpedaling away from the woman on the ground.

"You're fighting God, not the man…"

Paul spun and jogged to his truck, speeding off before anyone came to the witch's aid. As he drove through the access roads to the highway, he wiped the blood from his mouth.

My blood… my blood on her face. She has my blood in her mouth! Paul cleared his mind. How could such an accidental dosing mean anything? For didn't her God protect her tonight?

If that was her God tossing me across the parking lot, I need to steer clear. Paul didn't want to run into that invisible Force ever again, no matter what they called it. From now on, he would be careful.

19

When a disaster comes to a city, has not the Lord caused it?
Surely, the Sovereign Lord does nothing
without revealing His plan to His servants the prophets.
Amos 3:6-7

SARAH SAT AT THE INVESTIGATOR'S DESK AND WAITED for the young woman to return with coffee. After a twelve-hour hold, she'd been released from the hospital and the time had arrived to give a detailed report to the authorities. A police sketch artist had been assigned and any moment, Sarah would attempt to describe her attacker. The female officer returned and plunked down a Styrofoam cup brimming with black coffee. Barely five feet and soft around the middle, Gonzalez had an easy smile and gentle manner. She gave Sarah a moment to sample the brew.

"Thank you, Sergeant," Sarah offered.

"Please, call me Julie. Okay, you said you know this guy?"

Sarah set down her cup and took a deep breath. "Yes. I first met him when I was picking up a check at the church on Ryan Road..."

"The Methodist or the Baptist?"

"Methodist."

"Got it," Julie said, typing as she spoke. "And he told you his name was Saul White, right?" Sarah nodded. "And so that night and then last night. Is this the only two times you've seen him?"

"No. A few days after that night at the church lot, the same man came by my house. I spoke to him, advised him to seek after God, and then he left."

"You let him into your house?"

The cop did not mask her incredulity and Sarah sighed. Her spirituality sometimes put her in the *weirdo* category.

"Yes," she admitted. "I was compelled by the Holy Spirit."

"Uh-huh."

From there, the officer's responses became robotic and Sarah scaled back the God talk. "He went away and I didn't think I'd see him ever again."

"But I guess he wasn't done with you, eh?" Julie asked with an unspoken I-told-you-so.

"He must have followed me to the mall, because he was in the lot when I got to my car. He grabbed but didn't know I had my pepper spray in hand. I got a squirt off, but he dodged it, grabbed my sprayer and tried to get *me* with it. Thank God it wouldn't dispense."

Julie looked up. "He used your pepper spray?"

"Yes. Right before he pushed me down. I can't remember much after that…"

"But he grabbed your pepper spray," she stated. "Ma'am, we retrieved a vial of pepper spray at the crime scene." Julie picked up her phone, spoke urgently a few moments, and then hung up.

"What?" Sarah asked, smiling at the officer's sudden joy.

"Fingerprints," Julie said and kissed her fingers before pointing them to the ceiling. "We've been chasing a guy with a similar MO, but he never leaves fingerprints. He messed up this time. Bradley!" Julie shouted to another officer several desks away and he ambled over. "Prints of the Town Square Mall Attacker are being lifted in the lab. Get down there and stay on them until they're finished." The young man trotted away with purpose and Sarah smiled at God's providence.

"Okay, Pastor Tracey, the name Saul White did not turn up any easy suspects, so my sketch artist is standing by. Tell him what this character looks like and we'll nab him."

"Amen to that," Sarah replied and prepared to do her best.

Jonah's cell rang as he was getting off the first Montgomery exit. He tossed it to Jenn to better navigate the unfamiliar roadways. He'd been to the Montgomery PD, but it had been some years and the city had grown ten-fold since his last visit.

"Detective Speltz," Jennifer barked into the phone in her tough-cop voice, ignoring the smile that reached Jonah's mouth when she did so. Within moments, she pressed the speaker and a familiar voice filled the car.

"Jonah, it's Hank Addison."

"Hey, Hank, I'm his partner, Jennifer Speltz," Jennifer said and returned to her casual voice. "I'm afraid he's trying to maneuver this car through your town and he can't drive and talk at the same time. He's getting quite old, you know. You're on speaker."

"Hah! Join the club! So you're in Montgomery. Super. I have good news. If your old-man partner can listen while he's driving, tell him we got a hit on those fingerprints you faxed. The guy you're looking for attacked a woman a couple of days ago here in town. We're getting preliminary info right now. Does Grandpa Jonah know how to get to the new police station?"

Jennifer turned to Jonah who shrugged. She chuckled. "He doesn't. Where are ya now?"

"We didn't go far. If he can remember how to get to Madison, he can come toward where the old station was and he'll see us on the way. Still on Madison, but two blocks into town."

Jennifer forwarded the directions and hung up. She clasped her hands behind her head and gave Jonah a contended sigh. Jonah didn't take the bait so she cleared her throat to make him look over.

"What's with the dramatics?" Jonah asked with stolen glances, eyes on the downtown traffic.

"How about that? They're gonna help us nab our guy!"

Jonah chuckled. "Oh, I see. Pat-pat-pat. Good call, Speltz." Jonah returned his eyes to the road and thanked God in his heart.

◆ ◆ ◆

Paul sped down the interstate thumping the steering wheel. For a change of pace, he intended to go to his giant's house and meet the wife. Several thousand dollars in his bank account had given the big man pause. It seemed Big John might be thinking about quitting, and that would never do.

Paul glanced at the scrap of paper in the console denoting the Jenkins' address. He'd taken it from Tony's wallet and now allowed the truck's GPS to lead. It would be quite a night. First, he would meet John's woman and little boy. Paul grinned at the thought of John arriving home to find the baby in his arms. He'd arrive in less than an hour and Tony would be too far away to interfere. It was going to be great fun. Paul punched the accelerator and pushed the truck to eighty.

◆◆◆

There were four Saul Whites in Montgomery and surrounding area, and none had fingerprints on file. Jonah and Jennifer had returned to Montgomery for the third day in a row, despite a stern warning from their captain that their time was up. Jennifer put it best when the man threatened to reassign them. She told him to his face, *"I'm sorry, Captain, but I took this job to catch killers, and that is what I'm going to do. I'll let you know when we have the guy in cuffs."* Jonah laughed thinking back because Erkleson had been surprised enough to acquiesce and he gave them another week. The woman was powerful reminding Jonah of how much he liked her.

"Kranchez said we could ride with him. You coming?" Jennifer interrupted Jonah's thoughts and he nodded.

The three climbed into a marked police cruiser, Jonah and Kranchez up front, Jennifer in the back, and headed to the first address on their list.

Once underway, Jonah held the sheet of paper up to his partner in back and put his finger to the name across the top. *"Saul White.* Isn't it kind of weird that this name is so similar to Paul Black?"

"Oh, my God."

"Saul/Paul, Black/White. This could be the same guy. Stupid alias, but not as dumb as some I've seen."

"Oh, my God. I think you're right. I can't believe I didn't see that."

With one hand to the wheel, Kranchez pointed to the first address. "We went to this one already and no one's home. But we did some calling around and spoke to the Realtor. That gave me a red-flag right away because Saul White purchased this home with *cash.* Four hundred and twenty-nine grand. That's a hefty chunk of change for this part of the country. I know doctors and lawyers who couldn't round up that kind of cash if their life depended on it."

"That is curious," Jennifer agreed from her seat in the back.

Jonah remembered Tony Agricola and had a stroke of inspiration. "You spoke to the Realtor; did he mention another occupant living with Mr. White? I'm in contact with a man named Anthony Agricola who I think knows a lot more about my suspect than he let on. He's in Montgomery, but has been hard to locate."

"Sure, Mr. White was shown the house along with another man, purported to be his older brother. The Realtor described the second as scholarly and serious. Could that be your guy?"

Jonah twisted to catch Jennifer's eye and she nodded. "It could be. We have photos of all these guys. If I showed Paul Black's photo to your victim, I bet she'd ID him. Can we do that today?"

"We can try. Do you want to skip these other addresses and go on to see if we can catch her at home?" Jonah looked back to Jennifer and she nodded.

"Let's do it. Maybe another car can go to those other places just to X them out."

"You got it." Kranchez headed for the interstate. "Call the station and get them to check and see if she's home."

Jonah punched the number and waited for the desk to pick up. His pulse raced and he smiled. They were getting close, and soon they would put the case to bed.

◆◆◆

Paul rapped on John Jenkins's front door, his smile genuine. An attractive redhead answered, greeting him through an aging screen.

"Mrs. Jenkins? I'm Saul White. Your husband works for me." He'd found the right place; Big John's scent hung in the air as though he were still home. A quick check on the number of heartbeats told him that he and Opal were alone with the infant. *Wonderful.*

"Mr. White!" she exclaimed, blushing. "How nice!" Opal Jenkins was luminescent. A dainty barrette held her thick auburn hair in place and a simple shirt-dress disguised an assuredly petite figure. Paul cleared his mind, and focused on the night's goal.

"Is Big John home?"

"No, I'm sorry. He's at work." Opal unlatched the screen door and ushered him into the living room. "Please sit down. I'll phone Big and tell him you're here."

Paul gave her a new smile. "That'd be great."

"Can I get you something to drink? Some iced tea?" Opal hovered between the couch and the kitchen awaiting his answer and Paul shook his head. When she met his eyes, she shuddered, affected by his intense gaze. Then, snapping to attention, she gasped and placed manicured nails to her breastbone.

"Geez! I'm such an airhead. Let's make that call."

"Thank you, just tell him I'm here."

Big John would be mortified. Paul listened as Opal dialed and then looked up to make notice of her reactions.

"Babe? Hey! You'll never guess who just stopped by the house."

Paul watched and listened, picking up Big John's sentiments from where he sat.

"It's Mr. White!" A long pause followed until Opal sighed and handed the phone to Paul. "He wants to speak to you. Sorry if he seems grumpy. Sounds like he had a rough day."

Paul took the phone and cleared his throat for John to hear. "Hello?"

"What are you doing there?" John whisper-shouted. "This is *not* part of the deal. You need to leave *right now!*"

"Chill out, Big John. I met your lovely wife and she is *so sweet!*" Paul winked at Opal who blushed and excused herself to the back of the house. "Come on home so we can get started. I have something different in store tonight." John growled and Paul snickered.

"Are you going to hurt my family?" he asked much smaller.

"I don't think so…" Paul couldn't help himself and he added, "But hurry home, just in case."

"It'll take me ten minutes," John barked, his panic evident. "Don't do anything until I get there!"

Paul disconnected and called to Opal, who he overheard cooing to the baby in the back. "Your husband will be home in ten minutes. Bring that little John up here for a look-see."

"Sure," Opal responded. "Let me get him changed."

Paul stood to wait for her to enter. When she did, she handed over the mewling bundle. Mimicking the way John's wife handled the infant, Paul cradled the fragile child in both arms.

"You're a natural father, Mr. White," Opal remarked and lowered herself onto the sofa.

Paul sat beside her, carefully balancing the baby's head on his bicep. He watched John's son sleep; everything about the baby amazed him, from the tiny fingers gripping the soft blanket to the perfect lips that pursed in a dream.

Opal giggled. "You look mesmerized!"

Paul laughed and looked up to catch Opal examining him with intent. He held her gaze until she looked away. Opal cleared her throat before darting her eyes toward the door, finally sensing the danger.

"What do you do, Mr. White?" she asked her eyes on the door.

"Me? Everything and nothing. I guess you'd say I'm retired." Paul said, enjoying the spike in the woman's emotions. She wanted the baby back, but inwardly rationalized her unnamed anxiety.

"Must be nice," she said. "Before I met Big John, I had the briefcase, the suit, the whole nine yards. But now look at me. Little Susie homemaker."

"Don't sell yourself short. It's not easy keeping a household running perfectly." Paul cooed to the baby and his mind fluttered to his days with his master.

"I agree. So, you're married?"

"Sort of," Paul snickered. "I live with a whiny brother who tries to keep me on the straight and narrow."

Opal chuckled too loudly and looked at her watch. "Big's the one on the narrow path around here. Before I met him, I had no idea that there were two paths to choose from."

Paul didn't continue the topic and listened for John's car.

"God gave me a great husband and a perfect baby, and that's enough for me," Opal said her eyes still on the door.

Paul rocked the baby. "This tyke is *way* too tiny to grow into another Big John." Paul had never held an infant and the novelty had worn thin. Thankfully, John's car rumbled within his hearing and he stood. Opal followed suit.

"All the men on my side are average, so we'll see," she said and stepped close as if to take custody.

Paul ignored her hints and checked that the baby was cradled just right. "Does he have your husband's gray eyes?"

"Hard to say," Opal said and ruffled Junior's soft locks. "He has his grandpa's hair..."

A car door slammed and in the next moment, John Jenkins burst into the house, his face ashen.

◆

"Opal! Everything okay?" John's heart turned to ice at the sight of Paul holding his son. Opal stepped into his embrace. She seemed tense, but not frightened. Maybe Paul had behaved himself.

"Yeah, sure," she answered after he kissed her cheek. "Just getting to know Mr. White. He's very good with Junior. Look at that baby sleep!"

John stepped over to Paul, watching his eyes, and gently removed the baby from his hands.

"Here, babe," John said as he handed the bundle to his wife.

"Why don't you take Junior to see Nu-Nu."

"Can't. Nu-Nu's in Chattanooga," Opal said, nuzzling the baby's cheek, oblivious to John's agitation.

"Well, go *somewhere*. I need some privacy with Mr. White." John regretted his gruff tone, but hiding his terror took concentration. If he didn't get his family out of the house fast, Paul might attack them all.

"Okay, okay, geesh." Opal winked at Paul who offered an innocent shrug. "I'll run some errands and come back about six."

John looked at his watch and then to Paul. "No, make it eight. Our workouts take several hours." Paul grinned as John sent him a miniscule head shake. "*Liar-liar pants on fire,*" Paul teased in his mind.

Opal huffed, hugging Junior to her chest. "In that case, I'll be at mom's and you can just call me when you guys are done." Opal kissed John's cheek and headed to the back of the house.

Paul remained standing beside the couch and crossed his arms. Big John stood in the middle of the room, wondering what the evening would bring. Finally, in a low voice, he asked the question festering since he got the call Paul had arrived.

"Why did you come here? Why?"

"Because I can," Paul whispered. "Because I wanted to. You two preachers are not going to control me any longer."

John was silent. He had to get his family safe before engaging the vampire. Thankfully, Paul remained quiet as Opal gathered items from the kitchen.

She blew John a kiss and waved at Paul. "I'll take the Cadillac."

"Sure, babe. See you later." John held his breath; was Paul letting her leave? Opal grabbed her keys from the hook by the door and left the house. Both men listened to the big car's engine rev and pull away.

Paul spoke first. "Your wife looks delicious. I imagine she's the envy of all of your pals."

John bit his lip, expecting Paul to make snide and maybe even rude remarks. *What's going to happen next? God? Are You watching this?*

Paul smiled and reached behind his back in a quick movement. With dramatic flair, he brought forward a tooled leather scabbard.

"What's this?" John asked, afraid to hear the vampire's response.

"Have a look." Paul stepped close and unsnapped the leather pouch securing the dagger. John grasped the handle of the hefty knife to slide it free. It was a hunting blade, eighteen inches long and two and a half inches wide, with a serrated edge. The fat hilt had been carved with writhing serpents. Add to that, portions of the blade and handle were stained brownish-red.

Is this a murder weapon? Did it kill somebody?

"That's my blood, you big baby," Paul said and retrieved the leather scabbard to drop it onto the floor. "This is the knife that pierced my heart and compelled my master to transfer his power."

"Your master? You mean that guy in Europe?" John asked, wincing at the grisly mental image conjured by Paul's description.

"It's a shame you didn't meet him. He would terrorize you both into submission…"

John handed back the knife, hilt first, but Paul waved it away.

"No, Big John, that knife is for you. I'm giving it to you. And for our game tonight, I want you to try to kill me with it."

Paul did not smile or laugh, but the glint in his eye revealed that he really only wanted to be *attacked*. It was a game John wouldn't play.

"No way," John muttered.

"How about I give you some incentive? If you don't come at me with that knife, I will kill you, your wife, and your son." Paul put his hands in his trouser pockets holding his calm smirk.

Big John held in a gasp at the thought of Paul's hands on his treasures. Was God protecting them? Didn't God promise to protect those who loved Him? John asked God for help and shook his head.

"You've got to be kidding," Paul hissed, the now-familiar red glint in his eye. "You're telling me that if you found me in your bedroom tonight sucking the life out of your wife with your dead son at my feet, you'd simply stand by and watch? What kind of man would do that? Are you a man? Or a coward? You don't have to protect them because they belong to God?" John had no answer and Paul's anger intensified. "I'll tell you what your little buddy Tony would do. He'd protect them. He'd fly at me with this knife and try to slit my throat. How can he be a bigger man than you? A giant!"

John closed his eyes at Paul's screams, growing loud enough to attract the neighbors. He lifted his pleas to the Lord and in his mind, visualized his wife and son sleeping next to him on the bed. In this vision, Paul tried to enter the room and found no access. The meditative episode only lasted a few seconds, but when he reopened his eyes, he startled at the blind rage on the vampire's face.

John took a hesitant breath. "With all due respect," John began, praying for strength, "God is not going to let you anywhere *near* my wife and son. Not tonight or any night. He has placed a hedge around them that you cannot sweep aside."

John dropped the knife to the floorboards and fell to his knees, his hands coming together to pray. "You and your money can take a hike. I'm done with you. Be gone, devil!"

♦

Paul's eyes widened. *What does this fool think he is doing? Does he really believe that I'll leave him alone if he starts praying?* Paul made an attempt to interrupt the big preacher, but John had switched his tact from begging for a life raft to asking God to help Paul.

"O my God, this vampire is out to get me. Help him, Lord, and forgive him, for he does not know what he is doing…"

"I've had enough of this!" Paul made a grab for the knife and lobbed it in John's direction. The heavy dagger landed centimeters from the big man's thigh and embedded itself into the wood.

John didn't take notice.

"I didn't have to miss!" Paul shouted over the giant's supplications. Enraged, Paul slapped the man's face forcefully enough to draw blood from his cheek.

John continued to pray.

"Get up!" Paul grabbed his shoulders and wrenched the giant to his feet. As he prepared to deal a fatal blow, a car door slammed outside. Followed a millisecond later by a loud, official-sounding rap on the front door.

John stopped praying and opened his eyes. "I wonder who that could be. Could it be God coming to my rescue?" he asked and called toward the door before Paul could respond, "Come in!"

Paul stepped back and waited to see who it was, shocked that they would be interrupted at just the right moment. He had been ready to twist off the giant's head. Then he shied from the thought. *I don't want him dead… I need to get out of here!*

A tall, sturdy sheriff's deputy sauntered into the house, removing his hat along the way.

"Am I interrupting something?" The deputy crossed the room to introduce himself and shake John's hand. He nodded to Paul. "Do I know you, son?"

Paul scowled and shoved his hands in his pockets. The deputy watched him a little too long and Paul returned an unblinking stare.

The deputy finally turned his back on Paul and focused on the giant. "Everything okay, here, Mr. Jenkins? We had us a little noise complaint."

"Oh, thanks, Deputy Ray, but we were just having a little argument. Of course, I won." John flexed his pecs and the cop grinned. Then he motioned for Paul to leave. "Go along now, Mr. White. I don't expect I'll be seeing you again. Our contract has been terminated."

Paul looked the deputy over and cut his eyes to John. *"You don't think I could take you both?"*

John ignored him and closed him out as soon as his feet cleared the threshold. At first, Paul lingered, listening to inane small talk. Controlling his emotions wasn't easy but he finally shuffled toward his truck and got behind the wheel.

I love my preachers, but I might have to kill them.

Paul turned the ignition and pulled away from Big John's house. Over and over in his head, he recalled why he had gathered the two men to him in the first place. He had known Anthony was going to preach to him without ceasing. And hadn't he sensed the same spirit in the giant when he first looked into his face?

Why am I only attracted to these righteous men?

Anthony had said days ago that Paul was attracted because they were filled with the Spirit of God. He had also said that vampires couldn't have it because Paul was influenced by demons. But Paul didn't believe in demons and gods. Sure, some unseen force was at work, but it's wasn't God. It was magic, or alchemy. Not the God of that book.

Paul headed toward town, hoping to get lost in a crowd of strangers for a time. Maybe he'd satisfy himself in Columbus, maybe break Tony's zero-fatalities law. Then tomorrow, he would finish the job at the Jenkins's residence.

◆ ◆ ◆

Jonah sat across from Jennifer and Officer Andy Kranchez in the Waffle House sipping coffee and mentally reliving the events of the day. Jennifer's wristwatch beeped the ten o'clock hour and Jonah snapped out of his thoughts.

"We need a break on locating this White character," he said, stirring in another creamer. "The Tracey woman identified him even though he dyed his hair since this driver's license photo was taken."

"It shouldn't be long before someone spots him, right, Andy?"

Jennifer looked to the Montgomery officer who nodded. "We're going to get him. I feel it in my bones. If we have to, we'll stake out his house tonight."

Kranchez cleared his throat. "I can't work on this tonight. I'm sorry, but I've been up since ten *last* night. I gotta get home."

"And we should get back to Whitford City," Jonah said, stating the obvious. His partner hadn't faced the facts. "We have paperwork and we didn't have express permission to stay here so long in the first place." Jenn mumbled a complaint. "I know, but the MPD will watch him. If he pops up, they'll bring him in and call us right away. Right, Andy?"

"That's the way we roll," Kranchez offered and finished off his decaf.

"We go file our reports and keep tabs on the case long distance. They want to prosecute our guy on assault charges, so they're not going to take it easy on him," Jonah said. Jenn needed more prodding. "*And* now that we know he's our killer—they're going to add more manpower to the case until he is brought in. Okay?"

Jennifer didn't respond, but she took one last sip of her coffee and got up. Kranchez and Jonah stood as well and dropped some bills on the table for the waitress.

"I'd appreciate it if you'd keep me in the loop no matter how insignificant your progress. Will you do that?" Jonah asked Kranchez and Jennifer left ahead of them in a huff.

"Sure. I go on at 9 a.m. and I'll see what progress we've made. We'll get him. He's a wanted man in two states."

"I also want to watch Tony Agricola. Will you keep an eye out for him, too? He's wanted in connection, but I don't have anything on him. Just keep an unofficial eye out for me." Kranchez said he would and Jonah joined his partner in the car.

He didn't try to placate her further having already assured her as much as he could. At fifty years of age, he'd gained enough experience to know that when a woman is upset, speaking can make things decidedly worse. Jonah buttoned his lip and put in the Slim Whitman tape she liked.

◆ ◆ ◆

Big John ushered his wife into the house and locked the door. Paul had been gone for some hours, but John's anxiety lingered. The deputy asked some mundane questions and was gone. Just like that. John was convinced that God had intervened by sending the deputy at just the right time. Now, if he could only get his family away and safe before Paul returned to seek revenge.

"Hey, baby, did you and Mr. White have fun?" Opal set down the diaper bag toting Junior in his portable baby seat. When she glanced up to meet John's gaze, her grin faded. "Are you okay?"

John took possession of the baby seat to unbuckle the infant. He didn't respond, unsure of what to say. He couldn't tell her the truth and he didn't want to lie. As she asked him again what was going on, he formulated a few vague yet honest answers.

"Everything's going to be okay." John carried the sleeping baby to his crib with Opal following on his heels.

"Don't tell me that. Tell me what is going on. You look terrible." Opal watched John place Junior in his favorite sleeping position before she pulled his arm. "Come on, Big Daddy. Tell me what happened and you tell me now."

John returned to the living room and Opal lighted onto the couch beside him.

"Ope, Mr. White is no longer welcome here." John spoke carefully, choosing how to put an unbelievable problem into words. "I found out tonight that he's, well, dangerous."

Opal's eyes grew round. "Those cuts on your back..."

"Ope, let me finish," John gently admonished and took Opal's hand. "Tonight, Mr. White revealed himself to be a dangerous and unstable man. I want you to leave in the morning and stay with your mother for a few days while I straighten this out."

Opal shook her head throughout his instruction, and when he paused, she jumped in. "Big John Jenkins, no you don't! You're not putting me away so you can work this out on your own. You need to level with me, right now. No more secrets! What is going on with this guy? Why all the mystery? What did you get us into?"

"Look," John worked to keep his voice even. "I have it under control. You have to trust me and stay with your mother first thing in the morning." How could he tell her that he'd gotten them mixed up with a vampire?

Opal shook her head with more vigor. "No! I'm not going anywhere until you tell me what's going on. Don't make me guess, John." Opal crossed her arms and leaned back. "Level with me and I'll consider going to mom's."

John recognized Opal's resolute expression and sighed, his shoulders drooping. "Okay," he said, waiting for her to soften. "Mr. White was into some weird stuff. I knew it was weird in the beginning, but the money was so good, and it wasn't illegal, so I took the job."

"It's something you think God's against," Opal said flatly, showing how well she read her husband. John offered a half nod that ended in a shrug.

"Mr. White liked to, well, *wrestle*, and tonight, he took it too far." John glanced at the knife he had pulled out of the wood flooring and returned to its scabbard. Opal followed his gaze and picked it up.

"What's this?" she asked as she slipped the dagger from the holder to examine. "Is this Mr. White's knife?"

"Yes. He brought it because he wanted me to attack him. He said he wanted me to try to kill him."

"Oh, my God," Opal said in a soft voice.

"It was a sick game from a sick man. When I refused, he blew up; threatened me, us…"

"I can't believe it," Opal mumbled, still studying the weapon. "He seemed odd, but not psychotic…" She hopped to her feet and left the room for the dinette where her laptop was set up. Setting the knife next to her HP Pavilion, Opal called up her photo album. John stood behind her and watched the monitor.

"What? You know this knife?"

"Yeah, I've seen it before…" Opal scrolled through folder after folder of j-pegs. "A while back, the police called asking me about my cousin, Craig. The last time I emailed him was about this knife. Look." Opal leaned away and maximized the photo. "Craig found this knife in a gas station bathroom and he asked me to find a value for it." Opal held the hilt up to the photo on the computer monitor and John examined the two for similarities. "Look, even this nick on the top of this serpent—this is the same knife. Mr. White has Craig's knife…" Opal looked up and caught John's eye. "Craig, my cousin who was murdered last fall."

John's head swam. Opal had told him about the police finding her cousin dead in the woods, but what did Opal's cousin have to do with Paul?

"I better call that detective and tell him about the knife. He's gonna want it for evidence."

Warning bells sounded in John's head; the police? He and Tony had a lot to lose.

"Is that blood?" Opal gestured to the rust-colored stains on the blade and handle. John wiped nervous sweat from his brow with his bare palm and leaned against the wall beside his wife.

"Paul told me this was *his* blood…"

"Paul? Mr. White's name is Paul and Saul?" Opal asked.

"Saul's an alias. Oh, babe, I'm so sorry." John looked at the knife and then away again. "Paul said someone stabbed him with the knife you're holding. What if it was Craig who stabbed him?"

Opal bit her bottom lip. "I don't know him very well, I mean, could it have been self-defense? You said Mr. White is insane; maybe he went after Craig first."

"Maybe, what-if, maybe…Ope, don't call the police." John hated the look of disappointment in her eyes. But she didn't know what he knew, and he couldn't bear to tell her the whole truth; that he'd dragged his family into a dangerous battle with a demon. "Trust me, I have my reasons. Don't tell them about the knife."

"Big, we *have* to turn this over to the police. I can't believe you want me to withhold evidence."

"We need time. *I* need time. Mr. White is coming back here to try again." John pleaded with his eyes. "Go to your mom's and keep this to yourself for two days. Please." Opal's brow furrowed and Big John kissed her forehead. "If you have ever trusted me—do as I say. I promise I'll tell you everything when I can. Right now, it'll do no good. Please, trust me."

His emotions too great, John turned and left the room. On his knees in the bedroom, he asked God for comfort and wisdom. Opal joined him a few minutes later and allowed him to pray over her. Then John held her close, thanking God for his protection, and trying to forget that even with all of his faith, he was scared out of his wits.

Paul switched off the truck and peered over the steering wheel to the busy parking lot. He had driven to the shopping mall and sat to watch the patrons hustle to and fro, all with their various treasures in hand. He was still angry with Big John and tried to contact him telepathically. But somehow, the big guy was out of reach.

Paul sniffed and opened the door. Night had fallen and he would find some entertainment. He toyed with the idea of picking up a companion or two; a couple of head-bangers or socially destitute kids.

It wasn't hard to pick the easy prey out of the crowd. They were the ones who averted their eyes. Especially the black magic set. The Goth kids dressed in black wearing white make-up in an attempt to distinguish themselves as witches.

Paul had dispatched one of these in Atlanta before he found his preacher. It had been last winter, a month after Mark disappeared, and Paul had been despondent from the loss. He spent his evenings walking the dark alleys of downtown Atlanta, looking for trouble, or waiting for trouble to find him. One night, a thick lad of about fifteen bumped into him in the dark. The kid was dressed in black from head to toe, with deep black circles painted around his eyes. He was alone and Paul had asked him what he was doing.

"None of your business. And you better get outta my way before I stick ya."

Paul must have laughed, because the kid pulled out a small pentagram on a silver chain and held it up for him to see.

"Oh, no, ya don't. I may look like a stupid kid in his Halloween costume to the likes of you, but I'm more than that. I'm so much more than that…"

Paul smiled as he remembered the boy's brashness. There they were, all alone in the alley, past midnight, and the kid wasn't the least bit afraid. Paul had listened a little more to the kid's threats out of sheer amusement before draining his blood. It had been fun.

As Paul entered the brightly-lit shopping mall, he roamed the spacious aisleways searching for his type. They were plentiful tonight. He picked out a group of three that walked in a tight huddle in and out of the various stores. He tailed them for thirty minutes before attempting a meet and when he invited them to party, they accepted. Easy as pie.

◆◆◆

The Montgomery Police detective watching the White-Agricola place scrutinized the green pick-up that filed past him and then through the home's security gate. He checked the photograph taped to his clipboard and put his car into gear to follow the vehicle to the house. At the top of the drive, the truck stopped and a dark-haired man got out and came toward his unmarked cruiser. The detective exited his vehicle and met the man halfway.

"Evening, sir. My name is Detective Garrett Stephenson. We're looking for this man." He held out both photos his supervisor had handed him and gauged the guy's reaction. "We know this is his house. Can you tell me where to find him tonight?"

"Is he in some kind of trouble?"

"We need to speak to him, sir. Is he at home?"

"No, and I don't know when to expect him."

The detective motioned for his partner to exit the car and join him. The suspect was considered Priority One. They'd need to search the house, so he asked the man if they could.

"Sure, but I don't know what to tell you. He's not here. I haven't seen him since this morning."

The two detectives offered a cordial smile and followed the man into the house. The serious-looking fellow with the glasses didn't look guilty and he seemed to be telling the truth, but the officers wanted to be thorough. They would search the house, and if the man wasn't home, they'd resume their position watching the residence until shift change.

Just another day on the job.

20

Indeed, wine betrays him; he is arrogant and never at rest.
Because he is as greedy as the grave
And like death is never satisfied.
Habakkuk 2:5

PAUL STROLLED THE FAMOUS COLUMBUS RIVERWALK, smiling at strangers, devising schemes in his mind. The sky was blue, the sun shined brightly, and plenty of faces greeted him as they passed. Paul's smile was genuine; the previous evening had progressed much as he had planned.

The three lost teens he had attracted in the mall had followed him to his car, laughing and bragging on how hard they were going to party when they arrived on the scene. Nikky, the fifteen-going-on-thirty damsel of the group had slicked her long brown hair to her scalp and rolled the ends into a bun at her the base of her head. She wore a snug black tube dress with black tights and loafers. Her two friends were the same age, and dressed as if serving as extras in *The Matrix* with long black coats that flared in the wind as they walked. All three wore pale make-up and identical silver chain necklaces with a pentacle charm. Seeing that they were the antithesis of what Tony stood for, Paul couldn't help but wonder how he would minister to them if he were there.

Paul abruptly erased Tony from his mind before the memory ruined his enjoyment. He'd add Tony to the mix later. But now, Paul closed his eyes, reliving the way he handled the kids from the mall.

As the three had piled into the back seat of his truck, Paul overheard the girl boasting that her mother would never believe she had taken a ride from a total stranger. But it was okay. There were three of them. Paul drove the kids down Ninth Street, all the way to the end, where it forked into a quiet pastoral setting. The houses were farther apart, and several had barns with cows and horses munching away in the darkness. He turned onto a dirt road going nowhere, and when he came to a stop, the taller of the two males asked him where the party was. Paul had not spoken the entire ride, and now fear dawned as they realized that they had not been paying attention.

"Where's the party? You promised to take us to a party." The taller youth spoke again. Paul judged him to be the strongest of the three, which made him the immediate target.

"I decided to make *you guys* the party," Paul said and shut off the truck and then the headlights allowing the night to envelop the area. He stepped out and opened up the back door on the girl's side. "You guys run and see who escapes and who doesn't." The tall boy remained in place, but the other two kids laughed.

"That's stupid," the girl piped up, already rolling out of the truck seat and landing squarely on her thick-soled loafers. "This must be one of those pasture bashes I heard about in the sixth grade. Cool!" She walked away from the vehicle, peering into the blackness.

"Nikky, wait," the rotund kid said and stumbled after his friend. "There ain't no party out here. This jerk is playing with us. He's some kind of perv. We better get outta here."

"Mister, look, we don't want any trouble," the tall kid said in a brave voice. "If you'll just point us the way back to town, we'll walk. Don't try any funny stuff. We ain't helpless. There's three of us and only one of you."

He had not gotten out of the truck, and he watched his friends walk away. Paul pointed into the blackness that reached into the distance. The moon did little to illuminate the pasture, and the children would only be able to see a few yards at a time. "If you run that way for about an hour, you might get back to town…"

The girl turned to face her friends, a frown on her painted face. "Justin?"

The chubby kid held Nikky's arm and he watched Justin in the truck, impossibly cool, trying to reason with the stranger.

"Look, Mister, I'm not running anywhere," Justin said, finally opening the door on his side. He came around the truck to stand beside his friends. "We're gonna walk back to town and you better not give us any trouble."

Paul had been leaning casually on the front quarter panel of the truck waiting for someone to run when the tall kid met the others before him. It was risky attacking one and letting two go free, but hadn't the thrill gone out of his life? He was a supernatural wonder; a power beyond anything these kids could ever imagine. And what were the chances of the authorities ever fingering him for anything they might find in the pasture? He didn't live in Columbus. Only Big John and his wife knew he was in town, and he intended to take care of them tomorrow.

Plus, Paul considered, *it'll be worth it just to see the faces on these stupid kids.*

Encouraged by his subconscious, Paul grinned and reached forward, grabbing the leader by his upper arm. He pulled him into a headlock facing his terrified pals.

"Let him go!" Nikky yelled without stepping forward. She gripped her chubby pal's arm as they both stared at their attacker in horror. Paul laughed.

"You guys better run or you might see me killing your friend." Paul secured the youth in his arms, although the boy hadn't screamed. Paul watched the other two kids step away, eyes locked with their captive pal. Would they run? Would they fight? Paul was happy to accept either option. Finally, his victim spoke up.

"Nikky, Brett, you guys run back to town and get my dad. He'll know what to do. He knows the police chief. Y-y-you're in big trouble, jerk-weed!" Justin shouted, straining against Paul in a perfunctory manner. Puzzled by his lack of panic, Paul wrapped his forearm around the youth's throat and compressed his Adam's apple. "Go on! Get!" Justin squawked with rising fear.

"Yes, go get daddy," Paul teased, his face against Justin's cheek. Inches away from the boy's throat, he played with the idea of attacking him while his friends watched. Before he could decide one way or the other, the two frightened kids ran into the darkness. Paul called after them laughing. "Hurry! Your pal may not last very long. He doesn't look like he can take very much abuse."

Paul waited until they were out of his special sight, several yards away, before returning his attention to the boy in his arms. He'd sent Nikki and Chubby in the opposite direction from town. All that remained was to finish off kid three. Paul inhaled the urgent scent of adrenaline seeping from the kid's pores and whispered in his ear, "Justin, is it? What do you know about vampires?" …

In the pleasant sunshine of the shoreline, a cyclist zoomed by, tapping Paul on the head as she passed. "Ahoy, Matie!"

Paul snapped out of his reverie, his smile never wavering. Justin had met his end much like the rest of them do. People were such fools. He could easily kill them all. It would take barely any effort. But then who would be left to prey upon? It was an age-old vampire quandary, he surmised.

Paul looked up to the sky and then at his watch. It might be getting time to contact Tony and taunting the preacher gave Paul a lot of pleasure. After that, he'd head over to the Jenkins residence. Then the real fun would begin.

♦♦♦

"Preacher man, where are you!"

At the wheel of his truck, Tony blinked with surprise and winced. Paul's telepathic homing beacon had no volume control. In the quiet cab, Tony looked to the headliner.

"I'm at the bank! What do you want! I have a cell phone!" he barked, not sure if Paul would receive his message. Paul's next transmission chilled him to the bone.

"I'll race you to the giant's house! I'm going to kill him tonight..."

Tony cranked the engine and slammed the truck into drive. As he fishtailed out of the Regions parking lot, he fumbled in his wallet for the slip of paper he'd jotted John's information on. Even after turning out his entire contents, the paper was gone. Without missing a beat, he sped toward the house. He had John's phone number and address written in his ledger in his study. He'd grab the book and head to Columbus. It was all he could do to keep from screaming at God on the way.

♦♦♦

The unmarked police cruiser that had been tailing Agricola followed him toward the suburbs. Kranchez maintained a safe distance and with practiced precision kept the pick-up in his sights. The man had spent a short time at the Collegiate Bookstore in Cloverdale, an establishment the department had already traced to the White/Black character. Next, he stopped at Regions Bank. Minutes ago, he sped off a hair above the speed limit and reached his house in record time. Kranchez was thankful that he hadn't been spotted the way he had to cut corners and sometimes change lanes unexpectedly to avoid detection. Now that he had parked his Cutlass a short distance from Agricola's driveway, Kranchez radioed dispatch, keeping a sharp eye on the front door of the house.

"Get me Detective Jonah Miller in Whitford City." He only had to wait a few seconds before the connection was made.

"Miller." Jonah's voice sounded tinny over the State-provided radio system, but Kranchez recognized his calm tone.

"Kranchez, I'm tailing Agricola and he's in quite a hurry. He left the bank in a big rush. Went home, and…" Kranchez paused as he watched Agricola exit his house and jump back into his pick-up. "Here we go."

"He's on the go again?" Jonah's said, suddenly very alive.

"Yep. Heading north. I'll bet he's heading to the interstate. I'll tail him as far as I can."

"And if he leaves your jurisdiction?"

"Have I ever let you down?" Kranchez ducked as the green truck barreled past and he fell in behind, smooth as clockwork.

"Not yet."

"And I won't this time. I'll check back with you as soon as I have more information. Hey—Jonah…"

"Yep."

"Is your partner single? She's kinda hot."

"Too hot for you, Andy. Call me back. Miller out."

Kranchez laughed and hooked his radio in place. He knew as soon as he met Jennifer Speltz that Miller had a thing for her. Too bad it was a sad-old-man sort of thing, and not a sexy romantic sort of thing that *he* could offer. Kranchez refocused on the job at hand and monitored the police band.

Tony pushed his truck to seventy-five and then to eighty before easing off the gas. He had already calculated how much time it would take to reach Columbus, and he was afraid that he'd be painfully and—maybe morbidly—late. Praying the whole way, Tony tried to ignore the dash clock. He just needed to trust God. Put it upon the Lord and stop worrying about what was going to happen when he got there. *But could You work me a miracle anyway?* Tony sincerely hoped He would.

◆◆◆

Kranchez slowed to the speed limit and waved to the Alabama Statey that had agreed to pick up the tail on Agricola. Jonah Miller wouldn't like passing the buck like that, but what could he do? Jurisdiction had its purpose. Kranchez radioed in and requested a new patch to Jonah's phone and he hoped the guy was in a good mood.

What Kranchez didn't know was that although Bob Hartley had every intention of tailing the suspect, he hadn't foreseen what happened ten minutes after he parted company with the Montgomery detective. As Hartley watched the tailgate of the green pick-up a quarter of a mile ahead, his right front tire blew with a vengeance. Bob maneuvered his cruiser out of traffic and came to a shuddering stop on the shoulder. Cursing, he picked up his radio to call Detective Kranchez, but all he heard back was static.

"For the love of..." Bob mumbled, changing frequencies and hitting the trigger. *Nada.* His radio wasn't receiving at all. Bob dug around in the console for his cell phone and punched in headquarters. No signal.

"Am I in the twilight zone?" he groused, switching off the car with a jerk. Cursing the State for budget cuts that left him driving garbage, he prepared to change the tire. He'd just have to apologize to his Montgomery pal later. After all, it wasn't like they were chasing a murder suspect. It was just a person of interest.

Bob located his jack and got about changing the tire.

◆◆◆

Preparing to take his family into hiding, Big John checked the back door one last time and turned to see if Opal had followed him to the kitchen. She was still in the nursery with Junior.

"Babe? I'm only going to be gone for a half-hour. Get some things together and we'll leave as soon as I get back." John peered down the hall to see if his wife would reply. When she didn't, he plodded back to the nursery. "Babe?"

Opal held little Junior to her chest and stared at her husband. She did not understand all that was transpiring, but she agreed they should get away until White could be accounted for.

"I'm sure we'll be fine 'til you get back," she said, her voice stronger than expected. "I can be packed up in five minutes. Just hurry."

"I will, babe." John stepped into the room to embrace his wife and baby. She hugged him back with her free arm and then smiled as they parted.

"Leave your cell-phone on, Big." Opal looked out the baby's window and peered into the back yard. "At least the sun's out. It's a beautiful day. There's really not any chance he would try to come back and get us in the broad daylight, right?"

"Definitely not," John said with confidence. "I doubt he's hanging around, but if he tried to come back, he'd wait until nightfall."

"Okay. I'll be ready to leave when you get back." Opal shooed him off and John hurried through the door. He needed the cash he'd stored from the garage safe, and he'd need to turn over his pass-code to Sully if they expected him to run the business with Big John on vacation. He should be home in twenty minutes. John prayed for protection all the way to the office.

◆◆◆

Paul ducked in his white Tahoe as Big John's Caddy swerved past. He hadn't risked reading John telepathically for fear that he might alert him to his presence, and now he didn't know what the couple was up to.

Is it to be this easy? Paul thought as John left his wife and baby vulnerable to his attack. With the giant out of sight around the corner, Paul sat up and watched the house. Maybe John would be right back. Maybe that deputy was watching. Paul scanned the road both ways and saw only empty cars. No stupid deputy.

What about my preacher man? Paul pictured Tony in his mind and found him driving toward town at breakneck speed.

"Slow down, man. You'll get a ticket going that fast in Georgia..." He didn't receive a response from his partner although he sensed that the man was close.

Paul smiled and returned his attention to the small window on the left side of the house. He thought he'd seen movement in the kitchen area. Feeling secure in his hiding place six houses down behind a huge sleeping dump truck, Paul watched the tiny opening with interest. Timing was everything and Paul counted the minutes. His plan was good.

Tony glanced repeatedly at his cell as he drove, waiting for tower availability. *"Come on! Come on!"* he cried with building frustration.

He had already punched in Big John's home number in anticipation of the right moment to push send. As he crossed over the Georgia line, the receiving bars shot straight to the top.

Thank you, Jesus! he thought as he connected the call. The phone rang three times and just as he thought no one would answer, a female voice picked up the line.

"Hello? Mrs. Jenkins?" Tony spoke fast, certain that any second he might lose the connection. "This is Tony Agricola. I'm a friend of your husband's. Can I speak to John?"

"He's indisposed. Can I take a message?"

"Opal, I talked with you a couple of months ago; remember that first night Big John came to Montgomery? Remember?"

There was a pause and then a gasp. "Yes! Is something wrong?"

"I'm heading to your house and should be there in about fifteen minutes. Paul's coming, Mrs. Jenkins. I guess John told you about Paul?" Tony did not have the time or the energy to dance around the issues with John's bride. He hoped she knew *something* of what was going on.

"Mr. White? He's coming here? Now?" Opal's voice wavered. "Why are you coming?"

"I'm coming to stop Paul. Where is your husband? Can ya'll leave right away?"

""John had to run a quick errand." Opal lowered her voice to a whisper. "We're leaving when he gets back. Aren't you overreacting? I mean, it's broad daylight."

"I think he's already there. I'm coming up to…" The transmission broke up and Tony shouted into the receiver until the static cleared. "Tell John to get out of there as soon as possible. Tell John that he's c—" The connection severed as he passed through a deep mountain cut-out.

Frustrated, Tony dialed the number again several times in vain before tossing the phone into the console. He focused on the upcoming exits. John's was the second across the line. As he sped east, Tony prayed more fervently than he had in a very long time.

◆ ◆ ◆

"I don't believe this!" Jennifer growled as Jonah shared with her that the Statey lost Agricola over a flat tire. "We can't cut a break!"

Jonah's mind said, *calm down,* but knowing better, his lips remained closed. Anyway, he was just as exasperated. The POI that could possibly lead him to his prime suspect was again off the radar. He'd contacted every police agency between Montgomery and the East Coast and asked them to be on the lookout for Agricola's tags, but he couldn't tell any of them his need was Priority One; he had nothing but an earnest interest in the guy. It was a terrible bit of luck, especially since Jonah didn't believe in it. He depended on the fact that God was behind everything that transpired even in police work.

Jennifer took a deep breath and dropped into her chair, burying her head in her hands. "I'm going to close this file. I'm done with it." She peeked through her long bangs and saw Jonah look up to the ceiling. "Yeah—ask Him what we should do next, Jonah. Have you been asking Him all along because we're getting nowhere?"

Jonah forgave her mocking tone, but it hurt nonetheless. He kept his faith as quiet as possible and wasn't accustomed to being ridiculed for it. He slumped and pretended to look through a file. He didn't want her to see his eyes until he reset his expression and it wasn't clearing as fast as he would like.

"Jonah, I'm sorry. I really am. You know I didn't mean that," Jennifer whispered across her cluttered desk and Jonah didn't respond. "I'm just so tired of this stinking case. You know I'd never hurt you. I hate myself for even saying those things just now. I'm such a bitch. I told you."

Jonah met her eye, her apology sincere.

"So, Agricola left town. Are they going to watch his house to see if he comes back?" she asked.

Jonah nodded. "Kranchez is going to go by there a few times tomorrow. They can't dedicate any real man-hours for a stake-out, but Andy'll make a point to check on the house."

"I guess that'll have to do. So what do we do now?"

"Let's pull the Barbosa File. I told Erkleson we'd start it today. If the Nixon case is stalling, we might as well open a new one, eh?" Jonah's apologetic tone disguised his pleasure at beginning a new case. The mounting frustration of the past week had wreaked havoc on his temper and all but ruined his sleep. And recently, he'd been having nightmares about monsters with pointy teeth.

"May as well. I'm the sorriest detective alive, you know that, Jonah? If I was any good, we'd be doing real police work in the real world. Not trudging through cold cases, hiding behind dead leads and forgotten victims. I suck."

Jonah smiled and looked over his glasses at his partner. "Wait. I didn't get an invitation to your pity party. Will there be cake and ice cream like last time?"

"Hah-hah." Jennifer removed a pencil from her cup and bent it with both hands, keeping only enough pressure to flex but not enough to snap the wood. "And you can't come because you aren't pitiful enough."

"Oh, I am. I've been out of the game since 1998. I like it here in the cold cases. I got kind of scared when our Nixon case began to pick up steam. I hated working homicide and we were getting mighty close to that territory again, Jennifer."

His partner looked up when Jonah said her whole name.

"Retirement still looking good, eh? You *did* say the Nixon case would be your last." Jennifer kept her voice low enough that listening ears would not be able to overhear. Jonah smiled.

"You thought any more about coming with me?" Jonah didn't care who overheard. He watched her eyes; they were having a fairly intimate moment in a busy environment, and he didn't want to miss her reaction. He might have caught a hint of sympathy which wasn't the emotion he was going for.

"I've been so busy with this case that I haven't been able to think too much about it," Jenn replied, casting her eyes to her desktop. Before Jonah became disheartened, she threw him a life preserver. "But I am in no way refusing your offer."

"Good enough." Jonah sat up properly and tossed the Barbosa onto her desktop. "Tell me what you see."

Jennifer smiled and wiped her eyes with the back of her hand. Jonah liked to think her tears had been shed for him.

◆ ◆ ◆

"Mrs. Jenkins, do you have pink shutters?" Tony inched down Meadow Lane hoping to spot Big John's house without passing it. He spied the house number, but thought he had better be sure before he knocked on the door.

"Yes, are you in that green truck?" Opal asked, her face visible as she peeked between the blinds in the front window.

Tony said it was, clicked off his phone, and pulled into her driveway. There were no other cars around and he breathed a sigh of relief, eternally grateful that he'd arrived before his evil other half. We he reached the door, John's wife opened it before he knocked.

"Thank God I got here first. Mrs. Jenkins, I'm Tony. I'm so sorry about all this. I feel like it's all my fault."

"Please, call me Opal," John's wife said deadbolting the door. She gestured for the couch as she finished her thought. "I don't see how this could be anyone's fault but my husband's. He won't tell me the whole truth, but he has told me enough to know that he never should have gotten mixed up with your brother, no matter how much money he was offering."

"I hear you, but a lot of the responsibility lies on me, and I am so sorry. John's not back yet?" Opal shook her head. "John didn't tell you why Paul is such a threat?"

"He won't come clean until we're safe," Opal said, obviously exasperated. "Is your brother that dangerous?"

Tony didn't sit, his muscles too tense and his senses on full alert. He also didn't like being called Paul's brother. "Opal, this man is not my brother. I sort of work for him, like John, but in a different capacity."

"What capacity? Why won't either of you speak plainly?"

"There's no time. You won't believe it without lengthy explanation..." Tony stepped to the front windows and peeked through as Opal had done to see him. His heart broke at the thought of harm coming to John's family because of his selfishness. He decided to say as much, as if it would comfort either of them. "I'm sorry. I knew the risks, I should've told him. I only hope I can get you out of this mess without anyone getting hurt."

"Is the guy a murderer? A criminal? A monster?"

Tony met her gaze at her last guess. He steeled his jaw and returned his attention out the window. "Call Big John. Shouldn't he be back by now?" Had something happened to him? Had Paul nabbed him already? Tony's stomach lurched at the thought.

"Yeah, I'll—" Opal ceased speaking at Tony's upraised palm. They both heard a small sound from the back of the house. "Did you...?" she began, but was interrupted by a voice emanating from the baby monitor on the coffee table.

"Hey, Junior! Remember me? It's Uncle Paulie!"

Tony and Opal froze, looking at each other in disbelief. Finally after an unspoken suggestion, Tony sprinted down the hall and flung open the only closed door he found. Opal reached the doorway at the same time and cried out at what she saw in her baby's room.

♦

Paul was bent over Junior's crib, his hand on the baby's forehead when Tony burst in. He looked up and have him a wide smile.

"Preacher-man! Surprise, surprise." He stepped away from the crib to the center of the room.

"Hey, Paul. I'm here. Let me take you home," Tony said in a forced tone. "I promise. I'll make everything right." Tony positioned himself between Paul and John's wife, but Opal ignored his shielding and passed them both to reach the crib in four quick strides.

Paul watched amused and allowed her to scoop the infant into her arms, confident she wouldn't be able to leave the room before he grabbed her. To Tony he said, "Big John reneged on our deal."

"I know—" Tony said and gasped as Paul moved in a blur to grab John's wife, his arms encircling her body, pressing the infant into her chest and his cheek against hers from behind.

"But I really like Big John's family."

"Paul! Be cool." Tony stepped forward and Paul stepped back, the wall behind him.

"Stop, preacher-man. You don't want to get in my way. I've held up my end. Big John is the one who ruined everything. Not me." Paul inhaled at Opal's throat and grinned.

Opal screamed for help and Tony shook his head looking in her frightened gaze. "Don't scream. It only eggs him on."

Opal's eyes were huge and she struggled to be released, being careful to avoid crushing her son. "Please, Mr. White! Please don't hurt my baby!"

"Shhhh…" Paul tightened his grip around Opal's upper body, purposefully avoiding the infant, and she gasped for breath through compressed lungs. "I don't want that tiny thing. I want you. Set him down."

Paul maneuvered as a unit toward the crib and Opal placed Junior on his blanket while in Paul's grasp. Tony's racing heartbeat reached his ears and his stomach growled.

"Paul, wait," he begged. "Look over here. Come with me. I

promise I'll fix everything. I promise." Tony stepped closer, his hands out in supplication. "Let her go."

"Oh, Tony," Paul cooed and closed his eyes, breathing in the aroma of utter fear and desperation permeating the room. He had already won against his giant's God, captured the woman, punched a gigantic hole through the hedge that John claimed protected them.

Paul opened his eyes and fixed them upon Tony. The preacher was in anguish. It was such a welcome sight that Paul almost felt pity for him. The only expressions he had garnered from the man in the past were disdain and disgust. Now, the preacher was truly terrified of the power Paul held in his hands.

Is he offering me a substitute?

Barely had Paul finished the thought, before Tony came forward and with a swift movement, pulled a pocket-sized Swiss Army knife from his jeans. Flipping it open with one deft flick of his thumb, he plunged it into his throat, pulling downward, making a nasty gash.

"Please, let her go. I'll stay with you. I'll make it all better..."

Opal screamed at the sight of Tony's self-inflicted stab wound, but Paul lifted his brow, the aroma and sight of the preacher's blood more important than anything in the world at that moment. Releasing the woman, he surged forward and folded Tony into his arms. The outside world disappeared as Paul swallowed the blood exponentially sweeter because of the circumstance. Behind them, the woman scrambled out the door crying, the child in her arms.

In his embrace, Tony called after her. "Take my truck! Tell John to hide. Go!"

Paul smiled and drank on. The blood of a brother went down more smoothly as a gift than when stolen. He'd remember that.

♦

Tony spoke in stutters and gasps as Paul's savage attack wore on, happy to hear the front door slam and his truck crank afterward. Opal would heed is advice and make it fast. Paul wasn't letting up and Tony sensed his consciousness slipping away. He started a prayer, but didn't get very far before his brain fuzzed warning impending pass-out.

"Stop. Too much..." he groaned.

Paul feasted away. Then he spoke to Tony's mind. *"This is it, Tony! This is what I am, what I'm meant for! I will not be domesticated by you or any of you Jesus freaks."*

"You… can… still be… saved," Tony managed, although he wasn't certain he'd spoken. Spots filled his vision and he thought he might die. *Is this it, Lord? Am I done? Did I accomplish my task?*

"No, my beloved," Paul whispered in his frayed mind. *"You're staying right here with me. Until the end of time."*

The vampire might have said more, but Tony slipped away.

◆

Taking over the show, Paul tapped Tony's blood until the man was dead-weight in his arms. Then after tossing him over his shoulder, Paul walked to the front room. He draped Tony over the back of John's couch and peeked out the front door. The street remained deserted and not a soul worked or frolicked in the sunny yards. Smiling at his good fortune, Paul left the house, walked at a brisk pace down the block to reach his truck. Then he drove it to John's yard, over the curb and right up to the front door.

"I'm back. Did you miss me?" Paul joked to his silent preacher and went inside to pluck Tony up. On the coffee table, his knife sat in its leather scabbard and he tucked it into the small of his back. That done, he carried Tony to the truck, opened the passenger side door, and shoved him in. "Sleep on, preacher man. Your way sucked. My way is going to be a lot more fun."

Paul backed out of the yard and pointed them for the highway. There was one close call as Paul turned out of John's neighborhood onto the main drag. The now-familiar Deputy Ray was just getting into his car when he caught Paul's eye as he passed. The man nodded with recognition and then did something Paul found very odd; he winked. Paul cursed under his breath at the idiot lawman. His blood-gorged body tingled with pleasure and he allowed the delightful discomfort to distract him from Deputy Eye-Twitch.

After a few minutes, Paul glanced at Tony, leaning against his door as still as the dead. The plan was a good one and Paul couldn't wait to finish what he started.

21

Now you are under a curse and driven from the ground,
which opened its mouth to receive
your brother's blood from your hand.
Genesis 4:11

PAUL HELD THE HILT OF THE KNIFE IN PLACE WHERE
he had plunged it into Tony's chest. The man's eyes flew open at what
must have been an indescribable sensation that jerked him back from
oblivion. Paul grinned at the preacher's horror and focused down on
his task. He hadn't done this before and he had to get it right.

"Shhh, you're okay," Paul whispered, relieved that Tony remained
immobile. He needed no added complications. He watched what was
left of Tony's blood ooze out from the new wound. Minutes earlier,
he had contacted Mark about the process. His master had been no
help and inwardly, Paul fumed.

Why did Mark shut me out? Shouldn't he help me? I'm desperate! Paul
closed his eyes attempting to reach him once more, but hit the same
invisible brick wall. *He was there for a moment. He knew I needed him.* Paul
looked into Tony's pained face. *Mark didn't approve, so he cut me off.*

"It doesn't matter," Paul said, meeting Tony's astonished gaze, "I
know how it works."

Tony responded with a wet gurgle and Paul shook his head.

"Be still. This might feel weird."

He pulled the knife out in a swift movement, air escaping
through a collapsed lung and Tony's open mouth. Paul ignored the
man's anguished expression and sliced his arm to the bone.

"Now, you will be blood of my blood. Isn't that what Dracula
said?" Paul teased watching with awe as his blood poured into Tony's
wound, the overflow seeping onto the carpet. He gave Tony some
comforting words. "It's okay, you'll be fine in a minute…"

Tony's mouth formed words but no sound issued forth. Paul closed his eyes to memorize the moment. In his memories, his master performed the same procedure on him a few months earlier in a dark forest on a bed of wet leaves.

I almost died and Mark saved me. He used to love me. He used to adore me. Paul frowned at his inner monologue, hating his conclusion: *Now, he has gone insane.*

Paul opened his eyes to a tugging sensation in his arm. The deep gash he had made had healed, knitting together right before his eyes. With the injury erased, he leaned on his palms to watch the show. The preacher stared into his eyes with a glassy, horrified expression. He still had no spoken and Paul rejoiced to see the preacher's wound closing millimeter by millimeter. Paul's excitement filled his heart and he lifted Tony's upper body to his chest.

"Now you will understand this wonderful creature I've become! Now you will have first-hand knowledge of how difficult it is to remain chaste with so much delicious food within reach!"

Tony burbled something unintelligible and Paul continued.

"Shhh, hush now. Brother Paulie's going to take good care of you. No more rules. No more forbidden fruit. No more Bible talk. No more praying to your make-believe god."

"What... have you... done?" Tony said, finally able to make words.

"I think you know, but if you have any doubts..." Paul pulled Tony's fully into his lap. Cradling his head, he bit down hard on the inside of his right wrist and thrust the new wound to Tony's mouth. The preacher thrashed, but Paul succeeded in force-feeding his blood for several long moments before allowing him to slip free.

♦

"Stop!" Spitting and sputtering, Tony struggled out of Paul's grasp and pushed up on his hands and knees. Something was wrong with his legs. His lower body felt heavy and alien and did not respond to his commands. With a moan he dropped back to the carpet, rolling onto his back to stare at the prickled white ceiling. As slow as molasses, the transformation moved from his furiously pounding heart, down his spine, and into his hips and legs. He was changing, and not for the good.

This can't be happening...

"It's happening," Paul said in a low voice, sitting where Tony left him, blood covering his face and hands. "You play with fire long enough, you'll get burned. Didn't your mother ever teach you that?"

In another moment, Tony felt capable of sitting up and he did so with effort. "Jesus…" Meant as a prayer and not a curse, Tony spit as he spoke and gaped at the red droplets.

Paul shook his head. "No more praying now, preacher. You don't need Him anymore. You are god. You're just like me. Isn't this glorious?"

Tony crawled away from Paul to the door. He peered into the hall and then sat against the wall. He couldn't leave. Where would he go? He looked at his partner a long moment before allowing his eyes to roll closed, his head lolling against the wall.

Why is this so familiar? Why? Concentrating behind closed lids, he soon remembered what he'd forgotten. Almost a year ago, he counseled another man of God who had been force fed by a vampire. Dr. Mark Corescu had been a village priest, minding his own business, when the vampire sought him out and stole his life. Didn't Tony make it plain to the doctor how he would handle such as thing should it happen to him? *I told him I understood. I told him if I woke up starving for blood, I'd rationalize it, I said…*

But… I am not a vampire.

I'm not damned, he told himself and believed it. Still, he had contracted something evil from his slender nemesis, something vile and bloodthirsty. *How will this affect my relationship with God?*

God has not deserted me. I am not rejected. He is going to use this to some good end… Tony comforted himself with his thoughts. He swallowed, and along with the sensation of being parched, he recognized the coppery taste of blood still in his mouth.

But I can't drink blood. Tony endured a quick fantasy of attacking someone for their blood. *I could never do that.*

"You'll have to, silly," Paul interjected. "And if you ignore it, you'll attack without even realizing it."

Tony turned to prayer, promising again that his trust was in God.

"Amen!" Paul responded with a hearty laugh.

Tony did not react to Paul's sarcastic outburst but spoke more encouragements to himself. *I will not give up. I am a man of God. God will use this. I will not drink blood…*

When Tony opened his eyes, Paul's expression had morphed. The vampire wanted to be *thanked,* to be *exalted* for sharing such a wonderful gift with his preacher-man.

Am I hearing his thoughts? Tony narrowed his eyes. Either way, he wouldn't thank him. Paul meant harm, but God could turn it into something He could use. A song came to mind and Tony held Paul's eye with the first lyric. *"I am blessed among the people…"*

Paul's cheek twitched.

"I am blessed among the nations…"

Paul dropped his grin.

"I am blessed because I am loved by You…"

"Stop singing," Paul said low, remaining as he was, sitting beside Tony on the carpet.

"I am loved and highly favored!" Tony belted the lyric, off key but with gusto. Paul's face twisted into a grimace. *"Saved by the grace of a Mighty Savior!"*

Paul finally snapped. "Shut up! I command you to shut up!" Paul sprung to his feet and crossed to Tony in a blur. Grabbing him by the throat, Paul lifted him off the ground drilling him with his gaze. "STOP SINGING!"

Tony's airway was too compressed to breathe, but he managed a tiny smile and sent his thought with precision. *"I pity you."*

Roaring with anger, Paul spat in his face and opened his hands. Tony landed on his feet and rubbed his throat. He felt incredible, as if able to fly if he put his mind to it. Ten feet away, Paul seethed, his eyes rimmed red and his black thoughts spiking the room's energy.

Tony had one more jab and he said it with lowered chin. "And I forgive you…"

Paul shouted obscenities until his throat was raw.

PART TWO: THE MASTER

22

But as for me, I will always have hope;
I will praise You more and more.
My mouth will tell of Your righteousness,
Of Your salvation all day long.
Psalm 71:14-15

HIS PHYSICAL STRENGTH RESTORED AND EXPONENTIALLY amplified, Tony found his feet and placed his hands over Paul's at his throat.

"What did you expect? I could never be like you," he said curling his fingers around Paul's bloody hands.

With no small effort, he forced the vampire's hands loose and pushed him away. Paul took a swing, but he ducked just in time.

"My life is not something you control..." Tony surged forward and grabbed both of Paul's wrists.

Holding him tight, the vampire ceased struggling, likely planning his next move. Tony held his eye.

"You think you have all of this power and you want to exert it over your world. But you have no real power. What you have is what is given to you from Above. You are a puppet."

"If I'm a puppet, then so are you," Paul snarled, his eyes brimming with anger and what looked like concern, as if wondering if Tony was somehow stronger than he was. Tony did not have time to analyze and he hoped it to be true.

Tony stepped to the bed, pulling Paul along with him, and he forced him to sit, Tony taking a seat beside him, facing each other. "No, because I *choose* to help God. I'm a *participant,* not a puppet." As Tony's sense of conviction and faith grew, his empathy toward Paul grew in the same measure. "I *want* Him to control my life. You *resist,* so He moves you where He needs you to perform His will. Freedom is for those who submit. Puppetry for everybody else."

In a sudden violent move, Paul yanked his hands free and stood. Tony caught him by the forearm and Paul whirled around to face him, his eyes wild.

"Let me go!"

"Where are you going?"

"What do you care? You're leaving. I'll go wherever the hell I please!"

"I'm not going anywhere," Tony said, his voice grave. "You are my mission."

"I don't need a babysitter," Paul replied and made as if to take his arm back. He couldn't pull free, and when he tried in earnest, his eyes widened with revelation: his creation was stronger than he was.

Tony read his intentions and stood, twisting Paul's captive arm behind his back and forcing the vampire to his knees. Unafraid of breaking an arm, Paul struggled to get free. Tony sensed this as well and just as quickly fell upon him and held him to the floor with his body weight. His eyes fell upon the bloody knife a few feet away and he grabbed and pressed the blade against Paul's throat.

"Decapitation. That's one way to kill a vampire, right?" Tony whispered. He had no intention of harming Paul, but asserting dominance seemed necessary now that he could. Ignoring Tony's threat, Paul squirmed with vigor beneath him and Tony realized the extent of the vampire's increasing madness.

"I'm not insane," he sputtered. "I know you won't kill me." Paul fell still and turned his face to the side, lying flat on his stomach under Tony's upper body. "You feel sorry for me. You think I'm going crazy." Paul chuckled with an eerie inflection. "That's where you're wrong. It's *you* that's crazy. You and Mark and Big John. His stupid wife. That Bible witch. You're all deluded with the same notion, that an amazing and benevolent God is watching over us. Why is it that I'm the only one of us that can see that this is crazy?"

"Listen to yourself, Paulie. Everyone is crazy but you. Do you know how unlikely that is? If you're the only one that's sane, isn't there a big chance that you're actually the problem?"

Paul cursed aloud and strained again to rise. When he failed, he relaxed under Tony's weight. Then he laughed. When he didn't stop chuckling for several seconds, Tony became curious.

"What?" he asked and decided to let Paul up. The vampire rolled onto his back, looked at Tony's face and started laughing all over again. Tony stood, poked him with his toe, and put out a hand to help him up. "You've lost your mind."

Paul shook his head, and sat up on the carpet. "No, preacher-man, I'm just really excited to see your first kill. You have no idea what the bloodlust does to us. You won't be all holy then." Paul wiped his eyes. "It's going to be so fun to see you lose it."

Tony couldn't think of a smart retort as Paul had hit on a major concern. But leaving town took precedence. "Come on. Get up." Tony stuck out his hand again. "You have cops from at least two states after you. I need to get you out of the country." After a short staring contest, Paul accepted Tony's hand and was pulled to his feet. "We'll leave tonight," Tony said, using every psychology skill he possessed to calm Paul's ire. "Let me go tie up a few things at the bookstore and I will meet you back here to leave together. I'll take care of everything."

Paul looked away, his shoulders slumped as if pouting. "You don't tell me what we'll do. You are not my master."

"I'm not," Tony said quickly interjecting. "I don't want to be. Let's get going. I know you'll feel better when we're out of here."

Paul pulled the truck keys from his pocket. "Come on. I'm going to the bookstore with you."

Hoping to placate Paul into a better state of mind, Tony didn't argue.

An hour later, Tony was nearly done making arrangements for their departure. He didn't know how long they'd be gone, so there was a lot to consider. He had hired a young woman to manage the store and today would have been her first day of training. Now that he and Paul were departing immediately for Germany, she'd need to be brought up to speed. Her resumé gave him confidence that she could. She would arrive any minute and Tony needed Paul to lay low.

At that moment, Tony's ink pen took on an odd glow. Tony stared at it, entranced by the dance of light across the barrel, as if it he held a miniature light saber. Since Paul's most recent attack, his vision had been evolving, so much so that now objects seemed lit from within. Sitting in a chair against the wall, Paul laughed.

"The baby wakes up!" he announced with jazz hands. "It's a pen! Wow! Look at it!"

Tony broke his own trance and returned to signing papers. Downstairs, he thought he heard a car door.

"She's coming. She breathes like a piggy. Can you hear her? Have your ears caught up with your eyes?" Paul prodded.

Tony didn't take the bait. He needed Paul happy. "I hear her. I'll be quick. Wait up here and I'll take care of everything. Very shortly, we will be on our way." Tony paused to see if Paul would disagree, but when he didn't, he added, "Everything's going to be fine."

Paul only looked away. Tony shrugged off the silent treatment, too busy to worry about the vampire's inferiority complex. He would arrange to sell the bookstore and get Big John to take care of their estate, not to mention make sure he canceled his speaking engagements. Reaching across the desk top, he tossed a fat envelope to Paul.

"Heads up," Tony said, and Paul caught it without looking. "That's the title to your truck. See that it goes into the glove box when we get downstairs."

Paul didn't reply, but tucked the envelope under his leg for safekeeping. Tony hid his frustration. Since their last argument, Paul's every glare was filled with negative emotions. Tony didn't have to read his mind to know he was plotting. Tony only hoped he didn't snap before they reached Dr. Corescu.

He gave Paul a friendly grin. "Hang on a little longer. Can I depend on you to stay up here and behave?"

"Huh? I don't speak gibberish," Paul said and flipped the pages of his comic book.

Tony pursed his lips and opened the door. Downstairs, the woman he had hired waited at the locked front door. She sighed and Tony marveled. Before his transformation, such a small noise would not have reached his ears, but now Tony's every sense was increasingly amplified. He trotted down the narrow wooden staircase and went to the door. Was Paul likely to cause trouble in front of her? Tony hoped he didn't.

"Good morning," the young woman said as he pulled open the doors. "Mr. Agricola?"

"Just Tony, please," he said and locked the door after her once she entered. "And you're Rachel Fleming? How are you today?"

"I'm super. Ready to get started," she said, her friendly smile infectious.

"Good," Tony said and led her to the cashier island. Once there, he turned to face her and she blushed deep red. A powerful aroma struck his nostrils at the same moment, a mixture of floral perfume and laundry detergent. Then, a thumping sound vibrated deep within his skull. Tony's lips parted to speak, but before he could, Rachel's blush deepened and the thump increased its rhythm.

Oh, my God, that's her heartbeat. Tony frowned and looked through the file folder in his hand before handing it over to the woman.

"My partner and I have to leave urgently for Europe," he began before meeting her eye again. Her blush remained, and her heartbeat drummed steadily in his ears. Tony purposed to ignore both. A slight noise caused him to glance up at the office door. Paul stood on the threshold, watching them. Rachel noticed and waved.

"Is that Mr. White?" she asked and Tony mentally asked Paul to wait inside the office.

"Yes, but he has a cold, so I asked him to stay up there."

"Oh, thanks," she replied and peeked over the papers in the folder. "How long will you be gone?"

"I don't know yet, but I wanted to ask what you were capable of. Can you run the store without express training? It's a very basic retail system—would you feel comfortable with that?"

"I can," she said and pushed the keys on the cash register. "I'm familiar with this system. Sounds like you're leaving right now."

"Tomorrow at the latest." Tony heard Paul take a step down and he rushed to finish. "Another option is for you to keep the store closed and rearrange it or personalize the bookkeeping. Either would be fine. We plan on selling it soon."

"Oh, I guess this position is limited, then. That stinks."

Tony hadn't thought of that. He sighed. "I'm sorry. I understand if you want to rethink the hire. I should have considered your needs in this situation."

"No, I didn't mean it like that. I still get paid, right? Then I want to do it. It'll be great for my resumé."

Tony nodded and Rachel began a line of small talk that he only half heard. It took a minute for him to realize what it was, but an ethereal singing voice distracted him, accompanied by a strange pull in his gut. He looked up to where Paul had been standing, but he was no longer in the doorway. He glanced out the poster-cluttered front store windows, but no one approached. Still, the inexplicable tingle in his middle grew until it traveled to the base of his skull. Finally he heard the voice with his ears. It was Paul's giant, Big John Jenkins. John was almost there, fulfilling a compulsion to return Tony's forgotten truck.

The one Opal made her escape in.

Still reeling that he would have such foresight and telepathy,

Tony held up a hand to interrupt Rachel and he crossed to the door.

"What is it?" Rachel asked as a green pickup pulled into the lot.

"That is a friend of mine," Tony said and urgently unlocked the door. "Excuse me a sec."

Not only was it an entirely new sensation to predict and feel the approach of his giant pal, but he was shocked that the man would show himself. He had expressly warned John and his wife to lay low. Surely he didn't risk his life to return Tony's truck. It was a ridiculous notion. So, what was he thinking?

Behind him, the stairs creaked and Tony turned his head to see Paul descend the rickety staircase and head to the doorway. It was not good. He unlocked the door and met John's eye as he exited the truck. Hopefully, God would keep Paul from hurting any of them.

"John, what are you doing here?" Tony hissed in a whisper, hoping Rachel wouldn't hear. "Get out of here. I don't care about that stupid truck! Paul's here and he's none too happy with you."

John froze in place two steps away; as if he hadn't considered that his nemesis may be around. "I didn't think. I was going to leave it here and see if I could help you with him."

"Help me? How?" Exasperated and weary, Tony's tone was harsh. "It's not safe here. Already, an innocent woman is in there with Paul and now you, too? How am I supposed to protect you both?" Tony sensed that his severe gaze unnerved the big man, but he had little control over the nuances that accompanied his new condition. Would he be able to hide the fact that he'd been made over into Paul's image? If he could only get the big guy to leave...

"I'm just trying to do the right thing," John said and hung his head.

"I know, I know." Tony softened his tone and patted John's big arm. "It's almost impossible to know what the right thing is when impossible creatures are involved."

"I felt compelled to get here as fast as I could and see if you were okay. This is awful."

Tony shook his head. "It is, but you can't help me here, John. Please, get in the truck and go home. Paul's too unpredictable."

John had been meeting Tony's eye as he spoke, but as he finished, the big man did a double-take and took a step back.

"You do look pretty good for a man who faced the gates of hell a few hours ago. Opal said you were as good as dead." John lowered his voice. "She saw him drinking your blood. Paul's secret is out..."

Tony shook his head. "It happened really fast and she ran out before the attack was over. She can't know exactly what she saw."

"Tony?" Rachel called as she came to the open door. "You have a phone call. I think it's the bank."

"John, go home," he said under his breath and took possession of the phone. "Please. For the love of God." Tony took the call indoors and shook his head at John's folly.

♦

"I'm Rachel, the new store manager," Rachel said. "Are you coming in?"

John peered inside the bookstore, looking for Paul. The friendly brunette stepped aside and he gave her a smile.

"I'm Big John Jenkins, Tony's friend."

"Wow, you are *Enormous* John Jenkins!" Rachel smiled and shook his hand. "Forgive me if that was rude, but I've never seen a real life giant before. How tall are you?"

John chuckled, appreciating the easy-going nature of the youngster. And the fact that she obviously didn't know anything about Paul's dirty little secret.

"I reckon I'm about 6'6". And naw, I'm not embarrassed. I been big my whole life." John allowed himself to relax as he realized Paul wasn't going to jump out at him from behind the bookcases. Tony stood at the counter jotting something in his pad. Rachel remained at his side, gawking at his arms and chest. Things seemed normal. John breathed a sigh of relief and flexed his biceps to get a laugh.

"Look at that!" Rachel said rolling her eyes. "Like Arnold Schwarzenegger!"

"Bigger," John said with a wink. "So, you're working for Tony, eh?" John thought making small talk with the young lady would ease his nerves. She gave him a bit of her history and he kept a wary eye on Tony and an eye out for any sign of Paul. During a pause in her monologue, John interrupted her with a pressing question.

"Rachel, have you seen Tony's partner today?" Barely had he finished his question, when the hair stood up on his neck. Paul was directly behind him and he knew it even before Rachel's eyes averted that way.

"Big John Jenkins. What a pleasure."

John whirled around and looked down on the monster who had nearly killed his family the night before. The smile reserved for Rachel as he waited to see what Paul would do. To his surprise, he stuck out his hand to shake and John looked at it as if it might be poisonous.

When he failed to react to Paul's gesture, the vampire changed tactics and brought his fingers to rest on John's arm. "How is your wife? And Junior?"

Rachel had returned to her stool behind the counter and Tony was still on the phone, yet keeping a wary eye on all three from the counter. Knowing this comforted John, but he didn't know why. *It's not as if he can really protect me,* John reasoned, but the feeling in his heart was just the opposite. Somehow, the small and seemingly gentle Tony Agricola was the only one who *could* help him confront the evil in their adversary.

John didn't have a reply for Paul's questions. He couldn't even *think* of his family lest accidentally reveal their whereabouts to Paul, so he concentrated on his own trepidation.

Jesus! I need you! What should I do next?

John frantically searched his heart for the answers to his silent prayers. Paul's palm ran up his arm and massaged John's shoulder.

"It's about time somebody feared me, Big John," Paul whispered too low for Rachel to hear. "I want you upstairs with me, in the office. We'll talk this out."

"I had to protect my family," he whispered back, hoping to reason with the vampire. Paul's gaze was soft and the familiar evil grin had not yet touched his lips.

"I wasn't going to hurt your wife," Paul said in John's mind. *"It was all a ruse for Tony. A game. You know I can't leave him alone. He's too much fun."*

John exhaled the breath he had inadvertently stored up since Paul placed his hand upon him. He searched the vampire's eyes for malice; maybe he was telling the truth. He *did* like to mess with Tony. Could it have been an elaborate game to entertain a bored monster's mind?

"Come up to the office." Paul inclined his head toward the staircase.

John considered his options. Tony was still on the phone. Rachel thumbed through a magazine, now and then checking to see if the men needed her attention. John wondered if he could safely enter the office with Paul. Before he realized that he had made up his mind to follow, his left foot stepped in front of his right and started him toward the stairs.

"Excuse me," Tony spoke to his caller then raised his voice for John and Paul as they passed. "Paul…" He waited for Paul to turn and face him, and when he finally did, he finished his instructions.

"Why don't you go over that stuff with John that I told you about?"

Paul turned away from Tony and continued his forward motion to the office. John did the same, catching Tony's eye as he did. The preacher looked concerned, but not enough to hang up the phone. John took that as a good sign.

"Paul? Did you hear me?" Tony called out once more as the men were almost to the steps.

"Is he talking to me?" Paul asked John. "All I hear is blah, blah, blah, I'm an idiot, blah, blah, blah."

John smiled, but only from worry. Obviously, relations between the two men were strained more than ever. Deep down, John kicked himself for returning to the lair of the beast, no matter if it was the Spirit of God who sent him.

♦

Paul entered the small, oak-paneled office with John close behind. He gestured for the big man to have a seat in the sturdier of the two chairs, an ancient upholstered armchair. It creaked under the giant's weight, but held. Paul leaned his rear on the desk edge facing Big John. He considered the giant's broad build, his compassionate face, and steel gray eyes—he still wanted him. Paul had almost killed his most precious possession. Then, he had almost alienated him forever by trying to kill his wife. Tony's accusation regarding his sanity returned to his memory and Paul swallowed hard. If he could just keep his cool until they reached Mark. He had to keep his cool… Reaching behind him, he grabbed a yellow manila envelope and tossed it to John. "We have a new job for you."

John didn't reach out his hand right away. Paul read in the big man's eyes that he saw Paul as dangerous, hungry, and *unhinged*. Paul dropped his easy grin.

"Tony and I are leaving the country. We need you to manage the estate." Paul dropped the envelope onto the desktop, tired of waiting for John to take it from his hand. "Tony thinks you wouldn't mind arranging for the lawn care, housekeeping, you know, general custodial duties. For services rendered…" Paul paused dramatically, caught John's eye and licked his lips before continuing his sentence, "we'll have two thousand dollars a month deposited into your bank account. All of the details are in that envelope. We need you to be the physical presence for the property. We hired accountants and lawyers to take care of everything else."

John nodded, but hadn't spoken. Paul heard John contemplating the job offer in his mind; the big man was going to take it.

"Good," Paul said as if John had agreed aloud. "You noticed that you had to take a pay cut." John flinched and Paul smiled. "Why not? Your blood is much more valuable to us than a silly old house." Paul leaned forward, resting his palms on his thighs. They were headed out of town, maybe forever. Could he hypnotize the big man? Paul gave it his best shot. "For a thousand dollars, cold cash, right now. One more time. What do you say, Big John?"

John shook his head glancing toward the closed office door.

"I have the money right here" Paul patted his back jeans pocket. "I'm sorry for scaring you like I did Wednesday night. What do you say?" Paul stood off the desk and took one step toward Big John. So far, he hadn't said no. "I shouldn't have let my games with Tony spill over into your life. I made a mistake. I still need you, John."

"I don't know. I mean, maybe that's not such a good idea," John said aloud. In his mind, Paul heard, *One thousand dollars. Cold hard cash. Right now. What's the big deal?*

"Yeah, Big John. *What's the big deal? Just this last time.*" Paul responded to John's inner arguments and then spoke aloud in a gentle affectionate tone. "I'm going to Germany; I may never see you again. Come on. What do you say?"

"Right here? Right now? What about Tony and that girl down there?" John whispered. Paul had him on the hook, but then heard a number of disagreeing sentiments inside his mind.

"But what about the hedge? God got you out of that last scrape didn't He? And now you're going to go right back to the same sin you were delivered from before? John, stand up for yourself! You're more than food for a demon. You're a man of God. Stand up!"

Paul recognized the phrasing and cadence of speech: Tony! He looked toward the door to admonish the preacher, but John was speaking back to Tony telepathically.

"Tony? How can I hear you in my head?"

"You can choose, John. You can always choose."

Paul huffed and crossed to stand before where John sat and dropped to his knees. "John, don't listen. You can't trust him anymore." From the squat, Paul put his hands to John's knees. He hoped he would appear less intimidating and get that last hit of the man's blood. He could take it by force, but deep down, he feared Tony's reprisal. No matter how desperately he wanted his own will to be done, Tony had proven to be the stronger.

John turned his mind from Tony's instruction and looked into Paul's face. "What?"

"John, I care about you. I can't help that I'm different from everybody else. I take only what I need. Aren't you always okay afterwards? And as for Brother Tony, he's not the same man you left last week. Can't you see that he's different? You're communicating with him *telepathically.* Isn't that kind of odd?" Paul paused as his words sank into the giant's weary mind. "John, didn't your wife tell you what I did to him?"

John looked to the office door and back to Paul. *Why does he ask? And what is he trying to say about Tony?*

"I ask because we're friends. And you're my favorite..." Paul paused and listened for Tony downstairs. He had finally hung up the phone and was crossing to the stairway. He caught John's eye again and sent to his mind. *"You're Tony's type, too."*

As the truth began to sink into John's expression, Paul turned the screw as Tony's hand touched the doorknob.

"You'll need to have enough blood for both of us."

Tony pulled the door open with a jerk and John saw in Tony what Paul had been intimating. His friend's subtle, but seemingly impossible mental telepathy, his current eerie calm, and the way he had Paul a little more under his thumb...

When Paul attacked him last night, he didn't stop short. He took it all the way. He turned Tony into a... The realization was nearly enough to toss him over the edge. John squelched a scream with his big hand.

No! God, no!

Tony smiled kindly, his gaze filled with sadness. "Yes, God. Yes."

23

The Lord watches over you—
The Lord is your shade at your right hand;
The sun will not harm you by day, nor the moon by night.
The Lord will keep you from all harm...
Psalm 121:5-7

"PAUL, WHY DON'T YOU WAIT FOR ME IN THE TRUCK?" Tony walked into the office, pretending not to notice the look of horror on John's face or the look of apathy on Paul's. If Big John was going to know the truth, Paul certainly wouldn't be of any help.

"I'm not going anywhere," Paul insisted and placed himself before John's chair. "I want to see the show."

Tony took a shallow breath, readying to assert himself if necessary. With Rachel downstairs and John a few feet away, their safety was his paramount concern. He opened his hands, and gave it another try.

"Paul, please wait outside. I promise to get you to Mark as soon as I can. But we have to get away *clean*. Understand?" Tony switched to focused thought. *"The police have been to the house looking for you. They might come by here—this store is in your name."*

Paul crossed his arms at his chest. "Tell Big John." Rebellion in his voice and a smirk on his face, Paul leaned against the wall next to John. *"And if you try anything funny, I can kill him before you reach me. Got it?"*

Tony sighed and crossed to the rolling desk chair, his mouth a grim line. He flipped through the stack of papers before him thinking about how to proceed. After a long minute, Paul cleared his throat.

"Did you hear me?" he asked, scooting inches closer to John who stood with his back to the vampire, facing Tony with an expression of fear and disgust.

"Yep," Tony said, desperately praying for the next move. *Look busy, look busy,* he told himself as he neared the end of his pile. He sensed Paul getting antsy, working up a plan of his own, one with plenty of bloodshed.

"Tony—what's going on?" John asked, his voice trembling.

He knew. Tony gulped; his friend knew he was a vampire. How could he prove to the guy that he was not a monster just because Paul forced a curse on him?

"Ignoring me is not going to do anything. John and I will happily continue our business with you in here, flipping those papers like a little baby." Paul stood off the wall and with a hand on the big man's shoulder, spun him around. "What do you say, Big John? Can you help me out with that farewell kiss I requested?"

"Paul," Tony said in a low voice, "there's not going to be any kissing. You and John are through. Now, please go wait outside." Tony didn't rise from the chair as he leveled his gaze at his inhuman partner. He hoped that he looked fierce enough, but he doubted that he did. He decided to add a hidden threat. "If you need some help getting to the car, I'll be happy to assist you."

Paul laughed at first and then stopped to see if Tony was joking. *"You want me to walk out nice and easy, is that right? I could kill him before you could get across the room…"*

Before Paul finished his thought, Tony had gained his position and taken hold of his left arm. Paul's eyes widened but then a smirk spread across his face. Big John jumped at the sight and grunted with surprise, backing three heavy steps until his back was against the closed office door.

"John, I'll explain everything. Wait here."

The big man hesitated. "Tony," he said, his deep voice making the single word more a question.

Tony softened his eye, begging him to move aside and trust. Depending, Tony was sure, on their short history, John acquiesced, hugging the wall as he circled away, maintaining maximum distance between himself and Paul. Once the path opened, Tony pulled Paul's arm and walked toward the door.

He had no idea if the man would come, or if he would be able to *make* him come, but he followed his instincts. He hadn't known he could zoom across the room as he did, he'd barely even *thought* about taking a hold of Paul before he found himself right there, doing just that. Applying an angry scowl to his face that he didn't truly feel, he yanked hard on his partner's forearm.

Paul offered perfunctory resistance and when they reached the office door, Tony opened it and gently pulled Paul along behind him. Only exerting enough pressure that he thought was required, he and Paul waltzed past Rachel without raising her attention.

"I could cause quite a scene right here, couldn't I?" Paul sent over.

"And expose us both?" Tony whispered, far enough away from Rachel that she wouldn't hear. He reached the door to the stockroom and pushed it open. "Use some common sense, Paul. You act like a maniac."

Once inside in the relative privacy of the dark room, Tony stopped his forward motion and released Paul's arm.

"Look, Paul, you've won. I'll never be the same again. If you would let me explain our way out of this, we can leave, free and clear."

Paul was quiet a moment and then shook his head. "What did I win? You haven't lost anything but solid food. What do I get?"

"Me," Tony lied. He was so desperate to see Paul leave, he said the first thing that came to his head. "We're joined together—like you and Mark. I can't serve God like this, I can't serve man either. I have little else to live for than to go see Mark and find out what he thinks about all of this."

Tony waited a long minute as his explanation sunk in. He was inwardly hopeful that he might find a way for the Lord to cure him of his new malady, but for the sake of the innocents involved, he sincerely needed Paul to leave the building. Just because he couldn't find God in all of it right now, he felt sure he might find Him sooner or later. *Maybe in Germany when we have our certain battle over whether or not to inter Mark Corescu...*

"Yeah, I'm interested in finding out what Mark is thinking, too. He stopped calling me. He still talks to you, though, doesn't he?"

Tony nodded and waited again, his expression hopefully sincere and not as fearful as he felt inside. Paul sighed with a curt nod and made for the alley door. Tony headed into the store and listened for Paul's exit. When the squeaky alley door sounded, he smiled and made a beeline for the office stairs.

Tony walked past Rachel and hit the stairs running. When he entered the office, John was sitting at the desk with his head in his hands. Tony took a seat in the corner armchair and wondered where to begin. John beat him to it.

"You're a vampire."

Tony leaned over his lap. "John, I didn't do this and I would never be any danger to you, or anyone else for that matter."

John shook his head, but kept his gaze leveled on his friend. "I'm not afraid *of you,* Tony. I'm afraid *for you.* How will you continue serving God as a... *a mosquito?"* John had whispered the last word, even though it was a euphemism.

Tony shrugged. "I don't know yet, but I will. See, I was unconscious. I was protecting the innocent. I laid down my life for Opal and your baby. I thought I would wake up in the arms of Jesus." Tony's voice was melancholy and John's gaze softened with empathy.

"So this was Paul's plan, do you think? All along?"

"I don't know. Maybe." Tony looked at the planked floor. "He's not the planning type, especially lately."

Big John eyeballed Tony. *"How can he do it? How can he serve God like this? Should I be trying to destroy them both?"*

With John's private thoughts parading past Tony's consciousness, he frowned. "Don't go there, John. That kind of thinking won't get us anywhere."

"Stop peeking in my head," John said with ire. "Just because a stupid thought hits a man's head now and then, doesn't mean it's what he truly thinks or feels. You should know that." John pointed a thick finger to his head and hardened his tone further. "I'm bound to think something you don't like, so just stay out of here!"

Tony shrugged in apology. "I'm not doing it on purpose. I'm not even trying—it's like you're speaking to me aloud. I'm sorry." Tony waited for John's expression to soften, and then continued. "I thought I was a goner. I prayed to die so your family would live."

John covered his face with his hands. "I know and I feel horrible. I should have thanked you, but I have been so messed up. Geesh! I wish I'd never met you two!" John stood and walked toward the door.

"John," Tony rose and resisted the urge to jump to his friend's side and grab his arm as he had Paul's earlier. Instead, he took one step and stopped, hands open in supplication. "Wait, we need to talk. Can you give me a couple more minutes? Maybe you can help me figure this out."

John did not make a move, apparently weighing his options. Tony tried again.

"Pray with me. That isn't asking too much, is it?"

John huffed. "What can we possibly say to God? You've become an abomination." John was beyond mincing his words.

"How can you judge me so harshly? I haven't committed any sin. I need God's guidance here, more than ever. Pray with me and help me ask Him for divine insight."

The guilt trip worked. John took his hand off the doorknob and turned to face Tony fully.

"Okay. You're right. I've been jumping to conclusions." John offered a tentative smile. *"I mean, just because he's a vampire doesn't mean that he's been killing folks since last night…"*

"That's right. I don't intend to, either." Answering the big man's thoughts without realizing it, Tony went to his knees and waited for John to do the same.

"There you go again," John said, half-joking this time, and lowered his bulk to the floor. *"Don't bite me,"* John thought by reflex.

"I'm not biting anyone, John. Believe me." Tony reached out for John's hands. "I'm not turning into a monster just because the devil's trying to sink my faith." Tony closed his finger's around Big John's.

"I agree," John said with meaning, head bowed. "If anyone can lick this thing, you can."

"I appreciate that. Now listen… I've been going over this in my mind. …There are no such things as vampires." John raised his head and looked at him sideways. "Hear me out. A man made them up because at some point in the past, a demon caused a man to *appear* to be a vampire. What do you think?" Tony waited to see if John would come to a similar conclusion.

John scratched his smooth scalp and then conceded with a nod. "Go on…"

"This transfer of Paul's demon can't take hold unless I allow it."

"So you're *not* a vampire?" John asked, his voice hopeful. "Can you pray bloodlust away like a bad cold?"

"That's what I intend to find out."

John squeezed Tony's hands and they bowed in unison.

"Let us pray…"

◆

Weary and depressed, Hope sat at Glorie's kitchen table, elbows supporting her head, her eyes rimmed red with stress. Her twin's three boys played well together during the day, but by two in the afternoon, they were at each other's throats like rabid animals. Having very little experience watching children for such an extended time, Hope was going crazy, the three weeks feeling like three years. Daily meals, daily baths, daily playtime, daily TV-time, daily hugs, daily kisses—Hope pressed her face into the crook of her folded arms and screamed. For a split second she understood why her sister flipped her lid.

Stop it! There's no excuse for what she did!

Hope's unintentional rationalization gave her chills.

Is that how psychosis worked? Things get tough around a person until he or she can't take it anymore and they begin to make excuses for their behavior? So much so, that eventually, they feel the best answer is to kill their spouse or children or neighbor—whomever the cause of their trouble?

"Scary stuff," Hope whispered. Her twin had murdered at least two husbands and more than a few of her children before she was found out. Had Mark not told Hope about her sister's deeds, no one would have ever known; a consummate actress, Glorie never appeared unbalanced or even unhappy. Hope licked her lips. Her sister had been poisoning the three boys Hope babysat now. It was hard to swallow, that Hope's flesh and blood had been capable of such atrocities.

Hope rubbed her eyes and got to her feet. In minutes, she would need to prepare the kids' dinner. Hot dogs and Kraft Macaroni and Cheese proved to be the mainstays and Hope wasn't up to much more. As she pulled the franks from the freezer, the phone rang. It was Jimmy Hershey.

Please say you're coming back! she thought as she said hello.

"Hey, sis. Everything okay?" he asked and then barreled on without a reply. "I'm coming back early. The deal fell through so I'll be there in 48 hours. How you holding up? The boys behaving?"

"They're super," Hope said, rejoicing at the thought of turning over the parental reins. "I know this call is expensive, so have a safe trip home."

Jimmy spoke a few more minutes, mostly reporting on his trip. He was lonely and using her to fill-in for his dead wife.

How had he never noticed her homicidal tendencies?

When Jimmy signed off, Hope set the foodstuffs aside and ran upstairs to her borrowed bedroom. Would she scream, yell, or cry with relief? Hope flung herself onto her dead sister's guest bed and in time, did all three. When exhaustion overcame her emotions, she rolled onto her back and called Mark's name for several minutes.

She heard no reply.

24

The LORD is good to those whose hope is in Him,
To the one who seeks Him;
It is good to wait quietly for the salvation of the LORD.
Lamentations 3:25-26

PAUL'S RAUCOUS LAUGHTER FILTERED TO THE OFFICE from below. Tony and John stopped praying and looked toward the door. Rachel Fleming stood at the threshold, a look of embarrassment crossing her face as she considered the two grown men kneeling together with clasped hands. Paul's shrill and boisterous mirth grew in volume unnerving them all.

"Rachel," Tony said and got to his feet. "This must look pretty strange." John followed suit and dusted off his knees.

"This is why prayer rooms are usually locked," John said in a decent forced chuckle clapping Tony's back.

Paul's laughter continued and Tony heard his footfalls approaching the stairs. Whether he was coming to gloat over his prank of sending Rachel up at just the right moment, or to cause more trouble, Tony wasn't sure. He was more concerned with Rachel's safety and innocence—she didn't need to learn today that vampires were real.

"Oh, well…" Rachel said, a crooked grin in place. Tony squelched a tight knot of anger as Paul reached the top stair. In a split second, a dangerous psychopath would be in the room and inwardly Tony ramped up his prayers. "Mr. White said you needed me."

Rachel looked behind her and moved aside to let Paul into the office. He stood his ground and ushered her in ahead of him. Like a deer aware of a predator, she didn't fall for it.

"No, thanks, Mr. White. I'm going to split."

"No, no, no. Mr. Agricola has something wonderful planned for all four of us, right, Tony? I'm so excited! Don't you have a surprise for our friends?" Paul positioned himself between Rachel's back and the stair rail so she would have no escape other than to enter the office. He met Tony's eyes and smiled. "The doors are locked. We have the whole place to ourselves! Tell us your surprise."

"You are seriously pushing it. Turn around and you and I will leave together right now." Tony wasn't certain of his outward expression as he threatened Paul in his mind, but Rachel was still smiling and waiting to be excused. Aloud, he said, "You're such a kidder. Come on, let's go."

"No way. I want to hear the surprise. Aren't you hungry yet, little Tony?" Paul leaned closer to Rachel so his breath fell on the back of her head.

"Talk about hungry! I missed breakfast," John announced, rubbing his middle in an exaggerated fashion. "Who wants to come with me to the Waffle House?" As he spoke, John took two steps toward the doorway, as if to pass Rachel. But, already too close, she had nowhere to go. She clutched her hands to her chest and Tony sensed her rising alarm.

"John," Tony started, but John shushed him with a wave of his hand. He stopped just short of Rachel to look dead into Paul's sneering face.

"Paul, how about you? Won't you come with me? I know you're hungry. We'll leave these guys alone for a while to settle up business." John's head tilted to the side. "I'll get you the best breakfast ever."

Paul shook his head, eyes locked with Big John. "I don't know, Big John," he said and dropped his hands on Rachel's shoulders from behind. She immediately shrugged out from under his touch and crossed to stand beside Tony. Paul held up his hands. "What?"

"What's going on?" Rachel asked, her voice weak.

Tony put his hand on her shoulder for support and she stepped closer. "Ignore my brother. He has a weird sense of humor. John, head downstairs. Paul and I will be right behind you." Tony hoped that by acting normal, Paul might snap out of it and behave. It was a good wish.

"Tell them your surprise, preacher man," Paul warned, his eyes red. John bravely stepped around Rachel, put out his hand and took hold of Paul's slender forearm.

"Come on, Paul. What do you say? Join me for a bite?" John's euphemisms were crystal clear and Tony sensed a shift in Paul's thoughts.

"Yeah, okay. That sounds pretty good." Paul backed to let John pass. "We'll go get a bite." Paul had locked his gaze in Tony's and an unpleasant transmission trickled his way. *"I am done with the both of you."*

Paul turned to follow John and Tony said to Rachel, working to sound calm. "Don't come out of this room until we're gone, okay? But don't be afraid. My brother is very weird, always has been. But he's no danger to anyone," Tony lied and decided he better wrap up the excuses. "Just let me get him to the car."

Rachel offered a numb nod and Tony exited the office closing the door behind him. Halfway down the stairs, Paul stopped descending to turn and meet him. Tony took him by the arm.

"We're leaving," he said, his voice hard. "John, get the door. We're leaving thru the alley."

John scooted ahead of them, eyes wide. Tony twisted Paul's arm behind him and grabbed his other elbow as he flailed to break free.

"You'll never get me to the car," Paul hissed and stopped moving forward as they entered the stockroom. He spun out of Tony's grip and faced him, circling, hunched and ready to lunge.

"John, get Rachel out the front. I'll hold Paul here until you're both out of the building." When his giant friend hesitated, he tried again with more gusto, this time to the big man's mind. *"Now, John! I don't know how long I can hold him off!"*

John turned and left the storeroom tripping over his feet. As Paul and Tony faced off in the small lounge, Tony tried one more time to reason with the vampire.

"We can still leave together. Without any fuss. Without any fighting. Neither of us wants to get hurt, right?"

"Wrong. I'm ready to hurt you, preacher-man. I'm sick of you," Paul hissed and continued to circle Tony, awaiting his moment. "Mark and I will be together again. You can never have a part of us. I made a big mistake thinking you could ever be anything other than a nuisance."

Keys jingled in the front door lock and both vampires would have noticed. Tony thanked God; it looked like the innocents might get out unscathed. Now, he only had to deal with Paul.

"Think about what you're saying. Only minutes ago, you were sorry that you tried to kill Big John or me. You're not thinking straight." Paul had closed his ears, but Tony had to stall. "Let me help you. I'm sure I can help you get straightened out. I'm sure I…"

Paul snickered, his fingers flexed into claws. "All I want from you is your head crushed in my palms." He charged forward, but missed by a hair as Tony sidestepped his attempt. Undaunted and grinning, Paul lunged for him again.

"Paul, wait!" Tony yelped and jumped to the side a second time. For the moment at least, Paul sincerely intended to kill him—Tony read that in his bloodshot gaze. But God needed to pipe in. Tony called for help in his heart and continued to dodge Paul's mad attack attempts.

After the third lunge and duck, Tony swung at Paul as he passed, missing his head but striking the vampire's shoulder. The blow carried enough *oomph* to send the vampire stumbling backward, but he didn't lose his feet. The power at his disposal surprised Tony and by the look in Paul's face, the next time he came at him, he intended to end it. Paul's resolve noted, Tony sent up a new prayer. The sound of John's and Rachel's vehicles pulling away gave him comfort but the fight with Paul had only just begun.

"Thank you for getting them out, but Abba, Father, now help me. And help me help Paul!"

"I can't believe you're still praying," Paul said, his tone laced with scorn. "You're so utterly predictable." That said, Paul lunged for Tony's throat and this time, hit his target.

Jenn thumbed through the Barbosa file, her mind elsewhere. Across the desk, Jonah pecked away at his keyboard, pursuing safer avenues that led to safer criminals. The big lug had a lot going for him, but his disdain for adventure brought a frown. Would he really do it? Would he accept his pension and move out to the country? At the thought, Jenn's heart thumped.

What was that? she wondered, her eyes fixed on her partner's big hand rubbing his strong neck. She'd had other partners and she'd never had such a reaction to the thought of their eminent separation. The last time she felt such a surge was in college when her sweetheart left her for another woman. Was she so far gone that she'd fallen in love with Jonah? Jenn smiled and shook her head. Never happen. She had joined the force to make a difference and it was much too early to throw in the towel.

"I found a Facebook reference to a Dr. Corescu. How many

Doctor Corescu's can there be?" Jonah asked, waiting for her eyes to focus in his. Jenn startled, realized she'd been staring, and blushed.

"Oh? What's it say?" she asked. Maybe Jonah didn't notice her pink cheeks.

"Fran Booker posted, *Whatever. Lots of the ladies love Dr. Corescu.* She was responding to another woman who said before that, *your boss is so hot. I'll drop my dress for him any day.*"

"That's so wrong." Jenn shook her head. "I've got to see this guy in person." She pulled up the physician's driver's license photo on her laptop. "He looks normal, kind of dark, maybe he has a mysterious appeal that doesn't translate in 2D."

Jonah punched a few keys and nodded. "His name is Hungarian. He looks middle European, maybe from the Balkans."

"What do you know about the Balkans?" Jenn asked, smiling. Jonah had always been an enigma in the varied nature of his interests. He didn't go for sports and he didn't chase women. Instead he possessed knowledge on a wide array of subjects about which Jenn had never been curious. Had he been studying other cultures? He hadn't answered, but had returned to his typing. Jenn cleared her throat. "Well? What makes you think he's Balkan?"

"Oh, something about his brow, his dark eyes. My grandfather had a photo of one of his business partners in his barbershop and the guy looked like that. I thought he was a Gypsy, but Poppa said he had a proud history as a warrior for a landowner. A Count, no less."

Jenn laughed. "A Count? Like Dracula?" Jonah shrugged without looking up, the subject apparently closed. "Okay, Count Corescu. The name fits, eh?"

"Mm-hmm. They still have Counts in some of those areas," Jonah said and continued to type. "The government took claim to the land, but most of the time, the locals don't honor that, but instead cling to their aristocrats."

Jenn made a noise of interest and returned to the Barbosa investigation. Boring, but it was work. Jenn sighed and now and then, peeked at her partner's strong hands.

◆ ◆ ◆

His throat squeezed mercilessly in Paul's cruel grasp, Tony had a growing sense of power at his core. Blossoming from his gut, to his heart, and then up his spine, an electric surge set his nervous system vibrating with energy. With his air supply cut off, he inserted both forearms between Paul's and flung them wide; not only breaking Paul's grip, but simultaneously snapping his left ulna.

Paul screamed clutching his broken arm, his eyes wild with madness. "WHAT GOOD DID THAT DO?" he screamed, spittle flying. "IT'S HEALED ALREADY!"

Tony presented his palms and kept his voice stern but not loud. "Stop, Paul! Give it up. You'll never be stronger than us. It's no use."

"US? YOU AND WHO?" Paul responded, still shouting. He stretched out his healed arm and flexed his fist. "IT'S JUST YOU AND ME, AND I'M GOING TO RIP YOUR HEAD OFF."

"Paul, listen to yourself!" Tony added but Paul's murderous attitude seemed only to escalate. Then he had a thought—*maybe Paul's freaking out because God is trying to deliver him!* Tony changed tactics and hoped he was right. "Listen! I know why you're so enraged. I know what it is. Can I tell you? Will you listen?"

"NO!" Paul said and lunged for him again.

This time, Tony ducked below his arm and spun around to grab him from behind. Pinning his arms to his sides, he could barely keep Paul from breaking free. He spoke in his ear as calmly as he could, praying inside the whole time.

"Paul, it's the Holy Spirit. He's here right now trying to break through your defenses. Remember... Remember... you must have known Him in your youth. Think back..."

Paul screamed like a banshee and bent his knees. With all his strength, he pushed upward and Tony released and leapt back.

"SAY GOOD BYE," he screamed. "After you're dead, I'll go after that disgusting woman you hired. I will eat her up. And then John and his stupid wife..." Paul's breath caught, his respirations hyping. "I'll make a clean sweep. I'll start over. I'll revive my master by myself and never go near another stupid preacher again!" Paul made a half-grab and Tony stepped aside.

"Paul, listen! Mark is a preacher. He's a *priest,* for heaven's sake. He's not going to put up with this attitude any more than I will." Tony noted the pain in Paul's eyes as he was forced to agree. Turning the knife, Tony continued in a plaintive tone. "Let me help you. Your mind is running wild—I can share with you the greatest gift of all. God's love and God's peace."

"Let that be your last sermon, preacher-man," Paul sent telepathically. Growling low in his throat, he attacked in a blur of movement, again closing strong fingers around Tony's throat.

Tony gasped and dropped to his knees. Twisting his torso to the right, he brought Paul down to the floor with him. As Paul screamed with fury, the heavy steel door that led to the alley opened and spilled bright light into the dark storeroom. Paul and Tony both froze with surprise and gawked at the uniformed figure filling the doorway.

"Hey, guys, break it up…" A tall stout sheriff's deputy in a drab brown uniform stepped into the room from the alley, his flashlight handle still upraised where he had used it to push open the door. His eyes focused on the scene before him and his hand went to the butt of his gun.

Paul and Tony each released and hopped to their feet. One quick glance at his partner, and Tony noted Paul's episode had passed, the entrance of the deputy resetting his brain.

"Oh, sorry, Deputy…" Tony stammered and opened his hands to show he was unarmed. He couldn't see the deputy's face because of the light outdoors and he didn't want the man to do anything rash. "I'm Tony Agricola and this is my brother, Paul. We own this store."

Saved! Inside, he sent up new praises to God.

◆

Paul assumed his famous little-boy face and watched the officer move all the way into the space.

"Uh-huh," the deputy said and allowed the heavy door to close behind him. "We have a little problem with the noise, fellas."

Noise? Paul narrowed his eyes. *Is that the same guy?*

To the cop, he shrugged, grabbing his attention off Tony. "We were wrestling, that's all. It's not against the law to wrestle, right?" The fury that fueled his last few minutes had dissipated and to complete the farce, he ruffled Tony's hair.

The deputy lowered his chin and took a step forward, his hand still on his hip near his gun. "You play kind of rough, don't you?"

Paul gave him a fake grin. It was him, the same deputy from Big John's, but this time, his uniform sported the Montgomery County Sheriff Department seal instead of Georgia's Muscogee County. Did he have a twin? Then Paul read his tag—*Ray*. What did it mean? He watched Tony open small talk with the guy and gathered his thoughts.

"I'm sorry about that, Deputy," Tony said surely about to iron out the mess Paul's temper created. "We'll stop. We need to lock up and head out, anyway."

Paul overheard Tony praising God in his heart as he shook the deputy's hand. When the guy looked at Paul to agree, he nodded. "Yeah, Tony, I'm ready."

"Mr. Agricola, you look familiar. Have you ever preached at the Methodist church?" The deputy turned and showed Paul his back in a dismissive gesture that tweaked Paul's interest. He watched the two men jabber and wondered anew at the guy's appearance. If he had a twin brother, they would have the same last name.

He waited for a break in the inane church chatter and asked, "Hey, do you have a brother on the force in Columbus, Georgia?"

Deputy Ray turned his head only for a miniscule eye meet and returned his focus to Tony. "Nope," he said and picked up where he and the preacher left off in their conversation.

Paul sucked his teeth, not happy about being ignored. A minute ago, he wanted with his entire being to squeeze the life out of Tony Agricola. He had the power to do that right now. He had the strength to kill the stupid cop, too. But he didn't want to. Paul found himself ecstatic that they'd been interrupted; he didn't want Tony *or* John dead. Making a generous berth around the deputy, Paul reached the exit and pulled open the door.

"I'll be in the truck," he said and left. Inside, the men continued to talk about God and church and ministry. Nothing Paul had interest in. But he was interested in the coincidences: cop comes in time to stop him from killing John; *the same cop* comes in time to stop him from killing Tony. Something wasn't right.

Five full minutes later, Tony locked the alley door and climbed into the passenger's seat. Neither spoke and Paul pulled out of the alley and onto Narrow Lane. A mile later, he had to ask.

"That man stopped me from killing John the other night."

Tony looked over with an eye raise. "Same guy?"

"Yep." Paul paused and Tony resumed looking out the windshield. His next question only worked because he'd made the preacher into his image. He cleared his throat. "Did you notice he had no odor, no blood."

"Yeah," Tony said looking front, his mind far away.

Paul nodded thinking over the past hour. Why was he so unbalanced? It was like Tony accused—he vacillated between hating and loving his preachers like a crazy person. He looked into Tony's mind and only saw him praying. With a sigh, he decided to ask the one question for which he did not want an affirmative reply.

"Hey, Tony. Is that deputy an angel?"

Tony's response was to pop out of his thoughts and look to Paul with widened eyes. Then he jerked his head backward as if to the store, but it was two blocks away and there was no patrol car in sight.

"Geez. Maybe he was," Tony replied with awe in his voice. "He did smell weird. I mean, I noticed but thought it had something to do with transforming or the like…"

Paul slowed for a red light and frowned. Mark and Tony both warned him to avoid clashing swords with God, and now he'd been face-to-face with a supernatural creature that appeared twice to rescue who Paul attempted to erase.

Tony exhaled with a *shew*. "I guess you better behave," he said, but his tone hadn't been negative. Just touched with awe and wonder.

Paul remained mum, driving them home down the windy streets, pondering the existence of angels and wondering if they would compromise. And, of course, how to defeat them.

25

For I know the plans I have for you.
Plans to prosper you and not to harm you,
Plans to give you hope and a future.
Jeremiah 29:11

TAKING HIS ADVICE, PAUL SCOUTED FOR POLICE BEFORE turning into their private drive. If the authorities were coming, they hadn't yet arrived, so Tony suggested he park close to the front steps, both of them feeling the urgency of escape.

In his bedroom, Tony packed with haste, listening out for Paul's movements in the next room. Their conversation in the truck ended with the discussion of the angels and now Tony only wanted to get to the airport and out of the country.

"We're leaving in five minutes," Paul sent to his mind, his mental intonation bossy. Tony allowed it, although the strength in his spirit had multiplied since their run-in with the deputy. If the guy had been an angel sent by God, he certainly stoked Tony's spiritual flame.

What else could it have been? The guy saved John, too. Praise the Lord!

A loud bang sounded from the hall and Tony grabbed up his case and looked out. Paul had thrown his suitcase out of his room and it lay on its side against the wall. He went to the guy's open door.

"You okay?" he asked and Paul shot him a bird while slipping on his shoes. "Okay. Five minutes," he said, his voice neutral.

Tony returned to his room to brush his teeth and hair. He marveled how God's hand had covered their recent activities. A text from Big John assured that Rachel Fleming was fine. He explained everything in such a way that she understood and had lost her worry over her new bosses. John also said he would take care of the house and make sure she got the store going while they were gone. Tony thanked him and shut off his ringer. He didn't want the police to call him, but if they did, he didn't want to be notified.

As much as he wanted to explain such providence to Paul, Tony held his tongue for fear of starting another tirade. Paul had not mentioned their latest brawl and Tony had no idea what the man was thinking. He stared at his single bag sitting ready beside the door. It was time to leave, but he was spiritually exhausted. *Maybe I could relax a moment. Just a moment…* He sat on the bed and leaned against the pillows.

"Anthony…"

Tony sat up and pressed his right hand to the side of his head. "Dr. Corescu," he said low.

"Go to Paul, establish yourself. Right now. It will go easier for you if you do…"

"What?" Still speaking in a low voice, Tony couldn't fathom the old vampire's meaning. Establish himself? As what?

"As master. He is waiting for you to do so. He wonders why you haven't as of yet. You almost had him in the bookstore…"

Tony rolled to his feet and went to look in his dresser mirror. He marveled at the light emanating from his own outline and wondered again what it meant. He replied to the vampire in his mind simultaneously trying to shield it from Paul. *"I beg to differ. I was toast."*

"You were doing fine. Paul could never defeat you. Plus, I was with you. I was going to help you, but you had another there, didn't you?"

Tony agreed he'd had divine aid, but he'd been frightened to the core. The disturbing memory of that last second floated to Tony's mind when Paul took him by the throat. It might have been the end…

"My son is coming."

The raspy mental voice picked up the pace as stealthy footsteps sounded in the hall.

"Remember how he was subdued that night at my house. Remember. I will be with you. Subdue him and he'll follow you anywhere. Lead him here and we'll deal with him together."

With an audible "pop," the connection was severed and Tony looked up to his closed bedroom door. Paul was outside, leaning in, eavesdropping. His telepathic link with the man had resumed so Tony could nearly *see* what Paul was seeing… his face to the *outside* of Tony's bedroom door. Also, he could tell by the confusion in his partner's mind that he hadn't heard much.

"Come in." Tony stood as tall as 5'8" allowed and tried to smile. *Subdue him…*

His mind raced through the night at Corescu's house to recall how Paul was conquered that evening. The doctor intimated Tony could perform a similar trick.

But it's such a blur…

Tony had been almost killed—*twice*. He didn't pay much attention to what the vampires were up to while they were trying to terminate his life.

Subdue him and it will go better for you…

"What are you and Mark talking about?" Paul asked and sauntered in. He joined Tony at the mirror and they both looked at their reflections, standing side by side. "Did you tell him what happened at the store? Like how I almost popped your head off."

"He knows all about it and he's worried about you." Tony met Paul's eyes in the mirror and held his gaze. "Mark wants us there in one piece and you're behaving so irrationally, we might not make it." A tinge of repentance flashed in Paul's demeanor and Tony softened his expression to help him along. "What do you think?"

"Yeah," Paul agreed, "I'm not feeling normal."

"What do you feel? Maybe I can help," Tony prodded.

Paul shook his head. "I feel like I'm starving. I mean, *all the time*. And I'm bored. Bored to death. Sometimes my head feels as if it's going to explode. I don't like it. It's not supposed to be like this." Paul's shoulders drooped. "I want things back the way they were."

Tony offered a commiserating grunt and Paul walked away to sit on the edge of the bed. He watched the vampire's face, his countenance becoming more serene.

"Are you doing this?" Tony asked the doctor but heard no reply. Either way, Tony allowed it, because *something* was working and Paul continued to spiral into a new state of calm.

"I'm tired of squaring off with you," Paul said, his voice woeful. "I miss Mark, I miss him bad. I want to rewind this past year."

"I know," Tony said low and sat near him on the bed's corner. "We're gonna have to press on and get to the end. I don't have any idea what's in store, but I promise that we'll handle it together. I'm not leaving your side until whatever happens is done."

Paul looked up to catch Tony's eye. "I was so happy to see you at my apartment that first night… so relieved." The vampire's mind sent directly after, *"What happened? Why are we constantly at each other's throats?"*

Tony touched his arm, meeting his eye sideways on the bed. Paul had dropped the last of his flimsy telepathic block and he offered a weary smile. "You have to relinquish control," Tony said, surprised he didn't get an instant argument. "Until we see your master again, you have to let me call the shots."

Would he agree or would he fly into a rage like times past? Tony attempted to hypnotize Paul but had no idea what he was doing or how it would work; it simply occurred to him to try. He watched Paul's reactions, ready for anything, but eventually, without fuss, Paul turned his head and looked out the window.

"Paul, I've become your superior. I know you've sensed it." Tony spoke softly, waiting for the bomb to explode. So far, nothing. *"Are you going to let me lead you to Mark? I can, you know."* With a little focused telepathy, Tony finally got Paul to look him in the face.

"It's not fair." Paul fell back, lying cross-wise on the bed, his knees hanging over the edge.

A rush of empathy saturated Tony's being and he turned at the waist to put his hand on Paul's head. "No, none of it is fair, little Paulie."

In a wholly uncommon behavior, Tony stroked the vampire's crown. The Halloween dye had faded and Paul's summer-blond hair color had returned. Within moments, Tony began to feel disconnected and dizzy, sensing Corescu working his will through Tony bit by bit.

Paul closed his eyes at Tony's touch. *"I don't want to hurt you or my giant..."*

"I know. And I don't want to argue anymore. You and I are a team. We're brothers. We're going to work it out." Tony continued to stroke Paul's hair and speak to his mind, allowing the doctor to continue his magic through his hands.

"You reminded me of Mark just now," Paul said in a dreamy voice and Tony joined his gaze as he reopened his eyes.

Tony made a small nod and inside, Mark urged him to pull the guy into a hug. *"You're pushing it, Doctor. He's fine..."* Tony returned across the miles using new skills to prevent Paul overhearing.

"Trust me." The sentiment filtered in without words and because he'd submitted his will, Tony's body began the move on its own. Tony leaned forward to lift Paul into his arms in an awkward, manly embrace. The vampire he lived with didn't resist. As if expecting the move, Paul wrapped his long arms around Tony and clasped his hand's at Tony's mid-back.

"I know Mark is making you do this, but it's nice," Paul said low. "And yes, I agree with you. I need to let you lead, at least until we get to Mark. I'll behave. You'll see."

Tony held the movement another long moment marveling at the turn of events. The beast had been tamed. For the first time in months, Tony burned with real hope. The doctor's ethereal presence slipped loose and Tony sensed they were alone. Inside, he pondered God's providence and as if in response, his stomach growled. Low, longer, and then loud enough to break their hug.

Paul met his eye, rolling in his lips. "We better go."

Tony stood and led the way to the door happy the guy resisted a remark. *I'm not drinking any blood,* he said inside as his hunger developed the face of a poisonous snake ready to strike.

Downstairs the clock chimed and they moved in unison. Paul reached the front door first and pulled the knob, stepping aside for Tony to exit ahead of him. With a mischievous timbre, he warbled, "After you, *Master.*"

Tony peeked at his expression and caught his humor. This was good. Two hours to catch their flight and the vampire had found his smile. Tony hoped it would stick.

◆◆◆

Jonah answered his cell sideways, his face to the computer monitor. Nothing had happened with the Barbosa case and when his friend from Montgomery PD said hello, he snapped his fingers in Jennifer's direction.

"Andy! Anything to report?"

"I have good news and bad news," Kranchez said, moving on without awaiting small talk. "Good news is that there was a white Tahoe at your guy's place and one of the uniforms spotted Agricola walking through the yard. That was this morning. No sign of Paul Black, a.k.a Saul White."

"And the bad news?" Jonah asked, his partner now following the conversation with interest.

"'Member I told you that our captain wouldn't put any real hours on staking out this man's house? Well, today your White/Black character was downgraded. We were looking for a repeat offender in the Town Square Mall batteries, and a witness just made a positive ID on a guy we have in lock-up. That put your guy at a single assault. I'm afraid with three homicides and the mess from the tornado that hit Clanton, your guy has fallen to the bottom of the list. I was thinking about running by his house for you now. Maybe I can eyeball his truck. I'm about to be off the clock anyway."

Jonah grunted an acknowledgement and Jennifer jumped up to jog to Jonah's side.

"Wait, Andy, it's Jenn. We can be there in two hours," she said speaking into Jonah's cell speaker. He pushed it her way, but she ignored his offer. "Is there any way you could watch him 'til we get there?" To Jonah, she whispered, "Just this one last move, then we'll drop it. If it doesn't pan out, we'll close it for good. Okay?"

"I reckon I could watch him for two hours," Kranchez said. "I'll meet ya in front of his place unless you hear something new."

Jennifer gave Jonah the thumbs up. "We owe you one. See ya in two. Over and out." Jenn returned to her chair and grabbed her windbreaker. "Come on, partner. Let's nab is a bad guy!"

Jonah had no argument. He pulled on his jacket with a peek at the captain's office. The lights were out. Perfect time to slip away without questions.

On the way to the elevator, his partner elbowed his arm. "Try Agricola. Maybe he'll tell you what he's up to."

Jonah huffed a laugh and found the number. She was right, couldn't hurt to ask. The phone rang as they walked to the garage. The pep in his partner's step made him smile and he didn't mind that it was a hopeless homicide case that made her happy.

"This is Tony."

"Mr. Agricola? Detective Miller. We spoke the other day regarding Connie Nixon?" Jonah grinned, surprised the man answered.

"Sure, Detective. How is your investigation going?"

They had slipped into the Cutlass and he didn't start the ignition so his partner could overhear Agricola's end.

"Still working on it," Jonah replied. "Say, I'm heading into Montgomery. Can I meet you somewhere? I'd like to ask you a few more questions." Jonah sensed his partner's skepticism but she was grinning and nodding at his offer.

"Well, that might be kind of tricky. I'm about to get on a plane. I'll call you when I get back, if you want."

Jennifer's eyes widened in his gaze. "We can't hold him," he whispered to her and she gave him a lazy eye, probably to prod the guy some more. He cleared his throat.

"Listen, Tony, I'd consider it a great personal favor from one believer to another if you'd take a later flight and wait for me at the airport. There are a few loose ends we need to tie up." Maybe the man's guilty conscience would kick in like before. Jonah waited as the guy chewed his reply.

"I'm sorry, Detective, but I have a mission to carry out just like you have. God has put me on this track. He did it. Not me. I didn't choose any of it. But I'm a willing bondservant and I'm going to follow this trial through to the end..."

Jonah averted his gaze to the dashboard as Jennifer huffed in her seat. Agricola continued, his voice sincere.

"Do I feel bad about leaving you with a dead man and no answers? Yes. But I had nothing to do with that man's death. And I promise that before God. I can do nothing about your problems. I have to complete my mission. When and if I make it back, I'll call you and see if I can be of any further service. I'm sorry I couldn't be more help."

Jonah didn't reply right away. Agricola mentioned only one dead man and one missing man. That could mean he knew the whereabouts of two of the men Jonah sought. Add to that, one of those two killed Nixon. Jonah jumped in with that in mind.

"I appreciate your position, Mr. Agricola, really I do. But just now you indicated that you know where two of my missing persons are. Would that be Paul Black and Dr. Mark Corescu?"

Silence on the line and Jonah thought he heard another man's voice muffled nearby. Finally, Agricola replied, his voice more hurried.

"Detective Miller, I can honestly say I do not know where the doctor is. I seriously doubt that your superiors will bankroll your transcontinental pursuit of an innocent small-town preacher, and I think as a man of God you might just take my advice and let it go."

"Mr. Agricola—" Jonah said and was cut off.

"No, listen," the polite voice continued. *"I have my mission and you have yours. I don't think yours intersects with mine. Maybe it never should have. Think of all the unhappy coincidences that kept us apart. Maybe man put you in the way of my task and God has kept you out. Kept you safe."*

"That's pretty presumptuous, Mr. Agricola, don't you think?" Jonah said curious of the inflection the man put on his last word.

"Not at all. When I look at you in the spirit, I see a man raising his fists to the heavens and complaining because God continually foils your efforts to nab Paul. But if you could see yourself... step back and think about it. Is it God who compels you and your partner to hunt us down? Or is it your flesh?"

Jennifer growled and sent Jonah a new glare but he did not meet her eye. Jennifer didn't understand the God-talk Agricola spouted, but it made sense. *Aren't I really chasing this case for her?* Had God been the

One who killed the case in Jonah's spirit as well as for the captain? He returned to the call, happy the man hadn't disconnected.

"Mr. Agricola, I think I know what you're trying to say, but let me ask you a question. We think Paul Black murdered Connie Nixon in cold blood and left his body to rot in the woods off I-65. We have evidence he also attacked with intent to kill an evangelist in Montgomery. There's no telling what other mischief he's been party to. Are you telling me that you are taking care of this problem yourself? For God?"

Jennifer was having a fit trying to understand what was going on, but he had to let her stew.

"That's precisely what I'm saying. I have to go. The plane's loading. Pray for us. God bless." The line went dead and Jonah didn't speak for several long moments. Jennifer slapped her thighs and then the dashboard to get his attention.

"Jonah! What the hell was that?"

"Jenn…" Jonah raised his eyes to the upcoming exit sign and made a mental note to turn around. "We're going back. I can't prove any of it, but I think Agricola and Paul Black are boarding a plane, headed out of the country. He was being vague, but I get the feeling he is going to take care of Paul Black himself. He thinks he's on a mission from God."

"He's gonna kill him?" Jennifer asked, the answer in her eyes.

"Seems like what he was intimating. Nothing concrete to hang a warrant on, though." Jonah didn't need to justify anything, his partner's eyes said she was done with it. He gave a thoughtful sigh and added, "I'm pretty sure by the way he guarded his words that Black is with him."

"What a turd. After all our hard work."

"I'll put it all in my report and you *did* find out who killed Connie Nixon. That was good detective work."

"Hmph. I did no such thing. Lab matches, that's all. Nice try."

"The case is solved. Paul Black will go on the Wanted list. If he ever sets foot back into the country and surfaces, we have his prints and a particularly specific DNA sample to boot. We have done a good deed. Let's be happy and move on." Jonah didn't feel anything but cautious closure and his partner fell quiet on her side of the car. They rode without speaking for several miles and when she did speak again, she sounded like her old self.

"We solved the crime. Lack of Departmental support is to blame for not arresting that psycho. That's what *my* report's gonna read." She allowed a defined pause before adding, "My *final* report."

Jonah flashed her a look, eyebrows raised.

"Yep," Jenn replied and looked out the windshield.

Jonah nodded, holding back the question that tickled his tongue: would she come with him? Instead, he scratched his head and gave her a wink. "Did you think any more on your Count Corescu theory?"

Jenn's face was blank and then a smile crept in. "You mean, where did all the missing blood go? I don't think a Count Corescu theory would fly with the brass."

Jonah chuckled. "I'm not saying he's a vampire, but kick it around. Dead bodies piled up over decades, each one missing blood, some cases had a missing persons attached. It'd make a great novel."

Jenn laughed. "So, you're a writer, too?" She looked at her fingers and counted off. "You're a top-notch detective, a walking encyclopedia, a wannabe mushroom farmer, a great conversationalist, and a novelist. Pretty good for an old man."

Jonah grinned; her opinion of him was at an all-time peak. The time had come. "So, you're leaving the game? What will you do?"

Jenn looked away, a half-smile finding her mouth. "I think I'll go find me a job on a mushroom farm. I'm pretty good at shoveling manure. Did it for twelve years for the Whitford PD." Jenn turned to watch his profile and he gave a cautious smile.

"You wouldn't pull an old man's leg, would you?" She gave a tiny headshake and Jonah wiped his face with his hand, happiness threatening his tear ducts. "Okay. Mushrooms it is."

"Okay," Jennifer repeated and Jonah didn't mind if she noticed that his joy had leaked onto his cheeks.

26

May the words of my mouth and the meditation of my heart
Be pleasing in Your sight, O Lord, my Rock and my Redeemer.
Psalm 19:14

THE FLIGHT ATTENDANT PASSED PAUL'S SEAT ON HER way to the forward vending compartment and he touched her arm. She stopped, pasted on a huge grin, and turned to face her First Class, row 2 passengers.

"What can I get for you?" Attendant June asked with a wink.

"Yes, I'm sorry to bother you again, but how long until we land?" Paul used his sweetest voice and hoped he came off charming. Tony looked like death and her eyes flitted over to him more than once.

"It's no trouble, really, Mr. White. Let's see…" June checked her watch and did the math in her head. "We'll be in the air another six hours. But don't you worry. The weather is great and the skies are smooth. Is your brother going to be okay? We have some remedies."

Paul turned to see if Tony acknowledged the question but he didn't. Pale as a ghost, the preacher stared out the window, rolling and unrolling his leather-bound Bible in his hands. Paul had bugged the woman plenty on Tony's behalf already, requesting aspirin, Dramamine, extra pillows, and a blanket, but nothing soothed the emptiness in Tony's middle.

"He'll be fine after he takes his medicine. Thanks for the extra bags…" Paul pointed to the light blue bags she had handed him an hour earlier. She nodded and continued up the aisle. Paul prodded Tony on the shoulder and spoke low in his ear. "You look pretty bad. People are starting to notice. Don't you think you had better do something about it? You might start to draw the wrong kind of attention."

"Huh?" Tony responded without turning from the window.

Paul prodded him again. After the third rough shove, the preacher wearily met his gaze.

"People are starting to stare. You'll go crazy if you don't do something soon.

We won't land for another six hours…" Paul watched Tony's pained expression as his telepathic reiteration sunk in.

"Give me those peanuts," Tony rasped. In his peripheral vision, Paul caught five heads turning at the inhuman sound of the guy's voice. Tony would need to do something and soon.

Paul handed the nuts over, whispering through a tight smile, "You can't eat these, preacher-man. They won't stay down."

Tony glared, took the packet and turned his face out the window.

"Don't say I didn't warn you." Paul crossed his arms and leaned back, getting ready for the show.

♦

Tony ripped open the bag and popped the entire contents into his mouth. *All I need is protein…* He chewed the nuts well and swallowed. It had been thirty hours since Paul changed his life forever—*again*—and he hadn't had anything to eat since. Barely sixty seconds later, his stomach cramped with enough ferocity that he doubled over clutching his middle. A tiny groan escaped his lips, and in his mind, he yelled to Paul for the airsickness bag.

"I told you," Paul said handing it over. "What are you going to try next? Coffee and pound cake?" Paul clapped Tony's back as he gagged. *"You need blood…"*

"No!" Telepathically replying, Tony spit peanuts into his bag. His violent retching done, he wiped his mouth with his hand. Dropping the Bible into his seat, he stood and lurched into the aisle toward the toilet two rows ahead.

"Let me help you," Paul sent over but Tony didn't respond. He barely heard him anyway, the pain in his gut so acute. He fell into the tiny restroom, slammed the narrow door, and leaned onto the small metallic counter that graced the sink. In the mirror, he saw what the attendant and Paul had been trying to tell him: he looked like death. Sallow and sagging skin surrounded eyes like pits. How could he make it six more hours?

I'm not going to make it. Tony squeezed his eyes against the pain and crumpled to the floor. He had no room for his legs to stretch out, so he sat on his rear folding his knees to his chin. *What was I thinking? This pain is unbearable. I think I'm dying…*

A dull thumping reached his ears. Past the bellow of the plane's engines, beyond the roar of the wind outside, Tony heard his heart. Then, other hearts reached his awareness. To his horror, his inner eye visualized millions of blood corpuscles zooming through the systems of every passenger on board.

What do I do? What do I do? Verses of Scripture came to mind, but he couldn't grasp them. Paul rapped on the door, and Tony turned the lever without rising from the floor. Paul closed them in. The lavatory was made for one, so to fit, he leaned his buttocks against the opposite wall, his feet interlaced with Tony's on the linoleum floor.

"What are you going to do?" Paul asked, his sympathy evident. "We're thirty thousand feet up."

"I don't know. I don't know. I think I'm going to die." Tony's words came out in gasps and he shivered as a new wave of nausea overcame him. His vision dimmed and he covered his face with his hands.

Paul huffed with a sideways grin. "Just get up." His partner pulled Tony up with strong hands and pressed him against the sink counter so they stood face to face. "Put your arm around me like this." Tony would do nothing for himself, so Paul took his wrist and flipped Tony's arm so that it lay across his shoulder.

"No. Just leave me alone. I want to die…" Paul's intentions were clear and Tony watched through a haze as the vampire lifted an ink pen from his pocket and put the tip to his throat. He pressed it into his skin cupping Tony's head with his free hand.

"Stop being such a moron and drink." Paul forced Tony's face to the wound, but Tony didn't resist. His mind continued to loop the word no, but his tongue found the puncture and he latched on tight.

Instantly, a sense of calm rushed into his mind and body and Tony lifted his opposite arm to wrap Paul into an embrace. Holding their bodies together, he winced as inside his gums, an itch grew and his eyeteeth extended. He plunged them into the skin of Paul's throat and improved the volume.

"Hah!" Paul said with a laugh, but Tony didn't attend him. The vampire's blood coated his entire being with pleasure. Even when he was no longer hungry, he was still there, taking from a monster the very blood that was the root of his current trouble. Only when Paul grasped him by his hair and yanked did he stop. Even then, he was terrified by the realization that though he was no longer starving, he wanted more. The demon of bloodthirst existed and was visiting Tony with veracity. With a small noise of amusement, Paul released him and Tony couldn't meet his gaze.

"There's no reason to be embarrassed," Paul whispered in the tiny restroom. "What else could we have done?"

"You could have let me die…" Tony hissed finally lifting his gaze to meet Paul's bright blue eyes. But Tony wasn't angry. The vampire had done what he thought was best.

"I'm afraid Mother June was about to call you a doctor. Do you want to be hospitalized in this new condition?"

Tony shook his head.

"I didn't think so. Move over." Paul leaned left as Tony leaned right and he examined his throat in the reflective surface. "You're tidy for a newbie."

Tony grunted, misery creeping back even though he felt better than he had in years. Paul may have done what he thought was best, but Tony felt like he had been cast out of the Garden.

Lost… forbidden fruit… I'm a monster… Why me?

He dropped his shoulders and the tiny room grew quiet as they fell into their thoughts. Both startled when a loud knock sounded on the door.

"Are you okay? Do you need a doctor?" a female voice asked.

"We're fine, thank you. Coming out," Paul chirped through the door. He lowered his voice and took a hold of Tony's chin. "You look marvelous. See? It's no big deal."

Tony turned to see himself in the mirror and he saw that Paul was right. He looked better than he had in weeks. In fact, his face looked almost radiant. It reminded him of the glory of God.

"Hmmm, that's interesting," Paul replied eavesdropping on Tony's unveiled thoughts. "Maybe your god was a vampire."

"Don't go there." Tony's steely voice prompted Paul to open the door and step out.

"Ease up, I was just joking."

Tony stared at his reflection another long moment, occasionally pressing his cheeks and forehead as if it were all an illusion.

What have I done? I have sinned against God. The blood is the life…the blood is the life…do not drink the blood, for in the blood is the life.

Bible verses bubbled to the surface as a panic rose in his heart. In the Bible, every Pagan religion had blood sacrifices. Every demon craved human blood.

Because the blood is the life… What have I done?

He'd been half-dead the first time Paul forced him to drink his blood. This time? He hadn't resisted at all.

27

He will guard the feet of His saints,
But the wicked will be silent in darkness.
For by strength no man shall prevail.
1 Samuel 2:9

"IT IS NOT ENTIRELY UNPLEASANT. I HAVE MANY DREAMS, and most of them are quite heavenly…"

Weary but patient, Tony listened to Dr. Corescu in his mind, unable to ignore the connection. When he relinquished his will to the man to help Paul, he'd opened a nonstop tether between their minds. But it was one-way; the doctor could say *howdy* whenever he desired, but Tony lacked that power. Perhaps it had something to do with the age of the old vampire, but whatever the cause, he'd been sharing information about his time in country to Tony's mind since their plane landed.

"We'll come out in the morning. We have to wait for daybreak." Tony peeked out the huge picture window of their hotel room in Mausberg, Germany, the closest village to the estate Corescu owned in the protected forest. *"Paul's gone out, as I'm sure you know."*

Night had fallen and Paul was hunting. Tony had not even tried to stop him. How could he? It was his fault that Paul was on empty.

"He's fine. Can you see him?"

"Yes, I see him on a barstool in a dark pub. He's thinking about you." Tony pulled his mind away from Paul and sheltered his thoughts. Paul was sensitive to mental intrusion and Tony was trying his best to stay out of his way.

"Why are you afraid of him? He can't harm you."

"I'm not afraid of him. I'm afraid of myself with him," Tony said in the darkening room. He was growing sleepy and he wondered if Corescu would allow him to rest. "I'm trying to work this out. I'm not up to killing him if he defies me."

"Funny, isn't it? A year ago, you were trying to tell me how to live this life without sustenance and how to keep the commandments of God. I tell you, I have it figured out."

"Okay, you have said that many times these last few hours. What have you figured out?" Tony transmitted, then closed his eyes as he lay back onto the comfortable bed. He had no confidence the doctor had discovered a solution this soon.

"All three of us will go in the ground. We can't have Paul out in the world killing indiscriminately and you and I are not comfortable drinking blood to survive. You can make all of the necessary arrangements easily enough."

Tony didn't respond, not liking the suggestion. Didn't God promise to use him in this life? Use him to minister to His people? To spread the Gospel to the nations? If so, it could not be God's will that he go underground. That end might be fitting for the doctor or Paul, but it didn't sound right for Tony.

"I know what you're going through, but there's no other way. Like me, you are detestable now. A monster. How can God use you in this state?"

Tony thought that the doctor's mental voice sounded hopeful. Even *wishful.* He wanted very much for Tony to figure out a way to live out their lives above ground and with humanity. But so far, Tony had no insight on the matter.

"I don't know, but God has something planned. He likes to keep me in the dark until the last moment. I trust Him to show me what to do." Tony rolled onto his side. The sky was black now and he didn't want to think about Paul.

"Keep your eye on him. He hasn't moved from that spot. Some of the locals are getting curious. Pretty soon, one of them is going to approach him."

"That's what he wants," Tony said with no energy in his voice. He sighed and added, "You watch him, Doctor. I brought him here for *you* to deal with. I'm going to sleep. Please let me sleep." Tony sensed the other man's mind disentangle and slither away, and in less than sixty seconds, he fell fast asleep.

◆ ◆ ◆

The 747's wheels hit the rough tarmac jostling Hope from her restless nap. She gripped the armrests and peered out the window. Haze or smog blocked what might have been a beautiful view of the countryside beyond the airport. Hope diverted her attention from the disappointing panorama to the attendants preparing the passengers to disembark.

"*Erfassen sie bitte ihr gepäck.* Ladies and gentlemen, please gather your bags."

Hope stood as the plane came to a halt alongside the gate ramp and made a bid for her carryon. Traveling light, she'd packed a large canvas bag to serve as her purse and suitcase. With a hundred other travelers, she left the plane and mixed on to the busy concourse. German-language signs filled her vision and only every third offered a translation in English. Thankfully, the signs that led her toward the taxi-stand were in her native tongue often enough that she arrived with little trouble.

Finding a cabbie turned out to be very easy. As soon as she stepped to the curb, three swarthy drivers from three different cars approached and began speaking to her in thick dialects. Hope reached into her pocket and pulled out her wallet. "Whoever speaks the best English is my driver."

All three men then offered her a ride in English, but one of them reached for her carryon and tipped his grimy hat. "My lovely *fraulein*, let me help you with your bag. These scum..." the man gestured to the other men. "They rob you. Me? You can trust."

"Thank you," Hope said while the other men snarled and huffed to the next potential fare. Hope followed her driver to his cab and allowed him to open her door. "I need you to take me to the best hotel in Mausberg where lots of people speak English."

"Of course, fraulein."

Hope settled into the taxi's relatively clean backseat and flipped through her canvas satchel. One change of clothes in two gallon-sized zip-loc bags, her wallet full of credit cards and a fair supply of Euro dollars, a few toiletries, and a small five-by-seven First Aid kit. Knowing she might have to hike into the country to find Mark, she figured she might need a Band-Aid or two. Anthony's associate, John Jenkins, had told her by phone that the man she sought was in a wilderness. Hope's plan included coaxing a local resident, business owner, or even Realtor to tell her how to find Mark's property. Someone in town at least *knows* about such a large single-owner property. Hope counted on her internal logic and closed her bag. Less than thirty minutes later, the cab slowed before a squat multi-level stone hostel landscaped with flowering plants.

"Fraulein, this hotel is the best. You will like it here." The German driver pulled to the curb and hopped from the car. He opened her door with flair and offered to carry her bag into the hotel.

"No, thank you," Hope said and pressed more than enough money into his calloused hand. He grinned, revealing all five teeth.

"*Danke schoen, fraulein.* Thank you!"

Hope nodded and faced the hotel. Above the door, carved into a thick wooden plaque, read *Frische Rosen.* She discerned the word "rose" since the sign was encircled by a wreath of the dried flowers. The thing Hope hated most about world travel was not being able to understand the language.

A snappily-dressed doorman opened the door and she crossed to the counter. Night had fallen and she wanted to set off for Mark's at first light. There were phone calls to make and she needed a helpful German who understood her every word. She couldn't waste a single moment babbling about trying to find someone who spoke English. At the check-in counter, she asked point-blank for an interpreter. "…And I will pay whatever it costs."

The woman behind the counter picked up the phone. After uttering a few incoherent words in German, she pointed to a chair in the lobby. Hope thanked her and waited with her bag on her lap.

That was easy enough. Thank goodness that cabbie brought me to a tourist-friendly hotel. I'll bet they're not all like this.

"Madam? My name is Frederick Being. What can I do for you?"

Hope offered a relieved smile. He was fiftyish with a round belly, with short blond hair, and sparkling blue eyes. She stood and shook his hand.

"Hello. Thank goodness you speak English. Are you from the States?"

"Oh, what a compliment! No, I am from Hungary, raised in Berlin. I'm a professional interpreter employed by the city." Frederick reached for Hope's bag. "Would you like to see your room first?"

Hope thought a minute and shook her head. "No, this is what I need first." She reached into her pocket and handed the man a wad of folded bills. "Take this as a tip. I'll pay whatever the regular fee is too." He started to refuse and she barreled ahead. "No, *please.* I need some really good help right now, and it is worth all the money I have to get this business done as soon as possible."

"Yes, madam, I understand." Frederick palmed the money and shoved it into his own pocket without counting it. "I am all yours. What do you need?"

"Okay. A friend of mine owns a house in the Black Forest. He has no phone and I don't know exactly where he is. But I know his name and there's a good chance the locals know of him. I need to get that address. Then I need to arrange transportation to see him at first light."

Frederick Being gestured toward a hallway. "This way, madam. Come into my office. All this I can help you with."

Hope smiled and followed ecstatic with her luck.

Thank goodness! Is God helping me?

She didn't know, but appreciated it nonetheless.

Mausberg had one pub and Paul hoped to find his particular brand of entertainment inside. Selecting an empty barstool, he smiled at the barkeep and motioned for a beer. He didn't understand most of what was said, but every eye in the place watched him. He was a foreigner and that made him universally interesting. *All the more chance that they'll come over for some lively conversation,* he thought and accepted the local brew that the bartender delivered.

Paul held his stein with both hands and peered into the frothy liquid. The place was alive with boisterous locals and more than a few dark-skinned tourists. Several different languages and dialects were being spoken but none of them English.

Three men of German descent who had been eyeballing him for some time gathered their courage to approach. One of them hooked his thumb toward Paul slurring a epitaph that didn't take a linguist to decipher. Paul ignored them, a half-smile on his face, and continued to stare into his mug. After a few more moments, one of the three men—the short, squat one with the grimy bandage on one hand—prodded his shoulder.

"*Amerikanisch?*" A thick accent mangled his short question, and Paul assumed a serious expression.

"I am," he replied without smiling.

The thug breathed, "*Sie sind in meinem sitz,*" then translated, "You..." then with a rap to his chest he finished his sentence, "...Seat."

Paul wrinkled his nose with humor at the oldest way to start a bar fight. He would appear an easy target and two additional men ambled close with a drunken wobble and backed up their friend, cursing in their language. When the barkeep warned them in German and broken English to leave, Paul slipped off his stool.

"Maybe we should take this outside."

Whether they understood his English or his intentions, the three brutes nodded and followed Paul toward the door. *This ought to be fun,* Paul thought as he stepped into the cool night. None of the other patrons turned to see what might become of the slender blond American being bullied by the native roughnecks.

No one spoke until all four men reached the back yard area of the establishment. The structure abutted a thick forest and walking in the lead, Paul stopped before the tree line and turned. The leader with the bandaged hand caught up with Paul and grasped his shoulder. He spoke insults in his own tongue and Paul read their objectives in their inebriated minds. Not quite in the shadows enough for his needs, Paul shrugged loose of the guy's grip and took a wild swing, purposefully missing the man's jaw. The guy dodged and surged, and Paul pretended to run for the protection of the trees. In another few strides, Paul slipped into the dark seclusion of the forest where he would have privacy.

The two other men looked warily around for witnesses and grinned as they entered the woods after him. When everyone was in the dark forest, he turned to face the men forming a menacing circle.

Considering him easy prey, the taller of the three men stepped to the forefront and pulled out a switchblade that glimmered in the moonlight. Paul decided to take him first. The men didn't expect much of a fight, so their jaws dropped when Paul stepped forward in a blur, grabbed the tall man by the throat with both hands, and snapped his neck. The big man hit the ground and Paul winked at the two men remaining.

After a moment of paralyzed shock, these lunged at Paul in unison. When he ducked, both thugs stumbled past, again misjudging their intended victim's agility. Paul sought them out—who was weaker? He chose the man on his right, a roguish character of medium build with a scar through one eyebrow. This one's mind sent a beacon of cowardice, especially now that their largest pal had been dispensed. With a renewed grin, Paul zoomed around Scar-face and in an instant, held his head firmly between his palms. He shouted out in his mother tongue and Paul twisted his head nearly from his body.

The third man yelped and turned to run, but did not complete a single stride. Paul wrapped him up from behind, an arm holding him around the chest and his hand clamped over the man's mouth.

"Awww, come on. I'm not going to break *your* neck. Honest…" Paul toyed with him a moment longer, enjoying his fear. He moved to speak right against his ear. "What's the German word for 'vampire'?"

The bully's lips moved beneath his palm and Paul squeaked him a little room to say, *"Bitte! Bitte töten Sie mich nicht!"*[1]

Paul dropped his palm entirely and spun the man in his grip. The guy was his height and they stood eye-to-eye. He begged again in German, his voice small and filled with dread. Paul yanked him close, his mouth finding his favorite spot for a killing draw. His victim gagged and his hands gripped Paul's biceps as his fangs made their mark. With his voice barely audible, the man uttered one last word and it was one Paul understood.

"Vampyr…"

"Ja," Paul answered in his mind as the man expired in his grip. When Paul dropped the dead man to the forest floor, he trained his eyes to the clear night sky. He felt glorious, more fulfilled than he had in months.

"You should have been here, Tony. There was enough for both of us…" He received no reply from his partner at the hotel. His gaze fell to his victims and he pictured his master. *"Mark, there would've been enough for us all…"*

From his crumbling resting place, his old master sent a reply; a single word, but it gave him hope. *"Hurry,"* the voice of his beloved Mark urged from deep in the forest.

Paul nudged the nearest corpse with his toe and sent a new call to Tony. He would need help to clean up his mess and Tony had willingly taken the job.

♦

Tony opened his eyes in the dark, awakened from a lovely dream of days gone by, days before he met Corescu, days working in his dad's church with friends who loved the Lord. The images that crept into his more bucolic dream landscapes shocked him awake: the brutal and bloody murder of three strangers in a dark forest.

---

[1] "Please, don't kill me!"

Paul! What did you do?! He hadn't been calling the guy, but he picked up, laughing at Tony's distress.

"So this is what I have to do to get some attention! Hey, come out here and help me hide these guys."

Tony covered his face with one arm. Any policeman would connect the fair-haired American weirdo to the dead men in the woods. Wasn't the doctor supposed to be watching Paul? *"We are so close and you're taking these risks? Do you even think before you act?"*

"I was only defending myself." Paul transmitted his thoughts while dragging Scar-face deeper into the woods. Tony read his end goal—to cover them with leaves and hope to be gone before they were discovered. Tony looked to the dark ceiling.

"Do what you can. I'm going back to sleep."

Tony cut communication and shut his mental door, having no intention of helping him clean up his mistake. Maybe Mark would advise him, but Tony prayed for sleep and soon found it. Tomorrow promised to be a huge day for them all.

28

To obey is better than sacrifice,
And to heed is better than the fat of rams.
1 Samuel 15:22

THE FOLLOWING MORNING WITH PAUL WATCHING ON, Tony attempted in vain to explain their destination to the taxicab driver thru the use of a printed German-English Language Aid and an original form of sign-language.

"No, sir. We need the South end of...*Smeed.*" Tony glanced at the slip of paper in his hand. He'd scribbled the name down as Corescu spelled and pronounced it for him telepathically the night before. In the early morning light, Tony had forgotten how to pronounce it. *"Schmied?"* Tony said, trying again. He looked to Paul whose mouth curled into a smile.

Tony huffed aloud and collapsed backward into his seat. To the cabbie he pointed. "Just go. *Weitergehen.* That way!"

They had summoned the cab at 6 a.m. and it had arrived within minutes. Now, Tony was dismayed that the driver may have no idea where he wanted to go. Mark had indicated the last named street before they would have to get out and walk. The driver pulled away from the hotel porch and into the quiet street. He glanced at Tony in the rear-view mirror and winked his eye.

"I am sorry, Herr Agricola. I am having fun. I speak the English okay."

Not amused, Tony turned to gaze out the window and get a grip on his frustration. Beside him, Paul snickered.

"Herr Agricola? No buildings on that end of that road, just trees. Do you have the correct...*adresse*...er, address?" Tony nodded while still looking out the window.

The cab rolled steadily around the town, heading to the outer limits. They passed a bookstore, looking every bit like the ones back home. Instead of white walls, brown lattice covered the exterior of each building. Automobiles from many eras puttered past, and at least two gentlemen trotted by on horseback wearing the brightest red robes Tony had ever seen.

As the main drag petered out and they left town-proper, Tony narrowed his eyes at the tiny homes dotting the landscape, crawling up the hills like Billy goats. Only when the homes disappeared and the road narrowed to a grassy trail, did Tony snap out of his thoughts and think of what lay ahead.

They were in for a trying day and only God knew what would transpire once they found the doctor. Without opening his eyes, Tony apologized to the man for his rude behavior, stating that he was tired and hadn't slept well. The cabbie grunted and was silent. No one spoke the rest of the way and he was thankful. His head had begun to ache and there was a distinct rumbling deep in his gut. A rumbling not unlike the beginnings of a real hunger pang.

Mark thought to rise, but he didn't have the strength.

I never should have let myself degenerate into this condition. Now, his well-conceived plan was in danger of being altered. He began to ponder consequences and a few what-ifs came to mind right away.

Paul might overcome Tony and force me to be revived…

Tony might overcome Paul and bury me as I asked…

Then, *what if I want to be revived? What is so wrong with reliving my life? I could melt back into society. I could go back to the priesthood. I could return to medicine. Tony is going to go on. Why can't I?*

If I have changed my mind, will Tony fight me on it?

And if he challenges me, will I have the strength to have my will be done?

There were many things to consider and Mark went over each eventuality carefully as he waited for the duo to appear. Both men were reaching for him telepathically, but he shut them out, happy he still possessed the power to do so. At least so far.

The comedian taxi driver let them out at the head of a broken road and directed his fare to walk the rest of the way. The crumbling rock byway gave way to grass and then branched severely to the right.

"Which way?" Paul asked when they paused at the fork.

"This way," Tony said and started off.

Paul followed without a word.

"Watch your step. I almost slipped into that ravine and it looks like it runs right alongside this trail."

Paul stepped a little behind Tony to look into the chasm. It was over two hundred feet down and steep, possibly carved out by water at some point in history. Now it served as a booby trap for unsuspecting hikers.

If someone ever fell down there, they'd never be able to crawl out, even if they survived the fall, Paul thought to himself. *Even me. It would take even me a while to get out of there…* Stepping a closer to the edge and peering in, Tony stopped walking and came to his side.

"That's why I said watch your step," Tony said in a serious tone, overhearing Paul's thoughts. "Even if you survived the fall, the climb up would take forever…" He leaned over a smidge as Paul had, staring at endless shrubbery, copious leaf cover, and shadows. Paul leaned over another inch and with an introspective throat noise. Tony followed his gaze, also leaning a tiny bit more. "What is it? What do you see?"

"You," Paul quipped and shoved Tony as hard as he could, sending him flying a good fifteen feet before he started down. Tony's body rolled and flipped its way down the embankment until concealed by deep shrubbery. Paul made no expression but waited until the surprised screaming ceased and turned back down the path the way they were going. He got about three steps before he heard in his head what he'd been expecting.

"Paul! Come down here and help me. You could have killed me!"

Paul walked on. He thought of Tony and his righteous ways. Now he could preach to the chipmunks and birds. It would take him hours to climb out, providing he had the strength to heal his broken bones. His only fuel would be the blood he drew from Paul two days ago. Would it be enough? Paul didn't know, but he'd get to Mark first.

"How about that, God?" he said aloud in the quiet woods. "Your boy is in the ditch. Better get him out. Why don't You send that ridiculous sheriff's deputy? You're like a broken record with that guy. Now, leave me alone. I have some work to do." Paul picked up his pace laughing. He focused his energy on his master and spoke to the air, eager to hear Mark's voice, saying the words he had wanted to say months ago.

"Master! Hang on. Your salvation has arrived. We'll soon be back together. Like the old days. Let me be your Paulie again. I won't let you down …"

"*Come, then, little Paulie. You're almost here. Come to me. I will welcome you.*"

Joyful, Paul fell into a run.

John held his wife close as she sobbed. He'd taken his family to a Tennessee State Park. The luxury cabin afforded every comfort and was surrounded by the most beautiful mountains God ever created. The sliding back doors faced East and overlooked a lake, so every sunrise became a spiritual and visual blessing. The padded double hammock on the front deck meant he, his wife and son could recline in the heavenly view of the Creator's sunset. His vacation had barely begun when he decided to broach the most unpleasant topic between them: how to explain what had happened with Paul and Tony.

"This has to be a joke. I mean, Big, there's just no way." Opal didn't leave her husband's embrace, but spoke through her tears. "There's no such thing as *vampires!*"

"I know, babe, believe me, I know." Big John ran his hands through Opal's hair and kissed her head. "Do you understand now why I didn't try to explain it before? You said he sucked Tony's neck. That's about all the proof you'll get if I have my way."

John sought agreement in his bride's gaze. Her eyes were running water, but she *did* believe him on some level, and it didn't matter at this point about the semantics; she believed Paul was a killer.

"I want you to feel safe again. No more nightmares. No more crying fits. You're safe now…"

"How can you be so sure?" Opal refuted.

"He's gone. He won't be back. Trust me, it's over. I did what God wanted me to do. I'm done with them. Look…" Big John leaned out of the embrace to look Opal in the eye. "Life goes on. God protected us. We're completely safe. Okay?"

Opal nodded and snuggled back into John's strong arms. He held her a long time. Deep down, John wondered if it was truly over.

♦ ♦ ♦

Tony opened his eyes. He lay sprawled on his back, both legs bent impossibly to the side, and the hitch in his breathing told him he'd fractured several ribs. Without considering the consequence of possibly puncturing his lungs, he sat up with careful effort. He pulled the left and right thighs parallel and when satisfied that they were properly aligned, he fell back to the moist ground.

Maybe they'll heal if the bones are touching. Maybe... Jesus? Heal them for me, Your beloved son. If this new skin closes in seconds, surely bones fuse in only minutes...

Tony felt no pain and his mind ran rampant with a mixture of incoherent prayers and morbid observations of his condition. Without a doubt, if he'd been mortal, the fall would have killed him. In the same vein, his newfound *supernaturalness* actually came in handy. Tony grimaced as he recollected his abominable state, then closed his eyes to clear his mind.

Paul is going to try to raise his master from the dead. Lord, give Mark strength to fight the enemy. Forgive Paul for his misdeeds; he has no idea what he's doing...

Eventually, his frantic thoughts calmed and Tony fell fast asleep in the dark shadows of the ravine bottom. Tony dreamed and snored as his body repaired itself and night tip-toed upon the forest.

♦ ♦ ♦

Within ten minutes, Paul spied the house, obscured as it was by the dense trees enveloping it like a cloak. Night had fallen and before he set foot on the front stoop, he received a message in his mind.

"The door is locked, but press through, my son."

Paul smiled and twisted the old doorknob in his hand, simultaneously leaning into the wood with his weight. The lock gave way and the door creaked open. Paul entered, peering into the dark for the form of his master. His special vision picked up every detail in the gloom and he tried to prepare himself for what Mark might look like after so many months without sustenance. When his eyes finally rested upon his master's still form laid out on an old oak table, Paul gasped.

"Mark! What have you done?" Paul didn't approach for a few moments, but gawked, trying to discern the details from his position near the door. The once larger-than-life vampire master that commanded the universe only months ago had transformed into a husk, mere skin hanging over an impossible framework of bones. "Mark? Are you alive?" Paul asked again, his voice soft.

"Yes, Paulie. I imagine I look horrendous…"

Mark's reply came across telepathically and Paul realized he was unable to rise or speak. Paul stepped closer and his master completed his thought.

"I apologize for leaving you alone in the world. I should never have deserted you as I did. You have been making quite a mess of things out there."

"Have I done so poorly? It's not my fault…." Whining, Paul crept closer. "I was surrounded by idiots who didn't respect me or my power." Paul made it to Mark's side and peered into his sunken face.

"Why have you come?"

"To bring you back. I want to make everything like it was before. We had a good life, you and I, and we will have it again." Paul touched Mark's leathery cheek. "I don't think my blood is going to be enough. How far do you think it will take you?" As he spoke, Paul withdrew his hand and rolled up his sleeve.

"I called Tony here to put me in the ground. There is no room in the world for vampires, Paulie. You have seen this already. You will be challenged at every turn by the Creator of the universe. He has been matching you tit for tat ever since I set you loose."

"I don't care…" Paul brought his wrist to his mouth and bit down hard. "Let's see what two old monsters can accomplish before Tony's God catches up with us…"

With a seamless motion, he thrust the wound to Mark's slack mouth. Paul overheard Mark in prayer and he did not comment. His master was in no condition to refuse Paul's offer and he made no effort to do so. For several moments, nothing happened. Paul held position and watched his blood dribble over Mark's drawn lips.

"Mark, you'll…" he began, but before he could finish, his master jerked upward from his prone position and took Paul by the shoulders, his hands as claws. Paul gasped in surprise and then grew silent as Mark sought what he needed. Without ceremony, but with understood permission, Mark grasped Paul's throat with forgotten fangs. He pulled the blood with violence and sent words to his mind.

"Paulie… between us there is no God, no devil, no friends, and no foes— only the blood, and it reigns supreme."

Paul gripped Mark's rigid biceps, feeling no pain, but deep down, an irrational panic rose just as it had in the past. Somewhere, far back in his mind, he thought of Tony and how much he hated this act performed on him. Now Paul remembered why.

When it seemed the feeding would never end, Paul closed his eyes and accepted the possibility that Mark might kill him. Hadn't he been a bad creature since the night they parted ways? Maybe Mark had tricked him into coming close. Maybe if Tony had been present, they would have had that special protection from his God. Maybe if Tony had come, the two of them would have ganged up on Mark and chopped off his head.

"Stop!" Mark pulled away and laughed. Sounding more like himself, but still incredibly weak, he hushed Paul's internal whining. "Muster up some confidence! Listening to your misgivings reminds me of that poor little preacher you threw down the ravine."

Still holding onto Mark, Paul offered a half-smile. "He didn't know he could fly."

"How do you feel?" Mark supported Paul underneath his arms and watched his movements. "I just about used you up, didn't I? How do I look?"

Paul took stock of his body; besides general weakness, he felt fine. He would need to eat again right away, and Mark was far from healed. His face had filled out, but his once-penetrating eyes were sunken and almost invisible in the shadow of his brow. He didn't appear human or alive.

"You're not the man I remember." Paul looked around for a mirror.

"You forget what a marvelous creature I am. I can see myself through *your* eyes." Mark slipped off the table, balancing with care. In his mind, he was calculating how many victims he would need to be fully restored. Paul listened in and was pleased to hear Mark's opinion that Paul's blood had proven most helpful. Then he heard, *"if only Tony would be so generous..."*

"Tony won't be any help, master," Paul whispered. "With any luck, he's dead."

Mark laughed. "No, he's climbing out as we speak."

Paul gestured to the windows. "There are mortals in the forest," he offered in a soft voice. "I aim to have my old master back."

Mark's mouth turned up. "Tony is completely restored, carrying a chip on his shoulder the size of Cleveland." Mark patted Paul's back. "Let's go hunting and be restored ourselves when we face off with God. What do you say?"

"Yes," Paul said and followed Mark toward the door. Why did Mark even consider another battle? Together, they could easily destroy the preacher and be done with him forever.

"You still don't get it," his master said with a shake of the head. "You're not at war with that little man. You're at war with the Spirit inside of him. You can't win. All we can hope to accomplish is to escape with our heads."

"Then why try if we have no hope?" Sullen, Paul slowed his step as they crossed the overgrown yard.

"Because we are alive! Come. Two miles west." Mark broke into a shaky, but steady jog and disappeared into the trees. "I have been listening to a loud family of Gypsies for months. They sound delicious!"

Paul marveled at the conflict in his master's mind, wanting to please God *and* his flesh. But as they jogged through the brush side by side, his master actively put his divided heart away and sought to fill his belly. Paul contemplated another brush with Tony's God. No longer could he pretend He didn't exist; this God had real power and Tony seemed invincible. His God allowed him to be tortured, transformed, mistreated, and shoved down a cliff, but wouldn't let anyone kill him. God made no sense. He was unfathomable.

"You're finally getting it! The pot does not ask the Potter what He's up to," Mark sent telepathically. *"Let us have one more excursion in glory."*

And Paul agreed. It was all they could do.

♦♦♦

"Tony? Is that you?"

Tony opened his eyes to the voice of Big John Jenkins. Once his eyes focused, his fall into the ravine returned to his memory in detail. So where was John?

"Is this a dream or a vision?" the voice asked, again in Tony's head, but discerned as if the big man stood by.

Shadows flirted with the special light of his new vampire vision, and Tony looked into the sky. It had to be after ten and maybe as late as midnight. So… John. He decided to answer.

"John? Where are you?"

"I took Opal away a while. What's the matter?"

"I didn't realize this was possible…" Tony said aloud.

"Me either. And I can't move, I'm numb. This isn't natural…" John's

transmission did not waver. *"It's different than at the bookstore; I can see you. Are you lying on the ground?"*

"Yeah, Paul's sick sense of humor. He pushed me off a cliff. Let's see how I *am…"* Tony concentrated on his chest and took a tentative breath. No hitch, no discomfort, and he was able to fully expand his lungs. Next, he checked his legs; they also had healed.

"So you're okay?"

"Looks like it," Tony replied and walked around the clearing. "John, you still there?"

"Yeah and I can't move. It's like I'm chained down. I know I'm lying on the bed, but I can't make move…"

"Good. Be still a minute and help me figure something out," Tony said, still speaking aloud in the quiet night. "Paul wanted to slow me down so he could get to Corescu first, to return the vampire to his former glory. What should I do? What is the Lord telling you about this? I can't hear Him…"

"I've been praying for you since you left, but I haven't had any divine revelations. I need to tell you that the woman you mentioned is coming to Germany to find you and Corescu. Hope Brannen? I wasn't sure if I should have told her anything, but she was very convincing."

"What did you tell her?" Tony asked, a new dread permeating his spirit.

"I told her what I know. That the guy is in a house in the Black Forest and that you two flew over there to bury him. I think she said she was leaving for Europe immediately. Is that good or bad?"

"I don't know. I sure hope it's part of God's plan. Maybe she won't be able to find us. Maybe she'll show up when it's all over." Tony crossed to the steep wall of the ravine and craned his neck to consider the upcoming climb. His stomach rumbled and an arrow of panic hit his gut. He had lost a lot of blood and expended his energy healing so many injuries. To John he asked in a small voice, "What do I do now? I'm getting hungry…"

"Tony…" John's ethereal voice paused before continuing. *"You have to wrap your mind around the possibility that you may have to drink blood until you're delivered."*

"No, God wouldn't tell me to do that. He won't go against His own word," Tony argued, his mind racing on Scriptures pertaining to the drinking of blood.

"I don't know what He's doing!" John's words came faster and with passion. *"How can you know God's will? You just said you can't hear him*

anymore! Listen! God told Ezekiel to eat feces! He told Hosea to marry a whore! He can do what He wants to get His purposes across through His prophets. AAeeiiii!!"

Big John wrenched his mental eye away with a scream of discomfort, as if the connection had grown painful. Alone again at the bottom of an impossible ravine, Tony began his slow climb upward. And he ignored his stomach. For now.

𝕷𝖓

Those who oppose God, He must gently instruct,
Leading them to a knowledge of the Truth.
2 Timothy 2:25

MARK WATCHED THE GENTLE RISE AND FALL OF PAUL'S chest as he slept. They had spent the last few hours resting beneath the ancient trees of the forest after a horrendous, but delicious night of feasting on the Gypsy poachers. With a sardonic smile, Mark realized Paul's angelic countenance was entirely antithetical to his heinous actions of the preceding night. How could things have come to this state?

Mark stood without making a sound, unwilling to awaken him too soon. He needed a moment's peace, sorely convicted in his spirit for the previous evening's misdeeds. In the coming light of day, his soul swelled with regret. Mark stepped away from Paul's sleeping form, paced a dozen feet and grew still, staring at the purpling horizon. *I am fully restored. How can that be a bad thing?*

Three robust young men died to afford him such a glow and had not deserved death at Mark's hand. He had learned months ago that God had not hired him to be a judge on earth as he believed for nearly four centuries. Yet overnight he had done it thrice, and at the time, it had been enjoyable.

And I had Paul egging me on like a devil...

Mark sighed. Paul had been an innocent and loving youth. The horrid monster he had become barely resembled the carefree and honest young man he had been before Mark handed him the vampire's curse.

I didn't want to die... What could I have done differently? Mark's heart broke with remorse as he prayed. He placed his hands over his face and squelched a moan, not wanting Paul to know his state of mind.

He had to appear strong and sure. At least until Tony arrived.

You said that You would never test us beyond our limit. You said that You would give us a way out when we are tempted. Show me. Where was my escape? Show me… please.

Mark removed his hands from his face and peered into the distance again. The sun was coming and the eerie cobalt radiance that surrounded the elements in his vampire eyes receded to make way for the sun. Mark wandered back into his memory, back to the beginning. The night he was transformed into a monster.

He had been a content though poor village priest in a small Hungarian village. The night in question, he had been asleep when a fire broke out in the town square. He had sprung from bed and gone into the church to rescue his ward, a boy by the name of Miki, when he was confronted by the vampire in the sanctuary.

But Lord, he was much stronger than I. What could I have done?

Mark complained to the Lord as he recalled those minutes before he glimpsed the demon sitting on his boy's chest. Yes, he had been prompted to leave the building. The Holy Spirit had said clearly in his heart that he should leave and not look back. Mark squeezed his eyes small at the memory because that fiery night, he argued with the Lord and rejected His advice to flee.

But I wanted to save Miki. I should have listened. I made a mistake…

Paul stirred behind him and Mark turned to see if he had roused. He hadn't, but he would soon. Mark resumed his prayerful stance and continued to search his past for instances where God tried to dissuade him. He recalled being at the mercy of the demon-vampire for several days before it transformed him into a blood drinker. Mark looked again to the heavens.

How was I to get out of that? I tried, Lord. I ran. I did not want to kill.

Mark waited to see if he would receive a reply. More than a few seconds passed before he began to feel convicted that at the time in question, he had not prayed to be delivered.

But I did! he argued. In the beginning, he didn't want to drink blood. He desired to be cured, to be restored.

"But when the demon of bloodlust came over you, you chose blood over redemption."

Mark didn't breathe. Whether he had accused himself or whether it was God, the truth hit its mark. He had been insane with hunger and he listened to the voice of The Other instead of God. He didn't question the foul monster that directed him. Mark realized with mounting horror, that in effect, he had been led by the devil from that point onward.

I let the bloodlust control me. Bloodlust is a spirit, an addiction, a demon sent to destroy me and the work You have for me... The epiphany dawned clearer and Mark gasped at the wonder of it. The pieces were falling into place. The lust for blood, even when he wasn't hungry, the lust for power, even though only a few ever witnessed his super-human qualities, and the lust to be in control, when God is in control of all. Mark bowed his head, aware that Paul was awake and gaining his feet.

I know what has to be done. Guide me, and I will listen to You.

"Are you okay?" Paul asked as he approached.

Mark put on a grin. "Yes. Let's make our way back. Tony will reach the house very soon."

Mark laid his arm around Paul's shoulder and gave him a shake. He did not feel the affection of old, but he didn't want Paul to realized he had reconsidered. Mark protected his thoughts and pulled him along. He could pretend a little while longer, but when the time came, he would let Tony choose the next step. And Paul wasn't going to like that one bit.

◆ ◆ ◆

Tony collapsed onto the wet leaves covering the top of the ravine wall. It had taken five hours, but he had succeeded. Now he paused if only to decide what to do next.

A quick look at his filthy clothing and Tony huffed. The first light of dawn crept across the sky and he wiped muddy hands on an equally grimy shirt. *So, the climb took all night, which means those monsters have been out hunting.*

Without intending to do so, Tony picked up a few images from Paul. He and Mark traipsed through the forest after wreaking terror on a group of innocents.

Paul sensed him, and sent a mocking message. *"You're really late! Come on already and stop playing around."*

Paul's taunt rolled around in Tony's head. How simple it would be to run the other way. Hop a plane home and put the vampires behind him?

"Pick up the pace, Pudgy!" Paul said in his mind.

Tony sent no reply but grumbled and moved his feet. His mission remained: help Mark and Paul know God. Tony's personal comfort or misery had nothing to do with the end result. He decided to lob the vampire a peace dove.

"*I forgive you for trying to kill me, and tell Mark I forgive him for going against his word and giving in to the devil.*"

"*Tell him yourself. I'm not your secretary.*"

Not surprised, Tony closed his mind and resumed his trek down the lane. He made conversation with the air, but God was listening. By the time the sun had risen, he had reached the washout in the road, indicating his proximity to the house. With a heart of weary gratitude, Tony squat-slid into the steep gully. At the bottom, water trickled over his boots and he could not see over the edge. Then he heard an unimaginable sound—a car engine, and it was approaching at speed. No one would drive to this location on purpose so Tony waited for the vehicle to stop or turn around. They had to do one of the two; there would be no navigating the enormous ditch by car, and the abandoned road led only to the dilapidated house. Tony hugged the damp wall with his back and held his breath.

"*Not far now, madam. Climb through that ditch and follow the road to the house,*" a man's voice said from the direction of the engine noise.

Madam? With care, Tony's toe sought purchase in the slippery wall to heft himself high enough to see. *It can't be…*

The roof and then body of a dark green Jeep 4WD appeared as he peeked over the edge. The vehicle drove away toward town leaving behind a feminine figure who knelt to adjust her bootlaces. Upon standing, her face swiveled to Tony's. *HOPE!*

Tony ducked, but he had been seen. *Father! Why?! Do I have to fight for both of us?* Hope's soft perfume wafted to Tony's uncanny new nose and he worked to order his thoughts. He wasn't prepared to see her and he had no intention of sharing any of his new revelations. Plus, she shouldn't come too close; he was starving and one of the first things he recognized was her as potential *food.*

"I saw you! Don't try anything, forest freak!" she shouted with gusto impressing Tony with her bravery. Her footfalls approached in short breaks and he hated that he was able to hear her heart with his new ears. "Come out or I'll shoot," Hope shouted with the same ferocity. "One…two…"

Hope hadn't changed a bit, still as brash and bold as he remembered. He called out of the ditch, "It's Tony, Hope." Then on impulse he added, "Don't be afraid."

"Anthony?" Hope said and stepped to the edge. "Come out here so I can see you."

Tony climbed out of the gully, slipping every other step and calling a warning at the same time. "I look pretty bad but I'm okay. Don't freak out." When he had cleared the edge of the washout, his friend tossed her hands in the air and ran to hug his neck.

"Anthony! OmyGod! OmyGod!"

Tony returned the embrace, transferring mud from his clothes. When she stepped back, she gawked.

"God! What happened to you? Is that blood? Are you hurt?" She picked at Tony's shirt attempting to open the remaining buttons and Tony pushed her away with a gentle nudge. *God help me. She's so clean, and dry, and...full of blood.* Tony swallowed and stumbled backward.

"Stay back, okay?" he said and put out his hands. "You've walked into a snake pit. It's not just Mark, but Paul's here, too, trying to revive his past. And there's me—a lot has happened since I last saw you."

"Yeah, about that. Why didn't you return my calls? It hasn't been easy for me, either!"

"God had me watching Paul, to keep him from hurting strangers. Now you'll be in the way." Tony slapped Hope's hand as she reached through his outstretched arms to correct his flipped-over collar. "Please, from the bottom of my heart, will you please turn around and walk back to town?" Tony looked to the heavens and repeated his request to God.

"Stop being so melodramatic," Hope said and reached again for Tony's torn shirt. He grabbed both of her hands in his and held them captive. She frowned. "What happened? Why are you covered in blood?"

Tony ground his teeth and chose his words. "I fell into a ravine yesterday. Paul pushed me. It took all night to climb out and now I have to confront them. See how you have arrived at the worst possible time?" Without thinking, Tony brought Hope's hands to his face and breathed in her aroma. When his head swam, he dropped them to take an new step back.

"All of this blood is *yours?* Nobody can lose that much blood and live!"

"God helped me," Tony replied dragging out the inevitable.

"No, what's going on? You better come clean or I'll start guessing."

Tony sighed in weary frustration and met her eye. "I'm one of them, okay? And stay back. Paul did this. I'm not a killer, but I'm not feeling too friendly at the moment."

Tony didn't wait for her to respond; he turned and crawled back into the washout making for the other side, pointed for the house. Hope's stunned silence stretched into a minute and when he made it out, she was dropping into the gully to cross as well.

"Paul made you into a *vampire?*" she called across the distance he had built between them. It was only twenty yards, but at least he didn't hear her blood whooshing in his ears. "Anthony, answer me. Did Paul turn you into a vampire?" Hope jogged double-time and gained his position. She touched his arm, breathing with exertion. "Is that why you don't have any wounds? Is that why you're acting so strange?"

"Yes. Now see? I need you to go away and let me take care of this." Tony didn't turn to face her. He couldn't. He *shouldn't*. He sensed her desire to learn more about things she should fear. He hardened his tone. "I didn't figure you in. You can get hurt this time."

Tony finally turned and wished he hadn't. He told his feet to run, but they didn't. He held her gaze as she sputtered nonsense about how cool it must be to be a vampire and the entire time, Tony wondered what it might be like to taste her blood.

"What's it like?" Hope beamed and crossed her arms at her chest. "Did you drink someone's blood yet?"

"This is not an adventure! It's a nightmare!" Tony's voice had developed a marked rasp. *Oh, if she'd only offer me her blood...* Then, *No! Stop it! Where did that come from?*

"Come on, you're fine. Stop overreacting…"

"Hope! Get serious!" he barked and his eyes fell to her throat before he jerked them back up. "It's taking all my concentration to keep Mark from knowing you're here."

"Mark!" Hope looked toward the house a hundred yards up the scrubby lane. "Do you think he's in the house?"

"No, but he will be soon. Hope, Mark and Paul killed four men last night. The nightmare isn't over."

With incredible resolve, Tony resumed toward the house, ignoring Hope's protests and occasional snags at his sleeve. As he filtered out Hope's comments and prayed for help, he rubbed his middle. The black hole of his hunger consumed his consciousness. His impromptu blood meal on the plane came to mind as Hope yelped and fell to the rocky trail. He turned to look but didn't move.

She was bleeding. It was slight, but he picked up the heady scent of fresh blood.

"Help me up!" she said when he only stood there. "You're definitely not the gentleman I remember." Hope struggled onto her elbows and then tried to brace with her palms. "Ow!"

Wincing with fresh pain, she jerked her hands to her face. Both of her palms suffered abrasions and one a laceration. Hope sat on her rump and rummaged through her bag and Tony walked to her side and knelt down before he realized he had done so. He was too close, but there was no moving away; the sight and aroma of her blood fixed him to the spot.

"Gosh, where's my First Aid baggie?" Hope asked still pushing items around in her satchel.

With the very last measure of strength he possessed, Tony leapt to the side and crawled several feet away. Hope caught his eye and noticed he was staring at her hands.

"What? My blood?" she chuckled and returned to her hunt. "Must feel weird."

Tony whimpered. His tongue ran across his lips and he tasted her blood in the air. *Oh, God! Don't torture me, Your beloved!*

Giving up on finding a bandage, Hope giggled when she met Tony's eye and swung her injured hand behind her back. "Earth to Anthony. Do you read me? Are you freaking out? Do you need to drink my blood?"

Eons ago, in another life, Tony and Hope had spent dozens of evenings together watching vampire movies, laughing and poking fun at the bloodsuckers and their hapless victims. Tony clutched his stomach and lowered onto his back, the intermittent stones jabbing into his flesh. He didn't mind the distraction and he willed his hunger to pass while staring at the new sky, growing bluer as the morning arrived. He had focused down so ferociously that he didn't know Hope had drawn close and knelt beside him until she poked his side and said, "You can drink my blood. Here..." He peeked out and she showed him her wounded palm. "Look, it's already bleeding a little."

Tony closed his eyes and couldn't pray.

◆ ◆ ◆

"It can't be!"

Paul turned at Mark's exclamation, both of them coming to a halt. His master had cocked his head to one side, listening to a distant sound. Paul did too, at first picking up only the birds and wind, but then, he heard a woman's voice, far ahead in the direction of the house. It was Hope Brannen and she had said the word "blood." Mark whirled to face him, his countenance brightened and cheery. He clutched Paul by both shoulders.

"I'll meet you at the house."

And with that short statement, he dissolved from view. Paul huffed a complaint but his master had vanished. With his hands to his hips in frustration, Paul clenched his jaw to fume. Mark had been popping in and out of his face since the beginning, and Paul forgot, however momentarily, that he *could*.

He needs to show me this, Paul grumbled inside and resumed his trek to the house alone. When the Brannen woman's memory arose, Paul cursed and fell into a jog. She had stolen Mark's heart from their first meeting and thus had been the catalyst to rip Paul's world to shreds. He broke into a flat-out run and his anger burned hot within.

I'll kill her, dammit! I wished I had already. Paul estimated he'd be at the front door within thirty minutes and barreled on.

Translating his corporeal body to another location was a skill he'd never teach Paul; his master hadn't taught him, rather, he discovered it by accident over the centuries. Mark strode to the broken front window to watch the two familiar figures bickering a few yards away. Checking his shirtfront for dirt or dried blood, he found that he was relatively clean. His aroma was another story. Lying in the damp house unmoving had left him smelling like a wet couch. He'd wash later, for now… He opened the front door entertained by what played out between Tony and Hope.

"What's the big deal? It's already bleeding," she was saying holding a lacerated palm toward his head. Tony refused and thrashed away, his histrionics bringing a sad smile to Mark's lips. Tony kicked out of reach and yanked a cloth from his back pocket.

"Wrap it up. Wrap it up now," he said his voice quivering and Mark noted how difficult it was for him to not look at her wound.

"God, Anthony! You're so dramatic!" Hope coiled the cloth around her hand. She got to her feet and spun to face the house a few yards away. Mark met her eye. "Mark! Oh, my God! You're okay!"

Forgetting Tony altogether, Hope dropped her travel bag and

sprinted toward him and he walked down the path to meet her. When their bodies slapped together, she threw her arms about his neck with abandon and cried happy tears into his chest. She babbled her adventures in a rush, from searching for him in the States, to getting his info from Tony's friend John, to finding Tony in the ditch running from her bleeding hand. As she spoke, Mark stroked her silky hair, murmured words of calm and held Tony's eye.

"You'll be okay," he sent to the man's mind, but Tony closed his eyes and resumed lying flat on the ground.

"Oh, God! I can't believe you're okay! I thought you were dying."

Mark scoffed. "Have you forgotten all I taught you?" Inhaling deeply, Mark intended to enjoy every nuance of her scent. Exhaling with drama, he inclined his head in Tony's direction. "Let's bring Tony in the house."

Hope didn't release him at first, but held on tightly to his arms when he began to maneuver her away. When he succeeded, she followed on his heels as he walked to Tony's position and stooped down.

"Come in the house," he told him, but the preacher had shut down, despair eating his motivation. With a hand behind his neck and the other behind his knees, Mark hefted Tony into his arms. He turned for the house, and Hope wrapped her hands around his bicep and followed, jogging to match Mark's longer stride.

"Anthony said Paul made him into a vampire. Is this why he's so depressed?"

"He didn't ask for this trouble," Mark said and pushed open his front door with a toe. "But I am very glad you're here." He had looked into her face at his words and her beautiful return smile reminded him why he wanted to live. He set Tony on his former table-bed and examined Hope at arm's length, drinking in her aura.

From his recumbent position and in a near whisper, Tony offered his advice. "Paul's coming, Doctor, you need to get Hope to a safe place...."

Mark looked for Paul in his mind and heard nothing, like picking up a phone line but getting no response. Without turning, he responded to Tony in silence so Hope would not hear. *"I hear nothing."*

"You will. You will hear screaming and smell death before this is over." His mental voice sad and pitiful, Tony said the next aloud. "I'm tired. I can't take it. This is too much..."

In a gentle movement, Mark placed Hope at his side and turned to frown upon Tony's ravings. For such a stalwart man of God, the preacher had fallen into deep despair no doubt brought on by a hunger he couldn't ignore.

"God is ignoring me... My God! Why have You forsaken me? Now I sound like Jesus..."

Mark overheard Tony's prayers and had had enough. "Tony, get up." The man didn't move and Mark grasped his near arm and jerked him off the furniture. Tony's feet found the broken tile and then he stood, his knees wobbling but holding.

"Anthony, stop! It can't be that bad!" Hope said and Mark sent her a kind shush.

He touched Tony's shoulder. "You made it. Everything will be fine, you'll see. You and I will figure this out together." Mark waited and the preacher finally met his gaze, his sorrow deep.

"I want to die," Tony said low enough that Hope wouldn't hear. *"And Paul will be here in less than an hour. He plans on killing us all..."*

Mark again looked out the direction of the woods. Paul couldn't kill him. He also couldn't kill Tony—God wouldn't allow it. But if his plans had turned that psychotic, Mark would be on guard.

30

I will stand my watch and set myself on the rampart,
And watch to see what He will say to me,
And what I will answer when I am corrected...
Habakkuk 2:1

"THIS IS NO PLACE FOR MY PRINCESS. I WILL BUY YOU A castle..." Romance had never been his forte, but like a man set free, the *new* Dr. Mark Corescu was filled with notions of future, love, and courtship. Granted, his peculiarities would need attending but he would have Hope to help him work it through. After leaving Tony Agricola resting on the old oak table, Mark had taken Hope to the yard for a walk. He had not picked up Paul's thoughts since he left his side, but his ears worked, and the young vampire's footsteps did not yet approach.

"A castle is too big. I'm not much of a housekeeper," Hope joked unaware Mark was quite serious.

"We'll employ a full complement of servants. German maids. An English butler. I am embarking on a new life and for you, it will be like a storybook."

"Can we have a stable of show horses?"

Mark laughed at the innocence of Hope's request. It would be nothing for him to set her up with whatever she desired and a barn full of smelly beasts to ride upon would be no challenge. He steered them to the back door, picturing the future in his mind. When his hand touched the handle, Tony sent over, *"Paul's back."*

Mark stopped before entering and listened to the forest.

Has he learned to block me that well? Even so much as to muffle his physical existence? Then it hit him; Tony could read him. *What's going on? Have I lost so much power?* He did not want to ponder it and he gave Hope a serious gaze.

"Paul is coming in and there might be some unpleasantness before the dust clears."

Hope nodded once. "I'm ready, and despite what Tony thinks, I won't make things worse." He read in her eyes that she had come to do her part and he kissed her forehead.

"Stay behind me." Mark opened the crumbling door and entered ahead of Hope. "Paul?" he called into the musty space.

No one replied as the pair made their way through the kitchen and into the hallway to the living room. Mark received nothing telepathically and he called out again as they crossed the threshold. "Paul?"

"Yes?" Paul stood over Tony's prostrate body in the big front room, leaning on his hands so that his head hung down over the preacher's upturned face. He stared Mark down as they approached and lowered his voice. "Yes, *Master?*"

Mark moved Hope further behind him and lowered his chin; his former servant had become unhinged.

♦

"I'm not going through this again." Paul remained as he was, hovering over Tony, staring intently at the couple in the doorway. "I've had it a lot of ways since you gave me this gift and I decided which I like best."

"I imagine you have, little Paul, but you forget yourself." Mark stepped toward the table, happy that Hope remained in her spot at the room entry. "You forget that it's not about you. It has never been about you, or me, or Tony."

"Stop with the riddles!" Paul snapped, stroking Tony's grime-streaked hair. "You and my preachers… I suspect you may have lost your mind along with the rest of us. Seems we're all a little off since this party started."

Tony hadn't opened his eyes or reacted to Paul's threats. And as he had expected, the preacher's mental stream filled with prayers to his God, apologizing, repenting, and asking for deliverance from the vampire at his head. And his master… Paul expected him to do or say… something, but Mark had stopped his forward movement three strides out, his expression filled with emotion.

This is not what I want… Is Mark powerless? Has his slumber brought him weakness?

"Father, I love you, I serve you. What should I do? I will wait until You tell me to move. I trust You, Father. I have always trusted You…"

Tony's prayer reached Paul's mental ears and from Mark's eyebrow raise, it had reached his, too. Paul remained as he was and waited to see what either would do. Tony had summoned his God and in times past, that always resulted in adventure.

And Mark…

Paul recalled his master's power that night at his house. When he challenged Mark's decisions, Paul had been held to the floor by his master's mental power. Would he—*could* he—do it again?

"Have you decided what you're going to do?" Mark asked.

Paul nodded, but continued to veil his thoughts, happy he'd gained the ability. So far, he couldn't block Tony. No matter how hard he tried to prevent it, the preacher read it all. Paul imagined a broad nothingness and stood his ground.

Maybe I can do something unexpected and surprise them both.

"You'll have to surprise yourself, too, won't you?"

It was Tony's voice in his mind. Paul tore his gaze away from Mark and looked down at the face below his chin. Tony's eyes were still closed, but he had assumed a sideways smirk.

♦

A familiar calm washed over Tony's spirit as he readied for God's next move. His hunger had dissipated this gave him great hope.

"I wonder how fast I could rip your head off," Paul hissed in his mind.

"Not fast enough," Tony answered and opened his eyes to meet Paul's upside-down gaze. Grasping the edges of the table with his hands, he pulled to a sitting position. Out of the side of his eye, Hope moved forward but the doctor forced her to remain with a quiet "wait" gesture.

She whispered across the room, "I was afraid you had given up."

"He'll never give up," the doctor announced taking the last three strides to the table. He positioned himself to face Tony with Paul still at the head. "You came here to help us solve our joint problem. What does God tell you?"

"Yes, preacher-man, what does *God* tell you?" Paul asked, condescending as usual. He placed his hand on Tony's shoulder.

Tony slid off the table to his feet, in his mind reminded of the night he faced off to the same two men. Dr. Corescu had attacked him without provocation and Paul had held him fast as he did so. The situation differed, but Tony didn't feel any better equipped.

Mark lay a hand on Tony's opposite shoulder. "But you don't have to fight us, Tony. It's the devil inside of me that waffles back and forth. I'm on your side."

Tony manually removed both men's hands from his person. Neither resisted, and each smiled, placing their hands in their pockets.

"What does the Lord say?" the doctor asked, his eyes shining with interest. Tony waited for words and trusted God would do His part.

"The Lord would like this to end without bloodshed." Tony spoke to both men alternately meeting their eyes. "He would like everyone to repent and turn their lives over to Him." Mark nodded in agreement, but Paul only glared.

"How do we do it? How do we serve Him inside these cursed bodies?"

Mark's sincere question pierced Tony's soul and in the spiritually charged atmosphere of the old house, he half-expected God to give him an answer *right then*. He waited for the words to fill his mouth and as the seconds ticked by, he realized that either he already knew the answer, or God was waiting for a special moment to reveal it.

He listened to his inner monologue and nearly missed Paul's scheming behavior. The young vampire's mind had begun looping Mark's last question, asking inside, *"How do we do it? How do we do it? How do we do it?"*

"I am certain you and I will find a way," Mark said in a soft voice.

Tony nodded. "Maybe our mission is the same as it has always been…"

"…*How do we do it? How do we do it?*…" Paul's silent mantra continued.

"…Gather the harvest…" Tony continued and turned his face to Paul just as the man asked himself, *"How do we… get …her?"*

Then, Tony saw Paul's intention milliseconds before he leapt into action. In a blur, he bypassed Mark and Tony to grab Hope.

"PAUL!" Tony shouted and found himself beside him in an instant, gaining on the vampire as fast as thought. Paul wrapped his arms about Hope's body as Tony grabbed Paul's throat with both hands from behind. Hope gasped and fell silent; she had come prepared to fight.

"Let her go!" Tony growled in Paul's ear.

Paul changed the position of his hands by instead clutching her slender neck. She gasped again but did not scream, impressing Tony with her bravery. Time hit fast-forward and Tony caught the doctor's eye. The old vampire walked close and tilted his chin, boring Paul with his gaze. In a commanding tone, he said, "That will be enough, Paul…"

Tony intuited that Corescu expected Paul to crumple to the floor as he had that night in Georgia. But nothing happened. With no outward sign, he sent to Tony, *"Apparently, this is your show."*

Tony steeled his will.

"Let her go," Tony whispered in Paul's ear, "and I won't be forced to remove your head." As usual, he had no plan, but Mark's gaze reminded him to lean on his faith.

"Shut up!" Paul growled and laced his fingers tighter. "I won't let this woman ruin us again," he said to Mark. "I hope you will forgive me…" With finality in his tone, Paul squeezed.

Going limp, Hope feigned unconsciousness and Tony grabbed Paul by his hair, yanking his head back without restraint. As Paul choked his friend, Tony's teeth elongated into fangs. That sensation was all he needed. Whether it was God, the devil, or the return of his blind hunger, Tony fastened his mouth to Paul's throat. Blood, hot and viscous, flowed at volume into his mouth and he swallowed it all. Through a red haze, Paul released Hope and she tumbled to the littered floor. Tony didn't stop drinking the monster's blood. Inside, his spirit urged him to cease. Mark's voice entered his mind and his ear saying, "that's enough."

But Tony ignored them all and drank.

31

That they will come to their senses
and escape from the trap of the devil,
who has taken them captive to do his will.
2 Timothy 2:26

MARK STEPPED FORWARD, LIFTED A GASPING HOPE INTO his arms, and carted her out of the room. She rubbed her bruised throat with one hand and clung to Mark with the other. When they were safely out the rear door, he set Hope on her feet and supported her until he was sure she could stand.

"Take your time. Relax and breathe…" Mark slipped into doctor mode as Hope worked air through her aching trachea.

"Relax?" Hope rasped, her fingers still to her larynx. "What about Tony?" Hope paused between phrases to cough. "We have to help him…"

Mark pulled Hope into his arms stroking her hair to encourage her to slow her respirations. "Tony will be fine, catch your breath. He's on a mission. I do not see how he will fail before God wills it."

"But that's…" Hope said and cleared her throat. "He can't fight that monster by himself!"

"Hope," Mark said against her hair, "Tony will handle it." Although aware of her distance from Tony the past few months, he found her lack of faith surprising. "Where is your faith?"

"I guess I lost it when I was dying in there."

Mark smiled at her sarcasm, smoothing her long blonde hair once more. "You weren't going to *die,* Hope dear. I would never allow that to happen. See how your friend Tony jumped in to save you?"

"Yeah." Hope softened her tone. "Did Tony bite him on the neck?" Mark nodded. "Oh, God, I shouldn't have been so hard on him outside. How horrible. *Ugh.*"

Mark took Hope by the shoulders. "We must pray for Tony. Pray for God to help him. Pray now. He needs this most of all right now." Mark closed his eyes. Hope tried, he sensed it, but her mind could not release the image of her spiritual counselor feasting like a beast on a vampire's throat.

Tony had not ceased, still latched on. Paul swatted at him blindly, backwards fists making contact with his face more than once.

The furious vampire screamed in Tony's mind. *"You think you will have my master and the woman, too?"* But Tony held fast, his teeth embedded and his hands securing him as sure as iron. *"You can't kill me! What do you think you'll accomplish with this?"*

Tony didn't answer, hanging on now simply to keep Paul from killing him. The blood stopped flowing and the man's jagged throat wounds were closing around his fangs. Tony disengaged his mouth, but held on. Any false move could mean his death. Paul was a killer; he was not. *And why isn't Mark helping? Where did he go?*

"That's right, smarty pants. You can't win. In fact, you've already lost." Paul lifted clammy palms to Tony's wrists in an attempt to loosen his hold. When he couldn't, he swung his body to the side, smashing his attacker against the crumbling drywall. Tony endured the blow with a grunt and when he regained his balance, he released Paul and pushed away as hard as he could. Paul stumbled forward and caught himself, a wicked grin consuming his face.

"Big mistake," he sent over. *"There's no mysterious deputy flying in to save you this time."* Paul crouched and prepared to retaliate.

Tony assumed a similar stance and looked for a weapon. *I can't lose. I can't lose.* Taking in every inch of the messy floor, he found nothing to utilize in the battle, but his internal mantra gave him courage. *Lord, this is all You. I am at my end...*

At that moment, his knees buckled and Tony dropped to the floor. His actions startled even Paul, who rose from his attack posture.

"What the—? Pray, preacher man! Pray your heart out! It won't help!" Paul took a few steps forward, Mark's haunting words returning. *"You're not fighting that little man, but God inside of him..."*

"All Mighty God, You are the King of my heart. Father, You're my peace and my light. Spirit, You are the joy of my life..." Off-key but full of soul, Tony lifted his voice to the ceiling and closed his eyes against his attacker. In his mind, he drifted toward a glorious light. Tony sang to the Lord with abandon and forgot he was in the battle of his life.

32

As he journeyed he came near Damascus,
And suddenly a light shone around him from heaven.
Then he fell to the ground, and heard a voice saying to him,
"Saul, Saul, why are you persecuting me?"
Acts 9:3-4

Paul watched in disbelief as his opponent—still on his knees—worshipped. Shocked by his fortune, Paul thought to take a step toward him and found that he had not moved. He looked at his feet, but found no explanation for is immobility.

But this can't be happening! Paul concentrated as hard as he could and was still unable to lift a foot off the cluttered floor. A rumbling thunder roared from above and Paul lifted his eyes to the ceiling. Barely able to use his voice, Paul screamed once before he lost the ability to make a sound. He watched wide-eyed as in increments the room filled with blinding light.

What's happening? Mark? Tony? Is that you? Someone answer me!

There were no replies in his mind or in his ears and Paul turned his face further upward, so far that the back of his head met his shoulder. The light filled his consciousness and he could no longer see anything but the brilliance of it.

This can't be real! Mark doesn't have this kind of power, does he?

As the thundering persisted, Paul pondered. Something *other* was going on and deep in his heart, he realized who caused it.

"Is that Tony's God?"

Without realizing he had formed a coherent and answerable question, Paul discovered that the rumbling noise above him was in reality a voice. He closed his eyes and focused on the question again. "Is that You, God?"

"Why do you fight so? Why are you so stiff-necked and unreasonable? You

were not born this way…"

Paul released a short yelp of surprise and fell to his knees. He recognized the voice! It seemed familiar, yet he could not immediately place it. It was the voice of someone ancient and very dear. Paul covered his mouth and opened his eyes to the light.

"Do I know you?" Still barely whispering, Paul could not raise his voice. Was he still in Mark's run-down house? Had he been whisked away? Was he dead?

"Your Father in Heaven loves you. He would not let you go without a fight. He has fought for you all of your life. Satan has made a bid for you, but your Father in Heaven has prayed for you that you may be spared. My saints have prayed for you. The prayers of the righteous are powerful and effective, my son. Are you ready to make your choice?"

The disembodied voice thundered all around. It didn't travel simply to his eardrums, rather the words had substance. Like warm honey that landed pleasantly on his face and seeped into every pore. Paul covered his face and leaned over his knees.

"No, I'm not ready. Not ready!" *Am I being judged?* Not so long ago, his former partner Mark Corescu made a life's work of bringing sinners to Christ, by asking them to repent before he ended their life. Paul didn't think he was ready to meet God. Especially since he had never met Him before now. It wasn't fair…

"You know Me. I am the One. The Alpha and the Omega. I have been with you since before the day you were born. Without Me, you have no life. Why do you continue to fight Me so?"

The words began their work on Paul's heart and he collapsed face down on the ground now as tears welled in his closed eyes. Images of church, a measured distance between the minister and the flock— 1909, his father's church, where men and women gathered to worship the God of their fathers. Paul had attended, he'd listened to the sermons, he'd tasted the wine and eaten of the flesh. Hadn't he spoken to Jesus? That night his mother was hit by a carriage, didn't he ask Jesus to help her? And if He did, thirteen-year-old Paul promised to give his life to the church. How had he forgotten?

"I didn't believe!" Paul tried to say, but his paralyzed tongue refused. When he joined forces with the doctor all those years ago, he grew away from those beliefs, those ancient superstitions that his parents held dear. He was young and on a new adventure with a powerful vampire master. What need had he of salvation if he wouldn't ever die? Now he found himself in the impossible situation of having an incredible experience with his long lost Savior.

"It's too late; I haven't believed my whole life…"

"What do you believe now? I will hear your choice."

The rumbling voice calmed and the effect of the words seeping into his flesh comforted him. Lying flat-out on the littered floor, Paul's muscles relaxed as he accepted the river of peace that washed over his soul. He knew the answer to the question, but he rolled it about in his head before he replied. He wanted to get it right; he had the distinct impression that it was the most important question of all time. He mustered his waning strength and whispered the words into the blinding, thundering light-filled room.

"I believe you are God. I believe you are Jesus who died on the cross for my sins. I choose You, Jesus. Please forgive me. Will You take me back? Will You be my true Master? Please, Jesus…"

Thinking more clearly than he had in months, Paul tried to picture the Cross from the various paintings he had seen in his life. Nothing came to mind. He tried harder, feeling deep down in his soul that it was imperative he see the crucifixion before he heard the reply from the Lord. Just when he thought he would fail, he opened his eyes and gasped at what he saw.

Paul found himself kneeling at the foot of the cross. The Messiah no longer hung on the tree, but His blood soaked the ground around Paul's hands and knees, and buzzards squawked upon the mutilated bodies of two unfortunate mortals crucified on either side. Paul lifted his hands to his face and looked at the thick red blood that coated them. The blood was alive. Even though it had left the Man's body and hit the ground, even though some time had passed and His body had been taken away, the blood lived on. It pulsed with life. It pulsed with love.

And it was full of forgiveness.

"I see. I see!" Paul looked around in all directions, taking in the landscape and feeling every bit as if he had traveled back in time to wallow in sorrow below the tree where Jesus hang. "Jesus, I see!"

Paul craned his face to the gathering clouds as the first drops of rain hit his upturned cheeks. A bright flash of lightning speared the clouds and he squinted at the brightness. The thunder rumbled directly afterward, but this time, he discerned no words from the sky. On his knees in the blood-soaked mud, eyes shut, his mouth open in numbing epiphany, Paul awaited an answer.

What now? What now? Did Jesus accept me?

Paul moaned deep in his throat with no idea if he was on earth, in hell, or somewhere else. As the sound of the thunder receded, Paul cried as he never had before. When he opened his eyes, it was pitch black and he couldn't move.

33

"But love your enemies, do good, and lend,
hoping for nothing in return;
And your reward will be great, and you will be sons of the Most High.
For He is kind to the unthankful and evil."
Luke 6:35

TONY SCRAMBLED BACK TO CONSCIOUSNESS WITH THE vigorous shaking of his shoulder.

"Tony! Something has happened to Paul."

It was the doctor. Tony rubbed his eyes and looked about the room. He recalled the events that preceded his fainting spell as his eyes landed upon the still form of the vampire on his right.

Mark stood as he waited for Tony to do the same. "I heard a shout and found him like this…" Mark gestured but didn't go near. In response to Tony's quizzical gaze he added, "I can't get any closer. My feet won't go." He prodded Tony to hurry. "Check him. I think you're supposed to go check him."

Tony considered the doctor's words, *his feet won't move?* A moment later he realized for whatever reason, God prevented Mark from approaching Paul's body. Tony fixed his eyes and took a step forward. *So far so good,* he reasoned and closed the distance. Paul looked dead, lying spread-eagle on his back, eyes closed, lips partly open. He also did not appear to be breathing. Dropping to Paul's side, he touched his shoulder.

"Paul?" Tony's voice cracked with emotion, not knowing how to feel. He'd been rescued, but at what cost? "Paul? Are you alive?"

He received no reply. Tony's heart wrenched over the apparent loss of Paul's soul. Nearby, Mark held his breath in anticipation. Both men waited as if Paul might stir and prove to be still alive.

♦

"You are accepted, I love you, come home…"

Those three phrases filled Paul's soul with elation, but he still could not move, and if he tried, he endured the most excruciating pain of his life. His preacher had kneeled and leaned close so he mouthed words with no sound.

"I didn't hear you," Tony said, distressed and urgent. "What did you say?"

"Jesus…" Paul managed to whisper, choosing his words, knowing deep down that his time on earth was ending. "I… saw… Jesus."

"He said he saw Jesus!" Tony called aloud, assumedly to Mark. "That's good," Tony whispered with emotion and put a clammy palm to Paul's forehead. "That's good!"

"Yes," Paul said (or *thought* he said) and closed his bleary eyes. They no longer functioned and moment by moment, his body was shutting down. With a flash of memory, he recalled an important message for Tony. Paul focused his energy to utter his last words in the flesh. "Tony, forgive me and find…" Paul no longer felt his body, including his lips, as his soul slipped from his mortal shell.

But I have to tell them about the woman!

Desperately, Paul struggled to push the words from a paralyzed tongue. "Find…Sarah Tracey…"

"It is finished. Come home."

And with a relief saturating his every atom, Paul returned to the Father and found peace.

◆

Tony's ear was against Paul's lips, nothing else issued forth. He had heard the Reverend Sarah Tracey's name and his mind scrambled.

What in the world does Paul know about the Traceys? Has he ever met them? Was she the evangelist that the detective said Paul tried to kill? Lord, what does this mean?

Tony rolled off his knees onto his rump and grasped the sides of his head with dirty palms. "He's gone, Doctor."

"Dead?" Mark asked as if such a thing was impossible. Tony nodded and Mark move close, no longer stuck to the floor. He knelt at his friend's head and scooped him into a somber embrace.

"Jesus came to carry him home." Tony didn't feel like rejoicing although it would be appropriate. The Most High God took time out of His busy schedule to swoop in and take the man to heaven. *You can't beat that kind of grace. So why do I feel so crummy?*

Mark rocked Paul's still form and mumbled prayers of thanksgiving. Hope remained in the doorway and both men were glad she afforded them time to adjust their emotions.

Tony groaned and Mark turned to catch his eye.

"You don't feel resolution?"

Tony shook his head. The doctor's question had been no question at all. Neither of them felt it was over. Tony searched deep and found more adventure brewing, more monsters to quell, and more serpents to stomp into hell. He sighed and got to his feet.

Find Sarah Tracey…

Leaving Corescu on the brittle hardwood, Tony wandered out the front door, away from the doctor and the eyes of his friend. *Lord, what now? I know You have overcome the world, and I have nothing to fear, but what now?* In a minute, Mark joined him in the yard with Hope close behind.

"I thought if Paul found resolution, you and I might be…" Without looking up, Tony didn't end his sentence, too disappointed to complete his thought.

"Maybe He will. Restore us to the image of His likeness. It's not over. We're still alive," Mark offered, but maybe also trying to convince himself as well as Tony and Hope.

"Whose likeness am I now? Are we cursed?" He had advised the doctor a year ago on how to serve God as an abominable monster, but Tony couldn't fathom the answers now that the curse was upon his flesh. "I don't want to drink blood."

"I've never heard you be so negative," Hope chimed in and Tony did not look at her face. He had advised her as well, as long as they'd been friends, but now he did not have a word of counsel for anyone.

"You and I have a common goal and we will work together to discern God's will. I want you to answer my next question without thinking; God will supply your words… What's next?"

Tony appreciated his resolve and answered the first thing that came to mind. "I have to find Sarah Tracey. Before we left the States, a police detective said Paul attacked an evangelist. I guess that's what he was talking about."

Mark agreed. "Do you know her?"

Tony shook his head. "No, but everyone in the Charismatic Movement does. She and her husband have one of those million-follower social media accounts, bestselling Christian books, and a Zondervan Bible with Ira Tracey's notes in the margins."

Mark Corescu did not appreciate the depth of celebrity Tony described, but saying it aloud helped. He'd worked alone for the Lord long enough and at least his new "partner" also followed God.

"Can you get an interview with her?" Hope asked, her voice soft. She wanted to help, but how could she? Tony remembered to be patient; as an innocent bystander none of today's misadventures were her doing.

"Once I get back and clear the way with those cops..." Tony shook his head as if in disbelief. "I'll have to trust God with that, too. I don't think there's anything they can pin on me—I haven't done anything and if we dispose of Paul's corpse, this day never happened."

"He will never be found," Mark said with a reassuring nod.

"So I'll set up an interview with Reverend Tracey and ask questions..." His voice tapered off. Did Paul do something to her? Why else did he have to seek her out? Maybe Paul told her his secret. Then he asked the Lord in his heart, *"Maybe there is nothing wrong with her. Maybe You want me to join the Tracey's ministry team..."*

But the detective's words: "Paul attacked an evangelist in Montgomery." *Attacked...* To what extent? He wouldn't know until he found her. *No vacation for the cursed.*

Tony walked away from the others to weep.

34

The LORD is good to those whose hope is in Him,
To the one who seeks Him; It is good to wait quietly
For the salvation of the LORD.
Lamentations 3:25-26

"I DID NOT SEE PAUL ATTACK THE TRACEY WOMAN," Mark confessed as he and Tony shoveled dirt, filling in Paul's grave. They'd chosen a clearing thirty-five paces from the yard, enough in the woods to allow the body to return to dust in peace.

Tony met Mark's eye and said with strained levity, "That would be too easy." Mark offered a small grin. "I had no idea Paul was ever alone with her," Tony said and tamped the top of the grave.

Mark set his shovel aside and lowered his chin, his thoughts on sharing something he felt of utmost importance. Hearing the gist of the beginnings of it, Tony asked him to spill.

"Hah, spill I will." Mark licked his lips. "Concerning the bloodlust that you've already experienced..."

Tony indicated he was listening and Mark continued.

"When you sinned as a human, the grace of God hid you from the enemy, correct?"

Tony made a slow nod to show he followed. He had always hidden in the wings of the Lord because he trusted in Him. Now the doctor wanted to add a vampire into that equation.

"As a vampire, there is a crack in that hedge. When you drink blood, it widens and the devil will use it to torment you. I have experienced this firsthand and did not know how to explain it until my recent slumber."

"But I'm still protected by God," Tony asserted.

"Yes, but the temptation will be exponentially stronger than before you were a vampire."

"You're saying I'll have *supernaturally-strong* temptations?" Tony asked, his exasperated tone harsh.

Mark commiserated with his eyes and Tony squat to the earth and poked the dirt, grumbling about the past few days. The hunger on the plane had nearly ended him. How was he overcome it if it only grows in power?

"You will press through because of your faith," the doctor said and Tony guessed he'd been following his thoughts. But Tony again shook his head.

"Normal human temptation won over me all my life," he mumbled his gaze cast to the ground. "I didn't eat right. I never exercised. I procrastinated at my job." Tony huffed. "The hunger you're talking about—I can't face that again."

"The bloodlust is painful, this is a fact, accept it and let's move on. The blood of the saint belongs to God, but the blood of a vampire, belongs to the devil. You and I are walking a very thin line. We will need to keep our hearts pointed to God no matter how much blood we consume before we are delivered."

"Do you think that God will make me normal again?" Tony asked shaking the dirt from his hands.

"I don't know. I hope so."

Tony huffed. He saw that Mark wasn't asking to be delivered per se; rather, Mark sought permission. When Tony peeked deeper in the man's mind for why, the answer chilled Tony as it must the vampire: *Mark is 375 years old; will he turn to dust when made mortal?* It was a valid concern and Tony ran away from the topic rather than discuss it. He stood up and looked at the sky and Mark also fell into his own thoughts about the past hour's events. Then Mark cleared his throat and Tony looked over.

"I apologize for my behavior since you arrived. I have no excuse, I allowed my body to degenerate into such a condition that I was unable to put my flesh aside. I waffled on my resolve to do the right thing and I repented of murdering the men in the woods." Then Mark added, "I will add that Paul tempted me mercilessly."

Tony chuckled low. "God knows, he liked to do that. And you don't have to apologize. I'm a just as much a monster as you," Tony muttered without looking up. "God must think I'm superman."

Mark chuckled. "You *are* superman. For however long you're in this form, you'll be able to do amazing things. I can see God at work in this; think about it."

Tony huffed, not convinced. "What about you. What will you do now?" he asked sensing Mark's answer before he spoke.

"I have been reborn," Mark said. "And I have put the past is behind me. I have a new calling to start a free clinic on this side of the Pond. Hope has agreed to stay. She brings me much comfort."

Tony did not see how the man and his friend would work past his issues, but it would do no use to discuss it now. He had a much more serious problem and it grumbled as it came to mind.

Tony gestured to Tony's middle with a knuckle. "Paul's blood dissipated because you came in starved of sustenance. You will take my blood before we go in the house. When you get home—"

"I will not," Tony said, taken aback by Mark's certainty.

"…you can survive on the blood of animals. Cows, horses, pigs," the doctor continued his as if Tony hadn't spoken.

"And that's not going to happen." Tony shook his head at the moment a new pang of hunger stabbed his stomach like acid. He doubled over and waited for it to pass. It took too long. "Oh, God!" he cried, real tears springing to his cheeks.

Mark moved close and took his arm, stabilizing and preparing for the next inevitable conversation. Tony read snippets of it from his mind.

"I can't do it—and didn't we just spent an hour discussing temptation? How can you offer your blood after that?" Tony whisper-hissed the end of his query and Mark grew serious, standing close, still holding Tony's bicep.

"There are irrefutable facts that will not wait for you to be free of your curse." Tony again disagreed and he said a different way. "Hope is in the house. You and I are about to escort her to town. Do you think I would allow you near her when you're starving?"

Tony exhaled. She had slipped his mind. But now that he'd remembered, his new senses listened out for her, and mostly he wanted to hear her heartbeat.

"That is enough," Mark said seeing where his mind went. "My blood will hold you over for several days." Mark leaned forward and Tony leaned back. Mark frowned with impatience. "What else can you do? You want to get home, don't you?"

Tony didn't reply, the emptiness in his middle was building to the level it reached on the plane. Mark rolled up his sleeve and Tony grimaced as another pang hit hard. But take Mark's blood? I can't do it again, he said inside and the doctor presented the underside of his strong forearm. Corescu stood several inches taller, his other hand to

Tony's shoulder, he had the sense of a father feeding his son. Except this father figure didn't hold a spoon or fork, he wanted his son to bite his arm.

In his gums, the sensation returned as his new fangs slid into place. "Oh, God," he mumbled and tried to avoid hitting them with his tongue.

"Tony, our time is short," Mark said low. "Take from me so your flight home will go smoothly."

Tony looked to the house. *Can I make another thirteen-hour flight without any blood? No. A definite no.*

Beside him, Mark cleared his throat. "Do this. Once you're safe in your own little world, you can work out the details. But for now…"

"This lust is caused by a demon. I will learn how to cast it out," Tony said, his hand reaching out for the doctor's arm. *I can't believe this is happening!* Tony brought the man's arm to his mouth. "Just this once," he said and told himself *when I get home, God will deliver me.* With the flash-memory of this same vampire biting his arm in a similar fashion almost a year ago, Tony closed his eyes and prayed for a miracle up to the very last second.

It's just this once…One time, that's all.

Even as he convinced himself that this was the only way, he knew he was wrong. If he had enough faith, he'd walk away and trust God to figure out the way home. But his lips made contact with Mark's skin and in a near orgasmic sensation, Tony plunged his new teeth home. When the blood touched his tongue, with his whole heart and soul, it was all he ever wanted. Though he reviled the thought of drinking the vampire's blood, his senses rejoiced. And the centuries-old monster had been right about his blood. It contained power. It was alive. Even as it poured into his system, Tony was invigorated beyond his wildest imagination.

This has to be wrong. Anything this good has to be wrong. I hate it, but I love it, too. It would be good to let this be the very last blood he would ever drink. *Can I let God show me the way out? I will have to. I'm not going to live this way. No matter how delightful it may seem at the moment…*

Tony was glad that the doctor did not respond to his private thoughts; some situations had no easy solutions. Some questions had no easy answers.

Some never would.

END BOOK TWO

Please visit www.ellencmaze.com contact/newsletter
and sign up for her newsletter to
be alerted for every new novel release,
plus giveaways!

The Corescu Chronicles continues with Book Three,

Tree of Life.

Expected from Little Roni Publishers
in Summer 2020

As much as things change, they also stay the same. Tony's mission continues as he seeks evangelist Sarah Tracey, who the vampire, Paul Black, may have tainted before his deliverance in *Damascus Road.* Dr. Mark Corescu continues to back Tony up whenever possible, but he has his own troubles as Hope becomes increasingly difficult to please while falling further off the path of righteousness. The original vampire from *The Judging,* The Other, makes a big comeback in a borrowed body, wreaking havoc on them all.

The Tree of Life brings immortality; for Tony Agricola, there is no rest for the weary…or the valiant.

Stay connected! www.ellencmaze.com

More 5-Star Vampire Fiction from Ellen C. Maze

TWO VAMPIRE SERIES –
COMPLETELY SEPARATE, with an AMAZING & DARING
SHARED ELEMENT

Dive into both series today!

Rabbit: Chasing Beth Rider and *The Judging* are tied in a very unique way. The title character of *Rabbit*, Beth Rider, is the author of a provocative and bestselling vampire series entitled the *Corescu Chronicles*. Her first two books, *The Judging* and *Damascus Road*, are the catalyst that sets the vampires (the Rakum) after her in *Rabbit: Chasing Beth Rider*. dive in to both series' today, and please watch your step. Things get mighty hairy in my imagination!
Enjoy and God bless you,

Ellen C. Maze

Rabbit: Chasing Beth Rider

by Ellen C. Maze

#1 Customer-Ranked in Horror & Occult on Amazon.com

Whoever thought writing a bestseller could be so dangerous?

Author Beth Rider's second vampire novel has hit number one and she is flying high on her new-found fame. But at a fated book signing that runs late into the night, Beth is confronted by an evil she'd only experienced in nightmares.

Praise for Rabbit: Chasing Beth Rider

— "Maze's storytelling is fast and fun, overflowing with ideas and spiritual insight." ~ Eric Wilson, author of *Fireproof*, and *Valley of Bones (The Jerusalem Undead Trilogy)*

— "Riveting and eye-opening…a powerful testament to the often overlooked spiritual strength that lies within us all." ~ *Apex reviews*

Purchase anywhere you buy fine books. ISBN: 978-0615678306, Little Roni Publishers, 2017

Take a peek into ***Rabbit: Chasing Beth Rider...***

PG-Mild Language, Sexual Situations, Vampire Violence

Novel Excerpt: Rabbit Chasing Beth Rider

(slightly altered to make sense as a standalone for your pleasure)

⌘ The Book

"It's only three. You're not leaving, are you?" the handsome blond youth across from Javier said, his eyes wide. "You haven't heard the best part."

Javier hadn't yet taken Simon's blood and the boy probably feared he might skip it. Would he? Javier licked his lips before replying. When he arrived tonight, the youth had launched into reading part of a novel and before long, they were fifteen chapters in.

A grumble from Javier's middle sounded and Simon sat upright from his position on the bed.

Javier corrected him with his hand upraised, palm out. "No, read on. What happened next?"

Simon's expression relaxed. He loved giving blood but would settle for sitting under Javier's gaze a bit longer. His young friend was sharing the strangest tale Javier had ever heard and they'd only covered two-thirds of the story. He put both hands into his wavy black hair and massaged his scalp as Simon picked up where he'd left off.

With no human experience, the religious-themed plot made little sense, but Javier enjoyed the bloodthirsty nature of the main character. The storyline featured a priest who had been transformed into a vampire by the devil. The priest murdered a hapless mortal every night until the novel's protagonist, an aspiring preacher, convinces him to stop. The spiritual struggle of the protagonist intrigued Javier more than it should. Did such faith exist in the real world? Most bewildering of all, did their God *pop in* to save them as He did in this novel? Javier didn't know. In fact, he didn't know any gods. He'd never been to a church, synagogue, or temple, nor had he ever uttered a prayer in a time of need. Yet, as his favorite donor sat on his lumpy bachelor's bed, reading to him from this mortal woman's novel, something deep inside fluttered. For the first time in his long life, Javier experienced a desire to know this God. The sensation was peculiar, and he didn't resist. Instead, he watched Simon's lips move and concentrated on the words, the syllables, and sentences that built the suspense the author intended. When Simon reached the last page, it was five-thirty in the morning and Javier was stunned into silence.

Falling quiet, Simon closed the book, set it aside, and fell back onto his bed lengthwise. Javier chewed his thoughts, absently watching Simon watch the ceiling. Only when the kitchen clock rang in the quarter-hour did either of them speak.

"Sun-up in forty-five minutes." Simon rolled his head to the side to meet his pal's gaze, but Javier's face was red and his mouth a straight line. Simon sat up and threw his legs over the side of the bed. "What? Is something wrong?"

Javier clenched his jaw, losing the battle with the words that wanted so badly to exit. Rakum were not permitted to speak of mortal abstracts. There was no religion among the Brethren, yet something deep inside of him was proving stronger than the ancient tenets of his people. He looked into Simon's bright blue eyes and took a deep breath, ready to relinquish the fight. Leaning forward, he took his longtime donor by the forearm that he normally drew blood from and asked him point blank. "Will you tell me about God?"

There. It was out, and Javier was mortified. His people did not hold such frivolous and foolish notions. To do so would contradict the Ten Fathers, as well as the Elders assigned to educate them to adulthood. To do so would nullify his own deity, of which he had always been certain.

Until now.

Simon rubbed his eyes. "Sure. I mean, I never said anything before because I thought you weren't interested in that stuff. Do you want me to start from the beginning?"

"No," Javier sighed, sensing the unpleasant nudge of the sun nearing the horizon. He was disappointed that he would have to leave without finishing what he had started, but his time was up. "I'll come back tomorrow. Same time."

"I'll be here," Simon replied softly.

Javier nodded, stood, and turned for the closed bedroom door.

"Um, you didn't want..." Shyly, Simon lifted his forearm as well as his eyebrows.

Javier held up his hand. "Forget about it. I'll see you tomorrow." Simon's face fell, and Javier turned to leave. The kid's blood would ease his discomfort, but he had made his choices and tonight's preoccupation with the novel had erased any interest in a buzz.

Javier jogged the two blocks to his own residence. Once home and preparing to bed down, he thought about the characters from the novel and about the question he had asked Simon at the last. Mostly, he thought about the answer and what it might mean for him, his future, and that of his entire race. It meant *something,* but what? Had any of his brethren read the story? Did it move anyone else and wake something hidden deep inside of them? Was it ultimately going to be a bad thing that he peeked into the human concept of a Creator-God?

Javier slept fitfully and longed for the evening. To finish what he had started. Perhaps to learn about a God he had never known existed, one that would care for him and give him purpose. Ironically, he never knew he desired those things until he sat and listened to that silly woman's book. Beth Rider's book.

✄ Don't Bother to Scream

Bestselling vampire author Beth Rider reached her hotel room and sighed, collapsing face-down on the hotel bed. She had no energy to even turn on a lamp. She'd spent the last two days and most of both evenings in various bookstores signing novels for her readers. Her left hand was numb from the effort, but for the most part, each book signing had been a joy. Only the dark maniac at the Buckhead BooksAMillion left a sour taste in her mouth. She had put him out of her mind, but now, she shivered as she recalled the hellish encounter. Beth flipped onto her back, still lying long-ways across the king-sized bed. A furtive movement to her right, beyond the glow of the tiny nightlight caught her attention and she sat up. She was not alone.

"Is this the way you watch your back?" a husky whisper rasped.

Beth jumped to her feet and lunged for the door. Before she could take three steps, the dark form across the room grabbed her from behind.

"Don't bother to scream…"

As one steel-like arm wrapped uncomfortably about her chest holding her immobile, the other hand covered her mouth. Beth could not see her attacker, but it was definitely the tattooed monster from the night before. Beth prayed in her heart for help and went limp in her attacker's grasp.

"You're quite the nuisance. Have you any idea the trouble you're causing my people?" The voice paused and then continued in a guttural chortle that chilled Beth's soul. "I could handle this so many ways, Miss Rider. So many ways…"

Beth squeezed her eyes closed, unable to fathom the meaning of his accusation.

"Bel suggested I snuff you out, right here, right now." The stranger waited briefly for a response, but then continued his one-way conversation in a gleeful tone. "But Tomás, on the other hand… his idea intrigues me. Want to know what Elder Tomás suggested?"

Beth did not respond, still praying for divine rescue.

"He said you'd make a delightful Rabbit." The giant smacked his lips. "Hah! I haven't marked a Rabbit since… *damn*… it's been a long time. Would you rather die now or become a Rabbit for my pups to play with?"

Beth didn't attempt to answer, even though the thought was moot with her mouth covered. She opened her eyes and trained them on the outline of the curtained window across the dark room.

"I'll tell you," the man continued in a teaching tone, as if she had asked a question. "A Rabbit is a toy for my pups. You know, a papa wolf finds a rabbit, marks it with his scent, turns it over to his pups, and they play with it. They practice their technique on it. They attack it again and again until it's worn out, or insane, or both."

The man paused and Beth worked to ignore the rising panic in her gut. Somehow, she knew he was not going to end her life, but whatever he had in mind was going to be horrible.

"Most of the time, Rabbits give up *long* before we're done with 'em. I wonder how long you'll last? I wonder how many of my pups you can entertain before you kill yourself?" The man's tone turned wistful as he finished his thought. Still with his left arm around her from behind and that hand pressed firmly over her mouth, his right arm disappeared and she felt his fingers against her throat.

"Now, hush, this might sting a bit…" His fingernail pressed into the curve of Beth's neck and continue inward until the skin split and blood trickled out of the small wound. "Are you the quiet type, little Rabbit?" He encircled the wound with his lips, his tongue pressing against her skin.

Not even aware that she was going to do so, Beth leapt into action. With mighty effort, she pushed off with all of the strength she could muster. Although she didn't break free, the man's lips slipped away and she grunted victoriously. As she struggled to free herself from the death grip on her face, the man secured her once more with his strong right arm. His left hand shifted slightly and now covered her mouth *and* her nose.

"Can you wriggle free from this, you brat?"

Beth increased her attempts to break loose; she couldn't breathe and as panic crept in, all of her internal prayers ceased.

"I'm gonna mark you now. It'll only take a minute if you're still."

Beth continued to strain, all of her senses on alert. She was no longer a rational being, but rather a wild animal fighting for her life. Just as she thought she might lose consciousness, the man's hand slipped off her nose and she took in a painful breath. The man shuffled her to the bed and forced her into a lying position, his looming shape taking a straddling stance over her. Beth's eyes grew wide in the dim room and she thrashed wildly.

"Be still, you shit," the monster hissed and again, closed her airway with a slight movement of his hand. His weight over her abdomen caused enormous pressure to her diaphragm and Beth grew still.

"Move again, I beg you," the man rasped. "I don't like you enough to explore what else you might be good for."

Horrified at his vaguely sexual threat, Beth quieted every muscle.

"That's right, heheh," he chuckled, his putrid breath falling on her cheeks. "You're too school-teacher for me, but I have *lotsa* brothers." The monster leaned down to sniff her hairline. "*Yeahhhh,* I can think of three or four who like them clean and innocent..."

"Mmmm!" Beth mumbled into his hand, her eyes vainly seeking his in the dim light.

"My mark will change you, make you smell like me, and then *all* of my pups will like you—*a lot.*" He stressed the last two words and held her gaze. "I am about to uncover your mouth. Hush, submit, and this will be over quickly. Understand?"

Beth nodded, her eyes bulging with terror. She didn't know what he intended to do, but he said it would be quick. Beth held on to that assurance and closed her eyes. The man's clammy hand slipped from her mouth and a warm liquid touched her tongue and rapidly filled her mouth.

"I hope you're a swallower, Miss Rider," her gruff attacker jibed and pinched closed her nostrils. "All of it. *Swallow.*"

Beth's mind flashed to her novels. Her characters were forced to drink blood. Did this lunatic think he was a vampire? Is that what the entire ordeal was about? A psychotic and deluded fan of her novels acting out his fantasies? Even as her mind raced with comparisons, Beth swallowed to keep from choking. Immediately, the man removed his hands from her face and placed them down on the pillow to either side of her head. He looked upon her and now his fetid breath fell on her forehead.

"Wait for it..." the dark giant whispered.

He was waiting for something to happen and Beth opened her eyes to meet his glittering gaze. In the darkness, she saw only the reflection of the nightlight in her attacker's reddened eyes. Focusing on the man's scar, Beth worked to regain her composure. *What now?* Her mind was clearing, her morbid fear passing... What was he waiting for? Precisely five seconds later, Beth's stomach turned inside out.

"*Ugghhhhh!*" she groaned, writhing in pain beneath her monstrous enemy. The man did not cover her mouth as she twisted and strained beneath him, every nerve afire.

"*Shiiiiit...*" he chuckled, "that looks painful."

Beth made an attempt to conceal her discomfort, and soon, the acid burn in her middle subsided. As she settled her frightened but angry gaze into that of her attacker, her pain melted into nausea and then was gone altogether.

"You're hilarious," he said, spittle falling on her face. Beth didn't respond and the dark brute sat up, still holding his bulk up just enough to prevent crushing her. His right hand lifted and dropped to her shirt, dragging heavily across her breasts. "*Ehhhh,* so tender; my pups are going to be thanking me forever," he muttered. With one last lewd pass, he put both palms to his thighs and looked upon her. "Do you have any idea what just happened?"

Beth only glared, unsure if she could control her tongue if she spoke.

"Mad little bunny," the man chuckled and patted the top of her head. "My mark is on you and that makes you a Rabbit. Now, I am releasing you into the world so my pups can hunt you down. No matter where you go, they'll seek you out. Did you know that a wolf can sniff out a rabbit from as far away as a mile? My pups' senses are far greater than that and you will smell like steak roasting on an outdoor grill. You know how wonderful that smells? *Mmmmm.*"

He paused for Beth to respond, but again she refused.

"All of my brethren will want a shot at you. A juicy new Rabbit is a rarity they will exploit to the max and in every way imaginable."

As numbness seeped up her spinal cord, Beth realized she was losing consciousness. She watched the silhouette of the big man as he crawled away and then stood.

"Let's see…where is it?"

He reached for her purse on the nightstand. Through heavy eyelids, she watched him locate her wallet and pluck out a plastic card that glinted in the low light. Beth whimpered as he dropped the purse beside her, her driver's license in his possession. Beth's head swam. She was done fighting, but the monster spoke again and she made an attempt to comprehend.

"I like to know where my Rabbits are headed. Montgomery, Alabama? I have some pups '*round them parts.*" He spoke the last few words in a put-on Southern accent. "They haven't seen a Rabbit in a *long* time," he laughed to himself with a shake of the head. "My favorite lieutenant's in Montgomery; he'll find you first. You won't like him; he's horny and hungry *all the time.*"

Chuckling, the man backed toward the door and wiggled his fingers in Beth's direction.

"Sleep now, Rabbit. But tomorrow…" He opened the door and bright light spilled in from the hallway. "You better start running."

And he was gone.

Beth tried to thank God she was alive, but numbness overtook her brain and she slipped away, falling into a deep sleep. In her dreams, she was running and staying out of reach of the wolves.

Just barely.

✖ A Perfect Match

Jesse Cherrie opened his eyes in time to watch Atlanta fade into his past. Every Tuesday at sundown, he left his comfortable apartment in New York City for JFK, hopped a 747 to Atlanta, and then a regional jet to Montgomery, Alabama. Most Rakum used the Rakum-owned NCJ, but Jesse preferred comfort, and the human jets had the best amenities. So he headed south once a week to check his holdings in the southern companies and of course, to visit Jack Dawn's favored lieutenant, Michael Stone.

Jesse and Michael went *way* back, practically to the beginning. Raised in the same lair-house and paired up by the group proctor, they were a perfect match. With Michael's natural brawn and Jesse's mystical gifts, there was nothing they couldn't accomplish together. Delivered to Elder Dawn for Ritual training, they were made tough and successful, having graduated at the head of their class over a century ago. Since then, they had settled into separate and comfortable lives, co-existing with the cattle that populated the planet, enjoying what mankind had to offer in the way of luxury and comfort. ...*Well, Michael's not so much into the luxury...* Jesse sucked his teeth and pictured his pal's boring house, considered his boring job, and his pitiful bank balance. Rakum grunts worked as hard as mortals to earn a living wage, but where Jesse learned to multiply money on the Stock Market, Michael pursued work more in tune with his natural military leanings. Making barely $50K a year, he kept the humans in line as a law enforcement officer. Jesse grinned to himself; Michael seemed satisfied which was all that mattered.

Jesse increased the volume on his iPhone. It wasn't so much the music, but the distraction. He had an hour-long flight ahead and preferred being left alone. Because he purchased both seats, Jesse set his briefcase in the aisle seat and turned his attention to the music.

As he nodded his head with the beat, he thought about the night ahead. Maybe Michael would join him for a night on the town. Last week they'd gone to a bar frequented by twenty-somethings sipping dainty cocktails and fruity wine-coolers. What Michael saw in the

274

place, Jesse couldn't fathom. Well-known for his sexual appetite, Mike probably liked looking at the girls. But none of them were touchable and none were reliably alone. The one woman that maybe, just *maybe,* could have been convinced to sneak into the back with Mike for a snuggle ended up causing quite a stink.

Jesse glanced around the cabin, everyone was minding his or her own business. He closed his eyes and allowed the previous adventure to roll back. Michael Stone was fun to watch, especially when aroused by a potential buzz or provoked by a drunk idiot. The night in question, they enjoyed both extremes.

"Her," Michael had whispered, inclining his head toward a female at the opposite end of the bar. Jesse looked her over; she was petite and gentle-looking, like an elementary school teacher. Mike loved those—the meek little kittens. Jesse shook his head. He preferred his women confident, sexy, and a little frightening.

When Michael didn't make a move, Jesse comically widened his eyes. "Well? Go ahead. I'm not your daddy."

Mike grinned, hopped off his stool, and strolled the length of the bar. Jesse sipped his beer and watched the show. If his friend succeeded (which he most assuredly wouldn't in such a place), he would get her to either come to his car, or go behind the establishment where Mike would swoon her for her blood. A handsome Rakum lieutenant such as his friend should have no trouble. So far, Michael had game. The tiny thing smiled and nodded. Then she laughed into her hand when he made an idiotic joke. Jesse finished his beer and almost ordered a second when the woman slid off her stool and put her hand on Michael's arm.

"You have got to be shitting me..." Jesse sent to his mind. Michael was a miserable telepath, but read Jesse well enough. His friend grinned and sent him a wink. Jesse followed with his eyes as they headed for the front exit. Only when another patron approached from behind and roughly grasped Michael's shoulder did things go sour. Jesse grinned; so the woman had a date, and Michael loved besting bullies.

"Hey, asshole!" the rude man shouted, not nearly as drunk as he was pretending. "You got some nerve!"

The man balled a fist as Mike's new lady friend scampered away, her eyes huge. Mike dodged the man's ridiculously-aimed jab and lifted his hands in surrender, smiling like the hulky oaf he was.

"Hey, man, chill out. What's your problem?" he said as the angry guy reared back to swing again, shouting expletives. Michael caught the fist as it entered his space and held it, careful not to break any bones. "Fella, fella," he cooed, "chill."

Mike outweighed the man by fifty pounds and stood at least an inch taller. Jesse shook his head when his friend shot him an amused look.

"Don't hurt him," Jesse sent telepathically and with his mouth, which was unnecessary. Both of them would do whatever it took to avoid contact with the mortal authority.

Michael released the man's hand and the guy lunged into his torso, grabbed him around the waist, and tried in vain to wrestle him to the ground. Mike stood in place with his arms sticking out and looked at the other patrons with humor in his gaze.

"Hey, fella, I apologize—whatever you're mad about, I'm sorry," Michael said loud enough for everyone to hear. The crowd had grown four deep and Jesse finally left his stool to better keep his eye on the show. Finally, someone who knew the brawler struggled into the fray, attempting to stop the fight. The attacker still had Michael around the middle when Jesse reached them.

"Let's go, Mike," he said aloud and his friend lifted both hands, showing his palms.

"This man is in love with me," he said and laughed. "Not my type, but he's plenty cute."

Mike's teasing further stoked the guy's fire. Jesse intuited from the jilted lover that he would not soon give up his attack and he looked Mike in the eye. *"You'll have to end it."*

Mike chuckled and playfully squeezed the man's shoulder. "Hey, little fella, would you like to come home with me? I'll put a guy like you to work right away," Mike said over his attacker's head.

The brawler shoved violently away and shouted, "I'LL SHOW YOU LITTLE!" The man whipped out a pocketknife that he pointed with practiced ease. Jesse tensed, but needn't have. Without pause, Mike disarmed him with a painful slap to his wrist.

The man bellowed his anger and Jesse overheard the words, "Call the cops." It didn't matter who said it. *"Time to go..."* he sent Mike and stepped behind the angry gentleman. Jesse carefully grasped the mortal by the neck and pulled him back several feet. He flailed his arms and Jesse handed him off to some of the other patrons, arms straight and head back, as one might hand over a wild animal. He then took Michael's elbow and pulled him out of the bar.

He almost got the girl and he almost got arrested.

Jesse chuckled at the memory and shook his head. Michael Stone was and always had been a fun companion, but tonight, they'd try somewhere new and if he had his way, *drink* someone new along the way.

✖ Nip It in the Bud

Jack Dawn shoved Kite to the ground and beat his chest like a gorilla. He'd never been bested, not in twelve hundred years; no way this feeble pup was going to get the better of him tonight. Jack feigned toward him and the kid winced. It was good to be the king.

He'd begun his evening at a local brothel with a few of his brothers and now they were winding down, enjoying their nightly ritual of pounding each other until they collapsed or cried uncle. Kite endured a special beat-down for something he'd said over a month ago. There was no need to remind him of his error; it was more fun to slap the snot out of him and watch his eyes grow wide with fear. It would make the kid stronger. Jack was slapped around plenty when he was young and he recalled every excruciating millisecond.

"So, what about that Rabbit you marked?" Elder Tomás spoke with a thick Spanish accent, watching from a few feet away.

"What's to say?" Jack booted Kite in the shoulder to hear him yelp. When the kid fell silent, he turned to Tomás. "Well?"

"There's a whisper going around that Stone isn't playing fair."

"Don't you know better than to listen to gossip?" Jack approached his friend and punched his shoulder. Not quite as tall as Jack, but nearly as muscular, Tomás braced himself, effectively nullifying the jab.

"It's not gossip, Brother. Tyson said—"

"Tyson? That miserable waste of space? Come on, Tomás. Shut up about Tyson!" Jack growled and threatened the other Elder with a raised fist.

Tomás stepped forward and bared his teeth, wrapping strong fingers around Jack's closed hand. Jack pushed against him and soon added his upper body strength, leaning in to press through. Tomás matched his great physical might perfectly. As they tested each other, Tomás spat his next words into Jack's sweating face.

"Stone's gone soft," he grunted with effort. "Let's go down to Montgomery and check it out." Tomás clocked Jack under the chin. "If Stone's behaving, no problem. But if he's—"

Jack returned Tomás's uppercut with a powerful double blow to the kidney. Tomás crumpled to the ground, but didn't cry out. He remained on the carpet, drew up his knees, and caught his breath.

"Behaving? That's my *lieutenant,* you asshole!" Jack kicked the Elder's nearest shin hard.

Tomás made no notice of the blow. "If he's gone soft," he said in a forced whisper, "you're gonna want to nip that in the bud."

Jack frowned. "Seriously, what does Tyson know?"

"It's not Tyson alone." Tomás put out his hand and Jack pulled him to his feet. "Others sense the same thing. Don't you? He's *your* favored one—surely you've read his intentions," Tomás said and raised his fists, pugilist style.

Jack ignored the offer and turned, leaving the large room he'd modified especially for roughhousing. When he entered the kitchen, Tomás was right behind him, followed by a very bloody Kite. Behind him, entered Beryl, one of a set of twins Jack was discipling.

"What about it?" Tomás pressed as he pulled a beer from the fridge. He tossed the can to Jack who caught it without looking up.

"I got this. *Shit!* End of discussion." Jack popped open the can and drank the entire contents without pause. He tossed the empty to Beryl who dropped it into the trash. "I should have killed that woman and been done with it. Why do I always listen to you?"

"Blame yourself for lovin' me so much." Tomás smiled and then his eyes narrowed. "Did you hear Kilmeade's report?"

"Kilmeade..." Jack growled the name. Younger by centuries, Elder Kilmeade suffered under the delusion that he was greater than Jack. No Elder alive could realistically claim such a thing and merely looking upon the arrogant ass's face was infuriating. So, when the Elder sent out his latest Rabbit report, Jack had ignored it.

Observing Jack's surface thoughts, Tomás shook his head. "You should have listened. He's pompous, but he watches out for the Brethren."

"You can suck him off later, asshole. What did he say?"

"Maybe I will," Tomás chuckled. "He's more my type than your ugly ass..."

"What did he say?" Jack grumbled with a frown, his hand going to the deep scar over his cheek. He loved his face; if Tomás didn't, that was on him. *He* was the one always coming around. Tomás saw what he'd been thinking.

"Come here, precious," he cooed and reached for Jack's thick neck. Jack shoved him backward with more power than necessary and the brother hit the tiled floor, knocking into a daydreaming Kite on the way down.

"What did he say?!" Jack bellowed, leaning over his friend with a boot poised to stomp his middle. Tomás laughed and showed his palms.

"Our beautiful brother Kilmeade reported that he overheard two grunts planning to run away." He waited for Jack's expression to lose the irritation and reflect the seriousness of the situation.

"Overheard?" Jack asked and put out his hand to help Tomás stand. "Or read?"

Tomás tipped his chin. "Overheard—you know he hears better than any of us."

"SHIT, Tomás. Finish up!" Jack shouted and angrily sought Kite who stood to the side. With a sudden roundhouse kick, he sent the kid sprawling to the floor and met the other Elder's eye. "What did the wonderful and amazing Kilmeade say? Please, tell me."

Tomás grinned, obviously pleased he provoked Jack to such an extent. "Two of Emil's pups were plotting an escape. They spouted some religious shit and dropped off his radar."

Jack narrowed his eyes. "Dropped off?"

"Disappeared. Line severed." Tomás rubbed his face. "Hell, two of Bel's pups disappeared just tonight. And he described the same thing—the tether was gone. As if they blinked out of existence. That makes twenty Rakum so far that we know of."

Jack cursed and hit the wall with a closed fist. Powdered plaster filtered down from the ceiling onto his bald head. "This is *ridiculous*. Stone's a monster."

"His line still up?" Tomás asked, eyebrows raised.

Jack peeked inside and sought Stone's mental link. "He's there. No change. But twenty brethren? Has that woman unleashed some sort of disease on us. On my lieutenant?"

Tomás commiserated, his fists to his hips. "How are we to know? Thousands of years and nothing like this has ever happened. Should we request a meeting with the Fathers?"

Beryl cleared his throat and since he was an inferior, Jack sent him a glare. Not yet commissioned, over the past few years Beryl had earned his way into Jack's inner circle. When he sent Michael Stone to Montgomery, he moved Beryl and his identical twin brother, Meryl, right under him, intending to promote them to captain as soon as they had a few more years under their belts. Young, passionate, and impetuous, the boys performed as two bodies with one magnificent brain, and it was no use to separate them for long.

Tonight, Meryl was taking care of a mission for Jack across town and Beryl stayed behind. He liked to have one of them around at all times. He liked to watch them work. And he liked to watch them, *period.* Identical in every way, the boys had wavy brown hair and fawn-hazel eyes that mesmerized mortal and Rakum alike. The brotherhood considered the boys' appearance unmatched in their generation, with perfect facial symmetry, skin the color of creamy coffee, and a killer smile, and both with the disposition of their seed donor, the mighty Father Umbarto—also Jack's natural father. Ninety-nine Elders wanted them and Jack didn't share, never had and he never would.

Jack grinned inwardly as all this ran past his mind. As a fantastic telepath himself, Beryl appeared to have read him, a tiny sparkle in his eye as he prepared to explain his uncharacteristic interruption.

"You got something to add, B?" Jack asked, knowing his normally terse tone inevitably lifted when he addressed the twins.

Beryl carefully chose his words and in a voice as smooth as silk, he said, "Father Abroghia once told a story." He paused and met the eyes of each man. "Two thousand years ago, many Rakum fell away, grabbing onto a new religion circling the planet at that time. Abroghia was there."

Jack considered the tale. Abroghia was the only Father that went back that far. The other nine were old, no doubt, but Abroghia had seen at least two millennia and was widely respected as the ultimate leader of their Race. He nodded at the boy who returned a tight smile. It was the closest thing to affection that they had between them and it suited them both.

"Could be it's coming around again," Tomás interjected. "Twenty of the brethren gone underground. Hiding from us. Hiding from *you.*" Tomás headed out of the kitchen. "You need to go to Montgomery and eliminate that Rabbit. Hell, I'll go with you. It'll be fun."

Jack watched him go and then glared at Kite who stepped back, as if awaking from a trance, his marbles scrambled.

"We'll leave at sundown," Jack called to Tomás and then reached for Kite's upper arm. The boy knew better than to evade him and he stood under Jack's hard gaze suppressing a shudder. Jack eyed Beryl and he stepped behind the younger Rakum to wrap his arms firmly around his chest. Kite closed his eyes and pressed his lips together. It stunk being least in the kingdom.

End Excerpt

About the Author

Raised on Bram Stoker and Stephen King, Ellen read Frank Peretti's *This Present Darkness* in 2000, and has never been the same. Now she takes the horror/ paranormal /vampire genre directly into the heart of spiritual matters, pitting good against evil within the confines of biblical truth. Scripture is often bloody and the struggle to escape the claws of evil is real and personal. With writing as her passion and petting cats her main hobby, Ellen lives in Alabama with her family and does NOT have holes in her neck.

WRITTEN BY ELLEN C. MAZE

Rabbit: Chasing Beth Rider (Book One)
Rabbit Legacy (Book Two)
Rabbit Redemption (Book Three)
Anomaly: Beyond the Rabbit (Book Four)
Conundrum: The Lost Rabbit (Book Five)
The Vestige: Final Chapter (Book Six)

The Judging: The Corescu Chronicles Book One
Damascus Road: The Corescu Chronicles Book Two
Tree of Life: The Corescu Chronicles Book Three
Anathema: The Corescu Chronicles Book Four
Novus: The Corescu Chronicles Book Five

22 Sideways: Twenty-Two Bloodthirsty Tales
Loose Rabbits of the Rabbit Trilogy
Feckless Tales of Supernatural, Paranormal,
and Downright Presumptuous Ilk

ELLEN'S LINKS:

www.ellencmaze.com
Emails welcome: ellenmaze@aol.com
Twitter: @authorellenmaze
Facebook: www.facebook.com/ellencmaze
Ellen writes and illustrates children's books and nonfiction
under the pen name Ellen Sallas.

www.ingramcontent.com/pod-product-compliance
Lightning Source LLC
Chambersburg PA
CBHW071309170626
46809CB00001B/389